BLACKTHORN WOOD

PAULA HILLMAN

Paula Hillman

BLOODHOUND
— BOOKS —

First published in 2023 by Bloodhound Books.

www.bloodhoundbooks.com

Print ISBN: 978-1-916978-05-8

Prologue

W ould people have labelled me a murderer?
This is a question I've brooded over until it's become a dogged presence in my brain, and the only relief from it is to inflict pain. Nothing major; a sewing needle pushed under my thumbnail, perhaps, or a press against the muscles in my jaw. Then there's the Zopiclone. Self-harm or self-medicate? I wonder what the psychotherapist will make of it.

Getting help is my husband's idea. My chalky complexion and sleep-deprived eyes frighten him, I think. He doesn't know the half of it, doesn't know what I look like on the inside. The outside me is a glowering forty-year-old with quite good skin and soft brown hair, but something as ordinary as a face couldn't begin to convey what's actually going on. And I don't want anyone to know, so I've agreed to an overpriced package of psychotherapy from someone willing to come to my home. A *friend of a friend*, apparently, though I didn't think we had friends anymore.

'He's here.' My husband pushes his way into the study.

I look up from my laptop, glance outside for a moment. A

strip of peach-coloured light glows above the treeline in my garden. Skyscapes used to lift me up. Now, their weight is unbearable.

From the hallway comes a set of squeaky footsteps, then someone else is in the room.

'This is Freddy,' my husband says, with an enthusiasm I'm not feeling. 'Freddy Briggs.'

A blur of muddy brown dreadlocks and green anorak. I notice his boots: clean, but boots nonetheless. His hand extends towards me. I should stand up, stop being so snobbish, give the guy a chance. But the sight of him makes my shoulders ache all over again.

'Hi.' He grins. Overfriendly. 'Lovely bit of weather we're having, isn't it?'

I nod my agreement. 'Hello. Cassie Clifton.' He is my height. 'Good to meet you.' But it's not.

'I always think we love talking about weather because it keeps our feet on the ground,' he says.

Through gritted teeth, I ask him to explain. I can't help myself; he's hooked me already.

'Only that it feels tantalisingly insignificant to be a human in the face of the weather. A bit like looking up at the stars.'

'Oh.' *Cryptic*, I think, and smile sweetly.

My husband is backing away. 'I'll get the coffee on.' A shuffle of socks and he is gone.

'Sit down,' I tell Freddy, pointing to the sofa under the bay window. Sunlight slants into the room, creating a pool, dusty gold on grey. I back towards the safety of my chair. He is clutching a small black case. I watch as he smooths down his jeans: large hands, pale skin, and a pen between his fingers.

'It's a beautiful house,' he ventures. 'And overlooking that...' He tilts his head in the general direction of the wood. 'Have you lived here long?'

2

You're not a bloody estate agent, I think. 'Feels like forever. It was my grandparents' house.'

He lifts his chin. 'Lucky you.'

Do I detect a slight edge of sarcasm in his tone? This guy has no idea of my position in relation to Blackthorn. He'd better not be one of those fair-trade types: spread-the-wealth and all that. God, I'm struggling with this.

'Yes. Lucky me.'

My husband puts his head around the door. 'Milk and sugar, Freddy? I forgot to ask.'

'Please. Two sugars.'

I resist the urge to ask if he wants oat or almond milk. Not that we've got any, but he looks the type. And there I go again, making stupid assumptions based on a hairstyle or a coat or a phrase that probably isn't loaded. I swivel my office chair to face him again, try to be nice. 'Do you live locally?'

'I do,' he replies, tugging at the zip of his anorak. I notice the Berghaus logo. Expensive. 'I live over on Barrow Island, actually. Ramsden Dock Road.'

Everyone knows Ramsden Dock Road. If there's ever a television clip of our town, the sandstone tenements on the dock road are front and centre. Evocative they may be, but a *des-res* they're not.

'Not the flats, though,' he says. *How has he read my thoughts?*

'Not the flats?'

'No. I've got one of those terraced houses on the other side. Brick-built. With a forecourt.'

Why are we talking about houses again? Is this some kind of test?

'It's got atmosphere, that area,' I say. 'History.'

He agrees, then starts to unzip the case. 'Some of the stories I hear from my neighbours are unbelievable: ghosts, mad cat ladies, secret tunnels – it's all there.'

We both laugh. His is warm and rich but doesn't match his

age. I put him at late thirties. I'm doing it again. What does his age matter? Quite a lot, actually, if he's here to cure me. A notebook comes out of his case. He lays it on the sofa, then turns his flinty expression on me.

'Take your coat off,' I say, then add a *please*. Ever the teacher.

'Thanks.' He slides his shoulders out of the anorak and passes it to me. With it comes a homely smell, gingerbread, or burnt sugar. I want to frame this moment, then step away from it and let myself unravel. What I expected isn't what's happening. Where's the sanitised questioning? The soothing of my furrowed brow? This feels like I'm the responsible one, like I have to do all the running.

My husband comes back into the room, a mug in each hand. He puts them down on the small pine table by the fireplace. 'There you go. I'll take your jacket, shall I?' And off he shuffles. We are alone again, Freddy and I. The silence is a solid presence in the room. How these things work, I have no idea. Did he expect a wreck of a human being? Sobbing and ready to be saved? That's not how I am. Why isn't he saying anything?

I look over the top of his head and through the window. It's a copper-and-gold kind of morning. Meek and dove-soft. The ancient beech trees at the far end of the garden have started to shed their leaves, and the ornamental cherries have a halo of mustard yellow.

The sun picks out some red highlights in Freddy's hair. He stands up and reaches for his drink, then moves next to me, squinting through the morning light. 'That's some garden.' He tilts his head. 'Do you look after it yourself?'

'When I can.' I'm not quite sure what is going on here. Small talk fell out of my life more than two years ago. You need to be out in the world for small talk. I only do self-talk now; that, and writing.

He takes a sip of his drink. 'I hope you don't mind me asking,' he says.

I raise my eyebrows.

'Your *outside* problem. Can you get over to those woods?'

'Nope. Haven't been into Blackthorn Wood for more than two years.'

'Oh, I get it now. *Blackthorn*. Your house is named after the wood.'

I sigh. 'You're clever.'

'What about the garden?' he says. 'Can you get all the way down there?'

'I can do. Usually.' I wish he would get on with his job; we're paying by the hour, and three days' worth soon stacks up.

'Do you ever feel panicky when you're down there?'

'Sometimes,' I say, 'but it's not the same. I can always get back to the house.'

'Can we have a quick walk out? In the garden, I mean. Take our coffees?'

I have two choices here. I can flip out completely and send this guy packing, back to whatever *estate agency* he's come from. Or I can, for the first time in two years, take a walk in my garden, in the autumnal sunshine, with a person who is not my family and will expect me to behave in a normal, rational human being kind of way.

'Erm. Okay,' I say.

He turns towards the fireplace, stripped pine and shabby, and runs his attention along the mantel full of photos. 'Is this your girls?' The large photo, central and in a silver frame, shows me with a daughter on either side, same light brown hair, though theirs is longer, more bohemian. Our faces are almost identical.

'It is. There's a year between them, but you wouldn't know it. That manual for teenagers... they're on the same page. Blackthorn is resting while they're in York with their school.'

Freddy dazzles me with his smile. 'Family, hey. Can't beat it.'

I shrug and lead him out of the room. He admires the Victorian tiled floor in the hallway, then follows me through the kitchen and into the scullery. I slip off my indoor shoes and grab a pair of wellies from the rack. They belong to one of my daughters, but we're the same size now. These have pink flowers and a wide plastic tread.

'Do you want to borrow a pair?' I ask. 'The grass is quite wet after last night.'

I'd watched the torrents of rain streaming down the bedroom window until well past two this morning, while the rest of the house slept. It doesn't take much to upend my stability. Which is one of the reasons why I didn't want to talk to a psychotherapist: a fractured horizon is easily tilted.

Freddy shakes his head and points to his already booted feet. He hasn't quite understood the etiquette of *boots off in the house* yet. What am I thinking? It's my rule, not his.

I step outside, taste the earthiness of the season. He follows, balancing his coffee carefully and toeing through the carpet of beech leaves.

'Is it the tree that lets go of its leaves,' I hear him say, 'or do the leaves just free themselves?'

In the middle of the lawn, I stop. Does he want me to answer? Is it a kind of cryptic trap? 'Not one for biology,' I say with a petulant lift of my shoulders. 'And who could ever know the truth of it, anyway?'

'Just making conversation,' comes the reply, then he kneels and scoops up a handful of the elusive orange treasure. 'This place.' He inhales sharply, eyes roaming again. 'It's got presence.'

'It's more than a hundred years old,' I snap. 'So, it should have.'

We peer upwards at the perfect Victorian symmetry: four

bays and two gabled attic rooms, carved stonework and a tiled frieze like a Christmas garland, right around the eaves. But for me, there might as well be bars on every window.

'Are you feeling okay?' he asks.

My answer springs from my lips before I can stop it. 'I'm not an invalid.'

A small puff of breath escapes from his mouth. 'That's me told.'

'Sorry. Sorry.' And I am. 'But it was my husband who suggested I get help. I don't need a psychotherapist.'

'A *therapeutic* psychotherapist, I'll have you know.' His hand is on his chest, but he is laughing. 'And I'm a listener too. Everyone needs one of those.'

That's my line.

We walk further across the grass. It gives way softly, in a squelch of brown water and moss. I'm losing my purpose. I want to get back inside, back to my laptop. Not be in the incredibly unpredictable place that is my garden.

'Look.' I direct my small sigh at him. 'You know my background. Know what happened. I'm happy to just live with the consequences.' And I am. I've got my family. And Blackthorn. 'Talking about it will just make things worse.'

He shakes his head. 'No, Cassie. The opposite is true. I stopped your husband when he tried to tell me your story. I don't want to discover it through his lens. And you need to talk to someone who isn't biased.'

This is exactly what I didn't want. Some two-bit therapist telling me I need to talk.

'So why are we wandering around my garden then? If you wanted to talk?'

It's there. It's rising. Making my chest heave. I try to gulp it down. Freddy tilts his head to one side. His eyes are pale grey, with tiny pupils. They stare at me. Knowing. I hate it when people know.

'You tell me,' he says.

Who does he think he is? Speaking gently, patronising? He's years younger than me. 'The truth? I haven't left Blackthorn for two years. Okay. I've said it. What else is there?'

I stomp away, leaving a slosh of water in my wake. In the scullery, I sling my boots into a corner, then pad back to the study.

Freddy isn't far behind me. 'Two years, Cassie,' he says.

I look at his boots.

'Don't pretend everything's normal. People don't stay in their house for two years without some kind of medical problem.'

There is something about him, like a persistent Labrador. I find I can't be annoyed. But I don't need to be reminded of my plight. In fact, I am the one who has lived with it, who has changed it from rage and fear into a life choice.

I twist up my lips. 'There's no medical problem. And don't expect some stunning story of war-torn abusive childhood and battered wives, because there's nothing to see here.' I hold up my hands. 'Really, there's not.'

The last thing I want to do is dig into my brain and find words enough so a stranger might understand. It's become far easier to just pretend.

Freddy scratches at his chin. There is the faintest trace of blond stubble. 'Humour me,' he says.

'Oh, there won't be humour.' The snap of my voice changes his level of attention: it's completely trained on me now.

Chapter One

I nside the library, the air was heavy with heat. Cassie had the sensation of suffocating. It was partly anxiety. After six hours of being scrutinised from every possible angle, her self-esteem was in tatters.

The day had started with the usual rushing about and breakfast in Blackthorn House. Helli and Janey held on to the last minutes of sleep, leaving minimal time for anything more than a slice of toast and Nutella, eaten on the journey to school. Si had left them to it, kissing Cassie on the cheek and wishing her good luck.

When she'd arrived at school and peered through the window of her classroom, her children were swarming around another member of staff, and it felt slightly disorientating: what was a teacher without the validating needs of her pupils? *Not much*, she decided, as she'd waited around for her interview to begin.

She moved to stand by an open window and watched as the hordes charged across the yellowed grass of the playing field, intent on home. Where she wanted to be. In Blackthorn's back garden, with its cool green shade and its peace. Or in the wood itself, wandering between tinder-dry boughs of ash and hazel, hidden from the world by tall stems of cow parsley, their pristine white heads alive with flying insects.

The collar of her jacket had rubbed a raw patch on her neck. She tried to lift it away. Whether she got the job or she didn't, the interview suit was going in the next Oxfam bag. Along with the new shoes. Across the room, the other candidates looked cool and unruffled: Laura Pearson scrolled through her phone and the two men lounged next to her.

Laura would get the job; Cassie was certain. When the previous headteacher died, less than two years ago, Laura had been the one to step up and lead the school. Until Alison Harman took over.

A soft scrape of carpet, and the door opened. Catching their breath gave them something in common for a moment. Tina Armstrong tottered into the room, all pencil skirt and heels.

'I've brought you a drink,' she said, eyes on Laura, then her gaze moved to Cassie. 'Wasn't sure if you three wanted anything.' She put down a tall glass of orange juice and smashed ice.

You three? They were all frazzled from the events of the day. It wouldn't hurt the school secretary to look after each of them.

'I wouldn't mind a cup of tea, actually,' Cassie said. 'Would any of you like one?'

Silence.

'Oh, well.' Tina pulled out the chair next to Laura and peered at Cassie. 'You know where the kettle is.' She turned her back. There was a mumble of conversation. Tina was asking Laura how the interview went. Not that it was ethical, having a favourite. Tina's opinion held little sway. Only that she shouldn't be in the room, coating one candidate with smooth words and iced orange. There was already a mountain of tension. Adding to it would see them all cresting, then rolling down the other side.

As much as she wanted to, Cassie couldn't allow herself a wander to the staffroom for a cup of tea. Not when the results were due in at any moment. Instead, she glanced around the room, trying not to notice Tina and Laura's shaky-shouldered whispering.

Each wall in the library was fitted with light-oak shelves and low cabinets. Book spines poked out at untidy angles. In two glass-fronted cupboards were silver rose-bowls and trophies, handles tied with ribbons from a time when team spirit was encouraged.

Last summer's sports day had consisted of a beat-your-own-record competition, with no winners or losers. And everyone took part; one of Alison Harman's first changes to the Parkhouse tradition, though what the parents wanted was a good old-fashioned tug-o-war.

The door flew open again. All heads turned.

'Cassie. Could you come with me, please?' Becky Ripley, chair of governors, with her hard eyes and neatly bobbed dark hair. The grilling she'd given Cassie during the interview had felt personal. A moment in the room, then Becky was leaving again and beckoning her to follow. Cassie blinked, parted her lips to ask why. Until she realised. She was the one, the successful candidate, the new deputy head of Parkhouse.

'I... Me?' A quick look across the room gave her a view of Laura, open-mouthed. Tina scowled. Then, with a stretch of Becky's arm, Cassie was ushered away.

The door closed softly.

'Congratulations, poppet,' Becky said, once they were outside. 'You aced it.' A grin. 'Alison is waiting for you in her office. I'll talk to the others. That'll make me popular, won't it?'

At the end of the corridor, Cassie stopped for a moment. Was this what she wanted? What would have been the point of going through the application process, with all its gut-churning moments, if not to arrive at this ending? But she was genuinely shocked. Laura Pearson had her name on the deputy head's job – name, address and telephone number. Cassie was the outsider, the rogue choice. And with that thought lingering just below the surface of her anxiety, she let herself into the headteacher's office.

Alison was sitting at her desk, cheeks flushed and peering over the top of her glasses. Cassie hovered by the doorway, taking in the ambience of piled papers and dying houseplants.

'Hello. Come on in.' The glasses were slipped off. 'And congratulations. You were the only choice. Becky and I agreed, for once.'

'Thank you. But I honestly thought it would be Laura.' She hesitated. Should she be speaking her mind? 'Everyone was rooting for her.'

'What do you mean, *everyone?*'

Alison had been in post for seven months. If staff had opinions not in line with her own, she was onto it straight away. Cassie was starting to get a feel for this, after a few personal clashes.

'I just meant she did a good job. You know, when Mick died.'

'I'm not keen on her, though,' Alison said. 'She gave me the cold shoulder on my interview day. Those things stay with you, Cass. I know you were all struggling at the time, but I had a sense of Laura Pearson deliberately *not* cheering for me.'

And here was the truth. When Mick Ripley had died from an asthma attack the school community became mired in misery. Cassie had worked alongside the guy from the early days of her recruitment. A hard taskmaster, but in the few years before he'd succumbed to the attack, there had been a change in him. One that dragged everybody down. Apart from

Laura. She'd risen to the top, doing what she could, along with the admin staff, to keep the school afloat.

Alison's appointment put an end to all that. *New blood*, she'd been called, and most staff agreed it was needed.

'Well, you didn't get Laura in the end; you got me,' Cassie said. 'I'll certainly graft for you.'

Alison laughed. 'You will. I know I haven't been here long, but I've always felt like you were on my side. And you work in year six. That's where I want my most experienced staff. My seniors.'

Cassie backed towards the door. 'Senior or not, I need a drink. Can I get you one?'

'Please. Tea with two sugars.' Alison leaned down and picked up her handbag. 'I've got a KitKat in here somewhere.' She began to rummage. 'You go out there and test the water. I'm sure everyone knows by now.'

The corridors were quiet. When the children went home, they dragged with them the spark and flame of the school, leaving behind only a breath of stale air and a creeping sense of abandonment. Cassie headed towards her classroom. More than anything, she wanted to tell Jax the good news. Then she'd phone Si, let him know his wife had just been given a promotion, that he was now married to the new deputy head of Parkhouse School.

'Congrats, Whites.' Kevin Noble crouched outside his doorway, shirt sleeves rolled, laying pieces of dripping paper on the floor. 'Knew you'd get it.'

'Thanks, Nobbs.' Cassie turned to him. 'Has all been okay down here?'

'Fine. Jax had it under control.' He stepped towards her. 'Come here. This might be the last time I can give you a hug. Now you're deputy-dog an' awl.'

Cassie let herself be embraced. 'Stop with the American accent, will you? It's creepy.' There was a faint aroma of stale body odour and coffee about him. And the scratchy texture of stubble against her cheek. 'That's enough. Show some respect.'

'Will you two stop it?' Jax. She stepped into the corridor pushing her glasses to the top of her head and peeled Kevin's arms away. 'And congratulations, love. Although, I knew you'd get the job. Been trained by me, haven't you?'

Typical Jax.

'Your answers went down a treat, Mrs T. Thanks for the coaching.' Cassie peered into the classroom. Every table was neat and prim, books lined up, pencils standing to attention in their brightly coloured pots. 'How've the kids been?' If she'd learnt anything in her years of working with Jax, it was the value of a good teaching assistant: wordless support in the crazy arena of trying to hold thirty young minds for long enough to do some good; a last bastion when the well of endless enthusiasm finally ran dry.

'Put it this way: I told them I'd report them to the deputy head if they started anything.' Jax giggled. 'None of them knew who that was.'

What was she saying? Was *visibility* part of Cassie's role? If that was the case, she'd better go and make herself visible and allow people to voice their congratulations – for her benefit as much as theirs. And it wouldn't hurt to make an ally of Tina Armstrong, let her know the new deputy head was approachable. 'Make us a cup of tea, Jax. I won't be long, then we'll have a gossip about today.' She called over her shoulder. 'Could you make one for Alison, too.'

The door leading to the office was closed. Cassie lifted her knuckle for a moment then let it drop. Through the glass panel she could see the large desks that belonged to Tina and her new assistant, Denise Kelly. Their chairs were empty.

With a push of the door, Cassie let herself in. Then she heard the soft muttering of female voices. Laura Pearson. Pink faced and dabbing at her eyes, with Tina and Denise by her side. The three of them, huddled in a corner.

'Oh. Hi.' Cassie's gaze swept over them all. 'Sorry. I'll come back.'

No reply. If Cassie had expected a greeting, or an offer of congratulations, none came. Instead, Tina Armstrong let out the smallest sigh. A whispered exhale of breath. But it was enough.

Chapter Two

I f she'd thought about it properly, Cassie might have realised her first staff meeting as deputy head was not going to give her instant acceptance. She'd pictured herself, sitting alongside Alison, ticking off items on their freshly-typed agendas. Instead, there had been Laura Pearson, refusing to meet her eye and giggling with her teaching partner, Judy Barker. And Kevin Noble, sprawled on a chair, scrolling through his phone and sharing mints with some of the infant staff.

When she'd tried to put her points across, most were met with a kind of weary acceptance that begged for home. The only time any interest had been shown was when Cassie told the staff they were to send the children's data forms to the office to be checked. This was followed by mutterings that *Tina wouldn't like it*. Mainly from Laura. Kevin responded with a cocked eyebrow, making Cassie's cheeks flare red, and she wondered if she should just quit before she made a total idiot of herself.

The staff were not used to meetings: attending was part of Alison's new regime. Mick Ripley had insisted his teachers were in their classrooms or in their homes, which made him a popular head. On the day Becky Ripley telephoned to tell them he'd been rushed to hospital, unable to get a breath, his staff had clung on with him. Pointless, as it turned out. He hadn't made it out of accident and emergency.

After the meeting, Cassie caught up with Kevin in the corridor. 'Where was Joe tonight? Is he okay?'

Kevin huffed. 'I could do with a chat, *deputy head*.'

'Oh. Like that, is it?' She walked the few steps to his classroom, picking up a ruler from the floor as she entered.

'Shut the door.' He waited for a moment. 'I'm worried about Joe. Something's not right there. I asked him if he'd written out his half-termly reports and he burst into tears.'

Cassie sat down on the edge of a table. Joe Smythe had been her colleague for a few years. Theirs was a relationship close enough for teaching, but not for anything else. Visual cues were everything to teachers; if you looked okay, you must be okay. Time spent on asking after each other could be put to better use. Not good for helping with mental health, she realised now.

'Oh, no. Poor guy. Did he give you any clues? I thought there was something, but—'

'Nope. I just stood there, like an idiot, handing him tissues.'

'Where is he now?' Not that she could do anything.

'He went home. If he makes it to the end of next week, it'll be a miracle.' Kevin smoothed a hand across his chin. Scratched a little. 'I don't know if I should go round to his house or not.'

'Could do. But don't make him feel worse. And I can't really go now, can I? He'd think Alison sent me.'

Kevin pressed his lips together. There was something in the tilt of his head.

'What?'

'This might not be linked. And I'm not a stirrer, as you know.'

A raised eyebrow from Cassie. 'Oh?'

'Tina Armstrong came to me the other day. Said she'd had to have a word with Joe about collecting his dinner money. He keeps losing it, and parents have been complaining, apparently.'

'What's she telling you for?'

Kevin held out his hands. 'Don't have a go at me. I think she just wanted it sorting. She's asked him about it and got nowhere.'

'If Joe's got problems, the last thing he wants is admin staff on his case.' Cassie got up. 'I'll have to speak to them.' She lifted her shoulders and walked away. Joe in tears? Something was causing the guy to crumble. He was a strong part of their team, intelligent, and good at keeping on top of his paperwork. Unlike Kevin. Cassie had been Kevin's mentor, and he was a good teacher. But the mistakes he made in private were a constant source of entertainment for the younger staff, and of eyebrow-raising for the older.

Tina was locking the office when Cassie arrived.

'You're late tonight,' she said.

Tina tugged the strap of her handbag higher up her shoulder. She did not meet Cassie's eye. 'I had a few things to finish.'

'Ah, right. Could you spare five minutes now for a chat?'

'Not really.' Tina reached for the pass-coded door. 'What's the problem?'

'It's not a problem, exactly. I'm just information-gathering.' Cassie tapped in the code. 'Never mind. You get off. I'll see you tomorrow.'

Tina held the door open with her foot. 'Information-gathering? What does that mean?'

'Nothing. You go home; it's late. I'll catch you in the morning.'

They stood together in the doorway for a moment. Cassie thought back to her interview day, the way Tina looked at her, eyes narrowed, contempt visible but unspoken. There would be no cooperation from this woman, she was sure.

November 2015

Monday morning, seven o'clock, and Cassie arrived at Parkhouse. She stepped out of her car and looked up at the silhouette of the school. This week, she would find time to chat with every member of staff, get herself known a bit. And here was her first victim. No matter what time Cassie left for work, the site manager would be in the building before her. There would always be a yellow glow of welcome and the sound of the hoover. Dot. Queen of the Doc Martens boots and cargo belt.

'Hiya.' She looked up as Cassie walked into the reception area. 'Cold out there, innit?'

'Toasty in here though.' Cassie loosened her scarf. 'The tree looks nice.' She peered upwards to the place where the topmost branch of the twinkling Spruce bent sideways. 'Bigger than usual, is it?'

Dot gave a wink. 'You know me.' She ran a hand through red hair threaded with grey. 'The bigger, the better.' Which was exactly the right attitude for managing a solid Victorian building with gabled ceilings and an immense central heating bill. She kept the place spotless. Flawless, in fact, despite the wreckage potential of more than 200 sticky fingers and muddy shoes. 'How was your weekend?' Dot spread her hands along the tops of her hips. 'Do anything nice?'

'Work.' Cassie sighed. 'And sleep. What about you?'

'Took the little 'uns swimming. To give *her* a break, like.' She thumbed towards her invisible daughter; the one Cassie felt she knew so well. 'Then I did them all a roast.'

'No rest then, Dot. Now, back in here, cleaning up after us lot.'

But Dot had turned away, lifting the hoover hose again. 'Like to be busy, don't I.'

'You do. See you in a bit.' Cassie made her way along the quiet corridors. The old radiators blew out a comforting warmth and circulated the clean smell of the place. Her bags were heavy with a weekend's worth of marking.

Si was away offshore again, and she'd been on her own in Blackthorn, missing his easy company and good conversation. The girls had each other.

The next two weeks would be a frantic round of Christmas show rehearsals, parties, and communal singing. And that was before she could even start on her own preparations. There was a nostalgia to be found in singing carols and playing pass-the-parcel, eating ice-cream and red jelly, and wrapping thirty selection boxes, but sentimentality didn't prevent fatigue. She and her colleagues spent most of the December holidays recovering enough strength to teach the spring term, mangers and babies forgotten.

She flicked on the classroom lights and put her bags down by her desk. A glance at the clock told her she had about half an hour before Alison would arrive. Thirty minutes where she could just be Cassie Clifton, with no agenda, no role to play, no scattering of her edges.

Car headlights flashed through the window. Alison. Earlier than usual. Cassie hung up her coat, then sat down at her desk for a moment while her to-do list spooled in her head. A school was like a brilliantly polished diamond: solid and impenetrable, beautifully transparent but with enough facets to render it completely unpredictable. She would make tea and then she would wait.

In the staff kitchen, with the kettle set to boil, Cassie leaned against the counter and looked through the window at the rooftops and the glassy indigo of the morning sky. A solitary herring gull peered in at her. She heard footsteps, a dragging of heels on carpet. She recognised the sound. Alison. The door opened.

'Morning.' Her boss's grimace told Cassie something wasn't right.

'Morning. Are you okay?'

Alison checked around the room. 'Not really. Make me a coffee and meet me back in my office, would you? Please?' She backed away again.

'No probs. See you in a min.'

But Alison had already gone.

The kettle bubbled. Cassie found two mugs, dropped a tea bag into one and spooned instant coffee into another. Monday mornings hadn't ever been straightforward. Not even as a young and newly qualified teacher, with high ideals but low understanding of personnel issues. When Mick Ripley died, the town held its breath. How could anyone fill his shoes? But Alison Harman had stuck her neck out, *a brass neck*, Cassie thought, and she'd been taken on. Change caused panic, caused people to protect their empires. But nothing ever improved without change, so Parkhouse was enduring it. And Cassie was determined the diamond at its heart would shine even more brightly at the end of the process.

When she shouldered her way into Alison's office, the headteacher was sitting at her computer.

'Look at this.'

That tone, it was almost a command. Cassie didn't react. She was becoming used to it. There was an open email on the screen.

'I can't see it without my glasses,' she lied. Reading other people's emails felt sneaky, ferrety.

'I'll tell you then, shall I?' A pause. 'Them two. In the office. They've sent me an informal complaint.'

'About what?'

Alison exhaled loudly. 'They're telling me I'm not doing my job properly. I'm missing appointments and not getting returns in on time. That's not my bloody job, Cass, is it? That's admin.'

'They've got a nerve,' Cassie growled. 'Do they actually know what it takes to run a school?' She was picturing the two secretaries, competitive dieting and ridiculous heels, heads together, conspiring. 'You got us through the last OFSTED inspection. You, not them.'

And what a time it had been. From the hard-edged questioning to the patronising use of the word *dear*, the Parkhouse staff had fought for their lives. Three days and nights running on adrenaline and doughnuts, not to mention the gallons and gallons of coffee. And for what? To please three skinny women, who refused every school lunch they were offered.

'Well. I'm going to have that pair in,' Alison was saying. 'And you'll need to be there. I'll get some cover for you this afternoon.'

More barking out of orders. Cassie chewed at her bottom lip. This was her role now. Listener and do-er.

'That's fine,' she said. 'Those two need to be put back in their box. Not sure why they think they can even comment on how you run your school.'

Alison nibbled her thumb nail. The burgundy gel had all but peeled away. 'There's one more thing.'

'What's that?'

'Joe's phoned in sick. Could have predicted it, couldn't we?'

'I suppose so. He wasn't right last term. But we never found the time to talk to him.' Cassie didn't feel like explaining. 'Is there cover?'

'I've got someone for now. But we'd better presume we'll need a bit more.' Alison leaned back in her chair and rolled her shoulders.

'You think?'

Staff rarely went off sick when Mick had been in charge. Cassie glanced around the room, took in Alison's coat and bags, heaped on the small cluster of easy chairs in the corner, and the wilt of a weeping fig by the window. Was this woman on top of things? She wasn't sure.

'He's not been right for a while, Cass. I don't think this is a twenty-four-hour bug. I've asked Judy Barker to cover this week. She's worked in year six before, in her other school. Laura said she'll do the extra hours in their class.'

Cassie gritted her teeth. 'How did that go down?'

'Meaning?'

'Nothing. Only that those two usually do everything together.'

Silence. Cassie wasn't sure whether to add anything else.

Alison slapped her hands down on the desk. 'I'm telling you, Cass. I won't have staff questioning my decisions.' A pause. 'I don't mean you. But it's not up to Laura Pearson to decide what happens in this school. And Judy was fine about it.'

'Fair enough.' Cassie moved towards the door. 'Anything else?'

But Alison was already scrolling through her emails, distracted.

'I'll go then and catch you later.' She closed the door behind her and stood for a moment trying to picture her part in a showdown with the admin staff. Tina Armstrong in particular, with her sideways glances and tiny huffs.

Jax was in the classroom, curly grey head bent over a pile of children's books, Christmas earrings flashing.

'Morning, Mrs T.'

'Morning,' she beamed. 'What's occurring?'

'Oh, the usual. Mr Smythe has gone off again, so Mrs Barker is covering his class. And I'll be out for an hour this afternoon. Can you cope?'

Jax yawned. 'Course. What's wrong with him this time?'

'Not sure. So, we'll have to give our planning to Judy. I've got a feeling she'll be working with us long-term.'

'*C'est la vie.*' Jax turned back to her work. 'You're on morning duty so you'd better go. I'll finish up here.'

The classroom was warm and bright, and Cassie was reluctant to leave, but Alison Harman insisted her staff were visible in the mornings, especially after the weekend, when raw parenting caused a hangover for some children. She put her coat back on, looped her scarf around her neck and went to make herself another mug of tea.

'See you later.' Jax's sing-song voice crossed the room, but she didn't look up.

Terraced housing faced the school on every side, Victorian red brick with the added upgrade of UPVC, and a busy road thrown in for good measure. Cassie held her hands around her mug and blew steam into the grey morning. It had snowed across the Lakeland peaks overnight. None had settled in their coastal town, but she could feel freezing air rolling down from the mountains as if they were just next door, instead of thirty miles away. She wandered up to the front gate. No sign of any children yet; cars zoomed past, headlights splattering the gloom.

'Hi, Whites.' A voice behind her. She turned slightly.

'Nobbs. Morning.'

Kevin Noble. Early. Unusual.

'Cold one, isn't it?'

'It is.'

His cheeks were a mottled lilac colour under the weekend's greying stubble.

'Get a better coat.' Cassie looked at his brown sweater, a dress-shirt collar on view. 'That'd help.'

This was their relationship. Older sister, feckless younger brother. He pushed his hands into the pockets of his trousers, shivered a little.

'Anything new? Boss seems busy.'

'Joe's off again.'

Their usual mode of catch-up: snatched seconds in between the bigger events of the day.

'I think he's having some kind of breakdown.'

'Really? You didn't say anything?' Cassie frowned.

'It's the same for all of us at the moment, isn't it? New leadership and stuff.'

'I hope you're not including me in that?'

He shook his head, looked across the road and exhaled, blowing out a cloud of steam.

'Nah, not you. Her.' A finger-point over his shoulder. 'Some of the fuck-ups she makes, Cass—'

'Stop.' Cassie held up her hands. 'We have to support her. She's all we've got. Everyone makes mistakes when they're new.'

'She's not that new, though, is she?'

'Maybe not. But she's got us. To learn from, I mean. Tough as that is.' She hesitated. 'In other news, Judy Barker is moving up from lower school to cover for Joe. She's worked in year six before, apparently.'

Kevin's shoulders dropped as he let out a small sigh.

'What?' asked Cassie.

'Her. Judy. She fancies me, you know.' He lowered his eyes, smiled slightly.

'Everyone fancies you in your little world. She's a married

woman. With kids. You'll be fine.' Cassie gulped down her drink. Cold tea, her favourite.

She and Kevin stood shoulder to shoulder, alert for any sign of local rebellion. Further along the pavement, a group of children were crowded together, sprawling over each other, the royal blue of their uniform telling the world where they were heading. One of them was throwing something at the boarded-up windows of the Sure Start centre. Cassie stared for a moment, then winked at Kevin. 'That's us, Nobbs.'

'Sure is,' came the answer, and they moved towards the group.

In the afternoon and with her class hard at work, Cassie took a moment to mentally prepare for what she saw as her first proper personnel meeting. That the admin team felt aggrieved enough to complain wasn't sitting well; all the staff were being subject to change, Tina and Denise included. Alison needed to put these two women back in their box.

Outside, the grey pall of winter crept its way along the terrace of houses opposite the school. Car headlights flared. Two o'clock in the afternoon, and it might as well have been the middle of the night. Cassie's shoulders felt heavy with the weight of other people's problems. They pinched like so many unwelcome fingers.

'Miss. Someone's brought a note.'

Cassie turned back to her class and saw Lysette, one of her brightest pupils, talking to a smaller child, soft brown heads together, and the little one grinning.

'Pass it here please, Lysette.' She shook the water off her hands, then dried them on a turquoise paper towel. The note was from Alison. Time to meet with the admin staff.

'I'll have to go, Mrs T,' she called. 'Is that okay?'

Jax lifted her head. 'I'm sure we'll manage,' then to the children, 'won't we?'

'Y-e-s.' Agreement, but with little choice. A resigned tone.

She and Jax were a rock-solid team, without loopholes or chances for a flex of the rules. There was a security in their system; children drank in their low-level routines and used them for support when big things happened in their lives. It worked for adults too.

'You behave for Mrs T,' Cassie waved her finger, 'or there'll be trouble.'

'And you behave, Mrs Clifton.' Jax peered across at her. 'Let's hope the black stain on your shirt won't count against you.'

Cassie looked down. *Damn,* she thought. *I don't want to lose marks for my attire, not with the admin fashionistas on my case.* She left the classroom and made her way to the back office. The private one. Dot was in the corridor, down on her knees and scrubbing at a patch of something lumpy.

'And so, it begins.' She turned her head towards Cassie.

'Nice.' But it wasn't the time for small talk.

Alison was already in the office, informal, on an armchair. This was the place where parents came to have a good cry, and staff came to have a good rant. There was a small desk with a phone but not much else: cream walls, a few burnt-orange fabric chairs, and vanilla from a diffuser.

'Let's gather ourselves, then I'll buzz that pair in.' Alison was tugging at the hem of her black wool dress. A grey cardigan was draped across the back of her chair.

'Okay.' A hello would have been nice, though Cassie didn't point that out. 'What exactly is their problem?'

'Don't know.' Alison made a chopping motion with her hands. It emphasised each word. 'You've worked with Tina longer than I have. You tell me. Denise, I don't understand. She seemed quite happy when I interviewed her.'

When Cassie thought back across the time since Mick died, she could only remember Tina weeping with the rest of them, and bustling around, doing what was needed to keep the school running. With Laura Pearson at her side. Then Alison was appointed and there had been a collective sigh of relief, although it came with the realisation that she was nothing like her predecessor. *I lead from the back*, had been her first words at a welcome meeting. Some staff had emerged from the meeting with wide grins and the sparkle of freedom at their heels. But Cassie was wondering who'd be at the front.

'I can't get a handle on it myself,' she said. 'Only that Tina's a bit of a control freak.'

'Buzz them in, then. Let's hear what they've got to say.'

Cassie pressed a button on the telephone, brushed invisible pieces of fluff from her black teacher-slacks, and waited. Alison's nostrils flared and she sat forward in her chair, arms folded rigidly.

The door flew open.

Tina Armstrong tottered in, followed by Denise Kelly, blonde bob and pursed red lips. They perched together on the edge of the chairs directly opposite. Cassie wasn't sure if she should make eye contact. Was a smile the right thing to give? But neither of the women looked up.

Alison made her move. 'I've read your email, ladies.' A small cough. 'I must admit, I'm a bit confused. Are you saying you're unhappy with my admin skills?' Her nostrils were still flaring.

No response.

'Come on, let's have it.' A flash of redness crept up from the neckline of her dress. Cassie shifted in her seat, hoping her boss wasn't going to use the vocal tactics she'd witnessed when children wouldn't comply.

Then Denise was speaking. 'It's just… well…you're getting everything confused, Alison.' She picked at the clump of white tissues in her hand, glanced at Tina for a moment. 'Even though we send you lists of all you need to do.'

'You even missed that case conference last week,' Tina chipped in. 'We reminded you, didn't we? And—' She blinked at Denise, who nodded, emphatically.

Like an over-prepped actress, Cassie thought. *What was this fiasco?* But she said nothing. Silence was a great solvent, in her opinion.

'And we can't keep chasing after you, Alison.' Denise again. 'We've got our own work to do.'

Cassie watched the rise and fall of Alison's chest, the set of her jaw. She could see the muscles coiling. A snake, ready to spring. But there was more. Denise's lip-purse tightened. Tina pressed hers together, then let them spring apart.

'I've been running the school office for over fifteen years,' she began, 'and I like everything to be *just so*. I don't want my efficiency called into question. But I'm the one who has to cover and apologise when forms haven't been completed or emails answered.'

Denise interrupted. 'And.' A manicured hand on her chest. 'The other day I found my computer logged on with your passwords. Imagine how that could have ended.'

'Imagine.' Alison's eyebrows were sky high. 'I had to deal with an incident. It went on longer than I thought. That's all. I can't be in two places at once.'

Tina began again, all head tilt and saintly. 'I've never had to cover so many mistakes. When Mick—'

A breath was drawn on the name of Mick Ripley, and Cassie saw her chance to jump in.

'Stop,' she said quietly. 'I'm going to stop you there.' Her hands slapped onto her knees, and she leaned forwards. Tina arranged her thick black brows into an artful scowl. Denise shifted in her seat.

But Cassie continued. 'I'm going to stop you because you've not thought this through.'

Two frowns were fixed on her now.

'Alison pulled this school out of a deep hole last spring. She managed to prevent us from being plunged into special measures. Surely you knew that?' Cassie glowered. 'You didn't?'

Silence.

'The inspection team trusted her capacity to improve the school. Standards weren't up to the new expected high when the old head was in charge. And please don't mention him again. He's gone.'

Denise shredded her tissues with long red nails.

Cassie pushed on. 'It's Alison's job now. She's the headteacher. You don't need to fully understand pupil learning outcomes, do you? Well. She doesn't need to trouble herself with the running of your electronic diary, either.'

Tina raised herself up, puffing out her chest. 'We have to check every one of her letters for spelling and grammar mistakes. It's just not on. We don't have time.'

Denise agreed, dabbing at one eye with the clump of tissue.

'Yet you've got time to chase round after staff to collect their Avon money?' A bubble of anger came up from Cassie's stomach. Who did these two think they were? 'And checking for spelling mistakes in letters is absolutely part of your job.'

Tina's face crumpled in on itself, but she didn't reply.

'If I were you,' Cassie continued. 'I'd get on with the admin side of running a school. Including support for teacher – and headteacher – admin. If that's not too much trouble.' Cassie made her mouth into a straight line, something she did to the children in her class. They all knew what it meant. 'Actually, I think some of the admin jobs the staff are expected to do need to be handed over to you, ladies.'

'Such as?' Tina's eyes narrowed.

'Collecting dinner money, for example. Some of the teachers are struggling enough with their workload, without having to collect all sorts of money. Only to be criticised when they make mistakes.'

Alison shot Cassie a warning glance. 'Cass–'

'Sorry. But it needs saying. You and I are in charge here, are we not?'

Tina got to her feet. 'I'm not listening to this,' she spat. 'Who do you think you are? So good with words, aren't you? But that's all.' Then she stormed towards the door.

Denise stood up, tugged down the sides of her skirt and flung her clump of tissue into the bin. 'Sorry,' she mouthed at Cassie.

Nothing more was said as they left the room, one behind the other, the clicking heels telling their own story.

'They needed to be told,' Cassie said. Her boss was shaken, she could tell. 'What did they think they were doing?'

'What they were doing,' Alison sneered, 'was trying to place me under their control.'

'Well, that was a fail then.' But something had shifted in Cassie's trust, though she didn't say this. 'Whose idea was that little charade, do you think?'

Alison shook her head. 'Probably Tina's. But I'm surprised at Denise. She's one of mine.'

'Your what?'

'My recruits. That's all I meant. When I took the job, I expected some resistance from Mick's staff. I'd been warned. Denise was my personal choice. So were you. I stupidly thought there should be some loyalty attached.'

'There is.' Cassie hesitated. Loyalty worked both ways. 'From me, anyway. And as you say, Tina could hardly leave Denise out of that little panto, whether the poor woman wanted to be involved or not.'

'Bloody hell, Cass. I thought headship was about moving away from managing the day-to-day quarrels of the children.'

They both laughed at that, and the tension dissolved a little.

'You go and see your class off,' Alison said suddenly. 'I'll come down after.'

Cassie was being dismissed. She stood up. Tina's perfume still lingered. Expensive, but gone off.

'I'll see you later.'

She walked out of the office on shaky legs but pleased with herself. There could be no doubt about her management status now.

In the corridor, Dot stood, wearing a magenta anorak, a huge bunch of keys in her hand. Kevin Noble was leading a crocodile of children, coats on and smiling, and other staff hung around their classroom doors, wearing an end-of-the-day weariness.

'What's been happening, lovely?' Dot called to her, a lift of voice over the milling middle-tones.

Cassie stopped. 'What do you mean?'

'Nothing. Except that Tina's just stormed past me, telling me to *watch my back*. I think she's in there.' She gestured towards the staff toilet. 'She said the same thing to Mr Noble, too.'

Later, as Cassie pulled her car onto the drive of Blackthorn, she thought about those words – *Watch your back* – flying from Tina's mouth like poisonous darts. But why shout a warning to other staff if she felt herself to be the victim? *She's not implying I'm dangerous, surely?* Cassie giggled, but not with humour. Something felt off. Up until this point, Tina Armstrong had been nothing more than a member of the Parkhouse admin team. She hardly knew the woman out of her context: now, she felt like the enemy.

The house was in darkness, the street quiet. Cassie stepped from her car into the silvery chill of the evening and slammed the door behind her. The girls wouldn't be home for a while. Both were in their high school Christmas production, one on the stage, the other behind the scenes, so it would be cook-chill meals for them all, then making a worksheet about *adverbial phrases*. So much for deputy head highlife. She locked her car and stepped carefully up the three stone steps to her porch.

Watch your back: there had been something chilling about Tina's words. Did people really speak like that about each other, in a professional workplace? Perhaps they did. Cassie was management now. Maybe she should expect it.

As she opened the front door, warmth filtered out. She'd be without Si for a few more days, but the safety of the house wrapped around her like her granddad's arms used to. He had loved this house, and Cassie had been loath to change it much when they'd first moved in. Apart from new cherry-wood floors and central heating, the place was much like it was when her grandparents lived here. High ceilings and an old pine kitchen, a range cooker and a freezing cold scullery. There was a small front garden, and behind the house was a long stretch of grass with an orchard and a beech grove, then the various glasshouses where Granddad had grown his tomatoes and grapes.

He had loved his garden.

Cassie's swing was still there, attached to a thick beech bough. Her girls weren't keen on the outdoors. Electronic games and Primark were more their thing. But Cassie liked nothing more than to put on her walking boots and anorak, and stomp around in the garden, pruning and pottering.

And then there was the wood. Blackthorn House was set in a position high above the town, and looked out across a stretch of man-made woodland to the Irish Sea. It was prime Woodland Trust project land, and a popular place for dog walkers and families to enjoy winding pathways grown wild with blackthorn bushes and coppiced hazels, twisty ash trees and arcs of bramble and ivy. Cassie liked to pretend she owned the wood. Or that Blackthorn did.

She flicked on the Christmas tree lights and went into the kitchen to make herself some tea. She would telephone Si later, tell him about her day, about her encounter with the admin staff. Maybe tell him to watch *his* back.

But something was causing an itch, right at the edge of her consciousness. A niggle. A question. Why hadn't Alison Harman done anything to quell this small staff uprising?

Chapter Three

The supermarket on a dark Friday evening in the run-up to Christmas: it carried Cassie back to the time she'd taken a winter trip to New York. Before the girls. She and Si had walked along 34th Street, hand-in-hand, a rustle of padded jackets and enthusiasm. And they'd been steamrollered. Flattened into non-existence by packs of women made from leopard skin and arm-links. In Macy's, they hadn't been able to get anywhere near displays for the grabbing and grasping and elbowing of people who obviously felt themselves to be incredibly important. Just like Tesco on a Friday night.

'Hiya, Mrs Clifton.'

Cassie looked down the bread aisle. Two children in Parkhouse uniforms were zooming a trolley along, upsetting the tutting brigade.

'Hiya, girls.' She enjoyed their open-mouthed beaming. Teachers lived in the cupboard, didn't they? And they certainly didn't push a trolley full of wrapping paper around a supermarket. 'You're behaving, I hope.'

Their mother smiled a hello, then glided by, joining in with her children's glee at seeing a *teacher*. The joys of living in a small town: supportive, but no secrets.

Cassie looked at her watch. Three hours and she would be at the staff party. Two more and she would be home again, closing the front door of Blackthorn House and settling down for a less than traditional Christmas. One that didn't involve carol services and visits from Santa. Her girls were way past that now, thank goodness.

Kevin Noble with a pillow tied around his waist and wearing the school Santa suit had caused a collective shudder, although Judy Barker insisted on posing for a photo perched on his knee. Judy Barker, with her burgundy-rinsed hair and smocked blouses. And always a comment to make about television sport. She'd be part of their team next term, on a sabbatical from her relationship with Laura Pearson, but she'd be no substitute for Joe.

The next aisle was empty, apart from a woman peering closely at the display of baking products. Something about her stance caught Cassie's attention. Becky Ripley, bobbed hair tucked behind her ears and holding a shopping basket.

'Time for your legendary mince pies again, isn't it?'

The woman thumped her hand against her chest. 'Mrs Clifton. You bloody made me jump.'

'Sorry.' Cassie thought about a hug but settled for a smile. The other woman reached for her hand and brushed it lightly.

'You're right about the mince pies,' she groaned. 'The lads are coming home, and I can never keep them fed. Or their families. This'll be the first time we'll all be together at Christmas, since—'

Some things Cassie would never be able to get her head round. Finding strength to do the ordinary, while dying inside; that took courage to a whole new level.

'I don't know how you do it,' she said. 'You're so, I don't know, calm, about everything.'

'I have to be, poppet. Those boys are my life. More so since we lost Mick.' She said his name as a whisper. 'Anyhow.' She put her hand on Cassie's arm. 'What's it like being a deputy head? Do tell.'

'It's fine, thanks. Keeping me busy. Didn't see you at the last governors' meeting. Alison said you weren't well?'

'Oh, I'm up and down.' Becky glanced at her watch. 'Listen. Have you got time for a coffee? The café didn't look busy when I came in.'

'Course. That'd be lovely.' But in her head, Cassie was totting up time and deciding the staff party wasn't a priority compared to giving Becky what she craved. 'Now?'

'Why not. I bloody hate shopping, anyway. It feels lonely.'

The bright, boxy café was packed with tables. Most had been claimed by families and couples, people eating and talking and laughing. No wonder Becky felt lonely. They settled themselves, then Cassie pushed through the crowd to join the drinks queue. She gazed at the wilted slabs of Victoria sponge and cheesecake in the glass-fronted fridges but settled for two cups of coffee in chunky supermarket mugs. She added four UHT milk pods and some sugar packets to her tray, then handed over her money to the young guy operating the till.

Back at the table, Becky was scrolling through her phone. 'Look at this. My granddaughter. Isn't she gorgeous?'

Cassie peered at the photo. 'Oh, yes. Beautiful. And she has the look of your family. The *Ripley* effect, we used to call it.' The child had soft brown eyes and hair. And Mick's smile. 'Sorry. I didn't mean–'

'Everyone says that. She looks just like him, doesn't she?'

'She does. Have you got any other grandchildren?' Cassie slid a mug towards her.

'Yes. Both my boys have children and there's another on the way. I'll soon have four.'

'Do you see them a lot?' Her sons lived locally as far as Cassie could remember.

'I do. Thank God. I don't think I'd have coped. After Mick, and all that.' Becky stirred some sugar into her coffee. 'The job did for him in the end, you know.' Her expression hardened.

'I wish things had been different,' Cassie said. 'He loved his job.'

'Not in the last couple of years, he didn't. I blame *her*.'

What was she talking about? Cassie wanted to ask who, but the question felt too probing: she hardly knew this woman. Instead, she said, 'The job changed a few years ago. What with the *standards* agenda and everything. Mick's generation of headteachers took the fall for that.'

'Nothing to do with standards.' Becky's words fired out with a spray of spittle. 'It was that bloody Tina Armstrong. She never gave him a minute's peace.'

'Cassie. Cass, love. Wakey wakey.'

Cassie jumped out of a half-dream, felt a gentle touch on her cheek as the Christmas tree lights and the fire's orange glow came into focus: Blackthorn House. Her safety net.

'What time is it?' she mumbled, tongue thick with sleep.

Si knelt beside her. 'Time to get ready. If we're going.'

'We'll have to. I didn't say goodbye to anyone before I left.'

After coffee with Becky, there had been a bit more shopping, then a journey home, thinking about Tina Armstrong. The woman hadn't given Mick a moment's peace: what did that mean? Tina was pushy. Cassie had seen it for herself. And she needed flattening where Alison was concerned. Is this what she'd done to Mick; tried to get the upper hand?

'Well, it's past eight o'clock now,' Si was saying. 'By the

time we show our faces, there won't be any of the buffet left. So, quick, quick.' He reached down and took her hands. 'Up you get.'

Cassie found herself lifted into his embrace. He kissed the top of her head lightly, then stepped back. 'Are you okay?'

'I will be, when I can forget about work for a couple of weeks.'

'Those two office cows haven't been at you, have they?' He was taking her side, as he always did.

'No. They've been keeping a low profile. Well, kind of.'

In truth, Cassie felt she was being deliberately avoided. December was busy, with hardly time to eat or drink once each day began, let alone talk to other staff. There was something, though. Just a feeling. Oblique glances when she walked past. Loud laughter excluding her. Fatigue could push things out of proportion, she knew that. Then the morning she'd seen a small gift on Kevin's desk, bright in its Christmas wrapping and glittery ribbon. She couldn't resist having a peek at the label:

Best wishes from the admin staff xx

She recognised Tina's tiny handwriting. There was nothing for Cassie.

'Okay.' Si's voice pulled her away from her thoughts. 'Let's go and spruce ourselves up a bit, then get it over with. Back here by eleven, hey?' He smiled.

Cassie couldn't bring herself to think any more about Parkhouse. It was simply her workplace. The reality of her life was here, with Si and the girls.

'Eleven at the latest,' she said, then left the room.

Within half an hour, they were driving away from Blackthorn and through the sharp winter darkness. The streets were quiet. At the edge of town, they left the main road. Two miles of dry-stone walls and grey pastureland brought them to an unmarked junction.

'I never know which one of these roads to take,' Si moaned. 'They all look the same at night.'

Cassie yawned. The Clarence Hotel was in a small village, along a twist of unlit country lane. Almost impossible to access, yet fully booked for most of the year.

'We'll sleep late tomorrow,' he said.

'Yep. The girls will be up for that.' Cassie was looking forward to the four of them hunkering down for two weeks, with no distractions except food and the occasional walk. 'And I'm not going to think about work until after New Year.' She sighed. 'But then it will be all systems go. Did I tell you Joe's having some time off?'

Si looked puzzled. 'No. Why?'

'He's not well. Workload stress. He hasn't been coping for a while.' She was barely coping herself.

'Poor guy. Who's taking over, then?'

'Judy Barker. I don't know if you've met her.'

Si shook his head.

'She's been job-sharing in the lower school.'

'What's she like? Will you and Nobbs get along with her?'

Something she'd been wondering herself. Not so much because Judy had been whipped from under Laura Pearson's nose, but more because of the way the woman bounced up on her toes and clapped her hands together at the prospect of joining Cassie's team. And Kevin Noble's expression could have featured in a Da Vinci painting.

'I'm sure we will. She works hard.'

They pulled onto the gravel outside the hotel. Icicle fairy lights hung along the casement of every window and a pair of bay trees at the entrance glittered in their tinsel wrappings. Cassie opened the car door and climbed out, tugging the lapels of her coat across the floaty blouse she was wearing. A tang of silage hung on the frozen air and the surrounding fields lay dark and quiet. But inside the hotel was warm and bright. As soon as she and Si walked into the yellow glow, they were assailed by greetings and hugs and joviality.

'I'll get us some drinks,' he said. 'Which of us is driving home?'

'You have a drink,' replied Cassie. 'Just get me a lemonade or something.' She could see Kevin stumbling over. That blurred look. The last thing she wanted.

'Cass. Babe.' He held out his arms.

She let herself be hugged. His breath was rank with alcohol. 'How much have you had?' she asked, stepping away.

'Not enough... yet.' He moved to her side and laid an arm around her shoulder. 'Going back into town after this.' A wave of his hand at the gathered crowd. 'Don't want the boss to see me at my *best*. You look nice, by the way.' He leaned in and kissed Cassie on the cheek.

The smell of cheap cologne caught at the back of her throat. She pushed him away. 'Hey. I'm your superior, too. Show some respect.'

'After my wife... wives... you're my favourite superior, Whites.' He leaned in again.

'Piss off, Nobbs. And they're ex-wives, remember. You don't do commitment.'

He stuck out his bottom lip and staggered slightly. 'I am so offended. You have my full commitment. I love you.' He launched himself at Cassie. 'And him.' A swing of his arm towards where Si now stood, then an extended embrace to include him.

'Oi. Watch the drinks.' Si moved away slightly. He looked at Cassie. 'How much has he had?'

'He's on the *I love you like my family* stage. Watch out. He usually kisses you after that.'

She took her drink and peered out across the crowd. If she

could attract someone's attention, they might come and break the hold Kevin Noble had exerted. His head was resting against her shoulder now. Everyone seemed to be in groups, intent on conversation and laughter. Only one person was looking towards her. Judy Barker. Eyes squinting and mouth a hard line. Then she raised her chin and looked away.

What was that? Cassie wondered.

Si was trying to free himself from Kevin's clutches. 'Come on, buddy, let's get you sat down.' He slid an arm around his chest and hauled him upwards. They struggled towards the bar sofa, and Kevin was deposited. He fell sideways slightly, and Cassie laughed. Nobbs never could do things in half-measures. Except commitment.

The evening wore on in a bright fug of conversation and food and laughter. Cassie chatted to Alison and her husband, then to Jax, and to some of the colleagues she hardly ever saw. And all the while, she kept one eye on Tina Armstrong and Denise Kelly. Both had permanently turned backs. Not that she tried very hard to attract their attention. Using Christmas gifts to mark their territory? It came directly from the book of *playground mentality*. Clearly not everyone at Parkhouse had read it.

Kevin Noble sprawled across the sofa and seemed to be asleep. Cassie watched people go over and check on him, then walk away when they realised there was no conversation to be had.

By midnight, she had come to the end of her energy, and her face ached with smiling. But she was completely sober, unlike everyone else. She flashed a look across to where Alison's husband was deep in conversation with Si. He talked his way out, then came towards her.

'Ready to go, my darling?' he smiled, his expression smudged with heat and alcohol.

'If you don't mind. I've had it.'

'Course not. I'm only here for you.' He slipped an arm around her shoulder. 'Do you think we should take Kev home?'

'Go and ask him. If he doesn't answer, we'll take him.'

She watched her husband stumble away. Tall and dark, and her rock. He managed to fit in wherever he went. Unlike her. Parties were not her favourite thing. She could pretend a good range of social skills when they were needed, but she'd rather be out walking on her own, or with Si and the girls. They were enough. Now, Si was lifting Kevin from his seat and supporting him across the room. She picked up coats and her bag and waved a few goodbyes. Alison gave her a thumbs-up.

Jax was sitting on a faded red sofa in the foyer, face flushed, and fanning herself with what looked like a hotel brochure, her hair an untidy helmet of greyish-brown curls, damp and flat.

'Been dancing too much,' she laughed, winking at Cassie. 'I can't keep up with the young 'uns anymore.'

'Don't give me that.' Cassie sat down next to her. 'You'll still be dancing when the rest of them are well into retirement.'

Jax snorted. 'Don't think so. I'm feeling my age at the moment. Hormones.' She winked. 'If you know what I mean.'

'I do. Anyhow, have a good Christmas, won't you? We're off now. Taking Kevin home.' Cassie tilted her head towards her husband. 'And here they come.'

She stood up. Jax moved with her. 'He needs to be careful, that lad. Or he'll not see his fortieth birthday.' She gave Cassie a kiss on the cheek. 'You have a good one, my love.' Then she was gone.

'Give us a hand, Cass. Where's his coat?'

'He doesn't have one.'

'Don't wanna go home,' he was mumbling. 'Nothing to go home for.'

Cassie dragged Kevin's arm over her shoulder, then watched as Si grabbed at his waist to move him forwards.

Kevin staggered. They used his momentum to propel them all through the front door.

Outside, the air was jagged with cold, and the sky scattered with icy stars. Two people were standing in the shadows, heads together, breath in clouds around them. Tina Armstrong and Judy Barker. They turned at the sound of the door closing.

'Where are you taking him?' Judy could have been talking to anyone; Cassie didn't answer.

'Cassie? Where are you taking Kev?'

'He's had it, Judy. We're taking him home.'

Kevin's feet dragged and he mumbled something, then Si was pulling him away. Behind her back, Cassie heard the faintest of whispers. Something like *has to do what mummy says.* But she couldn't be sure. A snatched glance over her shoulder showed her a pair of blank faces, frosty as the night.

'Bye, ladies,' she called. No answer came.

October 2019

Freddy swirls the last dregs of coffee around in the bottom of his cup. Has he been listening, I wonder? I'm not the best at talking about myself.

'I think that's where everything started,' I tell him. 'All my *problems.*' The word slips out of my mouth and lands between us with a grim thud.

'Why are you saying "problems" in that tone?' His head snaps upwards. Those hard grey eyes again, with a yellow glint of sunlight. 'Nothing you've said so far suggests you had problems.'

I seem to remember I'd told myself exactly the same thing. Run-of-the-mill personnel issues: nothing a deputy head couldn't deal with. But something didn't feel right, even then.

And the more I put it down to my new management status, the less it rang true.

'And in my humble opinion,' Freddy is saying, 'if those women couldn't see they'd overstepped the mark, they had an inflated view of their position.'

I shrug.

'The place was in mourning, Cassie. You should have been working together.'

'I thought we were. Don't forget, I'd been locked away in my little world of classroom teaching for a long time. I hardly noticed anything. Then suddenly I found myself in the world of scratchy little staff issues.'

A memory comes, then. Walking into Mick's office on a grey February afternoon. Him, hunched over his desk and Tina Armstrong looming with an armful of papers. Neither of them speaking. She'd flattened me with her hard-set body language, so I'd backed out of the door with a muttered apology and wondered what I'd walked into. Though I'd forgotten the scene once I'd got back to my class, it left me wanting to ask Mick if he was okay. Our relationship never allowed for that, but I did care about him. We all did, I think. There's nothing quite so self-centred as a teacher working away at their craft. I can see this now I'm standing on the outside, shining in a light; the corrosive nature of being trapped inside the diamond.

Freddy starts to flip through the pages of his notebook. 'How were you feeling at the time?'

'Fine,' I snap. Nothing riles me more than being asked about my feelings. It's so bloody belittling. A little over two years ago, I was a robust human being with a handle on most things, a coper, a facilitator. This guy has no idea.

He stifles a yawn with his fist. 'Sorry. I bet you're thinking I'm so rude. I need to move about, that's all.' He holds the cup out and tilts his head slightly.

'Another?' I ask. Aware that what I've told him so far is low-level, that there's a long way to go.

'Please. I'm just going to write a few other things down, if it's okay.'

I tell him it is, but the creepy tone is starting to annoy me. I don't want to be petted, like a kitten.

In the kitchen, I fill the kettle and switch it on to boil, rub my socked feet over each other and wonder again why I am confiding in this stranger. How could he understand the workings of my mind? Even when he has all the facts. But I have made a promise. And I keep my promises.

I find Freddy standing at the window of my study. There is a squirrel on the lawn. A grey. No reds here.

'We get a lot of them at this time of year,' I say, handing him his coffee. 'They skim up and down the beeches, setting up their winter stores. Fascinating, aren't they?'

He thanks me for the drink. 'Can I ask you another question?' he says lightly.

'Go ahead.' I'm not keen on being the patient.

'Did your boss… Alison, was it? Did she ask you to put yourself in the firing line? You know, with the admin staff?'

I have to think about this. I'm not sure if Freddy wants a straight *yes* or *no*.

'She didn't ask me to, no. But I somehow found myself taking the lead, in the early days of her headship.' I wonder now about the sort of lead she wanted.

'Why was that?'

He's sharp, this guy.

'I didn't want the school to fail, I suppose.' God, how noble of me.

He inhales deeply. 'But you weren't in charge.' He lifts his mug to his lips. Two hands around it, like it is the most precious thing. 'Failure would hardly be down to you, would it?'

'I was deputy head. So it would, in a way.'

'Fair enough. Though I can't help thinking, from what you've told me, that she *let* you take the fall with these admin staff; so she was in the clear.'

I don't look at him: the thought had occurred to me at the time too.

'It's how we worked, Alison and I. She was a leader who drove from the back, so she told us all.'

'Did other staff take the fall for her too?'

'Your expression, not mine.' My jaw is tightening and I'm pressing my teeth together. 'It was just a new way of working, that's all.'

Freddy takes another sip of his coffee. He doesn't say anything else. I don't fill the silence; I'm not that stupid. He can work for his fee.

There are footsteps in the hallway. My husband pops his head around the door again, the picture of discretion today. 'I'm just going to the shops, love,' he says. 'Will you be all right?'

'Course,' I reply. I'm always all right.

The front door closes with a heavy clunk.

'We never changed that door,' I tell Freddy. 'It's the original Victorian one. We had it dipped and repainted, though. It's two-inch pitch-pine.'

'You're proud of this place, aren't you?' he laughs then glances around. 'I would be too.'

'Go and have a look,' I tell him. 'There's nobody in now. Except us.'

But he shakes his head. 'We need to carry on,' he informs me, as though I'm trying to avoid it.

I take his empty cup. It clinks on mine. 'Everyone needs a break. It's therapeutic.' He doesn't laugh. 'I'll wash these, then we can talk again. Go and have a quick explore.'

I love Blackthorn House. It's a protective place, a refuge.

The way its thick walls create a cool haven in summer but a warm cocoon during the cold winter months; the way every room has the echo of family stories from decades and centuries before; its strong, square sense of decorum. But it has me trapped as surely as if someone had nailed all the doors and windows closed, while I'm still inside.

'A quick look, then.' He smiles, and trots off down the hallway towards the bottom of the staircase. I'm relieved. I want him to see I am normal. With a normal house and a normal life. I am in control, and I have choices. I am not another case for a psychologist: nothing feels worse than that.

When he comes back downstairs, his first words are, 'You can see all the way across to the Isle of Man from upstairs. And over to Millom. No wonder whoever built the place chose this outlook. And the woods right across the road. I'd love to live here.'

I've heard this so many times. But I'm happy for Blackthorn to be praised: its success hides my failures.

'See,' I laugh. 'That was a good break from... proceedings, wasn't it?'

I lead him back into the study. And not for the first time, I wonder what the hell I'm going to gain from having this man trailing behind me, making me relive everything that happened. It won't change outcomes, I won't have a light-bulb moment, where I suddenly find myself free again. He sits down on the sofa and lets out a long sigh.

'Sorry if I'm boring you.' My words jump into the room and run around in front of me like boisterous children let out to play. Freddy can see them too.

'Sometimes,' he says, finally, 'the way you talk surprises me. You can be so measured, and then you snap.'

'Sorry again, then.' I turn away. Look out of the window. Watch the afternoon shadows as they collect at the end of the garden. What was golden is now a muddy brown.

'I'd recommend you snapped more often. *Better out than in,* as my mother used to say.' He waits.

I can't help but laugh. My granddad used to say that, too, though he wasn't referring to words.

'Okay,' I say as I sit down next to him. 'Let's talk again. Then I can bore you some more.'

'Your story is far from boring, Cassie.' He shifts his position, like a cat looking for a sunny spot. 'And this Tina sounds like she had issues around control. Every time you've mentioned her it's been as part of some alliance or other.'

Issues around control? We're talking about a school, not a bloody psychiatric ward. But he's right. Dead right.

'Look,' I say. 'We were all just trying to work through our feelings about the death of one of our colleagues. None of us wanted to scratch below that particular layer of misery. Scalp-hunting was just how Tina dealt with things. Well, that's what I thought, anyway.'

He laughs. 'I'm interested to know how it panned out with you and these colleagues of yours.'

Why not give me a sympathetic pat on the head, too?

'Well, for your information,' I tell him, 'I thought – naïve, I know – that Tina Armstrong was simply a bitch.'

Chapter Four

A jay squawked down from the thick bough of an oak tree, a flash of bright blue in the spectral woodland. Hoarfrost covered every surface, every branch and skeletal shrub. Cassie stumbled along the ice-rutted path. Back-to-school dread was hitting hard and had left her feeling as raw as the January weather.

'Quick. Helli. Get a photo.'

She put a hand on her daughter's shoulder. It was shaken off immediately. The girls were small-boned and delicate, with Si's dark eyes and pale skin, but their temperaments came courtesy of the teenage years.

'Why don't you get one?' Helli snarled then turned away.

'I'll try.' Janey held up her phone, just as the jay flapped out of their vision.

'Damn.' She smiled at her mother. 'I don't know how Dad gets all his brilliant bird photos. I can't even get a blurry splodge.'

'He sits for hours,' laughed Cassie. 'You two will never be dedicated enough. Or boring enough.'

'Hey. I can hear you, if you don't mind.' Si frowned. 'And

you're as bad. Tramping around the country lanes for hours on end.'

There was some truth in what he said. Whatever the weather, walking was therapy. She would follow the hawthorn hedges growing along the lanes on the edge of town. Bare and brittle, or lush and pale pink with blossom, they would accompany her as she solved problems in her head. Difficult children, new concepts, government diktats, all could be reduced to manageable proportions by a brisk march and gulps of fresh air. Or she would wander around Blackthorn Wood itself, enjoying the coppices of ash and hazel, the froth of blackthorn stems, picking her way through the ground ivy, hoping to find small treasures – an early snowdrop or a late celandine.

Christmas had been simple: food and drink and nights by the fire in Blackthorn's lounge, watching television or reading. Cassie had loved the normality of it all. But as soon as she'd laid her head on her pillow, fake conversations with Tina Armstrong would play themselves out. Cassie would be cajoling or angry, soft or vicious. But the outcome never changed. Tina would give her an empty stare, then turn her back and walk away.

Si grabbed her hand. 'What time are you going to Joe's?'

She glanced at her watch. 'Teatime, I said. I won't be long, though.'

The promised visit. Though she wasn't looking forward to it, and Joe seemed not to care either way.

'No worries. You go, and I'll get the girls something to eat.' He slid an arm around her shoulder. 'Poor guy. I feel for him.'

'I do, too. But Alison needs to know his long-term plans. Without actually asking him, if you see what I mean. She's not allowed.'

'So, she's sending you. As her spy.'

She pushed his arm away. 'It's not like that. I just want him to know he's not been forgotten. That the job will be waiting for him, when he's ready.'

Si raised his eyebrows then looked away. 'So long as you don't go making him feel worse. Never mind what *Alison* said.'

'It's my job and these are my colleagues, Si. Trust me to know what to do.'

The bubble of anger took Cassie by surprise. She held her breath for a few seconds, trying not to say anything else. Was there a conflict between her new role, and simple human compassion? The sane part of her knew that wasn't the case, but if Si felt the need to mention it, he'd noticed something.

'Sorry,' she said. 'I'll be careful with Joe. And not because my boss has told me to be.'

Si slipped his arm through hers. 'Do the job in your way, Cass, that's all I'm saying. Don't become anyone's mouthpiece.'

That word. It crystallised everything she had been thinking. Tomorrow would be a day for relationship building. On her terms. Alison Harman could do her own dirty-work.

'Let's walk to the edge of the quarry,' she called to the girls. 'You might get some sunset photos, if we're quick.'

A double groan.

'Yes. Come on, you two. You'll be missing your freedom this time tomorrow.' Si was already striding away, hands in pockets, breath hanging in ragged clouds behind him.

The wood opened out into wide grassland, blunted with frost-bitten tussocks, and blackened clumps of thistle and nettle. No more than 200 yards from here was a sheer drop. A deep sandstone crevice, and the flat quarry bottom, jagged with pieces of broken rock and brambles. But standing on the edge gave a stunning view across Walney Island, and over the blue-grey waters of the Irish Sea.

Cassie stopped. Held on to Si and the girls and stared into the draining light of the evening. The horizon was a strip of chilled gold, and above it, in layers of lilac, pink and rose, thin cloud hung in strips. The island's airport twinkled out a warning, as a plane lifted itself into the sky. This was her place. Their place. There was a strength in that.

————

When Cassie parked her car and knocked on Joe's front door, it was almost dark. She looked along the terraced street and thought about the last time she'd seen him, at the end of a long day in the autumn term. He'd shaken his head at the offer of a ride home, and shuffled off across the car park, lifting one hand, giving a small wave. He hadn't said anything. It was clear to her now that he couldn't.

But the Joe sparkle had been fading for a while before that evening. Boarding and cycling were his life. Both had been abandoned in the face of his heavy workload, he'd said, though Cassie found it hard to believe. Even on the weekends where school didn't infiltrate their lives, Joe had stopped going out. On their Monday morning catch-ups, when she and Kevin dropped hints about the latest forty-eight hours of freedom, Joe stopped chipping in. And now, he wasn't answering her knock.

There were no lights on in his house. Cassie waited. Wondered if she had the right place. Though the skateboard sticker on the inside of the window gave it away. She knocked again, then lifted the letterbox. And the door finally opened.

'Hiya, Mr Smythe.' She smiled brightly.

'Oh. Hi, Cassie.' Like he wasn't expecting her.

'How's things?'

Joe pulled the door open a little more. The smell of cigarettes filtered out. 'Do you want to come in?'

'If you don't mind. Just wanted to see how you are, that's all.' Cassie held up a carrier-bag. 'I've brought biscuits.'

There was no smile. He turned away and disappeared into the grey light of the hall.

The living room was at the front of the house. A television flared in the corner, and Joe was pointing at it with a remote control when Cassie walked in.

'Sit down,' he muttered. 'I'll put the lamp on.'

'Thanks.' She blinked as white light filled the room. Two black leather sofas were pushed together at right-angles, and he gestured for her to sit down. A table in the corner was piled high with papers and what looked like school exercise books. 'Nice little place you've got here.'

'Nothing like your spot though, is it?' Joe sat down beside her and lowered his head with a sigh. 'Sorry. That came out wrong.'

'Hey. Say what you like. It's me.' She shook the biscuit box. 'Any tea to go with these?'

'Yeah. Sure. Give me a minute.'

Cassie put a hand on his arm. 'I keep saying the wrong thing, don't I?'

'It's not you, Cass. I'm all over the place. Doc gave me medication and I swear it's making me feel worse.'

'That can happen, can't it? With anti-depressants, I mean. Is that what you've been given?'

Joe turned his head, glowering at her. 'Who've you been talking to?'

'Nobody. I just assumed, after last time. When you were off with depression, it was the same thing.'

'Yeah. It is.' Joe stood up again, tugged at the ruched-up legs of his joggers. 'Ignore me. I'm so touchy at the moment. That's why I'm best left to myself. I'll go and make tea.'

This room. It was all Joe: skateboards leaning against the wall and a framed photograph of a guy, mid-stunt, bicycle below him. She peered closer. Joe. She'd watched him perform a demo once, at a school fete, and held her breath along with the crowd. And now he was stuck at home because of a job he loved; with a nicotine habit she was sure he didn't have before.

When he walked back into the room with two mugs in his hand, he dragged the smell of burning tobacco with him.

'White, no sugar. That's you, isn't it?'

'Thanks.' Cassie put hers on the floor. 'Shall we start on these?' She picked at the cellophane wrapping on the biscuits. 'We don't usually get them to ourselves, do we. Not with Nobbs and his ever-hungry mouth.'

Joe shook his head. Gave her a lip-trembling smile. 'I miss him. You as well. But I don't think I'm ever coming back to Parkhouse.'

'Don't be daft. Once the medication kicks in, you'll see things differently. It's just your job and your workplace. It's not your family. And there's a lot we can do to make your workload less dense.'

'No.' Joe tilted his head towards her. 'My workload was completely doable. You know me. I've always managed to keep that balance.'

'I must admit I was surprised when Alison told me you were off. I thought you were over the worst.'

'You've been talking about me?'

'Only that she wants you back as much as we all do.'

'Can I tell you something, Cassie?' Joe put down his mug and shifted his position on the sofa. 'I need to tell someone. But it's confidential.'

'Course. But only if you want to. I don't want to be nosy.' The implication was that she shouldn't say anything to Alison. Which would be difficult.

Joe blew out a sigh. 'When Mick took me on, he knew I had an *item* on my DBS certificate. But he overlooked it because he wanted to give me a job.'

Cassie tried not to look surprised.

'Don't get into a flap, Cass. I was convicted of an assault. In my teens. At uni. I was involved in a drunken affray. Got a court appearance and a fine. Though we were all fighting, as far as I remember.' He pressed his hands to his face. 'This is really difficult.'

'If Mick trusted you, why does it matter now? It's nothing to get down about, is it?'

'It's not that.' Cassie watched his face, saw fear there. 'I've had a new DBS since Alison came. She hasn't mentioned anything about the conviction. But Tina Armstrong has.'

'What do you mean? What's it got to do with her.'

Joe chewed on his bottom lip. 'Nothing. But she files those records. And ever since I gave her my new one, she's been on my case.' He shook his head. 'I swear to you, Cass. There are the hints I've been stealing, the sideways looks when I'm using the phone. She's been finding fault in everything I do. Especially after—' he stopped, pressing his fingers against his temples.

'After what?'

'I walked in on them. Tina and Mick. They were kissing, Cass. I swear to you. They were kissing.'

Chapter Five

O n the drive to work, Cassie tried hard to rid herself of the disturbing image that was Tina and Mick Ripley locked in an embrace: Parkhouse was a school, not a soap opera.

One good thing to come out of her visit with Joe had been a growing sense that he could be persuaded to return to his job, with the right kind of support. Teachers like him were vital: he hated scandal as much as she did. Poor Joe. He'd been a crumple of tears and embarrassment when she'd left him yesterday. And he was angry. She'd made a promise not to mention what he'd told her. How could he go to Alison with something like that, he'd said? When Cassie had asked why he hadn't just confronted Tina and Mick, or at least told someone what they were up to, his answer had been chilling.

Get on the wrong side of Tina Armstrong? That's more than my life's worth.

The road into town was busy. Cassie joined the slow crawl of traffic and tried to get herself into the right frame of mind for a new term. Bright and bubbly was what she needed to be; fresh, eager. But behind her eyes was a pressure that felt new: she needed more sleep. At three o'clock this morning, she'd found herself wide awake and running conversations in her head, all linked to work. She'd crept out of bed and down to Blackthorn's kitchen to make herself a cup of tea. Then stood at the back door, breathing in the clean icy air as though it could somehow clear her worries.

And today, there was Judy to deal with.

When Cassie arrived, she was surprised to find the car park already full; staff never showed this much enthusiasm for a normal working day. Days reserved for training were like gold: glittering with possibility, attractive, but of no practical use.

'Happy New Year,' she called as she stepped into Judy Barker's classroom and put down her bags. 'Are you managing to get sorted out?'

Judy was standing in front of a bank of computers, squeezing a thick bunch of cables and shaking her head. But this still felt like Joe's room: his old armchair in the corner, draped with his stripy blanket; his library of storybooks and magazines; his plastic buckets full of stationery, even the twisted window-blind cord and the skateboarder figurines. A classroom took on the character of its inhabitants, but the heart of it was the teacher who resided there. And that wasn't Judy.

She turned as Cassie walked in. 'Happy New Year to you, too. It's a bit of a mess, to be frank, but I'm getting there. Joe wasn't the tidiest of guys.'

'How was Christmas?' Cassie perched on the edge of a desk. 'Family okay?'

Judy sighed. 'Ate too much. Drank too much. Spent too

much. The usual.' She wafted her blouse. 'I've had to wear my loosest clothing.'

They both laughed at that.

'Never mind. You know what January's like. You'll soon get the weight off again.' *God. Why did I say that? I'm trying to get this woman onside.*

Judy's mouth straightened, pursed a little. 'It's all right for you skinny people. I wonder what I'm doing wrong, sometimes.'

Cassie didn't reply. Couldn't. Not without causing more damage. She stood up again, lifted her bags, stepped towards the door. And in came Kevin Noble, clean-shaven but sallow, and wearing a grey sweater with the texture of a dishcloth.

'Happy New Year,' he called. 'The dream-team.' A punch of the air.

Cassie rearranged her features into a frown. 'Dream on,' she muttered, but he leaned towards her. With her arms tethered by bags, she could do nothing but submit to a wet cheek-kiss. 'Still hungover, I see.'

'Am not.' He put his hand against his chest. 'Whites. You do me a disservice.'

'Nobbs. I do not.'

Then Judy was coming towards them, face flushed and skipping lightly. 'Happy New Year, Kev,' she said, then grabbed at his face. When it was secured, she planted her lips on his. 'Gotcha.'

He staggered backwards. 'Easy tiger.' His eyes were wide, and Cassie matched the look. She watched as Judy ran her hand across the top of Kevin's arm.

'Had a good Christmas?' she heard her asking as she walked away.

What was that all about?

In her own classroom, she flicked on the lights. Here on the empty tables was the cold debris of a Christmas passed. One home-made calendar, bronze foil glinting, and two forgotten selection boxes. Coming back after a holiday was never easy. Today, it felt more hollow than usual.

She put her bags down. On her desk was a single Post-it note, pink and forlorn in the centre of the expanse of varnished wood. She let out a long sigh. This would be Alison. Five minutes back in work and the commands were being issued. This one asked for a meeting after lunch. So much for a training day. Kevin would just have to get Judy up to speed on his own.

The morning passed in a blur of printing and photocopying, chats to staff and stapling papers to pinboards. Jax was in and out of the room, hanging up nativity costumes and packing away the festive library. And there wasn't a single communication from the admin staff.

Just before lunchtime, Judy appeared in the doorway with some pieces of paper in her hand.

Cassie looked up from her desk. 'Hi. Are you managing to get the room sorted out?'

Judy said she was, then came towards her, waving the sheets. 'Tina's just dropped these in. Paper registers for tomorrow. And instructions. You know how she has to have everything just right.'

'Oh. She didn't bring one in for me.'

'I've got yours here. She didn't think you were in.'

Cassie was about to tell her that she'd been in the room all morning. But she stopped short; this was a junior colleague. 'Okay. Thanks.' She took the register. 'Have you got Kev's as well?'

Judy peered at her from behind black-rimmed glasses. 'No. Just yours. He must have been in his room. See you in a bit.'

Judy sauntered away, swinging her fresh-pressed hair, so that Cassie wondered if she'd missed something. The feeling of being deliberately excluded was starting to hit home. Surely

Tina and Denise would have to speak to her eventually. It wasn't possible to run the spider's web system that was school admin without contacting every person caught up inside it. But something was grabbing at her thinking, trying to make itself heard.

It is possible, and it's happening.

She needed a break. A glance at the clock told her it was lunchtime. Socialising might help. Or a sandwich, courtesy of Alison, and a large cup of tea.

In the staffroom, teachers and teaching assistants were already sprawled on the rows of easy chairs, tucking into sandwiches and other buffet treats, knees touching and chins wagging. Some looked up when Cassie came in, said hello, fired questions. She made herself tea and selected a few bites to eat, then sat down in an empty chair next to Laura Pearson, determined to strike up a conversation.

'Okay, Laura?' Cassie smiled at the other woman, who swung her legs away.

'Will be. When I get on top of things.' A cold look. 'Judy left me in the lurch, moving up to work with you.'

'You'll cope. We knew that, or we wouldn't have suggested it.'

Laura let out a snort and ran a hand through her long blonde hair. 'Yes, well. Being consulted would have been nice.'

Cassie frowned. 'You were consulted. Alison mentioned it to you last term. Didn't she?'

'She mentioned it, yes. I didn't agree with her decision, though. But we can't have anything disrupting the precious year six staff, can we?' Laura bit into a sandwich. Then started talking to the person on the other side of her.

Cassie looked at her plate of food, not sure if she could eat anything after all. Suddenly, the door flew open and in walked Kevin Noble. With Judy Barker just behind him, giggling, and cheeks red. He began making a show of putting a few sandwiches onto a plate, Judy hard on his heels.

'What's on the menu today then, ladies? Anything hot?'

Snorts of laughter. Everyone watching him now.

'Apart from you, Mr N?' Judy simpered.

Cassie looked away. He was a senior teacher, not a pantomime dame. When he walked towards the kitchen area, Judy trotted behind.

'Let me brew your tea,' she said, with a hint of innuendo that would have sat nicely in the script for a *Carry On* film.

That was enough. Cassie stood up and lifted her last sandwich from the plate, then stomped out of the room. Judy Barker couldn't make it any more obvious if she tried. Roll on tomorrow, when the children, not infatuations, would be top priority. Cassie pushed the sandwich into her mouth and lifted her eyes towards the end of the corridor. She would seek Alison out, talk to someone sensible. But ahead of her was Denise Kelly, deep in conversation with Tina Armstrong. Wearing their usual dressed-down glam – jeans and heels – but either they hadn't seen her, or they had and were ignoring her. Neither of them looked, as Cassie passed by. Only hooted louder.

'Happy New Year,' she said, with false brightness.

Both women snapped their faces towards her.

'Oh, yes. Happy New Year,' Denise replied.

But there was nothing from Tina; she had turned away. Cassie listened as the two women opened the staffroom door. She heard the screech of greeting, then a loud slam, and she was on her own again, leaving the chaotic bonhomie of her colleagues behind, and heading towards her boss's office. Where did she fit in? She wasn't sure.

I'm destined to walk the school corridors forever, like some kind of mad Miss Havisham.

Alison was sitting at her desk, wrapped in a chunky

cardigan, staring at a computer monitor and sliding a hand across the mouse. She looked up as Cassie walked in. 'Two hours ago,' she said, 'I was on my way down to see you. To wish you Happy New Year. This is as far as I got.'

'I thought you were going to restrict answering emails. New Year's resolutions, and all that.' Cassie lifted her eyebrows. 'Well?'

'I know, Cass. But. I don't want to miss anything. And it's a good job I looked anyway. I've had this email from county.'

She did the thing that Cassie hated; she swivelled the monitor around.

'Our Kevin has been head-hunted. Kind of. Becky's put him forward for an asthma awareness programme.' She picked at her thumbnail. 'In light of what happened to Mick, I guess.'

Mick again. It was an odd thing, the way his name still stood for Parkhouse. Alison must find it difficult.

'That'd be good for our staff and kids,' Cassie said. 'But can we spare him?'

Alison shook her head. 'Not really. I'll have to talk to him, though.'

'Just tell Becky no. She'll understand.'

'I'm not sure I can.' Alison leaned back in her chair and rolled her shoulders. 'God. One day back and I could do with a holiday.'

The door flew open, and a young man stepped through. Cassie took in the immaculate sports clothing and neatly trimmed beard.

'Sorry. Callum Graham,' he said. 'You asked me to come and see you. About some footy coaching.'

An awkward silence, then Alison smiled. 'Oh, yes.' She ran her hands through her hair. 'Cass, can you talk to Kevin about this asthma thingy; gauge his thoughts?'

'Will do.'

With a smile at Callum, Cassie did as she was told. Again.

Jax was in the classroom when she got back, mired in worksheets and glue sticks. The woman was pure gold. With a wave of her hand, she agreed to go and find some lunch for herself, leaving Cassie alone with her thoughts. She sat down at her desk and stared through the window at the car park. Every bay was full, every staff member present in the building, and busy. And here she was, looking out at the grey January afternoon, and wondering why she no longer felt at ease.

She wondered if Kevin was back in his classroom. He was always a good distraction, with his messy ideas and terrible sense of timing. She was surprised to find his door closed. Doors were only closed for teaching, or for private conversations. Or as a signal that someone was having a bit of a sulk. Inside the room, Judy Barker was sitting at a child's desk and staring across at Kevin, who was swinging backwards on his teacher's chair. The remnants of lunch were spread between them.

'Oh, sorry,' laughed Cassie. 'Am I interrupting?' *And why is the door closed?*

'Nah.' Kevin was sheepish. 'Just talking about rugby.'

Judy said nothing, elbows resting on the desk, hands pressed against her mouth.

'Well, rugby will have to wait. I need a word.' Cassie peered at him. 'Nobbs.'

Nobody moved.

'In private.' She looked at Judy. 'If you don't mind.'

The atmosphere thickened. Cassie felt trapped. Swamped.

Then Judy jumped up. 'Silly me. What am I doing? I'll go, shall I?'

Kevin contemplated the floor.

'Thanks. See you later,' Cassie said, teeth gritted.

Silence.

October 2019

Talking to Freddy is bringing to the surface all my buried angst. But to understand what happened, he has to hear how isolated incidents can join together and morph into something deadly; he has to hear me. By the time I returned to work that January, I wasn't myself. There had been years of happy-go-lucky teaching for me at Parkhouse. And then it stopped. Blaming my promotion to deputy head seemed the obvious way to respond.

'I don't mean to sound bigoted,' Freddy is saying, 'but you worked with some God-awful women, didn't you?'

When he sees my reaction, he holds up his hands. 'Sorry. But it needs saying.'

'Oh, I agree. But there's rogue employees in every workplace, aren't there. Mine was no different.' I glance past him. 'Well, that's what I told myself.'

He stands up and performs a series of stretches. I can't help but laugh, especially when one of them involves balancing the sole of his foot on the inside of his other knee.

He grins back at me. 'It's yoga,' he explains.

'I'm sure it is.'

'Join me?'

'You're all right, thanks. I won't.' When I lean back on the sofa and fold my arms, he moves into another pose, then overbalances and falls to the floor.

'Fuck me,' is his response, then, 'Oops. Sorry. If I was a schoolkid now, I'm sure I'd be given a diagnosis. ADHD or something. Not that I believe there's such a thing.' He sits himself back upright and shuffles across so that he is kneeling at my feet.

'Oh, there is. I've taught children with exactly that disorder, and I can tell you, it is very real.'

Freddy looks up at me. 'I didn't say it wasn't real, Cassie.

But giving a single diagnosis to a human condition that is multi-faceted...' He shakes his head. 'It's plain dangerous.'

I want to argue this point with him; my interest is piqued. But as I'm never going to be a teacher again, there seems little point. Instead, I ask him more about yoga. Then he entertains me with stories about the classes he goes to in the gym of a boxing club near his house, about the smells and the slippage of wind and the evening it was raided by police. And all the while, I'm thinking what an engaging man he is, and despite me wanting to hate him, I don't see how I can.

When he's finished, he climbs back onto the sofa next to me and reaches around to bunch up his dreadlocks, then tucks both feet underneath himself. 'So, a kind of inner-circle was being set up at your school,' he says. 'Were you ever admitted to it?'

Chapter Six

A gust of wind stung Cassie's cheeks. She'd positioned herself between the fence and the gable end of the building: good for overseeing all the action but a wind-tunnel, nonetheless. Children tore around, coats flying, enjoying a taste of freedom. Christmas was a long way in the past; what mattered to them now was the reunion of friendships and games invented only for the playground. There had been no lingering over artwork or clinging to teachers. The door was opened and off they ran.

While the children played, Cassie warmed her hands on a mug of tea and thought about the week, the evenings of marking and the slog of the teaching days. Something was missing. And whatever it was, had left a hollow feeling – something like homesickness – in her chest.

Judy Barker was across the other side of the playground, hood up and hands in the pockets of her raincoat. The woman was doing her best; keeping Joe's class in check and trying to make sure his absence didn't break the threads he'd so carefully sewn. But Cassie couldn't take to her, and she blamed Tina Armstrong for that. Every breaktime, every lunchtime, she would be in Judy's classroom, or Judy would be with her somewhere. The office, the staffroom, wherever Cassie went, she would find Judy and Tina, and sometimes Laura Pearson, heads together and whispering. Or that's how it seemed.

With a sigh, Cassie lifted her whistle to her lips and gave the signal for the end of playtime. At least the weekend was nearly upon them. One more session and the children would be heading home, and she could get back to Blackthorn House.

'Thank God for that.' Jax threw herself onto one of the children's chairs. 'What a week. And it was only four days long. I'm going to have a five-minute break, then we'll crack on.'

They sat together in the quiet classroom, elbows resting and fatigue across their shoulders. If Monday mornings were a big inhale of excitement, then Friday afternoons were the tiniest sigh of relief.

'Don't worry about it,' Cassie told her. 'We're on top of everything. I'm taking the marking home. Si's away and the girls are sleeping out with friends. The rest we can do next week.' She peered at Jax. 'Are you okay? You look tired.'

The teaching assistant rubbed at her temples. 'The little 'un isn't sleeping well. And her mother's gone again.'

She'd made no secret of her domestic situation. There was a younger daughter still living at home, and an unplanned but much loved, grandchild. Elderly parents nearby. Not demanding, but needy, nonetheless. Cassie was glad her own parents had chosen to live abroad. They had sun, sea and a great economy to stretch their pension. When they'd left Blackthorn House to her, more than fifteen years ago, they knew exactly what they were doing. They'd become parents-by-proxy: on the end of a telephone and always willing to listen, but at an impossible distance to offer practical help. The house itself was a joy, but at almost 120 years old, it was always going to soak up money.

'Where's she gone to this time?'

'Found herself another fella, hasn't she? So, Mother's left to pick up the pieces again.' Jax's chin wobbled a little, and Cassie reached out to her.

'Get yourself off home. It'll give you a head start. Who's got Meggy at the moment?'

'She's with her granddad. Until four.'

'There you go then,' said Cassie, getting up. 'Go home and get an hour to yourself.'

Jax pulled herself up from the chair and picked up her handbag. 'If you're sure.'

'I am. Go.' Cassie watched as Jax slipped on her coat and wound a thick scarf around her neck. They were both well past the age where they should have sleepless toddlers at home. And she'd done her fair share. Neither daughter had slept a whole night until they were toddling. She'd sleepwalked through the entire baby years, dazed and just about scraping herself together in the day. It had given her a deep empathy for working women with pre-school aged children. *Having it all* was a lie, peddled by celebrities and social media addicts.

As Jax walked out of the door, Cassie heard her calling a greeting to someone.

Becky Ripley.

'Not disturbing you am I, poppet?' she said brightly, pushing her way into the classroom.

First Friday back and face turned to home. Of course not. 'Hi.' She smiled as Becky pulled off her knitted hat and raked a hand through her hair. 'You look cold.'

'It was Kevin I wanted to see, actually.' She tugged at the zip of her anorak. 'But you'll be interested too, no doubt.'

'Is it about the asthma thing?'

'It is.' Becky slipped off her coat. 'He's going to do it, I gather. And Alison thinks there are some children who'll benefit, as well as their families. We'll need to publicise the event – could you get the local press involved? It'll sound better if the request comes from you.' She waited. 'There are so many kids suffering at the moment.'

'There are.' Cassie frowned. 'I've got Sophie in my class. Her asthma's that bad, we keep a spacer in the classroom. And of course I'll do your publicity.'

'Great.' Becky gave her a thumbs-up. 'And if kids know how to help each other, that can only be for the good, can't it.'

Cassie agreed. 'Scary though, isn't it? When they have an attack.'

'Oh, aye. Tell me about it.' Becky twisted her hat between white-knuckled hands. 'Scary doesn't come close.'

Cassie could have kicked herself. Saying to Becky that asthma was scary? What was she thinking? The poor woman had watched her husband die from an attack. If something like that happened to Si, there would be no brave coping or trying to find ways to help others: she'd be a wreck.

'Kev's just next door,' she offered instead. 'Let's go and have a chat, shall we?'

Kevin Noble's classroom was stuffy with the smell of too much breathing and not enough of the outside air. He and Judy were in their usual position; he, stretched out on his teacher chair and she at a desk, craning towards him. Surprise moved them both as Cassie entered with Becky not far behind her.

'Hi, you two.'

'Oh. Hi.' Kevin jumped up from his seat. 'We were just talking about the weekend.' He peered at Becky. 'Hello. I've been expecting you.'

But Becky was staring at Judy.

'Ah. It's all making sense now,' she said. 'Alison explained to me about a replacement teacher for young Joe.' She held out a hand. 'I'm Becky Ripley. Actually, we've met briefly, haven't we? At the gala?'

'Oh, yes. I remember.' Judy shook her hand lightly. 'I should get to know the governors a bit better, shouldn't I?'

'You're friends with that Tina from the office, aren't you?'

A pink flush spread across Judy's cheeks and neck. Cassie wondered where the conversation was going, but Becky pressed on. 'I've seen you in there a few times with her. During working hours, too.'

Was Judy about to get a telling off? Not from the chair of governors surely?

Kevin's voice cut across Cassie's thoughts. 'I've got some time now, Becky. If you want to fill me in on the details. Of the asthma roadshow, that is.'

'We'll leave you to it,' said Cassie. 'Won't we?' A glance at Judy, then she led her from the room.

Once she'd tidied around her classroom, Cassie filled her bag with exercise books, then lifted her coat from the peg behind her stockroom door. She'd meant to talk to Judy and Kevin about organising a trip out for their classes. Thanks to Becky Ripley and her unexpected visit, it would have to wait. The woman must be made of steel. To be leading the charge for the very illness that had killed her husband; it took guts.

As she moved to leave, Cassie saw Judy standing in the doorway, coat on and loaded down with books.

'Doing anything good at the weekend?' she asked.

'The usual. Si's away. Just me, my absent teens and Blackthorn.'

Judy looked at her. 'I must come and see this house of yours. It's full of fabulous Victoriana, so Kev keeps telling me.'

Does he? Really? 'Come anytime,' she replied. 'Nobbs treats it as his second home.' *Why had she said that?*

Judy let out a small sniff. 'Why do you call him *Nobbs*? It sounds so vulgar, if you don't mind me saying.'

I do.

'It started when he was a new teacher. I was his mentor. Cassie Clifton. Cliffs. White Cliffs. Whites. That's what he called me. So, I responded with Nobbs.'

Judy threw her head back in an explosion of laughter. When she recovered her breath, she took off her glasses and wiped them on the hem of her blouse. 'I'm all steamed up,' she grinned, and the laughter started again. It made Cassie wonder whether the unease she'd been feeling about this woman was justified. If Judy wanted to be friends with Tina Armstrong, or even Kevin, that was up to her. And nothing whatsoever to do with Cassie.

They walked out of school together, talking about how the week had gone, and about ideas for school trips. In the car park, Cassie clicked her key fob, then began to pile her bags onto the passenger seat of her car. But when she looked for Judy again to say goodbye, the other woman was standing at Kevin's illuminated window, knocking on the glass, and blowing kisses from her fingers.

Chapter Seven

January sunlight, silvery and without a trace of heat, slanted into Cassie's bedroom. One blink, and she was awake. The iron radiator in the bay window gurgled with a metallic warmth. She and Si had planned on rewiring when they'd put the new heating system in, but the money they had was never enough for the work they wanted. So Blackthorn House remained largely unmodernised, but to her mind solid enough for at least another hundred years.

The place had certainly been looked after by previous generations, the pearls-and-cream flock wallpaper in this room lovingly hung by her grandfather. She would never strip it away. An enormous wardrobe, dark walnut and gleaming, stood in the corner. The grainy faces she picked out as a child stared back at her, even now. And every bedroom had a bathroom. That was the Victorian way. But the attic rooms, once the place where housemaids and the boot boy had slept, had no such luxury, though each had an iron fireplace, original to the house and standing on solid slate hearths. She'd been offered hundreds of pounds for them by an antiques dealer; hadn't sold, in the end.

With a swing of her legs, she climbed out of bed. The room faced eastwards and had a wide view of the garden, then onto the roofs of nearby houses. There was something comforting about living high above the rest of the town, and in the evening, the eastern sky was an unpolluted star-scape.

Down in the kitchen, Cassie filled the kettle and set it to boil. She hadn't slept well. Thoughts of Judy Barker and her strange behaviour niggled away, leaving dark footprints across Cassie's consciousness. She had tried her best to include the woman in their small teaching team. But Judy's pursuit of Kevin Noble grated. If it was a pursuit.

Judy certainly hadn't been coming into Cassie's classroom every afternoon for a gossip, as she did Kevin's. Maybe that was understandable. She was the deputy head. Hardly the right person to sit down with and have a chat. Although Cassie thought of herself as approachable, maybe others didn't see that in her? Then there was Judy's friendship with Tina Armstrong. When had she and Judy become so close?

Cassie's brain had gnawed away for answers until the early hours. Then she'd finally fallen asleep. Perhaps she just needed someone to talk to. Si was usually her sounding board. He had insights into school politics that she often couldn't see because she was so involved. But how could she telephone him on the offshore vessel, and start moaning about school? And what would she say anyway? *One of the teachers is making a play for Kev, and I'm not happy about it? And she's been befriended by the school secretary.*

Those thoughts: they could have been lifted directly from the playground. She shook them away as she poured the boiled water into her mug. Today was for walking and daylight, not school.

Cassie ate some toast standing at the kitchen counter, then went upstairs to wash and dress. She found an old sweater and jeans, and a pair of her husband's socks. Perfect for a trudge through Blackthorn Wood. She lifted her boots from the scullery and pulled on her parka and knitted hat. At the front door, she stopped for a moment and looked across at the woods, breathed in the sharpness of the air. The winter trees stood grey against the glassy silver sky, beckoning her with their twiggy fingers. A walk would clear her head, put Judy Barker back where she belonged, on a shelf with Mills and Boon.

Across the road was a short gravel path, littered with ice and lumps of frosted mud. And here was the entrance to the wood. Signposted, and with a black and gold bin for dog walkers and picnickers, none of which were here now. Cassie was on her own.

Inside the wood, clouds of frozen condensation had become trapped between the close-planted trees. Sunlight glittered on the droplets. Cassie loved trees. Laying her hands against their bark and feeling their energy was one of her guilty pleasures: a tree-hugger, Si called her. Today, though, she was just lonely.

She walked on, feeling the creep of isolation across her shoulders. What would her workplace be like without the colleagues she was close to? It had never mattered before. There had always been an unspoken support, a quiet camaraderie, an assumption that everyone was fighting on the same side. Parkhouse School against the world. Something that Kevin Noble said quite often. Imagine being on the outside of that. Like poor Joe.

Cassie shuddered. Her breath caught in the back of her throat. A liquid flash of fear moved from her belly to her feet. What was there to be scared of? A couple of women making judgements about her? The fragmenting of her team? Shaking away those thoughts, she turned back, wanting to be home. Lack of sleep was unsettling; it magnified worries. With every step, she was conscious of her heart thudding against her ribs and pulsing at the base of her neck. She broke into a slow jog, ignoring the puddles of half-frozen muddy water. A stumble, then another. What was wrong with her?

And here was the house, at last. She leaned against the wall at the front of the garden and gulped down some breaths, told herself to stop being ridiculous, tried again to step away and take her walk. But she couldn't. Instead, she kicked her boots onto the doorstep and went inside.

When Monday morning came, Cassie began to feel anxious again. She hadn't left the house for the rest of the weekend. She'd paced through the rooms and told herself that she was just tired and a little bit overwrought because of her workload. But when the girls returned from their sleepovers, the relief had felt overwhelming. Thoughts of Judy Barker and her comments, and the way Tina Armstrong was ignoring her, were unsettling. But it was also what happened when large groups of people worked together in a stressful setting. *I can handle it,* she told herself. *I'll have to.* And now it was time for work again.

On the drive in, Cassie let her thoughts run over her tasks and teaching for the day. She was an adult, a professional woman, with years of experience. So why was her stomach churning at the thought of entering her workplace this morning?

When she pulled into the car park, the lights were already on. Which meant Dot had beaten her and would want a quick chat. Another welcome distraction. Cassie let herself in with her code, and went to find the site manager.

She was standing, coffee in hand, just outside Cassie's classroom. 'Morning, lovely,' she called. 'Good weekend?'

'Yes thanks, Dot. You?'

'I did.' She glanced around the room. 'I've been thinking

about the carpet in your room. Looking a bit grotty, isn't it?' She stepped into the classroom and flicked on the lights. 'I'm going to ask Her Majesty if the budget will stretch to a new one.'

She waited while Cassie took off her coat, chatting about carpets and money, a comforting presence and a welcome one.

'I'd better go and get on with my jobs,' she said eventually. 'Are you all right, love? You look a bit peaky.'

'I'm fine, Dot, honestly. Got a long day today, that's all.'

'Oh, aye. I've to get my cleaning done before your governors' meeting.'

Cassie's presence at these meetings was expected, but the thought of a full day's work followed by three hours of mulling over school issues with people who didn't understand them made her shudder, and Dot tuned in.

'Don't think too hard about it, love, or you won't go.'

'I haven't got a choice,' laughed Cassie, but Dot was right. Overthinking had always been one of her weaknesses. She would keep herself busy until Si came home at the end of the week. And she wouldn't let personnel issues cloud her judgement.

At eight o'clock, Cassie went to make a telephone call in the main office. The lion's den. Was the pack leader hiding somewhere, ready to pounce? To tear her to shreds with eyes and nails. But it was far too early for that woman to be a threat, and there were calls to be made. Better to do it now, whilst the office was empty, and she couldn't be classed as litter.

She tried three numbers for three different coach companies. None answered. She tried again, then left a voicemail. There would be no chance of getting to a telephone once the children arrived. And any messages would get back to her. Eventually.

At lunchtime, just as Cassie was about to slip on her coat and head off to supervise the playground, Kevin came into her class, closed the door behind him. A wry smile stretched across his lips.

'Got a minute?' He arched his brows.

'Yep. What's up?' Cassie moved towards him and sat down on the edge of a desk.

'You know what this is about, don't you?'

She shook her head. 'Not sure? But you've closed the door. That worries me.'

'No. No, it's nothing bad.'

'What then?' A glance at the clock said it all. There would be nobody on the playground, which always spelt trouble.

Kevin tilted his head towards Judy's classroom. 'It's her. Judy Barker.'

Cassie folded her arms, said nothing.

'She turned up at my house at the weekend. Bold as brass and twice as ugly.'

'Don't be mean, Nobbs.'

'Mean?' He coughed. 'I'm not fucking joking, you know. There she was. On my doorstep. All done up, and with a box of cake.'

'Done up? What does that even mean? Did you ask her to come?'

He shook his head vigorously. 'No, I bloody well didn't. I said I liked lemon drizzle cake the other day. Just a chance remark. And there she was, lemon drizzle in hand. And she had make-up, Cass.' He ran a hand across his face. 'Like you've never seen.'

A bolt of laughter, fuelled by a vision of Judy, all red lace and cleavage, rose from her empty stomach; she couldn't stop it. But Kevin didn't join in.

'Help me out, Cass. Please.' His face was pale, dirty with stubble. 'She's fucking married.'

That hasn't stopped you before, she wanted to say. 'Did you let her in?'

78

He tugged at his shirt collar. 'What do you think?'

'I wasn't there.'

'Look. I don't even fancy her. But she's somehow got the idea that I do.'

'And you don't know what's made her think that? Come on, Nobbs. She's at you whenever there's the opportunity. Don't start pretending you've not played a part in this.'

Kevin's face flooded with colour, right up to the tips of his ears. 'We work together. That's what colleagues do. It's the same as you and me, isn't it?'

Cassie jumped to her feet. 'I can't believe I'm hearing this. No, it isn't the same as you and me. Get a grip. You need to put a stop to it. Now.'

'I don't want to cause any upset, though.'

'Upset for who? There will be bloody upset if anything happens between you and her.' Cassie moved towards the door. 'I've got to go. I'll speak to her. Is that what you want me to do?'

'I don't know. What the hell would you say? We've got to work with her still, haven't we?'

This from a man who was at his most confident around women. Cassie shook away her disbelief. 'You should have told her there and then. But leave it with me. I'll have a think.' She began zipping her anorak. 'In the meantime, don't encourage her. No more closed-door conversations.'

The last thing she saw was the lift of Kevin's chin as she backed out of the room, surprised to find Judy, leaning against the wall, waiting.

'Anything I should know about?'

'No.' Cassie pushed past her and began to walk away.

'Kev,' she heard her say, 'I've been looking for you.'

On her way outside, Cassie made a detour to the school office. She hadn't heard from the coach company, which was unusual. If telephone calls came in during teaching hours, the admin staff would take the information down and deliver it by hand. There had been no hand-delivered message for Cassie that morning. She fully expected it to be waiting in her pigeonhole. But it wasn't.

Neither Denise nor Tina looked up as she walked into the office. She lifted the phone, then punched in the number for the coach company, and waited. The admin staff ignored her. A continued ringtone, then someone picked up.

'Hi. It's Cassie Clifton. From Parkhouse School in Barrow.'

The coach company manager said hello.

'I left a message this morning. About availability for February the nineteenth. I'm not sure if you got it?'

The coach company manager said that they had, that they'd tried to ring back, but were told, quite abruptly by a female secretary, that there was no Caron Clifton working at the school. Then the phone was hung up.

'It's *Cassie* Clifton. Not Caron. And I do work at the school. Sorry that happened. Shall I give you my email address? Then you won't have to communicate with them in future.'

Cassie looked over to where the admin staff were sitting. Tina was on the computer and Denise was tapping away at a calculator. Neither spoke, though they must have heard. Once the email address was passed over, Cassie apologised again, then said goodbye.

She took a deep breath. 'Who took that message? Tina? From County Coaches?'

'What message?' A flick of dark hair and red nails.

'You've just heard me talking to them.' Cassie tried to swallow down the rise of her own voice.

'Wasn't listening,' Tina said, then turned back to her computer screen.

At seven o'clock, when the sky outside the library window was midnight-dark and the streetlights flared, the governors' meeting ended. Cassie smiled across the conference table at Becky Ripley. A silent *thank you* to the woman who had stripped the timings down to an absolute minimum, which didn't make her popular with some of the other governors: those from the era of old school, whose lives revolved around agendas and addendums.

As Cassie left the meeting, Becky was just behind her, holding her mobile phone to her ear. She waved a hand, then Cassie caught a snippet of the conversation, which seemed to be about Becky's lift home.

'I can drop you off,' she offered, as the other woman followed her into the car park. 'It's a bit cold for walking. Has your driver let you down?'

Becky laughed. 'You could say that. Car's in for an MOT, and my pigging taxi's not coming.' She huffed. 'I'm not sure why.'

'Come on. You're only over the other side of Tesco, aren't you?'

While Cassie negotiated the evening traffic, Becky talked about Mick. About how he'd turned Parkhouse around and about how much she missed him. There was something about the intimacy of the conversation that made Cassie want to let out some of her own feelings. But how could she? There was nothing in her life to match the death of a husband. And shrinking it down to a series of Top Trump events wasn't helpful, anyway.

'I was so grateful for your support. In my interview, I mean.' She could offer that, at least.

Becky huffed softly. 'You were the best candidate, poppet. I just cheered you on.' She paused for a moment. 'And I wasn't having that Laura Pearson getting a promotion, anyway.'

'Oh?' Curiosity got the better of Cassie when really it shouldn't have.

'She's bosom buddies with Tina Armstrong. And as you know, I don't trust that woman.' Becky's words came out with such force that Cassie braced herself against the steering wheel, wondering if she was going to become hysterical. There was a resigned breath. 'Sorry. I can't stand her, that's all.'

'Me neither,' Cassie said, then wished she hadn't. Because it was unprofessional. And because Becky was leaning forward with interest.

'I guess you haven't made it to her gang,' she breathed. 'A scalp-hunter, that's what she is.'

Cassie wasn't sure how to respond. Could she trust Becky? Was it even about trust? A gang was a gang, no matter who was driving it; call them cliques and they weren't any better.

'Sorry, Cassie.' Becky interrupted her thoughts. 'I didn't mean to sound so vicious. Just watch yourself around bloody Tina Armstrong, okay?'

'Okay.'

October 2019

We are interrupted by a heavy *thunk*. The front door. Si, I expect. He has returned from his shopping expedition. I don't go shopping; haven't been inside a shop for a few years, and I don't miss it. Blackthorn House is my life now. Others worry for me, but I feel recovered. Digging up the past isn't something I want to do.

'Hello. I've brought lunch. It's only bread and cheese and stuff. Salad. Are you up for that, Freddy?' Si smiles in at us from the doorway. His cheeks are flushed from the outside. 'Bit late, I know.'

'Great,' says Freddy. 'I'm starving. It's been an intense morning.'

I flash him a warning. We agreed, the three of us. If I spoke up, nothing would be shared that I hadn't sanctioned. Si knows most of what happened. He became embroiled himself. But there are details I've kept to myself, out of shame, I suppose. We walk into the kitchen and stand around the dining table while Si unpacks the shopping.

'Anything I can do?' asks Freddy. When did he become one of the family?

'Put the kettle on, if you like,' I suggest. He's being paid by the day; why not make him work for his money?

We are soon seated and eating thick cheese and salad sandwiches and drinking mugs of tea. Freddy tucks in without a trace of self-consciousness. He is comfortable in Blackthorn. That goes in his favour. He and Si chat about pollarding trees and aerating lawns. I listen. And watch. The cuffs of Freddy's sweater are frayed a little, and there is a woven rainbow-coloured band on his wrist. He seems to know a lot about nature. Whatever Si tells him, he can match and add to. I have pigeonholed him as an activist, chaining himself to trees and cooking around an open fire. How can he be a psychotherapist?

When a gap in the conversation opens, I jump in. 'Where did you learn about gardening?'

He finishes chewing and turns to me. 'My parents had a farm. Over on the island. I worked on the land with my dad, until I went away to college.'

'On Walney? That island?' Si stands up and starts to collect our plates.

'Yes. Near the south end. They haven't got it now, though. They sold up and moved into town. I'm glad; I didn't want to be stuck working there forever. I... erm... farming's not for everyone.'

I follow Si to the sink, pick up a tea towel. 'Bit of a jump. Farmer to psychotherapist.' I drag the crumbs from the table.

Freddy laughs. 'I suppose it is. But the link is art therapy. I always drew and painted wildlife. When other people enjoyed my work, it gave me a real buzz. The rest, as they say, is history.'

'You specialised in art therapy then?' I am interested now.

Freddy gets up from the table. Brushes crumbs from his stubbly beard. 'I did. There are lots of things in this world that can be therapeutic. You must know that.'

I do. I really do. 'Like yoga,' I say, and he gives me a lopsided grin.

I'm not sure what is happening here. When will I start to feel better? That's not fair of me, I know, but all we're doing is having a nice time and a chat. Admittedly, I'm enjoying Freddy's company. He's an interesting guy, and I don't get out much. Does Si think simply telling my story to a stranger will lift it away from me? And that the old me will somehow emerge, shiny and fixed and ready to slot back into the gap I left?

'Want to stretch your legs?' I ask Freddy. 'Before we start again?'

'I'd love to have a look at the front of the house,' he says, too quickly. He's been planning this.

I lead him down the hall, then open the front door. Outside is bright and cold. We are only wearing socks, but the stone steps and path are dry. We pad down them and onto the street. Blackthorn Wood is just across the road. It was my favourite place to walk.

Freddy leans his elbows against the low garden wall and stares upwards. 'I can see why you don't want to leave this place,' he breathes.

'Are you trying to be funny?' I snap. *Why did I snap?*

'No. I mean it. It's like a world-within-a-world. A costume drama of a place.'

What is he getting at?

'It certainly has its stories,' I say. 'As we all do.'

He smiles up at me; does he think smiling solves everything? 'You make me laugh. The way you try to be all enigmatic. There are things that tell me you're not.'

'Like what?' I am spitting like a wronged teenager.

'Well, for one thing, you were kidding yourself about the events unfolding in your workplace. And pretending –to yourself as much as others– that they weren't having an effect. I know what my gut's telling me about this school of yours.'

I blink back my anger. This guy has known me for half a day. And here he is, pronouncing about what went on in Parkhouse. Then I remember. It was me who told him. Not directly, but I did.

'Look,' I say, my fists clenched but hidden. 'Si told you roughly what happened to me when he got in touch. I've dealt with the consequences as best I could. This is me, now. What the hell's difference does it make if I'm enigmatic or not?'

'And I like who you are now.' He straightens up, stretches his back. 'But don't pretend you somehow deserved what happened to you because you weren't diamond-hard.'

I blow out a puff of air then turn away from him, wondering how he's managed to unpick one of my deep threads when I've hardly told him anything yet. He is shuffling back up Blackthorn's stone steps. The tips of his hands are tucked into the pockets of his jeans. I follow, looking up at him as he speaks again.

'This Tina Armstrong character. Not everyone was taken in by her, were they? You mentioned Becky Ripley. A teacher, did you say?'

I shake my head. 'Not a teacher. She was chair of governors – still is, as far as I know. Unethical, when she was the old head's wife. But it's hard to be removed from a governing body. Mainly because no one wants to be on it.'

'And she wasn't a fan of Tina?'

'No.'

'Any idea why not?'

I have to think about this. There was never any proof of the affair between Tina and Becky's husband. I heard a few things but I'm pretty sure Becky had no idea.

'Apart from the obvious; and I don't think there was anything in what Joe Smythe told me. You know, about them kissing,' I say as Freddy holds the front door open for me. 'I'm guessing… and it is just a guess: she blamed Tina for Mick's death, in some strange, convoluted way.'

'What else had she sniffed out then?' Freddy looks puzzled.

'I'm not sure. Tina was just one of those people. There's a blurred line between love and hate, as you probably know.' And here she is again, my old, patronising self. 'I mean, from the job you do, you must know.'

Keep digging, Cassie.

Freddy is frowning now. 'It was a hell of a leap by her. To blame the secretary for your husband dying.'

'It was. Mick struggled with his health in those last months. We all saw it. And heard it. That awful coughing.'

'Poor guy. Was he getting treatment?'

'I think he was.'

We make our way towards the lounge. Freddy slides past me into the study and comes back with his notebook. 'This clique that was forming,' he says, flipping through the pages. 'Did your boss offer any insights? She must have noticed.'

'People only see what they want to see,' I tell him.

Chapter Eight

FEBRUARY 2016

'I could do with you back in class, Judy. If you wouldn't mind.'

Cassie stepped into the main office. Tina Armstrong was perched on her special chair, ankles crossed, and wearing a trouser suit pressed to within an inch of its life. Judy's head was bent towards her.

'Okay,' she said without looking up. 'I'm on my way.' A smirk at Tina. 'See you later.'

'There're quite a few kids in early, that's all. And nobody's in your room.'

Cassie waited for Tina to notice her; to acknowledge that another human being had come into the room. There was nothing. No greeting, not even a sigh. The woman swung her chair around and began tapping on her keyboard. This again. It made Cassie feel like she didn't exist, which was the point, she suspected.

Judy followed her back to class, silent now, apart from one long world-weary sigh. Cassie was hearing her do this more and more, especially when she pulled rank. The sound grated on her already-shredded nerves. Adrenaline overload was kicking in, leaving her mouth dry and sticky, and her stomach taut.

Taking other people's children out into the world caused a level of stress that couldn't be explained with mere words. Add to that a Lakeland setting and a pair of skis, and the situation became one which had to be experienced in order to be understood. And that was without the continual ignorance she was being treated to by Tina Armstrong.

'Don't worry, kiddywinks, Mrs Barker's here,' Judy called as they approached a group of boys, loitering in tracksuits and bobble hats. 'Did you miss me?'

Every one of those words tugged at Cassie's zinging nerves. *Just do your bloody job.*

Kevin was laying out risk assessments and first-aid kits on a table in his classroom. Cassie's stomach clenched tighter: there was nothing in those green bags that could fix a broken leg. Or head. But she should stop overthinking. Kids needed to get outside, to learn about themselves, to fashion their own risk assessments. Teachers, like parents, could only stand beside them with advice. And cushions.

'Thanks for doing that,' she said as she walked in. 'I've had to put me and Judy together for the sessions and leave you with Jax and Lucy. That way, there's a first aider and a senior teacher in each group.'

'No problem.' Kevin winked. 'Can you give me a list of who I've got?'

'I will. We'll do the first ski session while you take the others to the park. If that's okay? Then swap at about eleven o'clock.' Cassie rubbed a hand over her face.

'Calm down, Whites,' Kevin said. 'You've got everything covered. Your group has Judy for first aid. I've got me. And the skiing guys will have their own people, I'm sure. Nothing's going to go wrong. It's not even snow, is it. It's rubber matting.

And the sledding will provide some light relief. No danger in that, is there? He rolled his eyes.

Kevin was right. Overthinking didn't guarantee success. But if there was an accident, it would be for her to explain away. No one else. She inhaled deeply, then blew out the breath. The sooner they got the kids on the coach, the better.

'You know what I'm like,' she laughed, a toffee-brittle laugh. 'I call it conscientious. You call it nit-picking.'

Kevin looked at her. Moved in for a light hug. 'Well, we meet somewhere in the middle, that's why we're a good team. It'll be fine.'

As Cassie stepped away, she heard someone in the doorway.

'Everything all right?' Judy Barker. This woman had a spaniel's nose for private conversations.

'Yep.' Cassie picked up the risk assessments. 'I'll sign these and take them to the office.' A half smile at Kevin, then she escaped.

'Anything I can do?' Cassie could hear Judy's voice. Wheedling. Why wasn't she in her classroom? She didn't have a teaching assistant. Which meant every time she stepped out, her children were unsupervised. Cassie stopped at her own door.

'Mrs T. Could you watch both classes?'

Jax looked up from the sink.

'I'm just popping to the office.' Cassie tilted her head towards Judy's classroom.

'Will do.' Jax pulled some paper towels from the plastic holder and rubbed off her hands. 'Is Mrs Barker not in?'

'Oh, she's in.' Cassie pointed her thumb towards Kevin's room. 'There.'

Jax stepped through the doorway and positioned herself between the two rooms.

'Won't be a min,' Cassie called as she walked away. Time to brave the office. Again.

By nine o'clock, the coach was pulling away from school. As Cassie buckled herself into a seat at the front, she relaxed a little. There was an inevitability about this phase of any school trip. No turning back now. Into the abyss.

The landscape of the town centre soon gave way to open fields and the low, rounded fells of South Lakeland. Market towns flashed by. Children made their own entertainment: excited chatter, kicking the back of the chair in front and frequent requests for the sick bucket. There were exclamations at Whitbarrow Scar, renamed Mount Everest, and the River Leven became the Nile.

Cassie made her way up and down the aisle, thankful for the headspace allowed by her charges being fastened into their seats and under complete control. Not Judy Barker though. She had made her way down the bus and squeezed herself into a space next to Kevin.

The skies over Kendal were filled with low grey clouds, giving the light a grainy quality. It felt like evening. When the coach hit a curved bridge over the River Kent, Cassie's stomach went into freefall; soon, she would oversee sixty small lives while they threw themselves into a coveted new experience. It was one thing to take on this challenge with your own children; quite another to be answerable for someone else's. Was she overreacting? There had been many other trips over the years, but none had felt so painfully tense. There was no time to think anything further; the black rubber slopes of the ski club came into view, accompanied by a round of applause that made Jax grin and Lucy roll her eyes.

A group of people wearing heavy red parkas were waiting

in the car park as the coach pulled in. They waved their arms, making the children whoop in delight. Cassie smiled at Kevin.

Fuck, he mouthed, pulling himself up from his seat.

'Stay here, everyone.' Her best teacher voice. 'But start putting your coats on.'

As the coach doors slid open, a blast of cold hit her full in the face. Lakeland air, refreshing and sharp, and so redolent of her own childhood walks on the low fells. She pulled on her hat and zipped up her parka, then took the few steps down into the car park. A slim, bearded man stepped towards her and held out his hand.

'Hello. Cassie Clifton? I'm Steve Taylor. We've emailed each other?'

Cassie shook his hand.

'Get all the kids off the bus and we'll take them to the toilets and storerooms,' he beamed. 'Give you folk the chance to get organised. There's a café up there, too, if you need it.'

Kevin was climbing down the coach steps, first-aid bags held aloft. Children clunked off behind him, with a sway of rucksacks and excitement.

'Thanks.' Cassie turned to the first few. 'Follow Steve, everyone. And check you haven't left your coats or bags on the bus.' She took a deep breath.

Here we go.

When all the children were off, she clambered back up the steps, and lifted her own rucksack and clipboard of lists.

'Thanks,' she said to the driver. 'We'll be back here at half two. There's a café you can use, the guy said.'

She was treated to a wide smile. 'Good lass. Enjoy yourselves.'

Judy was zipping herself into a bright blue anorak. 'God, it's freezing,' she said. 'Might as well have gone to The Alps.'

Cassie shivered. 'Never mind. It'll be more authentic, sledding down the hill against the bite of the wind. Not.'

They both laughed.

'At least we can get a hot drink. There's a café.' But Judy wasn't listening. She was looking at Kevin, who was holding out a green first-aid bag.

'That's yours, Mrs Barker,' he said. 'For when I'm off site.'

Her smile slid. 'But I'm with you.'

Cassie stepped in. 'No. I need you with me. I haven't got a first-aid certificate. Mr Noble has. So, the TAs are going with him. You've seen the lists, haven't you?'

'I didn't look,' Judy muttered. 'But I'm going with Kev. There's plenty of people on site. There'll be first-aiders amongst them.'

Kevin wouldn't meet Cassie's eye.

'No. We'll stick to my plan. I did it like that for a reason.' Her heart thudded against her ribcage, and she gasped a little. Surely Judy Barker wasn't going to openly defy her. Some of the children were running back down the path towards them. Judy dropped the first-aid bag at Cassie's feet.

'You and Jax will need this. I'm with Kev.' Then she turned away and began to call for her own class to line up in front of her.

'Nobbs,' Cassie hissed. 'What's going on?'

He turned away and began to gather his own class, leaving her to do the same.

Jax came up behind her, cheeks red with the wind, and eyes streaming. 'It seems I'm staying with you, Cass,' she whispered. 'She,' a nod towards Judy, 'told me I was, anyway. Glad really.'

Cassie linked her hands together and tried to steady herself.

'Right, kiddos,' she called. 'Let's do this. I'm going to call out your names. And when I do, I'll point you to either my side, or to Mr Noble and Mrs Barker's. Please don't muck up my system.' Then to Jax, 'Any more than it's already been mucked up.'

Chapter Nine

Most of the children were asleep when the coach arrived back at school, heads pressed against windows or onto shoulders, faces aglow. They had ridden the day on a wave of energy that seemed endless, and as often happened, a little warmth and the lull of an engine had knocked them out.

Her own children were past that stage now. Prising them out of their beds was almost impossible. Lucky that their high school was only a five-minute walk away.

There had been no need for first aid, as it turned out, and Judy had been a great help with the turnaround and mobilisation of groups of children. But she had clung to Kevin's side, and he didn't seem to mind.

When the last of the children had been offloaded and sent on their way, Cassie and the other staff plodded back into school.

'I need a coffee,' laughed Jax, face wind-flushed and hair askew. 'Anyone else?'

'Oh, yes.' Cassie slung an arm around her shoulder. 'Get the kettle on, missus. I'll be down in a minute.' Kevin and Judy trailed behind, carrying buckets and bin bags and an assortment of clothing. 'Thanks, guys,' she called over her shoulder. 'Same time next year.'

'I'll need a double knee replacement first.' Kevin mimicked a stagger. 'Not as fit as I thought I was.'

Judy threw her head back and bellowed with laughter.

Get me out of here. But Cassie had decided: she was going to talk to Alison Harman about the events of the day, and her other worries.

The headteacher was waiting in the school foyer when they pushed open the front door. 'Good day?'

'Yes,' Cassie said. 'But I could do with a word. Can I grab us a drink, and see you in your office?'

'Course you can. Is all okay?'

The door banged behind them. Judy and Kevin.

'I'll see you in a bit.'

Alison tilted her head quizzically; the strain of a crazy afternoon showed itself in her flushed face and shirt sleeves, but Cassie was determined to share what was on her mind. Bottling things up was shredding her nerves. She followed Jax into the staffroom and put down her bag and coat, conscious of her colleagues' heavy footsteps behind her. Neither of them followed her in.

When the kettle boiled, Cassie made herself a mug of tea and coffees for Jax and Alison.

'I'm just popping in to see the boss, Jax. I'll be back shortly.' She passed the hot drink to her teaching assistant, who was already sprawled across two easy chairs, slipping off her trainers.

'Thanks. Everything okay?'

'Yep. Catch you later.'

As she passed Kevin's room, the low hum of voices filtered out. Judy was in there again. Cassie stuck her head through the open doorway.

'Haven't you two got homes to go to?' She kept her voice light but there was no mistaking her meaning.

'Yeah,' yawned Kevin, and as she walked away again, 'Hold up, Whites.'

Cassie had taken a few steps along the corridor before he caught up. She stopped, balancing the cups.

'Sorry about her.' He thumbed towards his room. 'Can't get rid.'

'What are you talking about? Just tell her.'

'How?' His tone became a whisper. 'She'll be out here in a minute. Tracking my every move.'

Cassie shook her head. She'd already offered to have a word with Judy, but in the end, he'd stopped her. Confrontation freaked him out, he'd said. Like it was something that only happened to him. 'You won't let me tell her. What else do you expect me to do? But I'm not going to forget about today, Nobbs. She shouldn't have defied me like that.'

'Oooo. Get you. Defied. You the big guns now, or what?'

'Do you know something? There's no helping you.' She turned away sharply, slopping Alison's coffee onto the corridor carpet. 'Damn. That was your fault.'

The corners of Kevin's mouth turned up slightly. She let her shoulders slump. 'Stop it, you idiot. It's not funny.' Judy appeared in the doorway.

'I'll message you later,' Cassie told him, as loudly as she could. Then hated herself for it. Her reaction to Judy Barker was turning her into someone she didn't want to be. Was it jealousy? An embarrassing emotion, and not one she'd had much experience of. No. Not jealousy. Something more corrosive. But too subtle to name. Better for speaking about, perhaps?

Alison was sitting at her desk, glasses balanced on the end of her nose. 'Hiya,' she said as Cassie walked in with their drinks. 'Long day? Your face is wind burnt. I bet you've had fun.'

'We have.' Cassie put down Alison's coffee and moved across the room to sit on one of the easy chairs. She sipped at her drink. How was she supposed to explain her worries to her boss, without sounding petty and whiny? Was it each individual event that bothered her, or the bigger feeling that she was somehow being marginalised? What did that even mean? She was the deputy headteacher. Did she still expect to be one of the girls?

'Spit it out.' Alison cut across her thoughts. 'What's on your mind?'

Cassie sat forwards in her chair. 'Have Tina and Denise been okay with you since... well, since we had that talk to them?'

Alison stretched her mouth downwards. 'They're a bit catty, but I haven't had a lot to do with them. Why?'

'I just get the feeling they're ignoring me deliberately. Not passing on my messages or emails, leaving me out of the admin loop.'

Alison's nostrils flared. Cassie felt like she had turned into something foul smelling, then reminded herself this was just one of her boss's ticks. 'They better bloody not be. Do you want me to have a word with them?'

But what would you say?

Cassie's gut was telling her that it would only make things worse. 'It would make me look like a telltale. I just wondered if they were giving you the same treatment.'

'You mean apart from sending me an email of complaint.' Alison lifted her hands. 'I've had the treatment too, don't forget.'

'Fair point. Do you think it's time we at least put Tina in her place? She's upset Joe as well.'

'Oh.' A sigh. 'Everyone's upset Joe. It's his state of mind, at the moment. Once he's better, he'll realise just how touchy he's been.'

Which was completely unfair. Joe had been very clear when Cassie had spoken to him. Tina had been on his case. This implied two things: Tina's rules had to be followed, and Joe had been a transgressor. Had this been the fate of Mick Ripley? And was it now Cassie who was stepping out of line?

'It's not only Joe though, is it?'

Alison narrowed her eyes. 'Meaning?'

'She niggled away at Mick, apparently.'

As soon as she'd said this, Cassie wished she hadn't.

'Oh, come on now, Cass.' Alison leaned back in her chair. 'It sounds like you're just dredging up anything because you're annoyed with Tina. And I get that.'

'You're making me sound like one of the kids.'

'Hey.' Alison's tone changed, became jagged. 'You're tired. You've just come back from a stressful trip, but don't snap at me.'

'Sorry.'

'It's okay. But there are some things, when you're a manager, that you must learn to live with. Admin staff belong to that group of *things*.'

Cassie took a sip of her coffee. 'It's annoying, though. Turning away when I ask them questions or say hello. They wouldn't do that to you.'

Alison pinched at the bridge of her nose. 'Just ignore them, Cass. They're not like us. They're caught up in their little world and don't see the bigger picture. The whole school. The kids. Everything is about their empire. Rise above it.'

The room had no outside windows. Cream walls bounced back white light from the overhead fluorescent tubes. Cassie felt trapped. She wanted to go home. To the warmth and space of Blackthorn. To Si. He wouldn't tell her to rise above anything. He'd be down in the depths with her. She jumped up.

'I'll try.' A pause. 'Now, I'd better go. I need a shower, and some food.' Then she stomped out of the room.

And I never even mentioned Judy pigging Barker.

Flakes of snow fell across the windscreen, lilac against the grey of early evening. The wipers cleared a space and Cassie craned to see the road. Her neck and shoulders hurt. The tensions of the day lay deep in her muscles, and she wanted nothing more than to be home. When Blackthorn House emerged, solid and watchful, through a swirl of white, she relaxed. The lights were on, and Si would be waiting.

She pulled the car onto the drive and carried her rucksack and parka into the warmth of the house. She slammed the door behind her; Judy Barker and Tina Armstrong couldn't get to her here.

'Si. It's me.'

Her husband came into the hallway, tea towel in hand. 'Hiya. Good day? Any broken legs?'

Cassie tried to speak, but no words came.

'Hey. What's happened?' Si moved towards her, but she stepped away, shook her head, then walked into the lounge and threw herself onto the sofa. A log fire burned in the grate. It spat and crackled, illuminating the black marble surround. There was a comfort in this place, a softness; it lifted her away from what was becoming a rigid and bewildering workplace.

Si knelt in front of her. 'Shall I make you tea. Then you can tell me?'

Cassie watched his back as he walked away. What was wrong with her? Crying wasn't something she did very often. Behaving in a professional manner was her trademark, yet here she was, blubbing at nothing more than the actions of her colleagues. She pressed her hands to her cheeks. This situation wasn't going to escape from her control. It was gaining too much momentum. And the perfect way to stop it in its tracks was to add words.

Si came back into the room, carrying two steaming mugs and a handful of kitchen paper. He flicked the floor lamps with his toe. 'Better?' he asked, handing her a mug. 'This is not like you.'

'Better now I've let go a bit. But something's going on at work, Si, and it doesn't feel right.' Cassie gulped down a mouthful of tea, hid her expression behind a hand.

'Can you tell me? Are you allowed?'

'I can.' Another gulp. 'It's nothing to do with the children, though. And I know, as soon as I explain, it'll sound petty.'

'Tell me anyway. I'll decide if it's petty. And what if it is?' He lifted one shoulder. 'It's obviously bugging you. That makes it important, in my book.'

Cassie put down her drink and took the wad of paper from him. She dabbed at her face, blew her nose.

'Both the admin staff have decided to ignore me. They don't pass messages on. Don't inform me of stuff when they should. And they're in cahoots with Judy Barker, I'm sure. She's been chasing round after Nobbs. Throwing herself at him. It's embarrassing.'

Putting words to her fears had exactly the effect Cassie thought it would. Two women sulking at her, and another flirting with a close colleague. The ebb and flow of any functioning workplace, she was sure.

But Si looked thoughtful. 'They can't just refuse to do your work, can they? You should tell Alison.'

Cassie lowered her head. 'I have. She thinks I should *rise above it*. Bloody cows. They're so blatant.'

Si rocked back on his heels, then stood up. 'You're senior

management, Cass. Just tell the pair of them what's what.' He picked up another log from the basket by the hearth and threw it onto the shrinking embers. 'You're normally quite tough. Why are you holding back?'

This was something she'd been asking herself. 'I don't know.' A shake of her head. Confusion. 'I don't think I've been so openly ignored before. It's weird.' Was she really scared of being ignored? Schoolkids did it to their teachers all the time. *All behaviour is communication,* they had been told during their training. What were the admin staff trying to communicate to her?

'And what's Nobbs been up to?' Si was asking.

'Oh, it's Judy Barker. The one that's come into our year group to cover for Joe. She's chasing after him. Turning up at his house. Having cliquey little meetings with him. He doesn't like it, so he says.'

Si walked back across the room and sat beside her, took her hands in his. 'That's not your problem though, is it? I know he's a friend, but he should be dealing with it, not you. She sounds a bit insecure, to me. Best leave well alone.'

Si shouldn't have to listen to this rubbish, Cassie thought. It sounded like playground squabbles. And there were no words to explain what Judy was doing. It wasn't the flirting; it was the relationship building. With Nobbs. Leaving her out. The very thing she was having to deal with every day when the older girls in the school had their tiffs.

'You're right. Let's not talk about it anymore. I think I'm just stressed after the trip. I need something to eat. Then we can have a walk in the snow. Just a short one, though. I've been skiing all day.'

Her husband stood up. His knees clicked, and he rolled his shoulders backwards. 'I think you should talk to the admin staff. Hit the problem head-on. Otherwise, it'll fester, run to poison where you can't see it.' He walked towards the door.

'Now. Poke the fire, would you? I'll go and dish up. And, Cassie?'

'What?'

'Don't worry. A good meal and a sleep. That's what you need. You know how worked up you get when you're tired.'

Chapter Ten

MARCH 2016

The school hall was filled with excited voices and the shuffle of 200 feet. Benches to sit on meant only one thing: an important event. Something that would transform the monotony of the day. At the front, Cassie waited for quiet and kept one eye on the doorway, while the other staff fidgeted in their seats. Then Kevin Noble peeped through and gave her a signal.

With a whoop of music and voices, the door was flung wide and in came something that resembled a Victorian bathing machine, accompanied by two men dressed in hospital scrubs. Becky Ripley brought up the rear, her tidily bobbed hair and equally tidy dress sense replaced with something Wonder Woman might wear. The children didn't need much encouragement to join the flapping arms and cheering of these adults. Cassie could only stare as Kevin followed, arms above his head and clapping.

'Well, kiddos,' he shouted as he reached the front of the hall. 'Are you all up for a treat? Some fun?'

The loudest cheer came from Judy Barker.

'You are?'

More cheering.

'Then let me introduce *Andy's Attack on Asthma.*'

Cassie cringed at the slapstick of the occasion, but the children were captivated. With a wave of their hands, the fake doctors gained complete control of the crowd.

Kevin took advantage of the silence. 'This is going to be a bit of fun, with a serious message,' he trilled, pretending not to notice the mimicry going on behind him.

He's loving this.

'So please give a big round of applause and all your attention to,' he faked a drum roll, 'Andy's Attack on Asthma.'

What followed was an hour of singing and dancing, acting and joining in. Cassie found herself drawn to the compelling atmosphere of live theatre, the weaving of stories using dramatic movement and the timbres of the human voice. Children waved their hands to be chosen. The audience inched forward, some got to their feet. Cassie and Jax did their best to control emotions, especially when Kevin, now everyone's favourite teacher, taught a song-and-dance routine that would serve as a reminder of how to deal with an asthma attack.

At the end of the performance, a glowing Becky Ripley came to kneel by Cassie, while Kevin talked everyone down with information about sponsored events and further help for asthma charities.

'You were brill.' Cassie smiled at the woman. How difficult must the show have been for her?

'I do my best,' Becky replied. 'I saw you having a sneaky little clap-along and cheer.' Sweat trickled down from her headband. 'The guys have it just right, don't they? I can't wait to deliver the show to other schools.'

They listened while Kevin droned. It had the desired effect. The energy of the room collected itself together and settled around the children's feet. They sagged on the benches, and hands began to go up.

The sound of a door, pushed against its frame, sent all heads turning. In walked Tina Armstrong, Laura Pearson and a tall man carrying a camera. Tina's forceful heels propelled her towards the front of the hall, while Kevin scratched at his chin, and watched. Laura and the cameraman followed.

'This man wanted to get some photographs, Mr Noble. Of the show.' Tina peered at the children. 'Would that be all right?'

Cassie shifted in her chair. She'd asked the press photographer to come, and now she was going to have to talk to him. Or perhaps Kevin would.

'And I've brought Miss Pearson down, too,' Tina was saying. 'With Mrs Harman being out, I thought she could do the press release. She always did it, before—' This word aimed straight at Cassie; a barb of poison shot straight from shiny red lips.

Cassie felt Becky's hand, hot on her thigh. 'Don't react,' she whispered. 'Just smile sweetly and pretend you're grateful.'

'Bloody cow,' Cassie snarled, trying to make herself do what Becky suggested, when what she wanted was to get up from her seat and kick Tina Armstrong's legs from under her. 'This is driving me mad. I'm sorry, Becky. You shouldn't have to listen to me moaning.'

'Don't worry about it,' came the reply. 'I've seen how she operates, believe me. And how hurtful it can be. Anytime you want to offload, you know where I am.'

Cassie smiled her thanks with a clenched jaw: offloading wasn't an option, however tempting it felt.

Across the room, Judy Barker, pink faced and giggling still, was gathering some children together for a photoshoot, under Laura's direction. Cassie looked at the pair of them. And what she got back was a smirk that made her want to scream.

Later, with the children gone and the school quiet, Cassie tried to settle to some marking. But thoughts of Tina Armstrong hammered at her brain. Why was the woman so against her? There had been the smallest tinge of embarrassment on Laura Pearson's face when she'd been wheeled into the hall earlier, in place of the deputy head. Why wouldn't Tina just leave the situation alone. Or accept it. The energy it was taking from all of them would be much better spent doing the thing they were actually paid for; their job.

Cassie put down her pen and headed for the classroom door. Some fresh air might help. There was at least an hour of work to do before she could head home to Blackthorn, though the draw of the place was almost too much to bear.

Somewhere in the distance, a hoover buzzed, but the corridors were empty. Most teachers were at their desks, head down and planning for the long tomorrow. Cassie pushed open the door to the playground and stepped outside.

She shivered, hugged her arms around herself.

Once the children had gone home, this was an area of quiet. Of waiting. A place with no purpose, aside from the containment of fun and laughter and energy. And here was Denise Kelly, emptying the contents of her desktop shredding machine into one of the recycling bins.

There was no way of avoiding conversation.

'Hi,' called Cassie, hopeful.

'Oh. Hello.' Denise hesitated. 'It's a bit cold to be out here.' She looked at Cassie's blouse. 'Without a coat, I mean.'

'I see you've got yours on,' Cassie laughed.

'Silly, aren't we. Telling the kids to wear coats, when we don't.'

Cassie was confused. She hardly knew this woman, could find no common ground. She hesitated. 'I–'

But Denise interrupted. 'I've been wanting to talk to you.'

'Oh, yes?'

'I feel bad, you know, about what Tina is doing.'

Cassie frowned. 'And what is she doing?'

'She's been so annoyed, ever since you got the deputy's job. Finding things to moan about. Saying you are clueless. And Alison.' A glance at the playground door. 'Tina wanted Laura to be deputy head.'

'Why? What's wrong with me?'

'Nothing. Laura's her best friend, that's all. And she'd all but promised her the job.' Denise's chin was trembling.

'I'm a bit confused, Denise.' *That was an understatement.* 'How could Tina have promised Laura the job. She's not the headteacher; she's not even close.'

What Cassie wanted to mention, and what hung in the air between them was the slippery status of the school secretary: it lay somewhere between teaching assistants and the manager of the site, yet its power was immense. When the school admin systems failed, the institution failed. Everyone kowtowed to the secretaries, didn't they?

'I don't think she's been happy since the other guy – Mick Ripley wasn't it – since he stopped being the head. She always goes on about him. Comparing him to Mrs Harman.' She rubbed her arms. 'I'd better go in. It's freezing.'

'I'll walk with you.' Cassie looked towards the door. 'And, Denise?'

'Yes?'

'Sorry if I sounded harsh. The other day. When Alison had you both in.'

A snort. 'That email was Tina's idea. She said it was how things were done. Formally, I mean. I didn't dare argue. And anyway, she had a point. Alison is so disorganised.'

Didn't dare. Those words stayed with Cassie as she walked back towards her classroom. Now she knew of three people who had showed an irrational fear of Tina Armstrong. And one of them was dead.

Chapter Eleven

Cassie stood at the bedroom window. Overnight, more snow had fallen, and the back garden of Blackthorn was smothered. A strip of orange light was edging up behind the beeches: peach icing along their boughs, and the promise of ear-tingling cold. Si was asleep, all of him under the duvet apart from one foot. This, he claimed, was a throwback to when the girls were babies and he needed to always be ready for them.

Cassie ran a finger over his heel. 'Tea, I think.'

'Please,' he mumbled from the blur of sleep. 'Do you want me to make it?'

'I'll do it,' she laughed. 'You'll be shovelling my car out in an hour anyway.'

He groaned, pulled the duvet over his head.

They had breakfast together, then Cassie dressed for the weather: heavy sweater and woollen trousers, not the standard blouse and slacks.

Though the pavements and gardens were covered in a soft white layer, the roads around Blackthorn were clear. Si shovelled away the snow from behind her car, and she rolled down the drive carefully, waving to him as she pulled away.

Her nerves were on edge. Adrenaline again. This morning, as soon as she had the chance, she would have that difficult conversation with Judy. Si was probably right: the woman was insecure. But she needed to realise the consequences of stalking a colleague. If it was stalking. Cassie wasn't convinced. That Kevin Noble liked the attention she didn't doubt, though his words suggested something else. Either way, things had to change. Especially the closed-door chats. They annoyed her the most, for reasons she couldn't explain, except to say she felt excluded. And then she was back to calling herself immature again.

On the roads, the traffic moved slowly. Cassie gripped her steering wheel as the car up ahead of her sent out a spray of slush and pink grit. Heavy grey clouds hung across the lighted buildings, and people shuffled along the pavements, heads down and hands thrust deep in pockets. But the children would love it. She remembered what the atmosphere was like on a snow day. There weren't many of them. Not in a coastal town like this, but not much teaching happened when there was a magical world just outside the window.

The school was in darkness when she arrived. No Dot. But she did live quite a distance away, over on the island. Walney was a fourteen-mile-long spit of land, formed when the mouth of the River Duddon had dropped it as silt, almost twelve thousand years previously. Now, a good chunk of the town's inhabitants lived there, and travelled onto the mainland via a rickety Victorian bridge, which was probably where Dot was stuck, right now, along with hundreds of other drivers.

Cassie searched through her bunch of keys for the one that would let her into the building. The place felt strange without children or staff, full of echoes and trapped energy. A bit like her, this morning. She deactivated the alarm and let herself through the pass-coded door. Then she flicked on the lights and walked towards her classroom, to wait.

Dot arrived, swishing into the car park. Then Alison. And two of the lower school staff. Laura Pearson. Jax. And finally, Judy Barker's car pulled in. Cassie's heart jumped against her ribs. Was it a good idea to confront the woman? On Nobbs' behalf or even her own? Probably not. But the incident at the ski slope cut deep. Judy was a junior colleague. She couldn't just make rules and change plans because they didn't suit her own needs.

Cassie listened while Judy let herself in to her classroom and began bustling about, listened while she walked out again and along to the staffroom. She'd be getting herself a drink. There were voices. Greetings. Then Judy was back again. Cassie took her chance. She left the pile of worksheets she was trimming and stepped across to the other woman's room. She closed the door loudly and waited to be noticed.

'Hi.' Judy was lifting a dry-wipe pen from her board. She unclicked the lid. 'Everything all right?'

'Yes, thanks. Have you got time for a word?' Cassie took a few steps towards her. Swallowed down her nerves.

'Sure.'

'It's about Kevin, among other things.'

Judy walked towards her desk, sat on her chair then put the pen down in front of her. 'What about Kevin?' She dipped her head.

'Well, for a start, the skiing. Going off with him when I'd already sorted out arrangements. And those little chats with the door closed.' A pause. 'Taking cake to his house.' Cassie could feel her heart banging against her ribs. Time for Judy to do some talking.

Silence.

Then she picked up the pen again and began drumming it on the desk. There was grey hair in her parting, iron against strands of dark red. 'He told you about that?' She jutted her chin. 'How *cosy*.'

'There was nothing cosy about it. He's worried. He doesn't want to start anything with you.'

Judy inhaled sharply and ran her hands across her face. 'Oh, poor Kev, I don't think. You've got a cheek. Coming in here. Accusing me of things. You need to get your facts straight. You know nothing.' She rolled the pen between the fingers of both hands.

'I know you seem intent on pushing me out to the edge of this year group.' Cassie waited. Then, 'Why would that be?'

Judy slammed down the pen. 'What? You wanted me to pull this year group out of a hole. That's what I'm doing. Can't you handle it?'

'And taking a cake to Kevin's house. How does that fit into this rescue mission?' Cassie's plan hit a wall. Every word she was saying patronised, like the worst kind of conciliatory politician. *I'm telling you for your own good.* She almost said it, then decided on a change of tack. 'You don't have to huddle up with Nobbs. You can talk to me.' *Oh God, that sounded just as belittling.*

'How fucking kind of you.' Judy's words smashed across the room, then she shoved back the chair and stood up, glowered at Cassie, lifted the pen again and threw it, so that it skimmed past her shoulder. 'What has any of this got to do with you?' The words came out like an explosion of fireworks, each with a flourish of energy.

Cassie opened her mouth to speak again, but Judy stormed towards her, finger wagging. More explosions.

'You only want him for yourself. I've seen you. Simpering bitch. Nobbs this. Nobbs that. Tina said–'

Cassie didn't hear anything else. Judy stamped away and was gone. Cassie followed, heard the slam of the staff toilet door. The lock clunked. Then all was quiet.

What have I done?

Jax poked her head out from the staffroom. 'Morning. Everything all right?'

Cassie shook her head in horror. 'No,' she choked, hand on her chest. 'I'm going to have to see Alison. Cover for me if there's anything. Please?'

Jax stared out her agreement and wafted her hands. 'Go. Go.'

At Alison's office door, Cassie hesitated. What could she do but admit she'd caused this situation? Tell her that Judy Barker had locked herself in the toilet, that she was probably banging her head up and down on the wall? But she had to do something.

'Morning.' Alison was peering at the computer screen. 'Three hundred bloody emails, again.'

'Morning. Look. I've done something stupid.' Cassie's voice was trembling. With rage or fear, she wasn't sure. But emotion was threatening to spill out, however hard she was trying to keep cool.

Alison's head snapped up. 'Oh no. You look pale. Sit down.' She dragged her chair away from her desk. 'Now, tell me.'

'I tried to talk to Judy about something, and she took it the wrong way. She stormed out and locked herself in the toilets.'

Alison's nostrils flared. She put her hands on her thighs and drew in a deep breath, making Cassie feel about five years old. 'You'd better tell me everything very carefully,' she breathed. 'And don't leave anything out.'

As she explained, a red flush crept from Cassie's chest to her neck and face. This was like being a miscreant, dragged in front of the headteacher. But the more words she said, the more bleating the whole thing sounded. Like she was making excuses. Like she was incompetent. When she'd finished, Alison chewed at her lip for a moment, then swung back around to her desk. With a click of her mouse, she closed down what she had been working on, and stood up.

'I'll go and talk to Judy. Give me ten minutes or so, then go back to your classroom. I'll come and see you again later.'

And that was it. Cut down like a naughty schoolgirl.

Cassie put her head in her hands and listened for the door closing. No matter what else happened, she would not put herself in this position ever again. Deputy headteacher, moaning about a badly handled personnel matter, having to ask someone else to sort out her mess. Never again. She felt utterly humiliated.

When enough time had passed, Cassie slunk back towards her classroom. Still a day of teaching to get through. And the repercussions of this ridiculous incident. There was a tightness in her chest, as though no air was getting in, and a wave of hot acid sloshed in her stomach. As she rounded the corner of the corridor, she could see into the staffroom. Inside, Judy Barker was sitting on the easy chair nearest the door. Kneeling in front of her, offering a box of tissues, was Tina Armstrong. Laura Pearson was there too, holding out a mug of tea. As Cassie neared, Tina caught her eye. That look. It made her want to turn and run.

October 2019

'Woah,' exclaims Freddy. He leans back on the sofa. 'These people. They sound like something out of *Stepford Wives*.'

I laugh bitterly at that. 'Not quite. There was nothing submissive about that trio, believe me. But they did seem to be controlled by some collective hatred, that's for sure.' I look at the notepad on his knee. The first thing he'd picked up when we came back into my study, after lunch. 'What is it you're writing down, if you don't mind me asking?'

Freddy clears his throat and closes the notebook. His face is pure frustration. 'Stop apologising. Or asking permission. That's the sort of thing I've written, actually. Themes keep popping up. Like everything you tell me comes with a rider, that you must have been at fault, somehow.'

'That's what I felt.' I can't add anything else; when Judy threw the pen at me, I knew I'd pushed her over the edge. I stand up. 'One more cup of tea before you go? The girls will be home soon. You could meet them, if you don't mind mouthy teenagers.'

Reliving those days and months is making me feel antsy. And I've been so content. Safe in Blackthorn, with family, my writing. How could scratching around in the actions of the past be of any benefit now?

'I'm completely at home with *mouthy teenagers;* we have empathy.' He chuckles at his own joke. 'But let me make the tea. I think I know where everything is.'

I follow him out to the kitchen, watch him fill the kettle and rinse out the cups. The dreadlocks of hair reach halfway down his back, and with his small and slim stature, he could be one of my girls, bustling around the kitchen, though they would never wear cargo pants and a hand-knitted sweater. And here I am, telling him things that I've never described before, even to Si. But he doesn't seem shocked or surprised or even slightly on my side. Rather, I feel like an exhibit, something to be studied, commented on in note form.

Freddy is running his socks across the floor tiles. 'Are these original?' he asks. 'I mean, from when the house was built?'

I peer down at the terracotta-and-black octagonal tiles. Chipped and worn, but part of Blackthorn's unique style. 'They are. We could get them replaced. Like for like, but newer. I don't want to, though. They could tell some tales, these tiles.'

'I've got something similar in my hall,' Freddy tells me. 'Though they've got blue and white bits mixed in, too. They're indestructible, aren't they?' He passes me over a mug of tea and sits down opposite. 'This Nobbs guy sounds a bit of a flake, if you don't mind me saying. Why do you think Judy Barker was attracted to him?'

What does that matter? 'Not sure,' I say. 'Her own husband was a good guy. A family man. Isn't that what counts, in the end?'

As far as I'd thought about it, Kevin was attractive in a crumpled, used kind of way. Not that I ever see him now. The last I'd heard, he was having a relationship with one of the new teaching assistants, younger and probably oblivious of his track record. I receive the odd text message from him, checking I'm okay, but I never text back. My social circle has dwindled to zero; I'm only alive in Parkhouse's past.

'It doesn't make sense. Here was a woman – Judy, you called her – an experienced teacher, with so much to lose. And she made a play for a guy like that.' He shakes his head. 'Anyway. That doesn't excuse her behaviour. Did you report the fact that she threw a pen at you?'

'I did, in a way. I told Alison what had happened, as I said. But I always got the feeling she thought it was my fault. Perhaps it was. I should have just left well alone.' I run my hands over my face. 'I tried to. I really did.'

The afternoon sun is almost gone. I get up and switch on the kitchen lights. I lay a hand on the range. It is cold. Iron cold. 'I'd better light this,' I say to Freddy. 'This room has never had a radiator. The range keeps it warm. When we remember to feed in the coal.'

'Do you want me to do it? I'm great at fires.'

You would be. 'Sure. The logs are just there, in the basket. And there's coal in that brass bucket. Are you staying for tea?'

He hesitates. 'I shouldn't, really. I've a dog to walk and I want to make some further notes. But… I'd love to. Can I pop and use your loo? Funny word that, isn't it? Loo.'

'You can.' I point in the direction of upstairs. 'You're not vegan or anything, are you? It's probably going to be sausages and mash?'

'Great.' He steps out of the kitchen and into the darkness of the hallway.

What I don't tell him, when he's so much in admiration of Blackthorn House, is how much the place traps me. Where once it had been a safe-haven, now its purpose is to hold me back from the outside world. That I've been the cause of the problem is clear; but Blackthorn played its part. And now the house and I are like runners in a three-legged race: we want to win, to untie, but individual falls bring us both down.

When Freddy eventually comes back, I am peeling potatoes. The kitchen table is spread with newspaper, the range is warming up and the girls have arrived home from school.

'Oh. Hello,' he says to Janey.

She is standing in front of the open fridge, eyes scanning. 'Hi.' She slides her gaze to me. *Who's that,* she mouths.

'This is Freddy,' I say. 'Freddy… Janey.'

'It's Mum's *therapist*,' Helli chips in from the doorway of the scullery.

I look in her direction. 'That's Helli.'

Freddy leans against the countertop and gives a strange wave. The conversation dips, then Helli pipes up again.

'Which car is yours?'

'I'm not sure what… I-I don't have a car.'

'We were looking at that flashy black one parked further down the street.' Janey has a can of Coke and a yoghurt in her hand. She fishes around for a spoon. 'It's not been parked there before.' She turns to me. 'I'm having this then going down to Nina's. Okay?'

'I'll need a bit more than that. It's a school night.'

She drops her shoulders and exhales in the way only teenagers can. Freddy presses his lips together, keeps his gaze on the floor.

'It's down the road and we're painting,' she grumbles. 'Her mum's doing us a pizza.'

I have to smile at her comment. These girls have kept me afloat in ways they can't imagine. I am their mother, a satellite in their universe, and as long as that role ensues, they don't worry. We have spent time talking about what happened at Parkhouse, but their questions took the form of changes it might bring to their lives: I made sure these were positive. That I'm having *therapy*, they can understand, but the word belongs to the world of adults, and they're not there yet.

'Janey is working on a GCSE art portfolio with her friend,' I tell Freddy. 'You're a bit of an artist yourself, aren't you?'

'I am,' he says. 'Though I have nothing as grand as a GCSE portfolio. It was just a few pieces pinned up in the art room when I got my first qualification.'

Janey composes her face. I've seen her do it many times. The expression she goes for is *polite disinterest*. I've taught her well.

'He's done art therapy, so he's not as *unqualified* as he's making out.' I am determined to keep the conversation going. 'Janey wants to be an art teacher eventually.'

'Mother. You don't have to explain me. Explain Helli, instead. She's much more interesting.'

Freddy bites his bottom lip, but a smile is forming. 'Fair point. Enjoy your art.'

'Thanks. See ya,' Janey says, then heads for her bedroom, pushing the yoghurt-pot lid into the bin as she passes.

Helli is sitting at the kitchen table. 'What about you?' I ask.

'Freddy is staying for tea. It would be nice to have your company.'

'Okay,' she says. 'Call me when it's ready.' She gets up. 'And Janey's right, for once. I am the interesting daughter.' With a swish of her blonde ponytail, she is gone. Freddy and I are alone again, and the zinging energy in the room settles itself.

'To be that young again, and know what I know now.' He pushes his hands into his pockets. 'Anything I can do to help? I'm a rubbish cook. Good at washing-up, though. And eating.'

'Sit down and keep me company, if you like. Si's down the garden.' I tilt my head towards the back door. 'But it's a bit cold out there. And dark.'

Freddy pulls out a chair, settles himself and puts his hands behind his neck. 'You seem so together about everything,' he says. 'So cool. You can't be though, can you?'

'Why not?'

'Well, I'm here, for one thing. Your husband wouldn't have asked for my help for no reason, would he?' He cocks his head at me.

I huff. 'Look, Freddy, I agreed to talk to you because he wanted me to. I have accepted that my *disability* is a small price to pay for surviving the things that happened to me. I can live with it; other people can't.'

I throw the last potato into a pan of water and lift it onto the top plate of the range. Then sprinkle on some salt from a dish on the shelf and turn to face him again. 'Boiling potatoes takes an hour on this thing. The sausages will be cooked then, too. Shall we go and light a fire in the lounge?'

I make my way through, draw the curtains and switch on the two electric lamps. The room is instantly aglow with red and orange light. Freddy kneels by the empty grate and runs his hands up the black marble pillars of the fireplace.

'This is beautiful,' he breathes. 'Look at the grain.'

'Nero Marquina, it's called. Spanish, I think. It was highly prized by the Victorian monied classes. Si doesn't like it, though. Thinks we should get underfloor heating and a reclaimed pine surround.'

Freddy begins laying firesticks and logs. 'Can I ask you something, Cassie?' Coolness in his gaze.

'Um-hum.'

'Has anyone ever mentioned agoraphobia to you?'

This. The thing I don't want to talk about. A middle-aged woman's curtain-twitching affliction. A mental illness. Nothing to do with me or my life.

'*I've* mentioned it to me. In my head. And then moved on. It's not for me, I'm afraid.'

A frown spreads across Freddy's smooth forehead. 'You've had a trauma. A stress injury. Why would you be worried about a symptom? It's treatable, as most symptoms are.'

What is he talking about? Stress injury? Trauma? He makes it sound like I've been in a car crash. I sit down on the sofa, tuck my feet under my legs, and shake my head. 'Do you think I've got a mental illness? Come on. I've got everything going for me. And one day, when I want to, I'll go somewhere away from Blackthorn. But not until then.' The same old story. The one I tell myself every day.

Freddy sits down on the marble hearth. Hugs his knees. 'Your husband mentioned a nasty text message,' he says. 'Tell me about it.'

Chapter Twelve

A slant of golden sunshine was coming through the classroom window. Four o'clock, and still light. Comforting, after the long weeks at winter's end.

Judy Barker stood at the head of a group of tables. Pacing and giggling and smoothing her cat-patterned blouse. Cassie pulled out a chair at the other end and sat down. The classroom was warm, and fragranced with fake oranges. She rarely came in here. Never came in here, actually.

Sitting along one side of the table was Kevin Noble, coffee cup in hand and a month's worth of beard growth. Next to him was Laura Pearson, in an efficient Dorothy Perkins trousers suit. Then, two teachers from a neighbouring primary school, male and tired-looking. Along the other side of the table sat the literacy adviser for the county, all sharp-cut grey hair and chunky silver jewellery, chatting to two women Cassie had never seen before.

This was Judy's big moment. Her assessment for passing a middle leader qualification, and Cassie had been ordered to attend; she could hardly refuse, when deputising for the headteacher was an operational part of her job.

Since the pen incident, there had been no communication from Judy, no greetings or farewells, no shared planning or joint projects: Cassie was simply ignored. When business that concerned their year-group arose, Judy would work with Kevin, and he would pass the information on. Or vice versa.

Cassie didn't dare try and clear the air again. Having to humiliate herself in front of Alison had been one of the worst moments of her career. Trying to explain a subtle power struggle to someone who didn't believe in power, was impossible. Especially when it had come out as a small-minded attack on a junior colleague. She certainly wasn't going to allow that to happen again. Ever.

Now, Judy was puffing out her chest and straightening her collar.

Here we go. I'll try my best to be professional.

'I'd like to welcome you all to my little presentation.' A livid bloom was creeping up from Judy's chest. 'I hope you like the project. It's worked for me, in my school. There might be some ideas that you can take away, too.'

Cassie gazed at the assembled audience, but no one was looking at her.

'Let's do introductions first. I'm Judy Barker. Year six lead teacher, and this is my wingman, Kevin Noble.' A glance at Nobbs.

She wasn't a lead teacher. Why had she said that? Wingman?

Kevin lifted one corner of his mouth and gave a half-wave, like a salute.

'Then we have Laura Pearson,' Judy continued, 'another partner of mine, and second in command at Parkhouse.' Her fingers put inverted commas around those words, and Laura blushed. 'Then Colin Andrews and David Fell, from Rosse Side School.'

Cassie tried to swallow down her incredulity. *Second in command?* Had Tina Armstrong written Judy a script?

But Judy didn't miss a beat. 'And I'm pleased to welcome Janis Starkey, from county. And Marianne Bower. And lastly, Janine Jones. Also from county.' She pointed her remote control at the overhead projector, and the presentation slides flicked up on the screen. 'And here I go.'

Cassie's pulse pounded. Had she just been completely overlooked? The deputy headteacher? Why hadn't Nobbs said something? Why hadn't *she* said something? She wanted to get up and walk out. But she was trapped. Like a prisoner, in a room full of people on a different side. Invisible chains tightened around her chest. She tried to breathe smoothly, but her body didn't understand. It sucked in air at an alarming rate, then sent it out with such a force that Cassie was sure one of the others would peer at her, all judgement and finger-pointing, and tell her to shush.

Judy's voice droned on. She used her remote control to scroll through slides, talked about herself, praised her school.

Cassie hunched down in her seat. She had to get out, or else she would slide under the table and disappear that way. Suddenly, there was a burst of laughter, an interjection of agreement and excited chatter. This was her chance. She dived for the door, escaped, and closed it behind her. She leaned forward over a small table in the corridor and tried to steady her breathing.

I need to go home. I can't do this anymore.

She stumbled her way to her own classroom. Jax was there, elbow resting on a table, eyeing a pile of marking.

'Oh. That was quick. I thought you'd be an hour. I was getting stuck into the maths books.'

'Yeah. Judy didn't need me, after all. So, if you don't mind, I'll get a flyer.'

Jax flashed a look at her. 'Everything okay?'

Cassie was pulling on her coat. Her legs trembled. She hoped Jax couldn't see. 'Fine. Yes, everything's fine. Got a headache, that's all.' She didn't trust herself to say anything else. 'I'll see you in the morning.'

Jax waved her hand and turned her head back to the books.

Cassie hurried along the corridor, not wanting to be seen by anyone, not wanting a single emotion to escape before she got back to the safety of Blackthorn. Her mouth felt as though it was full of the turquoise paper towels used to dry tiny hands. And she couldn't get her breath. If either of the admin staff were in the office, she didn't see. She fumbled with the coded door, then escaped from the building and onto the car park. Two clicks of her keys let her into the car, and she was away.

The drive home flashed by in a blur of traffic lights and shopfronts, grey trees, and pavements full of people. But Cassie couldn't engage. It felt like someone else was in control of the car, and she was just an anxious passenger. When Blackthorn appeared, she let go of her breath and it came out as a desperate sob.

Si was in the front garden. He stopped digging when she pulled up, then rested one wellington boot on his spade and peered at her. The sight of his scruffy fisherman's sweater, shirt collar hanging out of the neckline, made her want to cry. She could not have explained why. Except to say the quicksand of her life was shifting in a terrifying way, and Si was her safety rope.

'You're early, darling,' he called as she climbed out of the car. 'What's happening?'

Cassie shook her head then stumbled up the drive and into the house.

'Cass. Cassie. What's going on?' Si was behind her. She heard the rubbery clatter of his boots, then soft footsteps as he followed her into the lounge. 'It's not those bloody cows again, is it?'

'It is.' Gritted teeth. 'Judy Barker. Again.'

'This is not right, Cass.' He stood in front of the empty fireplace. 'What has she done this time?'

As Cassie explained the way she'd been overlooked in the meeting, her husband rubbed his muddy hands together then pushed them into his pockets. He shook his head. 'That's fucking terrible,' he said, when she'd finished. 'Pardon my language. You need to tell your boss.'

'I can't. It was bad enough last time. I felt like some whining schoolkid. And I've almost convinced myself that's what I am.' Her voice cracked and she couldn't say anymore.

Si took her hands in his. 'You're not. You're being bullied. This is bullying.'

Cassie bit down on her bottom lip, tried not to let the tears come. But they came anyway. 'I'm an anti-bullying champion for the kids. How can I be a victim?'

She'd had this conversation with herself so many times over the past few weeks and months and knew exactly what was happening. In her head, she'd used that word: *bullying*. Then she'd dismissed it as an impossibility. She was a forty-year-old woman, an experienced and confident deputy headteacher, held in high esteem by many. How could she be the target of a bully?

'There are bullies in every workplace, Cass,' Si said. 'You have to play them at their own game.'

She ran her hands across her face and felt the sting of salty tears. 'How?'

'Give them the same back.'

'No. I can't do that. I couldn't bring myself to victimise someone.'

Si moved to sit beside her on the sofa. 'I didn't mean that.' He hesitated, scratched at his chin. 'Take today's happening, for example. You should have made a complete show of Judy Barker. Given a loud shout about who you were and how she'd forgotten to introduce you. Made her look like an idiot.'

'I'm not being ungrateful, Si. But it's easy to suggest things like that when you're not in the situation. I tried to stand up to her once before, remember. That didn't end well.' But Cassie was beginning to understand how some of her own pupils must feel when teachers told them to ignore snarky comments from their peers, or give the same back, or even to talk to a trusted adult. Lip service. That's what it was. None of which would make any difference to the person with a grudge.

What she couldn't find an answer to was why Judy would have a grudge. Tina Armstrong and Laura Pearson, she could understand. She'd undone her collar and laid her neck bare for them to take a swipe, but she'd given nothing but support to Judy Barker. Or she'd tried to, at first.

'I blame Nobbs for that.'

Cassie snorted.

'Sorry, but I do,' he continued. 'He shouldn't be begging you to get this woman off his back. It didn't work though, did it? He's probably been encouraging her anyway. You know what he's like.'

She certainly did. Lovely guy but no backbone, and certainly nobody's wingman. Why had Judy Barker used that expression? Cassie's anxiety was fading, her brain-fog lifting. And the scales were falling from her eyes.

'What?' Si tilted his head sideways. 'I know that look.'

'I don't think she's a bully, Si. I think she's jealous. I think she wants to be me.'

'What do you mean?'

'She wants my job. Wants Nobbs as her buddy. And her friend to be the deputy head. How strange. She's even said she'd like to see Blackthorn.'

'Creepy.' Si shuddered. 'Well, she can't have me.'

Cassie laughed, felt suddenly lighter. If it was a simple case of jealousy, there were things she could do. Stepping away from Nobbs was one of them. As was reinforcing her position as a senior colleague and deputy head.

She leaned her head against her husband's shoulder. 'No, she can't have you,' she whispered. 'Not when you make the best cups of tea and light the best fires.'

He kissed the top of her head. 'Glad to be of service. Now, go and get changed, and let's forget about Parkhouse for a while.' He slid onto the floor and walked on his knees across to the hearth. 'Chuck me some logs in, would you, on your way.'

Blackthorn settled around them. The wrap of ancient bricks and family stories. The safety of knitted sweaters and wellington boots, beech trees and applewood fires. Here was a place where Cassie could be herself, without the press of other people's thoughts or their grasping needs.

Upstairs, on the dark landing, she stopped. Peeped into the girls' bedrooms. Soaked up the quiet energy they always left behind. And in her own room, she clicked on the bedside lamp and walked over to the wide, draped window. The faded evening sky stretched away over the townscape of her life. Creamy blue and pearl: a match for the bedroom walls.

She wants to be me? Well, she can't.

Chapter Thirteen

'Where'd you get to yesterday, Whites?' Kevin Noble stood at the doorway to Cassie's classroom, a wry smile spreading across his lips. She looked up from the sink, put down the water jug and tried to contain her seething.

'Needed the loo. And then I got caught up in something else. Did everything go okay?' Having to ask the question grated on her nerves; she'd wished for an almighty fail.

He wouldn't look at her, chose instead to shuffle his feet. 'Soz about what she did. The lies, and stuff.' A tilt of his head towards Judy's classroom. 'It was rude. Nerves got the better of her, I think.'

'Nerves? Are you having a laugh? That was deliberate.' She dragged a paper towel from the holder and began dabbing at the pools of liquid that had splashed onto the draining board. 'But it was no more than I expected. I did laugh when she called you her wingman, though.'

Kevin moved further into the room, closed the door behind him. 'That freaked me out, too. I've not given her any help with her project.' He frowned. 'I don't think.'

'You didn't step in and introduce me either, did you?'

Cassie snapped out the words, and he backed away. There was something shabby-looking about him this morning, something that poked at her stomach and made her feel sick.

'I thought it might embarrass you even more. She's a bitch, isn't she?'

'Your word, not mine,' Cassie said. 'You need to make up your mind.' This was Nobbs. Her friend and confidante. Was she begging for his support? They'd been through tricky work situations, survived groups of children whose needs would have been better met at a pupil referral unit, but she could feel the trust slipping away as easily as the water that was now running through her fingers.

'I don't do ultimatums. You know that about me.'

'Sorry? You don't do ultimatums?' She stretched her eyes. 'There's a lot of stuff you don't do, isn't there?'

'Meaning?'

'If you'd put Judy Barker in her place when she first started stalking you, I'm sure we wouldn't be having this conversation now.' That last word came out as a broken gasp and Cassie hated herself for her weakness.

Kevin opened the door, propped it with his foot. One leg in her world, and one somewhere else entirely. 'Don't be like that. I was trying to give her a chance, that's all. And I feel bad about how things worked out. You know, when you and her had that talk.'

'Told you all about it, did she? So much for confidentiality.'

'No, actually. But she did apologise for making me feel uncomfortable.' He lowered his voice. 'I just wish you and her could get on. It's not good, being stuck in the middle.'

Stuck in the middle? Cassie spun around to face him. From the bottom of her lungs came a huge growl. 'You poor thing. I tell you what: if I remove myself from your weird human equation, there'll be no middle, will there?'

He stepped across the room towards her, holding out his

hands. 'Cass.' A patronising whisper. 'Don't be like that. It's just so fucking awkward.'

'Oh. Just get out of my room,' she hissed. 'We're done.'

Their eyes locked. His narrowed. 'Okay,' he stretched the word, then turned on his heel and stomped away.

Cassie took a deep breath and let it out with a slump of her shoulders. Where was Jax? She needed her like never before. A glance at the clock above the doorway told her there was half an hour until the children started arriving. And no sign of Jax. Which was odd, considering she was usually early, arriving after dropping her granddaughter at nursery. Or there would be a text if she was running late.

Cassie dried off her hands and stepped across the room to pick up her phone. No messages. Nothing. But she'd better get on with the jobs for the day, starting with a letter to be faxed. Which meant a trip to the office; perfect, considering the mood she was in.

Tina Armstrong was taking her coat off when Cassie arrived. She turned her back, giving no morning greeting, just a flash of cerise wool, and the faintest hint of Black Opium.

'I'm just going to try and work the fax machine,' Cassie snapped at her. No response. She slid the document into the feeder and began hammering away at random buttons. Nothing happened. Behind her, she could hear Tina moving about. The start-up tone of a computer, then the first play of the day's voicemails. The fax machine appeared to be ignoring Cassie too. She changed the position of the document, bashed some different buttons. Still no response, though a blue light began to flash.

'I'll leave this letter here, Tina.' Cassie didn't turn around. She kept her voice sharp and clear. 'Fax it when you can, please.' That last word hung in the air, reproachful as an out-an-out lie. Then she stormed out of the office, Tina's over-exaggerated sigh following her through the open doorway. This was what she'd been reduced to. Begging for admin to be done. Assuming it wouldn't. And having to massage the fragile egos of her colleagues in case they broke open and she was left with nothing. Well, she wasn't going to put up with it any longer.

Jax didn't arrive.

When the children began to filter in, cheeks red from the raw morning air, throwing down coats and bags, Cassie stopped missing her and the focus shifted to keeping everyone entertained and listened to. The learning would be harder without Jax, but she'd turn up eventually.

At breaktime, Cassie made herself a coffee and stuck her head around Alison's door. She was leaning over an open file on her desk. Two more were stacked beside it, with a line of half-full cups queuing for attention.

'Hello.' Cassie smiled across at her boss.

'Oh. Hi, Cass. I haven't even had time to come down this morning. Is all okay?'

'It is,' she sighed. 'Kind of. But Jax didn't turn up. It's not like her.'

Alison looked at the ceiling and let out a breath. 'She telephoned me, to say she's ill. Nothing serious. She'll be back tomorrow, probably. I asked Tina to let you know.'

Cassie said nothing. Backed away. She was not going to let Alison see her reaction.

'Sorry, Cass. Sorry. I should have come down to tell you myself.'

The door closed heavily.

Cassie's feet wanted to take her to the office; to hold her upright while she grabbed Tina Armstrong and shook the malice out of her. Instead, she walked back to her classroom, and sat on one of the children's chairs, sipping her coffee and struggling to gain control of her breathing. This was war. And she had no idea what the outcome would be.

In the weeks that followed, Cassie hid away in her classroom with Jax. When she needed administrative tasks completing, or information from the office, she sent the teaching assistant. If Jax wondered why, she didn't ask. Nor did she comment about Cassie's abrupt answers and dismissals when Kevin Noble was around.

Cassie had decided: she would no longer be a player in the game of her downfall. She was the deputy head. Junior colleagues would always be snapping at her heels, adoring or jealous. She would do her job, and make sure that there wasn't one *t* uncrossed or one *i* undotted. But her nerves were on high alert. And the only place she could relax was Blackthorn.

On a sunny lunchtime towards the end of the spring term, when clumps of daffodils bloomed in the wooden planters that edged the school playground, and the children faced the afternoon lessons with a renewed energy after a half hour of handstands and fresh air, Cassie sat at her desk, trying to catch up with some admin tasks. She looked up from the memo she was typing. Another set of instructions for Kevin and Judy. This was the easiest way to communicate now. Pieces of coloured paper with dates and times; teamwork reduced to its lowest form. Jax was zipping up her fleecy school jacket.

'I've written everything down about the end-of-school concert,' Cassie told her. 'Can you give it a quick scan. Don't want Mrs Barker to find any typos. I sent her a phone message about it this morning, but she didn't reply.'

Jax came to stand beside her. She bent towards the screen of Cassie's laptop and laid a comforting hand on her shoulder while she ran her eyes over the screen. 'That looks fine. I had noticed things aren't exactly sweetness-and-light between you and them.' She waved her hand towards the other classrooms.

Cassie coughed loudly. 'That's an understatement. Judy

hates me and Kev's an idiot.' She clicked print on the open document, and walked out with Jax, to collect the paper copies.

Once the memos were in Kevin's and Judy's pigeonholes, Cassie took the remaining copies and dropped them onto her desk. There was just time to eat her sandwich and have a cup of tea, before an afternoon of planning with her boss.

She grabbed her bags and made her way to the staffroom. From her own schooldays, she could remember these were sacred places, where no child ever ventured. And any that did were treated to the poisonous fug of coffee and cigarette smoke. Teachers lurked there, only motivated to leave by the sound of a loud bell. Then they had to face their pupils again.

At Parkhouse, most staff were on duty at break or lunchtimes, and even if they weren't, there was always something that needed doing or a child demanding attention. And children came first. Thank goodness. When Cassie had broken her arm falling off some swing bars in her own childhood playground, no teacher had come out to look after her for twenty minutes, by which time she'd attracted the attention of a crowd of passers-by with her screams.

She dropped a tea bag in her mug and spooned coffee into Alison's. She doubted the headteacher had even had time to make herself a drink, let alone eat any lunch. She shoved an open packet of biscuits into her handbag, and set off towards Alison's office.

A child was sprawled across the easy chairs, sobbing, with Alison sitting beside him, rubbing his back.

'You just chill out,' she was saying. 'And here's Mrs Clifton, look. You don't want her to see you crying, do you?'

Cassie put the drinks down on the desk. 'Come on, Rhys,' she said softly. 'Mrs Harman's trying to help you here.'

Alison mouthed a thank you.

The child continued to sob, but sat up, arm across his face, elbow pointing skyward. He was ten years old. Life was unfair.

'Do you want a drink?' Water. A universal solver of problems.

He lifted his elbow away slightly. 'Yeah.'

Alison rounded on him. 'Yes what?'

'Yes please, Mrs Clifton.'

'I'll go and get you your very own bottle from the tuck shop.' Cassie moved towards the door.

'But it isn't open,' he gasped, between sobs.

'Mrs Clifton has the magic key.' Alison held up crossed fingers.

'I have. Count to sixty, and I'll be back.'

Within seconds, Cassie had lifted the tuck shop key from its hiding place, let herself in, grabbed a bottle of water, and locked the kiosk back up again. Rhys had reached forty when she arrived back, though at forty-nine, he magically went back to thirty again.

'Can I go back out to play, Mrs Harman,' he was saying. Cassie handed over the water. 'I'm feeling better now.'

'You can, sunshine,' she laughed. 'But stay away from Kaci. You know how she winds you up.'

'I will.' He ducked through the door in a flash of royal blue sweatshirt and large white teeth.

Alison let out a long sigh and scratched through her brassy blonde hair. 'Put the meeting sign on the door, would you, Cass? Or we'll never get anything done. The girls will buzz through if there's any emergencies.'

When did Tina and Denise become 'the girls'?

Cassie took a laminated sign from Alison's shelf and Blu-Tacked it to the outside of the door. 'Done,' she said, sitting down next to her boss. 'Now. Drink your coffee. I've got biscuits, too.' She rustled the plastic. 'Then we'll make a start.'

Alison went back to her desk and moved a stack of files across to the low table between the easy chairs. She carried her cup over and sat down.

'Shall we start with staffing? Your year group should be all right for the summer term, but Mrs Shaw from year five has put in a request. She's been offered a term's secondment, and I want to let her take it.'

She talked through her ideas for covering the absence, and then they worked their way through the other changes that would be needed. They heard the children come in from their lunch break, the voices of teachers marshalling them along the corridors, and finally the school fell silent again. Cassie thought about Jax, with her class. There would be no problems. There never were. But Cassie wanted to be there. She was a teacher. The bureaucracy of headship would never suit her. The classroom was her place. The chalk-face. Though there hadn't been chalk for many years.

Suddenly the door burst open, and Judy Barker pushed her way into the room. Her face was the colour of over-whipped cream, and she clutched a mobile phone. 'I'm so sorry to barge in.' She looked at them both, hopped from one foot to the other. 'But I've done something stupid.'

Cassie watched her carefully. Something about the moment felt expansive yet so confining. Alison gave the faintest cough.

'I've sent a text to you, Cassie,' Judy croaked, 'and I just want to say it was in no way a nasty jibe. Or sarcastic or anything.' Her bottom lip trembled. 'It was meant for someone else.' Then she spun around and charged out of the room, leaving Cassie and her boss sitting in confused silence.

'Have a look.' Alison tipped her head towards Cassie's handbag.

She leaned down and rummaged around for the phone. A flush spread across her cheeks. Adrenaline was zooming around her body, doing its worst. Her heart was trying to punch a hole through her ribcage, she had to gasp for breath.

'Don't worry about it, Cass,' said Alison. 'Keep calm. Read it out to me, if you can.'

Cassie looked at the screen of her phone. There was the text. She scanned across the words, pressed a hand to her chest.

'What is that bitch Clifton doing now? Sending out her orders on a piece of paper. Who the hell does she think she is?'

Alison's mouth fell open, and Cassie expected a response. None came.

'Nasty that, isn't it?' she whispered.

October 2019

An ember explodes from the fire, and I jump up from my seat. I take the brass hand brush from a bucket by the hearth and sweep the glowing crumble of wood back into the grate. That I was already in a bad place, before the text message was sent, is something I realise now. Reliving each moment in glorious technicolour is helping me to see what was lying just below the surface; my low mood. I'd seen every move made against me through a lens of adrenaline-fizz, caused by the previous moves. Not that it makes any difference, now.

'I guess you're going to say exactly what Si and my daughters said.'

'And what's that?' Freddy's eyes gleam. His brows meet across them.

A nice face, I think. Intelligent.

'Judy Barker should have been sacked, there and then.' I shake my head and let out the smallest of sighs. 'But I didn't want that. I felt sorry for her.'

It is Freddy's turn to explode. 'What? You're not telling me you felt sympathy for the woman? That's not natural.'

I walk over to the bay window and pull the heavy curtains across. It is way past the time that he should be here, passing comment on me and my life.

'It wasn't sympathy. When I read that text, I just wanted to run.' I sit beside him again, inhale deeply. 'Sympathy didn't come into it.' Exhale.

'You said you felt sorry for her?' Freddy is writing on his notepad again. I imagine his words: *This woman is talking nonsense. She's quite mad.*

'Part of me could imagine how Judy felt, trying to break into the relationship between me and Kevin. Nobbs. To fit in, to be included. We were very tight, Kevin and I. And I know for a fact that Tina was cheering her on; she'd been doling out make-up and hair-do lessons, by all accounts.'

Freddy's face takes on a startled expression.

I can't help but laugh. 'Creepy, isn't it. Judy dolls herself up on Tina's advice, then sets off on her quest for Kevin Noble.'

He shakes his head. His cheeks are flushed, and I can understand if it's embarrassment. We're talking about a bunch of civil servants here, not the all-star cast of an American soap.

'The guy didn't stick up for you though, Cassie. That must have hurt.' He clicks on the lid of the pen, then closes his notes. 'Was it him she meant the text for?'

I snort loudly. 'Oh no. It was supposed to have gone to Tina. Judy blamed me later, for being next to Tina in the conversation thread. She'd pressed the wrong name. Laughable, really, when we hardly communicated.'

'Well, I hope she was treated to a disciplinary hearing, at the very least.' He stands up. That warm smell again. Vanilla and clean cotton. 'Thanks for tea, by the way. Now, I must be going. The dog will be trying to dig himself out.'

I stand with him, flicking my hands through my hair. Hanging over the fireplace is a huge antique mirror. It is in the shape of a flattened archway and has a mock-iron frame, with carved leaves at its highest point. It has watched our family in this room for as long as I can remember. My granddad used to twist holly around it at Christmas, and he would lift me up to touch it. We would wave to ourselves. Blow kisses. Freddy and I are reflected in it now. Side-by-side and similar in height. I catch his eye. He smiles back at me.

'That's a beautiful thing.' His hand reaches out and touches the wood. 'I thought that was metal. It jars your brain when it doesn't feel cold.'

'It's never been moved. Not for as long as I can remember. That wallpaper,' I run my hand over the gold-and-blue peacock feather design, 'was there when my grandparents had the house. I think it must have been expensive.'

'This place is a time capsule,' he says. 'In a good way. It's beautifully preserved.' Then, 'Would you mind if I gave you some homework?'

I would mind. But I don't say so. I nod and smile and keep my true feelings to myself. I'm an A-star student at that.

'Good.'

'What is it, then?' I gape at him. 'Something difficult? Will I need Helli and Janey's help?'

'It's pretty simple, actually. Just have it ready for tomorrow. I am coming back tomorrow, aren't I?'

'You are. I'll fetch your coat.' *Bloody homework. Is he trying to be funny?*

Si is sitting at the kitchen table, tapping away at his laptop.

'He's going,' I whisper, punching the air. 'You stay there.' Si is trying to get up and follow me out. I put a hand on his shoulder, press down. 'Stay.'

Freddy is already at the front door, slipping his feet back into his boots. He lifts his face to mine.

'I want you to write down five things you kept hidden when all the stuff was happening to you at school. Can you do that?'

I twist my lips up into a smirk. 'Yes.'

He pulls open the front door. Cold wind knifes in. He tugs at his zip. 'I'm going to run; it'll only take me a half hour.'

I don't offer him a lift; I haven't driven a car for two years. Si could take him, but it's not my place to ask.

'Thanks for the food,' he calls, jogging away. 'I'll see you bright and early tomorrow.'

I'll be here.

I step outside for a minute, look across to Blackthorn Wood. The trees are thickly silhouetted, joined together as a living, breathing entity. The sky behind them is a dark shade of blue, and full of stars. My breath hangs in soft clouds: tomorrow there will be a frost, the first of the season. I yearn to walk in those woods again, to be free. But no one knows this. They think I am happy with the life I have now. It is one of the things I keep hidden. Freddy is very perceptive. He recognises a person living a lie.

Back in the kitchen, Si is making hot chocolate. 'Might help you sleep,' he offers. 'Today is bound to have stirred up stressful memories.'

I thank him; put my arms around him; think about the things I have hidden from him. He knows every detail of what happened in my workplace. But I've never explained my irrational fear of being away from the house. I'm too ashamed. There's another thing for Freddy's list.

'I'm going up, if that's okay.'

Si stretches. 'I'll lock up. You go.' He's hardly ever away from home now. He changed his job when I left mine. We both took a hit financially, that year, but we get by.

From the bedroom window, I look out across the garden one last time, then draw the curtains. Sometimes I need to pretend there isn't a world out there because it's too painful to focus on what I'm missing. But I can't help dwelling on Freddy, stepping away from Blackthorn without it clawing at his coat-tails; running light and free, through the evening streets. Why can't I do that? Because the house has trapped me, that's why. There's another one for his list. I climb into bed and try not to remember how much of a stomach punch the dreaded text had delivered. It had filtered through my body as surely as if it was a poison; it's with me still.

When Alison talked to Judy Barker about sending it, she'd implied it was my fault. And my boss had been startled by that fact. Which caused her to make a suggestion: Judy and I would meet for a formal discussion, and we would air our grievances. Hilarious, considering I was the victim. But I agreed. I didn't want Alison to think I was spiteful, so I agreed. That meeting shook me to the core.

'How are you feeling? After today?' Si lifts the duvet and climbs in beside me, minty and warm.

A shake of my head tells him to leave well alone. He lifts the latest William Boyd from the pine cabinet beside his bed. Clicks on his lamp. 'Fair enough,' he mutters.

'Sorry. I wasn't being awkward. Don't be in a mood with me.'

'I'm not,' he sighs. 'Go back to your reading.'

Of course he's not. That's just me. Hyper-worried about everything and anything, always on the lookout for any trace of a negative reaction in case I've upset someone. Not the best mindset for a school manager, it turns out. Or did that only happen later? I can't be sure. Either way, by the time I left my job, I was monitoring every small change in body language, every nuance of voice, and every choice my colleagues made. Then assuming the worst. Something else to tell Freddy, I suppose. Not that I expect to change my mindset now. I'm way beyond saving. And I don't want to be saved. I have carved out a life for myself where there is no threat or challenge. Where I have my family around me. I feel well. My nerves seem to be mended and I'm not living in that black hole anymore. I'd rather not be upended.

Agoraphobia indeed. Who does Freddy Briggs think he is?

Freddy arrives the next morning, cheeks aglow and the smell of cold autumn dragged with him. He stands on my doorstep with his hands thrust deep in the pockets of an old army jacket with a furry collar.

'Chilly today,' he beams. 'Are you feeling okay?'

I hold the front door open for him. It's a kind of welcome; I'm keen to talk to him.

He sniffs as he walks in. 'Real coffee. That smells wonderful.'

'I thought I'd treat you.' I smile. Something feels different. I allow a memory. Those days. When the air is so heady with autumn sunshine. A chestnut crunch under your feet and the promise of winter huddling. Stepping out, freedom fizzing through your veins like a drug.

'Great.' Freddy bends to remove his boots. 'And I want to know what happened at this so-called disciplinary meeting.'

Chapter Fourteen

APRIL 2016

The private office had no outside windows and Cassie could feel the dismal lighting as a weight pressing onto her shoulders. Had agreeing to this meeting been a mistake? Alison warned her not to expect a hearts-and-flowers ending, which was rather insulting. Cassie had been dealing with the complexities of the school world for many years, she hardly needed reminding that human beings didn't behave according to plan. Judy and Tina certainly proved that. But her head was pounding, and a catch of anger was gathering at the back of her throat. Whatever else she'd deserved, it wasn't the text message.

Alison's voice, brittle with fatigue, dragged her from her thoughts. They sat at the circular table, peering at each other over a jug of water and a box of tissues. 'Are you ready?' She looked at her watch. 'I've got to be at a case conference by three. I don't want this to take up the whole afternoon.'

Oh, so sorry. This had become Cassie's fault, somehow. 'Yep. Ready.' Her heart jumped. Alison buzzed Judy Barker through. In she came, red-eyed and clutching a wad of tissues. As soon as Cassie looked up at her, words began to spill out.

'I've been thinking about that text,' she spluttered. 'All weekend. I know why I sent it, now.' Her bottom lip trembled. 'You've been making my life difficult, Cassie. Working with you has been awful. It was just a reaction to that.'

When she gasped for a breath, Alison interrupted. 'Sit down. Please.'

Cassie blinked back her surprise, said nothing.

Judy pulled out a chair, and threw herself down, dabbing at her tears. Alison poured her a glass of water then slid it across the table.

'Can we just pause for a moment?' she said. 'It's important that we deal with the facts, rather than personal feelings.'

Judy harrumphed and took a sip of water.

Alison continued. 'Can you explain exactly what Cassie has been doing to make you feel excluded?'

Cassie kept quiet. Let this woman do her worst.

'It's how she is, with Kev. All over him. They're all *Nobbs this* and *Whites that.* I don't get a look in, and we're supposed to be a team.' Her voice had a croaky edge.

Cassie shook her head slightly and dropped her eyes.

'Any specifics?' Alison said, glancing up from her note-taking.

Cassie ransacked her memory. Was there anything?

'I can't think.' Judy was sobbing now. 'I've been so worried. Tina's been telling me to report my worries. But I didn't want to cause any trouble.'

Tina. Again.

A pink flush crept across Alison's cheeks, and she pressed her lips together. Sympathy? Or something else? Cassie wasn't sure. But it was time for her to have her say.

'And how was sending that text about me supposed to help? You've clearly been discussing me at some length.' Cassie shook her head. 'If you had a problem with me, you should have talked to me.'

Judy flashed a glare. Seething with something. 'Couldn't get near you. You're always with him.'

Cassie wasn't having that. She pulled herself upright and pointed her face at the other woman. 'The truth is, Judy, you're obsessed with Kevin Noble, aren't you? The cosy chats in your classroom, with the door closed. Changing my plans on the ski trip so you could be with him. And then that awful presentation last month. You introduced him as your wingman, Laura as the deputy, and didn't even acknowledge I was in the room.'

'It's you that's obsessed with him,' Judy wailed. 'And you hate me.'

Shredded tissue fell onto the table. Cassie couldn't believe what she was hearing.

But Alison was slamming her hand down. 'No. This is too personal. I'm not having it.'

'And I'm not having her saying that,' Cassie fumed. 'I was Kevin Noble's mentor, many years ago, and we're close. Always have been, but I'm not blind to his faults, as you seem to be. He's a *player*, Judy, and he's played you. It sounds like Tina has, as well.'

Alison held up her hands. 'Enough. Cass, I don't know what's been going on in your year group, but what you're both saying is worrying me. You're professional people. In charge of children. This needs to stop.'

I've only just started.

Judy began to make a different sound. A kind of spoken exhale.

'Have a drink, Judy,' Alison said, and topped up her glass. 'Get your breath back.'

Cassie watched. How had she become caught up in a situation like this? It felt like childish squabbling, and she was sure that must be how it looked. But there was something else. Another layer. One she couldn't get access to.

And now Judy was trying a different tack. 'This is all my fault,' she cried. 'I've changed. I don't know what's come over me recently. That's my only excuse for everything I'm being accused of. I feel like I'm not in charge of myself anymore.' Then her head went down, and she sobbed into the silence.

The atmosphere in the room shifted. Cassie looked at the top of Judy's head. No grey roots this time. Just a shiny, burgundy wash. And the blouse looked new, too. Principles best orange chiffon.

She's just a person, trying to survive. Like we all are.

Alison yawned into her hand. 'You need to apologise to Cassie for sending that text, Judy,' she said.

The sobs continued.

'Mrs Barker, I'm talking to you.' Alison held out her hands.

Judy stood up with a sudden force, and her chair toppled backwards. 'Sorry. All right?' A spit of words, heavy with meaning, but not with conciliation. Then she stormed out of the room.

Alison put her head in her hands. 'I don't need this, Cass, I really don't.' She scratched at her scalp. 'Let me get the other one in.'

She pressed the telephone buzzer and in tottered Tina Armstrong. No wad of tissue this time. She picked up the fallen chair, and sat herself down neatly, eyeing Alison through thick black lashes.

'You know about this text, I take it?' Alison was using a different tone. Cold.

Tina lifted her chin. 'I do.' Her flesh-coloured make-up creased on itself. 'And it's nothing to do with me.' She tapped her nails on the table, making Cassie want to get a pair of scissors and cut them off.

'Judy had told us that she sent it to Cassie in error. It was meant for you. Was this a regular practice, slagging off my deputy by text?' Alison's voice sliced, and Cassie jumped. 'Well?'

Tina let out the tiniest of snorts. 'No. It was a one-off.' She added nothing else, nothing that would incriminate her further.

Alison moved swiftly. 'Why would she send it to you, Tina? Why you?'

'No idea.'

Cassie could see Tina's eyeballs moving, under the lowered lids. Waiting. But she didn't dare add anything. Every time she chipped in, she ended up making herself complicit, somehow.

'I hadn't realised you were that friendly with Mrs Barker. Tina?'

'She's friendly with everyone. I've got to know her through Laura, and I like her. We've been out a few times.'

That word. *Like.* It slithered out of her mouth, Eve's serpent, making Cassie shudder. She needed to get out of this room. Its magnolia walls reflected back every emotion, every loaded word.

'Well, you'd better go and see her now then,' Alison said with a sigh, 'she's in a bit of a state over all this. And I'm warning you.' A pause. 'If I find out there is any bullying going on in my school, I will be dealing with it; same as I would with the children.'

There is, and you're not. Cassie sat on her hands, kept her mouth shut.

Tina stood up and click-clacked over to the door. 'Thanks.' She flung out that word, then left.

Alison was still writing her notes.

Cassie watched the pen and wondered what had actually made its way onto the paper. And what would happen to those words. But she was certain of one thing. The situation was far from over.

Chapter Fifteen

Easter came in with spikes of green and pink and gold. The front garden of Blackthorn glowed with forsythia and flowering currant bushes, and early daffodils bathed in the warmth of the April sunshine. Cassie sat on her doorstep and pushed her feet into her boots.

Si leaned on the wall, his face to the sun. 'Are you sure you're going to be all right?' he said. 'We can just stay in the garden, if you don't feel up to walking.'

'No, I'll be fine. I need to get back to normal before Monday.' She tugged at her boot laces and stood up.

Since the meeting with Judy Barker and Tina Armstrong, Cassie's health had been suffering. Subtle things, at first. Tiny heart palpitations and breathlessness. Noticeable, but not enough to prompt a doctor's visit.

She would lie awake at night, worrying about every glance or whispered word from her colleagues, every incident of hard-edged ignorance. Judy had formed a tight team with the admin staff. And they made sure that Cassie was left trying to get a grip on their icy wall.

That her other colleagues knew about the text message and

subsequent meeting, she was sure. Far from it being something that might mute Judy's resentment, or dampen Tina's grudge, it had morphed into a lie that she couldn't reshape. Which meant that every day spent at work was a day full of anxiety. And that was taking its toll.

Cassie took Si's hand, and they stepped across the road from the house, and onto the path for Blackthorn Wood. The beech trees at the entrance were covered in pointed and pale green buds, and dark leaves of oak and ash, open early, muted the vivid morning sunlight. Purple crocuses grew tightly together in the leaf mould, and clumps of narcissus, faces like poached eggs, waved their heads gently. The blackthorns were showing early signs of flowering, delicate white flowers jarring with the darkness of their winter boughs.

Cassie stepped carefully, avoiding puddles of water and soft chocolatey mud. 'I wish I didn't have to go back to work, Si. I just don't like it anymore.' A simple truth.

But he was having none of it. 'Don't be daft,' he laughed. 'What would you do? Besides, we need the money. We could sink a fortune into Blackthorn, and we would still need more.'

'It would make life easier with the girls if I was at home. And I could write. You know I've always wanted to do that.' Cassie could feel her anxiety rising. It happened every time she was away from the house. It would start with the tiniest of dark thoughts, then claw its way out from a place in her brain, fighting with her heart and her breath, making her want to run.

'You? At home all the time? Not teaching?' He shook his head. 'I can't see it, Cass.'

Here was the anxiety again. Her feet were trying to carry her back to Blackthorn.

'Cass?' Si turned his head and peered down at her. 'You've gone pale.'

She clutched at her throat, gasped for breath. 'Can we go back?' It came out as a croak.

'Course.' He linked his arm through hers, guided her in the direction of the house. 'I knew you weren't right. You have to see a doctor.'

Cassie inhaled through her nose to stop herself from gasping and tried to swallow down her fear. Though what she was afraid of, she couldn't quite say. Judy Barker and Tina Armstrong weren't likely to appear in these woods. But her nerves were telling her something different.

'Sorry. I'm sorry,' she stammered. 'You carry on. I don't want to ruin your walk.'

'You're not ruining my walk. But I'm worried about you.' The house came into sight. 'We're here now anyway.'

And Cassie's anxiety began to calm. Safety. But the damage had been done. Her legs trembled and a dark fog clouded her thoughts, a mix of guilt and terror, when all she'd been doing was walking with her husband, on a sunny afternoon.

'Sit on the step and I'll fetch you a cuppa,' he said. 'Maybe we'll try again, in a bit.'

She listened as he unlocked the front door and kicked off his boots. What was wrong with her? Ever since the dreaded meeting, she'd felt as though her skin had been peeled back, so that even the slightest change in tempo of her world caused pain. Emotional pain.

Did Alison no longer trust her? Was Judy Barker plotting something else with Tina Armstrong? Had her colleagues been told about the text message? Was she being blamed? These thoughts dragged at her well-being, like swampy mud, and she couldn't free herself. Only inside Blackthorn's walls did she feel she could be her old self. And on Monday morning, she would have to throw herself to the wolves of her thinking, again.

Cassie turned the keys in the ignition, but she couldn't make herself pull the car away. She'd been dreading this day. Everything was ready, marked, prepped and polished. She just had to get herself to the school building now. A ten-minute drive. But it might as well have been a flight across the Amazon in an open-topped plane with a drunken pilot, such was the fear fizzing through her. If she could just get there, talk to Dot, get on with her day, she'd be okay. Raw, but okay.

With her foot on the clutch, she tried to empty her mind of the worries that flew freely there. The car moved slowly down the drive. She revved the engine and let herself get into second gear, leaving Blackthorn behind.

The pounding started up. Behind her ribs, then inside her head so that she couldn't focus. There was danger in driving like this, but she had to get to work.

When she reached the main road, Cassie joined the crawl of other cars heading into town. Here was normality. Nothing could happen. Just an ordinary workday, with the usual push of children and tasks, chattering colleagues, and the smell of jacket potatoes. So why did she feel like she couldn't breathe? And what could she do about the fear pressing so hard at the back of her eyes, it was impossible to focus?

At the traffic lights, she almost turned back. To the safety of Blackthorn, the end of her anxious feelings. But the car somehow knew its way; that was how it seemed. She was soon pulling into the school car park and wondering how she'd managed to get there.

Some lights were on; Dot was here. Someone to talk to, a distraction. Her panic was subsiding, and it would soon be at a manageable level if she could just keep her racing thoughts in check until the school day began.

'Morning, Cassie.' Dot spotted her in the entrance hallway. 'How were the hols? Go anywhere nice?'

Cassie put down her bags, said enough to get Dot engaged,

then stood in silent battle with her breathing, while she listened to tales of Blackpool and the beach and Dot's grandson. But it worked. Her brain cooled. She was able to slip into her deputy head persona once again.

The classroom smelt musty with the shut-in air of a fortnight minus children. She clicked on the lights and pulled open one of the huge windows that looked out onto the car park. Daylight, and just before eight in the morning. That had been a long time coming. A strip of buttery sky sent the townscape into silhouette, a familiar sight for so long. Why had she even been considering leaving her workplace? Her school? The one whose ethos ran through her veins, and whose families she had worked with for so long. She wasn't going to let a handful of vindictive colleagues ruin her career; she could do this.

As she turned away, she caught sight of a car pulling through the school gates. Alison Harman. She was early.

Cassie hung up her coat and unpacked her bags, flicked on the computers, then stepped out of the room towards the staff kitchen. Tea first, then photocopying.

'Morning, Mrs Clifton.' Alison stood at the end of the corridor, coat on, and bags in her hands. 'Pop up and see me as soon as you can, will you?'

Cassie's heart flipped over. *What now?*

'Okay. Do you want coffee?'

'Please.' Then Alison was gone.

The corridor suddenly felt intimidating, a long walk to her next episode of doom.

In the kitchen, she filled the kettle and flicked it on to boil, then waited. She should stop feeling like a transgressing child and remember that she was almost the boss of this large primary school, sometimes was the boss, in fact. *Rise above it*: those were the words Alison used. So why did Cassie feel like an escaping bird, cats snapping at her legs and pulling her to the ground, no matter how hard she tried to save herself.

Alison was sitting at her desk, tapping at her keyboard. Her face was slightly tanned.

'There you go.' Cassie put the mug of coffee down on her boss's desk. 'You look like you've had a good holiday. Where did you get to?'

'Thanks. We've been to Santorini. It was beautiful. Then I've come back to this.'

Cassie's heart jumped against her ribs. 'What's happened?'

'Two things, actually. Denise's mother is ill. She wants to reduce her hours.'

Cassie waited.

'And,' Alison cocked an eyebrow, 'Judy Barker has emailed me. She's leaving.'

October 2019

'Fuck's sake. It's like a cheap television drama.' Freddy laughs, and I giggle too, despite being one of the actors.

'Si often said you couldn't make it up. But it happened, and I was so relieved.'

Freddy sits at the kitchen table, scribbling away on his notebook.

'Top up?' I ask, craning to see. He is so at home in Blackthorn. This is what the house does. It wraps its brick and slate arms around you, gives you a security, which transforms into something more toxic if you're not very careful.

'Thanks.' He holds out his mug. 'You might have been relieved, but the psychological impact of what was happening, was already taking hold, from what you're telling me.'

I lift one shoulder, then shake my head. I don't want him to think of me as a weak person. I'm growing to like him. Today, his dreadlocks are loose around his shoulders, and he wears his smile at a jaunty angle.

'I'm not mentally ill, you know,' I snap, then wish I hadn't.

'Sorry, Cassie, but you are.'

I am horrified. How dare he? I have kept myself well and safe in Blackthorn for years, taken up none of the National Health Service's resources, supported my family unconditionally. Let bullying colleagues off the hook.

'That's just your opinion. You hardly know me.'

'But this isn't about you, personally. If you'd broken your leg or had a brain tumour, you wouldn't try to keep it hidden, would you?'

'Like you're the first person to ever say that to me.' I spin away and tip my coffee dregs down the sink. I hear him sigh.

'You're intelligent,' he says after a moment. 'So I expect you already know your type of personality is highly susceptible to stress.'

'So what?' I snap. 'I didn't cause the stress, did I?'

I brace myself against the sink and look through the window into the yard area of the back garden; breathe deeply. A pair of collared doves are scratching around at the margin of concrete and grass. I watch them, and try to get myself out of my own head. This is how I cope. Living in the moment and leaving the past where it belongs. Wouldn't a psychotherapist give exactly that advice? I suddenly feel so weary of talking to Freddy about things he can't change. We have to find something different.

I step across to the kitchen table. 'What are you actually writing? If you don't mind me asking.'

He spins the notebook around then pushes it towards me. I'm not sure if I want to see the words I've spoken, set down on a page, captured in black ink. But what I see is a picture. Swirls and flowers, jigsaw pieces and arrows, with three-dimensional block letters at their centre.

'Do my ideas match up with yours?' he asks. 'Are those the things you've kept hidden?'

I allow myself to view the page, feel like an intruder. And there, in solid black, with a shadow behind each letter, are these words: *trapped, perfectionist, hypervigilant, nature-lover, bottom-of-the-list, ninety-seconds.*

A heat comes into my face. It burns at the edges of my self-respect. Here I am, on a page, and I hate myself.

'Nice.' It's all I can think of to say. I watch Freddy's hands as he reaches across the table and takes the notebook back.

'Sit down, Cassie. And let me tell it like it is.' I hear a patronising tone but know that isn't him.

I do as he asks. 'You're seeing my world as *you are*. Not as *I am*. Isn't that what you lot say?' My words are a growl. I cannot help the sound they make.

I see interest in his expression, not sympathy. 'I'm not saying you've caused your problem. But as I said, your personality hasn't helped you. Lazy, disinterested types rarely suffer from trauma. Things might happen to them, but they don't care.'

I am genuinely shocked. At his use of language, as much as at what he is saying. How can he call himself a therapist, then write off groups of people, as though they are not worthy of his help? He must sense my disbelief because he reacts instantly.

'That didn't come out exactly right. But I stand by what I've said.' He leans towards me, then takes another sip of his coffee. 'And your perfectionist tendencies probably made you a target, anyhow.'

I open my mouth to defend myself, but he continues.

'I'm absolutely on your side here, Cassie. Don't get me wrong. There are some unenlightened people out there. They have issues with themselves, and they damage others because of it.' He pauses for a moment, and his face loses focus. Then he comes back. 'You got tangled up in that. But I want to concentrate on you, now. Not try to punish them. They do that well enough to themselves.'

My hands are together, in front of my mouth. I chew on my nails. Then I look at him again. 'What does *ninety-seconds* mean?'

'I knew you'd ask that. It's one of the things that I think will pull you out of your permanent comfort zone. Your brain loves a challenge.'

I smile slightly. 'What can I say? Tell me.'

'Neuroanatomists have discovered that emotions only last for ninety seconds. After that, you feed them yourself.' He waits. And watches. 'I'll just let that sink in.'

His comment strikes me. Punches me in the gut, in fact. Is he saying that every bit of adrenaline-fuelled worry I've ever felt has been exacerbated by *me*?

'Oh well. Silly me. I wasn't aware of that, back then.' A machine-gun of words, fired straight at him. But he doesn't duck. Instead, he meets me head-on.

'Cassie. Don't you see what I'm saying. That's an ideal scenario, for someone who likes to keep control of themselves. It's your way out.'

'How?' I am interested, despite wanting to pick up his notebook and sling it across the kitchen. 'How is it my way out? Sorry. I don't understand.'

But he is beside me, taking my hand. His is large and rough-palmed. 'Stop apologising. You're allowed to be angry. You don't have to swallow down your feelings. Be an emotional mess. It's fun.'

I laugh. Quietly, at first. My head tilts forward, onto his shoulder. Tears come, but not sad tears. He is full of humour, this guy. I can laugh with him. And he's right. I'm all about keeping things hidden. Making sure that the outside world sees only the glitter of many things that are not golden.

After a moment, I lift my head and wipe at my cheeks. 'Talking of emotional messes, you should have seen Judy Barker on her last day.'

Chapter Sixteen

APRIL 2016

Cassie stared at her boss.

'Leaving? When?'

Alison laughed. 'Close your mouth, Cass. And try not to look so happy about it. End of term, she's going.'

'I suppose I'll get the blame.' Cassie hadn't meant to say those words, and as soon as they escaped, she wanted to scream. But how was she supposed to react.

'You won't, actually.' Alison picked up her coffee. 'She was going to leave, about a year ago. Her husband's firm wanted him to relocate, to Dublin, in fact, but Judy was having none of it. Now, she's changed her mind. I don't know any more than that, but I suspect all is not perfect in their relationship.' She made a drumroll of fingertips on her desk. 'Don't quote me.'

Cassie ran a hand over her face. The thought of September, a new term, without Judy Barker and her divisive intentions, that was wonderful. But she had to be careful, say the right thing and hope people would feel Judy had got her just desserts.

'We'll have to recruit, won't we? For the autumn term? Or we'll be a teacher down.'

Alison peered at her, distracted now. 'No. Joe's coming back, according to Tina. Judy is going to let people know today or tomorrow. We'll have to get a leaving party organised.' She turned back to her computer.

Cassie stepped away. 'Has Tina spoken to Joe, then?'

'Only to ask him about his sick note.'

'How was he?'

Alison lifted her glasses and locked eyes with Cassie. 'He bit Tina's head off, apparently. But he's insisting he'll be back in September.'

She would make time to go and see Joe again. Find out what support he needed to get back to work. He was not going to become another victim of Tina Armstrong's cat-and-mouse games.

As the day unfolded, so did the reaction to Judy's announcement. Cassie had to witness huddled gatherings and hugs, heads shaken incredulously and encouraging words. Judy had been part of their team, whatever else she had become. Most staff had no idea of what had happened between Judy and Cassie, and for that she was grateful. Placing a distance between herself and others meant safety. And then she could get on with her job.

When Cassie returned from settling her class into their lunchtime routine, she noticed Judy's classroom door was closed. And Tina Armstrong's back was pressed up against the glass panel, head bobbing and arms waving. This was it. The perfect opportunity for a chat with Denise. And Alison had handed her that gift: a reason. Cassie jogged along the corridor and pushed open the office door. Denise was sitting by herself, sipping at a glass of water. Sliced lemons floated on its surface. She peered over Cassie's shoulder, then smiled.

'Hello.' Cassie lifted the box of index cards. 'Just looking for an address.'

Denise made eye contact.

Cassie took the chance. 'Sorry to hear your mum's ill.'

'Thanks. But that's not the only reason I want to cut my hours.' Denise hugged the glass to her chest.

'Oh?' Cassie continued to flick through the card-index.

'It's her.' She gestured towards Tina's desk. 'I can't be what she wants me to be. I'm looking for another job, if you must know.'

'Oh, I'm sorry. Is there anything I can do to help?' She tried to sound nonchalant, but focused on every word Denise was saying.

'Don't mention it to Alison, will you?'

'I won't. But I don't think she'd want to lose you.'

Denise exhaled softly. 'I like the work. I wouldn't even need a cut in hours to look after Mum, if I'm being honest. But working with Tina – it's not pleasant.'

'I thought you two were friends. Have I got that wrong?'

'She can be lovely, she really can.' Denise shot Cassie a smile, stretched, and not quite real. 'The way she makes you feel important and included. God help those she takes against, though.'

'Like me, you mean?'

Denise was about to answer when the door opened. Tina. She gave Cassie a lingering sneer, then moved towards her desk.

'I'm going to get a sandwich.' She rummaged in her handbag. 'Do you want anything, Denise?'

Cassie turned her back and fled. Her gut instincts hadn't been wrong, but there was little she could do in response to Denise's claims. Not without getting herself into more trouble. She was not going to give Tina any more opportunities to get her claws out. Cassie planned to keep her head down and her thoughts to herself. So, when Kevin Noble came into her classroom at the end of the day, she was ready for him.

'What's happened there?' he asked, tilting his head towards

Judy's room. Jax was slicing the ragged edges from some large paintings, while Cassie spread them with glue and pressed them onto brightly coloured pieces of sugar paper. She peered up at him. This was the first day back after a two-week holiday. He looked as though he'd spent every one of those days behind bars. And he probably had. But not prison bars.

'Hasn't she told you?' The words burst from her lips. 'She's been around everyone else?'

Kevin pouted. 'She has. Her other half is taking that job in Ireland. For two years, she said.' But he was gesturing with his thumb towards the open classroom door.

What? mouthed Cassie.

'Something in my room. I want to show you.'

That old trick. One they'd used so often, but not for a long while. She looked at Jax. 'I'll just be a minute.'

A small snort of air escaped from her teaching assistant's nose. Cassie followed Kevin into his classroom. It smelt of sweat and plimsols, despite the freshness of the afternoon.

'Don't you ever have these windows open?' Her nose twitched.

'Don't change the subject.' He walked away, then positioned himself behind his desk. 'What's really happened with Judy. Why's she leaving?'

Cassie hesitated. She wasn't sure about Kevin anymore, not certain of his loyalty or his reactions. Judy had made sure of that. 'What has she told you?'

'The long or the short version?'

'There are *versions*? What the hell does that mean?'

Cassie's heart fluttered. Once again, the ribbons of this story were unravelling, while she stood by, unable to catch hold of their slippery fabric.

'Oh, Cass. You should have been there.' Kevin sat down. He rested his forehead in the palms of his hands. 'She shut the door, then threw herself on me. Bawling. Snot everywhere.

Saying she couldn't work here anymore, when the senior management hated her.'

Cassie listened, her expression frozen.

Kevin continued. 'You've had it in for her since she moved into year six, apparently. And she wants a fresh start, away from you. Has something else happened? Y'know, since—'

'Since what?'

He'd better not know about the text incident. Judy was told the matter was being treated as confidential.

Kevin backed off. 'Don't have a go at me. We both know what she did to you in that meeting. I wondered if you'd said anything to her.'

But Cassie found her trust in him was gone. There had been a time when she'd always told him her thoughts and feelings, and snippets of school business that she needed to offload. Now, the words wouldn't come. They were stuck fast, in a place somewhere between lemon drizzle cake and wingmen. All she could hear was his own need to find out what had happened, and if he was any way to blame.

She stared at him, almost choking on her words. 'Do me a favour. Ignore all the bad stuff you hear about me over the next few weeks. Or better still, flatten it.'

At the door, she stopped for a moment. To leave now, with anger occupying the space between them, might mean they could never get their relationship on track again.

'Cass. Don't be like that,' he called. 'You know I'm on your side.'

She let the door slam behind her.

Chapter Seventeen

Cassie stood in front of the long wardrobe mirror and checked her outfit was appropriate: her best yellow dress, unapologetically cheerful. Today, Judy Barker was finally leaving. There would be a lunch and gifts and tears. A celebration for the woman who had caused her so much angst. And she would have to smile along and wish her well.

Early sunlight slanted through the bedroom window. There was a softness to the morning, and the lawn was layered in dew. A perfect day for pottering and planting and reading in the shade of her favourite horse chestnut tree. Instead, she was having to fix a smile on her face and bite down until her teeth hurt.

Judy wasn't giving up without a fight. She refused any kind of communication with Cassie, and everything had to be organised via Kevin. Which had its problems. Then there were the huddles, usually with Judy or Tina at their heart, and never open to visitors. But today, Joe was coming back. That had to be an improvement.

Driving away from Blackthorn was becoming difficult. From the moment Cassie climbed into her car each morning, she would be overwhelmed by a kind of panic, a crowding of thoughts from which she couldn't get free. And now, those feelings were transferring to many other daily trips. An invisible hand would grip her stomach as she stood in a supermarket queue, or sat in the hairdresser's salon chair, speeding up her heart rate and making her breath catch in her chest. She would try to swallow down the feelings, only for them to fight back, even harder.

Today was no different. By the time Cassie reached the school, she was struggling to focus. Alison's car was already in the car park. That represented a moment of relief. An escape. There would be conversation and distraction, human contact that didn't require expert navigation.

In the reception area, Alison was wrestling with an armful of helium balloons while trying to type in the door code.

'Morning. Let me do it.' Cassie leaned past her and let them both through. 'Those are for Judy, I take it.'

'Don't be like that, Cass. We can't just let the woman leave without any kind of send-off. I thought you were okay with it.'

With what? With accepting the damage Judy had caused, now she was clearing off? She didn't trust herself to say anything. Instead, she gave Alison a grim smile and walked away. Locking herself in her classroom with only excited children for company was going to be the way to get through this day. That, and a hug from Joe.

Lunchtime loomed. Cassie had spent the morning watching Tina storming back and forth, a flash of red floral dress, and arms full of flowers. Then with the caterers in tow. And finally with invited guests: a handful of governors, Dot, then Joe. His fingers waved her a greeting through the glass panel in her classroom door.

With her class gone, led away by Jax for their final school meal of the year, Cassie could find no further excuse to avoid the staffroom. She would paint a smile across her lips, remember her position in the school and pray for three o'clock, when she would never have to see Judy Barker again.

The staffroom was solid with the smell of cucumber and coffee, and the press of hot bodies. People stood around, balancing plates of sandwiches and trying to talk as well as eat. The easy chairs had become a haven for flowers and gifts, and in the centre of it all sat Judy, raw-faced and wafting a handful of tissues. Joe hovered over the platters of food, picking at crisps and eyeing the door.

'Cass. Look who's here.' Kevin Noble, his mouth full of cheese savoury, peered at her from behind a pillar. 'Smiggy-boy.'

She walked across the room and fell into Joe's embrace.

'So good to see you,' she whispered. 'You've no idea.'

'Kev said the same.' He stretched his brow. 'There's dirt to be dished, I gather.'

'There is.'

'I can't see *Atilla the Hun*. Where's she got to, then?'

A splinter of crisp caught in Cassie's throat. 'Can't think who you're talking about.' She coughed. 'I'd better go and mingle. Let's meet up later once madam's gone.' A tilt of her head towards Judy.

Across the room, Becky Ripley had crammed herself on a seat between three pink helium balloons and the door. She waved her hand and beamed out a smile. Cassie returned the wave. Talking to Becky would be safe; Laura Pearson was already sending out knife-blade looks and snarly words.

Conversation flowed.

Alison came into the room. Then Denise. Judy blinked tearily at everyone and accepted the occasional hug.

With her coffee cup balanced carefully, Cassie made her way over to Becky, and crouched at her feet.

'How are you?'

Becky tucked her hair behind her ears and grinned widely. 'I'm fine, thanks. Haven't seen you for a while.'

'Not since the asthma drama,' laughed Cassie. 'And what a drama it was. The kids loved it.'

'It's been such a great way to remember Mick. Not that–'

Becky didn't finish her sentence. The door flew open, knocking into Cassie and toppling her forward. The coffee cup flew upwards, slopping its steaming contents from the neckline of her dress to its hem. She yelped in surprise. Beck jumped up to help her, but all Cassie could see was a flash of biscuity calf and red floral dress. And Judy Barker shooting a grin across the room to a target just above her head.

Chapter Eighteen

Weeds sprouted between the pieces of rectangular paving, and two black dustbins stood by the front door, lids askew and spilling out rubbish. Becky's house. Modern, but not what Cassie thought it would be. She'd got the woman down as a nurturing type, a home-bird who knitted sweaters and made apple pies. Ridiculous, really. Who went around typecasting women in this day and age? Anyone could be anything. She should know better. But still, the house seemed far less welcoming than the woman.

She climbed out of her car. Getting this far from Blackthorn had been a trial, especially when memories of spilt coffee and humiliation still lingered. Becky had saved her from a total meltdown. Though there'd been a mumbled apology from behind the huge bouquet Tina was carrying, the shrieks of laughter from Laura and Judy, and the flash of tension across the room, had sent Cassie running in blind panic. And it'd been Becky who followed, mopped her dress and calmed her with a comic deep-breathing routine.

Now she was going to return the favour, in the form of some company and a large bottle of fizzy wine.

Outside the house, Cassie took a few moments to steady herself, then stepped between the weeds and up to the front door. It opened before she had the chance to knock.

'Cassie, poppet. You look nice.' Becky plucked at the hem of her own T-shirt. 'I don't bother anymore.'

Cassie handed her the gift. 'No coffee stains today.'

'Lovely. Thank you.' Becky put the bottle down on a small table behind the front door. 'Not nice that, yesterday, was it?' She stepped away and beckoned her in. 'Are you okay?'

'It's becoming a habit. You, asking if I'm okay.' Cassie followed. A long hallway, dark, and smelling faintly of wet dog.

'In here.'

She waited as Becky opened a door at the end of the hall. And out clattered a large chocolate-coloured Labrador.

'Don't mind Mini,' she laughed as the dog almost snapped itself in two, wagging and sniffing. 'Doesn't get out much.'

Cassie knelt in front of the excited animal and rubbed behind both of its ears. 'I'd love to have a dog,' she said. 'Wouldn't be fair to leave it all day though, would it?'

'This one would just sleep,' Becky replied. 'And yes. It is becoming a habit. You go through.' She pointed towards another door. 'I'll get you something to drink.'

Cassie let herself in to what she assumed was a lounge, the room a featureless box with flat windows, and glass doors at one end, giving a view over another patch of garden: a tangle of ferns and long grass this time, a wall of choked climbing roses at its furthest point.

She glanced around, then sat down on the sagging cushions of a sofa so big there was hardly room for any other furniture. Except a fireplace with a wooden mantel, jam-packed with photographs, and a domed clock. Blackthorn House suddenly felt extravagant and more than a little self-conscious. There was an aura of sliding neglect about this place.

'Don't laugh, but I've made you a coffee.' Becky shouldered

her way back into the room carrying two mugs and a plate of biscuits. 'Oh, that was mean, wasn't it?' She giggled.

'I can laugh about it now,' replied Cassie, accepting her mug, 'but I felt such an idiot yesterday. Thanks for helping me out, Becky. I'm grateful.'

'Bloody Tina Armstrong. She did that on purpose, I guarantee it. I watched her look through the glass panel before she walked in. Cow.' Becky's words fired from her mouth with a spray of spittle.

'I can't disagree with you there,' muttered Cassie, over the rim of her cup.

'And she runs, you know.' Becky reached for a biscuit and dipped it in her drink. 'Who, apart from athletes, goes running? I'll tell you who, shall I?' She bit on the biscuit mush, then wiped her lips. 'Someone who wants a trim figure as currency, that's who.'

Cassie wasn't sure where the conversation was going, but she needed to change its direction. 'Or perhaps,' she said, 'Tina's in training, so she can run away from all the people she's offended.'

Becky snorted and had to put down her coffee. 'You're a right one, you are. Cheeky. That's why I'm surprised–'

'Surprised?'

'That you don't stand up for yourself more. You never said a word when that Laura character was wheeled in after the roadshow, but I could tell you were upset.'

Stand up for myself? Surely I do that? 'I've been told to rise above it. By my boss,' Cassie said. 'That, and to keep an eye on my position in the hierarchy. Alison's a great fan of the moral high ground.'

'Alison bloody Harman. She's not a patch on my Mick.'

How could Cassie follow that?

Becky leaned forward and ran a hand over her face. 'Sorry. That's not something I should be saying. Ignore me.'

She glanced towards the clutch of photographs. 'I just miss him.'

'Course you do.' Cassie put a hand on Becky's shoulder. 'He was a good guy. I didn't know him well, but he was always kind to me. Especially in the early days, when I was clueless.'

Becky laughed lightly. 'He was everybody's favourite, that's for sure.' She jumped up from her seat. 'Still. Life goes on, doesn't it, poppet. Now, you've got green fingers, so I've heard. Come and have a look at this garden of mine, would you, and give me some pointers. I've done nothing out there since Mick passed, and it's looking a little shabby, wouldn't you say?'

For the rest of the afternoon, Cassie was able to forget about Tina Armstrong; she was able to send Judy Barker into the wide blue yonder on her metaphorical aeroplane. But it was much more difficult to stop her swirling recall of Joe's revelation. *I walked in on them. Tina and Mick. They were kissing.* Did Becky have any idea that Mick and Tina could well have been having an affair?

October 2019

This is the first time I've told anyone else about that deliberate shove from Tina Armstrong. I wonder now if it gave me permission for what I ended up doing. It was certainly a turning point in my relationship with Becky. That she was lonely, I understood very well. Her real reason for befriending me wasn't clear until much later.

'To be fair, this Tina Armstrong's behaviour sounds far more worrying than Judy Barker's,' Freddy is saying, from his position at my kitchen table. 'She was showing the classic signs.'

'Of what?'

PAULA HILLMAN

'A narcissistic personality disorder, I would surmise. But don't quote me. Don't ever tell anyone I said that.'

'Oh, Freddy,' I say, running my hands across my eyes. 'It doesn't matter now. She's been out of my life for more than two years. They both have.'

He is wearing checked flannel today. I doubt he owns an iron.

'What I don't understand,' he says, linking his fingers together, then cracking his knuckles, 'is why your boss... Alison Harman was she called? ... Why she didn't see what was happening? She must have, Cassie, surely?'

I am standing at the kitchen door. It is a beautiful morning. Liquid gold sunshine and the collared doves now on the lawn, pecking at the dew. Si was out early, cycling to work.

How must that feel? To climb onto a bicycle and ride along the beauty of an autumn morning. 'Alison Harman never stuck up for me. How could she?' I turn to face him. 'On the few occasions I asked for help, she told me she couldn't take sides because that would create cliques. Headteachers had to remain impartial. I got that.'

'Cassie.' His voice is raised, just a little. 'Stop being so bloody reasonable. Tina Armstrong was a bully of the worst kind. I wouldn't want that behaviour in my workplace, if I was a boss.'

'But you haven't been a boss, have you?' I snap back. I've had these conversations so many times. With Si. With my girls. With myself. 'The truth is, I was trapped. By my personality as much as by what was happening. If I said nothing, it gave *carte blanche*. If I stuck up for myself, it gave a reason to carry on.'

Freddy gets up from the table. He stretches his arms above his head and yawns loudly. 'Let's go outside,' he says. 'We could try Blackthorn Wood, if you like.'

That one sentence flips a switch in my head, but I have a

168

choice. The same one I always have. Lose my temper, shout and scream, ask him if he has understood anything I've told him. Or glide, swanlike across the surface of his cruel suggestion, then disappear into this life I have created for myself. I choose the swan.

'No thanks. You go,' I say. *Even though I'm paying for every minute of your time.*

'I want you to come.'

'I said no.'

'It's only across the road, Cassie. Come on.'

'No.'

'Why not?' He is standing beside me now. That warm vanilla smell.

'I don't want to.'

'Course you do. It's a beautiful morning. Everyone and anyone would want to.'

'Not me.' My jaw is hurting. I am biting down hard on my own teeth.

'You don't fool me, Cassie. Stop hiding what's happening. It's simple. People recover from phobias every day. Even the most stubborn ones: I should know.'

He lays a hand on my arm, tilts his head slightly. And that is enough.

'If there's one thing I cannot stand,' I shriek, 'it's being patronised. You know nothing about me, or what I actually feel. So, stop being a shrink, and go.'

I drag my arm away and walk out of the kitchen. My breath is coming too fast. I don't want to lose control. I've spent two years avoiding the hammering of my heart and my wish to escape. But I am already in my sanctuary. Blackthorn House. Why have I let someone so disruptive into my sanctuary? Yet here he is, just behind me, standing at the doorway of the study.

I spin around. 'Please can you just go. I don't want to do

this anymore.' The words catch in my throat, as though I have been running. The last one comes out as a sob.

'No. I'm not leaving. I want you to come across the road with me. Put on your boots and come.' A hand is held towards me. Freddy's hand. 'And don't call me a shrink. It's so American.' His lips curl upwards, but I'm not finding him funny.

'You can't make me, and I've said no. You can keep on all day, but I won't change my mind.'

'God, you're controlling.' He is muttering, but I hear what he says.

'Nice.' I sit on my couch and bring my knees up to my chest. Hug myself a little and rest my chin. 'You're making me into a sulky teenager. Stop it.'

'Well, you are.' He kneels next to me. 'Let your body do something it wants, for a change. Instead of always letting your brain be in charge.'

I blow out a small puff of air. 'Go and do your psychotherapy on someone who cares,' I say.

'That'll be you, then.'

'Oh, get lost.' I can feel my anger rising now. A splurge of stomach acid and here it comes. But I'm safe in my house, so I decide to set it free. 'I mean it,' I screech. 'Get out.'

But he just keeps kneeling, staring at me. I jump up and stomp down the hall towards the front door. I listen for his footsteps. They don't come.

'I said, "Get out". I'm throwing your boots outside.' A pause. 'And your coat.'

No response.

'I'm doing it.' I pull open the door and push it hard against the wall. He must have heard. 'Out go your boots.' I pick them up and fling them. They go over the front garden wall and into the road. 'And your coat.' It lands in a heap on the holly bush. I'm panting now. But I don't feel scared. I feel strong. Powerful.

Freddy isn't coming out of the study. So, I march back in. He is sitting on my sofa, doing that infuriating head tilt again.

'Your stuff's in the road. Could you please follow it?'

He shakes his dreadlocks.

'You're trespassing,' I growl. 'I'm going to telephone Si.'

The shrug he gives me makes me want to scream. I do scream. 'Stop it. Just stop it.' Louder. But then I'm not doing it anymore. That shouting. Shrieking. It felt good. My anger is shrinking. I smile, just a little, but Freddy sees.

'Enjoy that, did you? Losing control?'

I am about to argue with that summary of my actions, but I hesitate. He's right. I hate it, but he is. My breathing is back under my control again. My stomach has freed itself of the serpent.

'I did, actually.' I slump down on the sofa beside him. 'But your stuff is all over the road.' We both begin to giggle. It's not a nervous giggle. It grows into genuine laughter. 'Shall I go and get it?'

'Do that,' he says. 'I dare you.'

'Don't be stupid,' I tell him. 'I can go out into the road.'

He widens his eyes. 'Okay.' That word stretches out. 'I'll put the kettle on.'

I pad out of the room and down the hallway. A dart of cold air has entered. It smells of freedom. I drag Freddy's coat off the holly bush. There are dog hairs around the cuffs. White and wiry. His boots lie together in the middle of the road. I trot out and bend to pick them up. Small boots, probably my size, with worn, crumpled leather and traces of dubbin. He is the sort of person who would repair and recycle. I like that about him.

As I stand up, I can see the wood just at the other side of the road. The beeches are a dying orange, and each hazel coppice stands golden-green between them. There will be the last of the cob nuts lying along the paths, and crisped mud, adding to the crunch underfoot and traction for the walker. Autumn is my favourite season. I edge closer to the pavement opposite, breathe in the woodsmoke-and-red-clay fragrance, and think about what it would be like. But Blackthorn House pulls me back.

'Sorry,' I say to Freddy when I find him in the kitchen. 'But your coat and boots have survived. It was all a test of their durability. I work for Berghaus, you know. That's why I threw them.'

He is stirring the drinks, clinking a teaspoon against the side of each mug.

'You are quite an amusing woman,' he laughs. 'I could get to like you. And don't be sorry. I bet you feel better after that rant, don't you?' He hesitates. 'Got any biscuits? I'm starving.'

Blackthorn's kitchen has a huge pantry. The pine door reaches from floor to ceiling. It is like another room. I walk inside and find a packet of chocolate digestives.

Freddy is just behind me. 'Wow,' he exclaims, looking upwards. 'It even has a borrowed light. That always reminds me of being a kid. Every one of the rooms in our house had a borrowed light above its door.'

'Here,' I say, pushing the biscuits into his hand. 'These'll keep you going until lunch.'

We make our way into the lounge. It is west facing and chilly in the mornings, without a fire. I kneel in front of the empty hearth, start to lay firesticks, coal and logs. Freddy watches me, sipping his drink and munching on dunked biscuits.

'To heal from your trauma,' he says, between mouthfuls, 'you need to rewire your brain. Stop thinking of your reactions as bad things. Failures.'

I strike a match and throw it onto the firesticks. Nothing catches, so I do it again.

He continues. 'But you've got to allow those failures. Not run away from them. Cassie? Are you listening?'

I'm listening. But I'm not hearing anything new. How many times did Si tell me to face up to what was happening to me? My daughters told me the same.

'If you knew what went on after Judy Barker left, you might not be telling me to face my fears.' *God, I'm so dramatic.*

'Tell me, then,' he says.

Chapter Nineteen

SEPTEMBER 2016

R ain pattered onto the bunches of cellophane-wrapped flowers outside the shop. Standing under the green-striped awning gave no protection. Cassie could feel needle-sharp droplets of water along the gap between her collar and hair. A distraction from the fierce thumping of her heart. Though the florist was less than a hundred yards from school, the fear-fuelled symptoms of panic had started the minute she'd stepped away from the car park. But it was Jax's birthday, and she deserved something. Roses, perhaps. Cassie lifted a bunch of creamy yellow ones from the bucket and shook off the water.

Inside the shop, she rummaged around in her pocket for her purse, while the assistant smiled her patience. The potent smell of lilies, cloyingly warm and sweet, reminded Cassie of Tina Armstrong's perfume, and that was enough. She shoved a ten-pound note into the other woman's hand and fled.

As she dashed back across the road, the rain pelted against the shell of her anorak and splashed around the heels of her boots. And it did nothing to enhance the grey, litter-strewn streets of the town centre.

Spending the summer at Blackthorn House had gone some way towards repairing her shattered nerves, had taken the sting out of her adrenaline burnout, but she hadn't left the place without Si. There had been walks along the shore and through the woods, shopping trips and runs to the pickup point for the girls' summer camp. Each one of these missions had been completed, but each left Cassie feeling like she should have stayed at home. Then she would berate herself for being weak. And Si would talk her out of it, and back into reality.

When the day had come to return to Parkhouse, he'd even offered to drive her. She'd refused; if she could just get to the building, there would be distraction, and the panic symptoms would subside. When Si suggested he would check up on her once enough time had passed, she'd laughed, but wanted to cry. Had she become an invalid? Not able to manage even the smallest change to her mental state? The drive to work had been difficult, but she'd done it. Visiting the flower shop had been much trickier. They'd had long conversations over the summer about the whole Judy Barker episode. Si wanted Cassie to document everything and go to her union. She just wanted to forget, and start afresh, hoping her nervous condition would heal itself once she didn't feel she was living under constant fear of attack.

'You're talking like I've been working in front-line emergency medicine, or in the field for the British Army,' she'd told him. There had been laughter at that word: *attack*. But the adrenaline burnout was the same in both situations, she suspected.

As she pushed her way through the front door, Cassie glanced at Tina through the glass panel of the reception area. If the woman saw her, she didn't look up. There was no greeting, no asking after the six weeks that had kept them apart, and certainly no pressing of the entry button, so that Cassie had to scrabble with the coded door.

Jax was in the classroom, sitting in her usual place, with a pile of books in front of her.

'It's terrible out there,' Cassie said, as she stepped in, breathless, but trying to sound calm. 'I hope it's better tomorrow, or we'll be dealing with the smell of wet dog all day.' A consequence of having twenty-two children walking to school in the rain, then sitting all day in damp clothing, while their soaking coats and shoes hung around on the backs of chairs and under radiators. She pulled the bunch of roses from behind her back and shook them a little. 'Happy wet birthday, by the way.'

Jax looked up. 'Oh. Thank you. I'm trying not to think about it. Don't want to be an old woman.' She carried the flowers over to the sink. 'I'll lay them in here until they've dried out a bit. Thanks.' She buried her nose and sniffed. 'They're gorgeous.'

Cassie took off her coat and gave it a shake. 'How are you getting on with the labels?' She read down the class list on her desk. 'I can't believe how boy-heavy we are this year. Seventeen boys and five girls. How did that happen?'

Jax exhaled sharply. Rolled her shoulders and ran her hands through her salt-and-pepper curls. 'It's not necessarily a bad thing. But one name on that list bothers me. Ian McIntyre. He lives across the road from me and he's a little devil.'

She pronounced it *divil*, and Cassie laughed. 'He's come in from the Catholic school around the corner. Why, I wonder? Especially as it's his last year.'

'It doesn't take a genius.' Jax frowned. 'But he'll get no special favours here.'

In truth, her teaching assistant was a superb behaviourist and children with difficulties in managing themselves thrived in her care. Between them, they'd soon have the measure of this Ian McIntyre.

'Anyhow.' Jax yawned. 'The labels are nearly done, and I've

just got the trays to do. Look at the state of me. I've been up half the night with Meggy. First day of school tomorrow. She's on the ceiling.'

'I'll go and get a vase for the flowers, and bring you a strong coffee.' Cassie wanted to avoid sitting at her desk, wanted to get rid of the jitters from the shop visit. 'I think there's one in the staffroom cupboard.'

Kevin Noble was already there, sprawled across three chairs, wowing two young teaching assistants with a story about his summer trip to Poland. His face and arms were lightly tanned, and he had six weeks growth of grey-and-dark beard.

'Whites.' A flash of blue eyes. 'How's it going?'

'Good, thanks.' Cassie grinned at him. 'Nobbs.'

The teaching assistants giggled.

'Seen anything of Joe?'

He shook his head, eyelashes batting at the crowd.

'Could do with catching up together at some point today. Part of our training, and everything.'

'Did I hear my name?' Joe stepped through the door. 'Only being used in a good way, I hope.'

'Joe, you're here.' A hug. Cassie asked after his health and Kevin chipped in with comments about extended holidays and shirking; they laughed and postured for the young women, made coffee and had an exaggerated hunt for biscuits.

Cassie enjoyed the normality of the situation, then Jax was calling to her from the corridor. 'Be back in a min. My boss wants me.'

A float of soft laughter followed her out of the room. Banter. How she'd missed it in the previous year. No agendas. No asking Jax to pull the knives from her back. Just camaraderie. A tangible antidote to the stress of being confined with hundreds of children every day.

'What's up?' Her teaching assistant was standing in the classroom doorway.

'It's your hubby. He's tapping on the window.'

Cassie waved at him, then ran along the corridor towards the reception area. Poor guy. If nobody was in the office, he wouldn't have been able to get in. Husbands weren't allowed to know the door code. But Tina Armstrong, wearing pristine jeans and a sharp-cut blouse, was in her usual place behind the glass partition, tapping away at her keyboard. Cassie let herself into the waiting area and slid her arms around her husband's waist.

'You checking up on me?' she laughed, looking into his face.

'I had a few jobs to do in town, that's all. Thought I'd pop in and see you. I've been sat here for ages, but she just ignored me.' He pointed towards the glass. 'Bloody cow.'

Cassie felt a shot of adrenaline buzz through her body. She stepped away from Si and pushed open the office door.

'Did you not see him waiting?' This to Tina Armstrong.

No response.

'Tina. I'm talking to you. Si has been waiting out there for ten minutes. You would have seen him. Why didn't you buzz him through?' Cassie tried to ease the tension in her jaw as she spoke.

A flash of matted mascara. A red sneer. 'Didn't see him.'

'You must have. Or heard him, at least. That door bangs every time anyone comes through it.'

The keyboard tapping continued. Cassie wanted to walk across the room, grab Tina by the shoulders and shake her, watch her head rattle backwards and forwards. Then throw her to the floor. It might give her a taste of the damage she was inflicting, albeit in a cruelly invisible way. Instead, she swallowed down her rage, though the size and shape of it clogged her throat.

Silence.

Tina looked at her computer screen. Her cheeks were livid,

and she wiggled her toes so that her black suede high-heels slipped back and forth.

'Tina. Answer me.' Cassie's words came from the place where adrenaline burned.

Then the sound of footsteps on carpet. Small footsteps. Alison Harman appeared at the office door, scruffy, in jeans and a long cardigan and with a pile of books in her arms.

'Hello, all.' Announcing herself. She glanced at Si. 'Is everything okay?'

'Fine,' smiled Tina. 'We were just chatting.' A sucked-lemon voice.

'Oh, that's good.' Alison put the books down in front of Tina. 'I've some things to work through with you. Admission forms and stuff. Now's all right, isn't it?' She slid Denise's chair across to the edge of the desk and sat down.

'We'll leave you to it.' Cassie pulled at Si's hand and led him out of the room. The effects of the adrenaline burst were wearing off: now she felt shaky and raw.

'Come and say hello to Jax,' she hissed. 'At least she'll be happy to see you.'

October 2019

The fire is starting to crackle and find its life. Freddy wipes the melted chocolate from around his mouth.

'Don't lose it again with me when I ask you this, Cassie,' he says.

What now?

'Do you think women employees had some sort of problem with you? Because you were in a position of power?'

I'm shaking my head, not trusting myself to speak.

'It's an accepted thing, you know. Women can be quite vicious, despite their sometimes,' a pause, 'meek appearance.'

I'm not having this. From a man with a hint of education and empathy. From any man.

'This must be a trick,' I say. 'You're a *misogynist* now?'

He shakes his head. 'Far from it. But I am a mirror. I'm reflecting back the things you must have asked yourself, given the situation.'

'Meaning?' I pull back my head. But he is exactly right. I did ask myself whether Tina or Judy just didn't like women in managerial positions. Though both would have been happy to see Laura Pearson in my role.

'Meaning,' he says, 'that despite Kevin Noble acting in an unprofessional way, you accepted it, never broke faith with him. Were you more exacting with the female staff, I wonder?'

I can't answer this. Jax and I had a wonderful relationship. We worked hard, acknowledged our strengths and weaknesses, would never have resorted to back-biting. But, yes. I demanded that from her. And in return she got loyalty and support. Nothing to do with her being a woman. I liked to think it was because we were friends as well as colleagues.

'What I'm saying, Cassie, is basically, were those women jealous because you kept them at a distance? Made them feel inferior, somehow?'

I hold my hands up to my forehead, spread my fingers and push down. 'So many questions. I don't know what went on in Tina or Judy's head. Nothing much, I suspect.'

These women have been trapped inside a box for two years. And now Freddy has loosened the string and lifted the lid.

'I rest my case.' He scrunches up the plastic wrapper of the biscuits then throws it at the fire. It misses. 'You looked down on them, Cassie. And they wanted to make you pay.'

'You weren't there,' I tell him, though I think he has a point.

'Then it's up to you to shine a light,' he sighs.

Chapter Twenty

The door sprung open, and Cassie's new class sauntered into the room, bringing with them the usual faded tans and enthusiasm.

'Hi, Mrs Clifton.'

'Where do I sit, miss?'

'It looks so bare.' Faces staring up at the walls.

'Cheeky,' she laughed. 'Mrs T and I spent days covering all the boards in colours we thought you'd like; we'll soon fill them.'

Cassie had made a pact with herself after the incident in the office. No matter what nasty acts of subversion Tina tried to pull off, she would put the woman in her place. Not doing so with Judy Barker had been a mistake, one she didn't intend to make again. And she would try to be more friendly towards Denise.

Jax matched children to lockers while Cassie took a register and chased up the arrangements for lunch. A few late-comers straggled in, a daze of the first morning get-up blurring their faces. They had her sympathy. She'd seethed into the early hours herself, after Si's humiliation yesterday, and after waving him off on another twelve-day shift offshore, she'd found it difficult to pull the car away from Blackthorn. But she was here. That would have to be enough, for now.

One last scan of the class list told her that the newcomer, Ian McIntyre, was yet to arrive. She looked at the clock. Five minutes until her assembly. Alison rarely led them these days: there was usually a pressing meeting with a parent, or an urgent telephone call. Cassie always prepared, and this morning was no different. Her new class would have to get used to being punctual. Jax could deal with Ian McIntyre, if he arrived.

'Okay, everyone.' She peered at the eager faces spread around tables, the pristine uniforms and grown-up hairstyles. 'Here's a thing you'll have to get used to. I'm taking the assembly today. And you're going to help me.'

A low groan.

'Year six.' She held up her hands. 'That's how it is. Some of you will want to be prefects. You'd better get used to helping teachers, even if it is uncool.'

Laughter rippled.

'So,' she stood up and straightened her collar, 'let's go.'

The children pushed their way into a line in front of the door. She looked at the adoring puppy faces and smart black shoes, mainly lace-ups. There would only be a tiny female-faction this year. And one of those was Georgia. Or George. Though her mother dressed her in grey skirts and braided her long dark hair, George wanted nothing more than to fight her way onto the football pitch and excel.

'Okay, George?' Cassie smiled down at her. 'Going for the A-team this year?'

A slight nod.

'In everything?'

Another nod, and a wry smile. 'Course.'

As Cassie led her class along the corridor, she could see two adults walking towards her, with Tina Armstrong and a small red-haired boy just behind.

'Ah. Mrs Clifton. This is Ian. He's joining your class.'

There were no smiles. Cassie looked at him, and then at the parents.

'Hello. I'll catch up with you at some point.' Then, to Tina. 'Mrs T is in class. She'll look after Ian. I've got to do an assembly.'

The parents glared.

'S'a bit fucking rude,' growled the man, all Regatta anorak and a switched-off e-cigarette in his hand. The woman was a smaller version of the same. Cassie didn't turn back.

Get your child in on time then. But she'd catch up with these new parents later when she was less pressed. Her time was spread thinly, stretched across hundreds of children and their needs, as well as her own class, and all the intensity that required. Then there were her colleagues. When things ran smoothly, a simple word, flattery or praise, would keep them at their best. But most of the time, things didn't run smoothly.

Cassie got her own class settled on the floor of the hall, chose one or two of them to help her, then began to set up her PowerPoint slides and some music. The first lines of children began to patter their way in. Teachers ambled along behind. Spines were straightened and legs were crossed.

This is me. The thought made her smile. *Where else would I be?*

***

Ian McIntyre proved his reputation within a day.

'I don't read,' he told Jax. Then the reading book she'd given him was thrown across the classroom. It made a beautiful arc then landed at Cassie's feet. The children slid down in their seats, shoulders hunched and wondering how Mrs T would react. But one or two of the boys thought the situation was quite amusing, thought they might even try it themselves. And Cassie had been forced to do something she rarely did, especially on a first day. She showed them all a flash of temper, ending her wish for calm and control.

Lunchtime had caused some problems too. Ian decided that he didn't like the meal choices. This reaction was usually dealt with swiftly: the unhappy child given one of the sandwiches kept in reserve by the cook. Ian didn't like sandwiches. He'd thrown his in the scraps bin, all the while staring down the lunchtime supervisor who'd tried to help him. Her challenge was met with a string of swear words and a threat to tell his parents about her.

Alison had been sent for, but she'd batted the problem back to Cassie, which did nothing to improve any of their relationships.

At half past three, when a feather-soft silence descended on the classroom, Cassie and Jax were sitting at one of the children's tables, thinking about strategies to deal with this new little boy. Rectangular slabs of September sunshine lit up the tables by the window, where the curled-up first attempts of some seaside art was drying.

'We can't let him dictate what happens,' sighed Jax. 'He gets his own way far too much, from what I have seen.'

Cassie put her head in her hands. 'It was the way the others watched him that bothered me. That sort of influence we can do without. Especially in a class full of boys.' She pulled back her chair. 'Let's see what tomorrow brings. It was his first day, after all. The rest of them know each other. He probably just wanted to make his mark.'

Jax stood up. 'Well,' she smiled, 'boy-politics is our speciality. So, his mark might not be what he wants it to be.' She winked at Cassie. 'I'm going to get some backing paper for those monstrosities.' A tilt of her head towards the paintings. 'Black?'

'Yep.'

They both turned as Kevin Noble put his head around the doorway. 'Phone call for you, Whites.' A thumb in the direction of the office. 'Tina said.'

'Could she not have told me?' The words burst from Cassie's mouth, and slapped Kevin around the face.

He raised his hands. 'Hey. I was just passing. She asked me to fetch you.'

'Sorry, Nobbs. Sorry.' She looked at Jax. 'I won't be a minute.'

In the office, the phone receiver lay in a tangle of wire, along the side of Tina Armstrong's desk. She didn't look up, didn't tell Cassie who was calling, just kept writing. Cassie picked up the receiver and moved as far away from the desk as the wire would allow.

'Hello. It's Mrs Clifton. Who's speaking, please.'

A male voice. Angry. 'Jason McIntyre. You our Ian's teacher?'

'Oh, hi. Yes, I am. Is everything okay?'

'No, it's fucking not.'

Cassie's stomach hit the floor. She pulled everything that had happened with the red-haired boy from her memory. 'Sorry to hear that. What's the problem?'

'Call yourself a teacher.' A vicious growl. 'Can't even spell his name right.'

'I'm sorry. What do you mean?'

'He's come out tonight, in tears. Every fucking book and locker. Everything. Got his name spelt I-a-n. It's I-a-i-n. I want it sorted.'

She doubted Iain had gone out of school in tears. His face had hardened, tight as rock, when she'd told him off about

PAULA HILLMAN

throwing the reading book. He didn't appear to have mentioned that to his father.

'Oh dear. I apologise, Mr McIntyre.' She turned to face Tina. 'It must have been spelt wrong on the list we were given.' Not a flicker. 'I'll go and change everything right this minute. Now, is there anything else I can help you with?'

But the line was dead. Mr McIntyre was gone.

'Better change the spelling on your records, Mrs Armstrong,' Cassie muttered as she put down the receiver. 'You gave us a wrong spelling of Iain's name.'

For a few seconds, she thought her words hadn't been spoken, that they were still clinging to the back of her throat, fighting against her wish to keep them hidden. But, no. She had said them. Though there was no response, just the scratching of Tina's pen.

'Tina? Do you want me to write down the proper spelling? Jax spent ages yesterday labelling everything. We assumed the list would be correct.'

Tina didn't look up; her voice was ice. 'It was correct. I don't make spelling mistakes. You must have read it wrong.'

'I doubt it. Jax doesn't make errors like that.' Which was true.

Tina smashed her pen down on the table. 'You really are a bitch, aren't you?' She blinked heavy lashes at Cassie. 'Are you going to be on my case, now you've got rid of Judy? I'm not in the slightest bit interested in Kevin Noble, if that helps.'

Heat flared across Cassie's face. From the time she'd sat opposite Judy Barker and listened to her attempts to excuse the nasty text message, she'd wondered what had been said about it. And now she knew.

'Judy Barker did a very good job of getting rid of herself,' she said with a calm she wasn't feeling, 'though that isn't your business.' She picked up the pen and grabbed a bright pink Post-it note, then scribbled down Iain McIntyre's name. 'But

186

this is.' She pushed the note down onto the top of Tina's writing pad, laid the pen carefully next to it. 'And it would be very helpful if you could stop ignoring me. I'm finding it rather petty.'

Tina darted a look at the door. 'I've only just started,' she spat. 'You'll be right behind Judy, if I get my way.'

October 2019

'I wanted to slap her face at that point,' I snarl from the sofa. Freddy is doing one of his stretching routines. 'Whether I was her superior or not.'

But shockwaves had run from my head to my feet when it finally dawned on me that Judy had been just another pawn in Tina's long-game.

'Then you would have lost your job,' he snorts. 'So, let me get this right. You think that Judy Barker had been manipulated by Tina. To get at you.' He lets out a small whistle. 'She was some player, wasn't she? In fact–'

But I don't let him finish. 'There's no *think* about it. Even Judy admitted she'd changed. Oh, I know she had an obsession with Kevin Noble. For Tina, that was perfect. She could use its energy to keep Judy's focus.' I groan. '*Eastenders*, or what?'

'There's nowt so queer as folk,' he says.

'Helpful.' I grimace. But I am long past being uppity with him. It's exactly as he says: he's the mirror and the light.

I get up from my place on the sofa and lift another log from the basket on the hearth. I hold it up to my nose, breathe in the rich soil fragrance. 'It's one of the boughs from the oldest apple tree in the garden.'

Freddy lifts his chin and frowns slightly. I take his meaning.

'Oh, I know, burning unseasoned wood isn't the *done thing*, but we don't do it very often.' I lift another from the basket and crumble the bark with my nails. 'And besides, it's really dry.'

'Not bothered about the wood, Cassie. But I'm wondering why you didn't slap Tina Armstrong's face. At least metaphorically. I would have.' He slides himself forward, perching on the edge of the sofa. 'Keeping that level of annoyance inside is corrosive.'

I shiver then hold my hands out to the weakly crackling flames. It is past lunchtime, according to the German clock – dark wood and as old as my grandfather – on the mantelpiece. The bright sunshine of the morning has faded. It didn't make it to the front of the house. I may have to switch on the heating. I don't usually sit for this long. I tend to write for a short while, then move about. There is always something to be getting on with in Blackthorn.

'Shall I make us some soup?'

'Sounds good,' he says, 'but don't avoid the question. What did you do about this, quite frankly, bitter and vindictive member of your staff?'

'What could I do?' I walk away. 'When I tried to put her in her place, she came back twice as hard.'

He follows me into the kitchen. It's warmer in here, with the range fully stoked. 'You could have talked it over with your boss. She had ultimate responsibility for staff welfare. Mental as well as physical health. That's employment law.'

'You've never worked in a school then, have you. There's barely enough time to draw breath, let alone have in-depth conversations about your feelings.' I make inverted commas with my fingers, and Freddy cringes slightly, shakes his head.

'Don't start that. It's not a luxury to focus on your mental health. It's vital.'

I step into the pantry and lift out two tins of tomato soup. 'This okay?' I jiggle the tins in front of him.

He takes them from my hands. 'Tell me one thing,' he says, 'then we'll break for lunch proper.'

'What's that?' It will be good to stop feeling like a specimen for ten minutes. I rummage around in one of the kitchen cupboards and pull out a small saucepan. Freddy comes to stand beside me. He's good at invading personal space. I've stopped minding so much now. He slides an elbow across the wooden countertop, rests his head there and squints at me.

'When did you make the connection between what was happening at work, and your own mental state?'

'After I'd left.' I've been ready for this question. So many people have asked me the same thing. Asked me why I never told anyone I was struggling, why I didn't reach out for help. All that showed is that they didn't know me at all. Or understand the situation. I cock my head at Freddy. Does he understand, or not?

He hesitates. 'I think your brain had already changed itself well before then. Always hungry for a challenge, our brains. They never think of our bodies.'

He gets it.

'I have to ignore mine sometimes. Like, now. My body needs food. I'm done thinking.' He takes the spoon from my hand and begins stirring the soup. 'You make some sandwiches,' he laughs. I like his laugh. It's from my present. Not my past.

I find half a loaf of bread in the bread bin. White and stodgy, but nobody in my family likes bread with bits in. I grate some cheese and cut three rounds of sandwiches. Pure comfort food: Heinz tomato soup and cheese sandwiches.

'I made a fruit cake last week. There's some of that left, too. Would you like to try it?'

'If you insist,' says Freddy, his mouth full of cheese and bread. 'Love a bit of fruit cake.' He sniggers. 'Love cakes generally, actually.'

I have to laugh. I've realised something about Freddy. He's clever enough to get away with acting daft. There's something innately trustworthy about him. Like he knows the world, like nothing can faze him. How else would he be here, listening to someone as guarded as I am, and somehow getting to the heart of me.

'Cheeky,' I say, then, 'let's eat.'

We sit at the kitchen table, with no airs and graces. We just tuck in. Spoons chink against the edge of bowls, and we slurp. But I am relaxed in a way I haven't been for a long time. Somebody else knows, and they have taken my side. I haven't felt this before. Even Si, who supported me through everything, often made me hate myself for the mess I'd created. And he never even knew. Which is just as well: he'd have been mortified.

'Is there a Mrs Freddy?' I ask, when we have finished.

'What?' He beams. A soup-rimmed smile. 'Are you asking if I have a partner?'

'Call it what you like.'

He shakes his head. 'There was someone. Elena. She was from Spain. Went back there, in the end.'

'Did you not want to go with her?'

His face colours a little. 'I did, but it turns out there was a boyfriend over there, too. She liked him more.'

I am embarrassed. I've no right to this information. 'Sorry.'

'Don't worry about it. But, Cassie, she was gorgeous.' He gets up. 'Not for me, though.' He picks up our bowls and plates. At the sink, he gazes out of the kitchen window. 'What's through there?' he asks.

At the end of Blackthorn's back garden is an old wooden gate. My granddad knocked a hole in the wall and put it up. I remember the day, exactly. Hot and humid, and I was wearing my silvery dress and a pair of white sandals, no socks. He and my dad pulled down a section of the wall, brick after red brick, sending up clouds of dust and making my grandma call me away. But I wanted to join in. Instead, I had to sit and sip lemonade, and be crooned over by the women of the family. Every alteration, every addition that Granddad made, is logged in my heart. I knew Blackthorn would belong to me one day; even then, I knew.

'Oh, just the back street,' I say. 'It leads to the road eventually. It's where we put out the wheelie bins.'

'Can we have a wander down the garden for a bit? Let our dinner settle?'

'You go,' I tell him. 'I'll catch you up.'

'S'okay. I'll wait. Dry up. Have you got a tea towel?'

I point to a wide drawer at the bottom of my pine dresser. It was Grandma's dresser, actually.

He slides out the drawer. 'I love this place,' he says, and not for the first time. He selects an old towel with faded bleach marks, clean but not exactly *Homes and Gardens*. Then picks up the crockery from the draining board and sets to, wiping and chatting. He is good company. Our conversation moves between houses and the town, natural history and the more social kind. Finally, we are done, and he hangs the tea towel over the handle of one of the range's ovens.

When he sees my smile, he wobbles his head slightly, flicks his dreadlocks. 'Go on, say it. I'd make somebody a lovely wife.'

'I'd never say anything so sexist,' I tell him. 'But you are pretty domesticated.'

'That's life on a farm for you,' is all he says.

At the back door, I hesitate, then lift a jacket from the scullery and slip on my boots. Freddy pushes his feet into his. 'Borrow a fleece, if you like. It looks chilly out there.' I get one down from the peg.

'It's fine,' he grins. 'I'm made from tough island stock.'

'Walney? Or Baz I?' I laugh. The nickname for Barrow Island, a chunk of the town that has docks on three sides.

'Both.' He pulls open the door and we are greeted by the taste of an autumn afternoon, woodsmoke with a swirl of perfectly damp grass.

It takes all my effort to step outside. This can't happen. I would normally just shut the door again, do something else.

'You coming out, Cassie?' His hand. Pale pink with the odd freckle. Why is he holding it out towards me? I'm not an invalid. But I don't move. The *thing* starts. Chewing away from the centre of my brain. Telling me what will happen if I take that step. I'll get a rush of blood, a race of heart, a choke of breath. Everything I hate. The numbness in my jaw comes first today. I say nothing.

'Cassie. Stop thinking. Focus on this second. What can you hear?'

'Your voice,' I say. A wry twist of my lips.

'What does the air smell like, Cassie?'

Woodsmoke, I think, *and earthy, dying ferns.*

'Where are you standing, at this moment?'

I frown. 'That's pretty obvious, isn't it?'

'Tell me. Look at your feet and tell me.'

'What are we doing?' I'm getting cross, now. These stupid questions. Is he some sort of Buddhist healer? I don't say that, though an image slips into my mind: Bald head and scarlet robes, the Manjushri monks from the priory nearby.

'What does my voice sound like, to you, Cassie?' A tilt of his head. His face looks grainy against the faded afternoon light.

'Like you're an idiot.' I can't contain my emotion, but it comes out as a small laugh.

Freddy laughs, too. 'Harsh,' he says.

More emotion bubbles up from my stomach. 'Get out,' I say, then follow him.

Our feet squelch against the wet moss that passes for lawn in some places. I put my hands in my pockets.

Freddy inhales deeply. 'It's so quiet. Glad you came, now?'

'Yep,' I say, but a haze of failure is moving through my body. How must it be to just go outside, without the grey spectre of fear standing in your way?

He takes my hand. Pats it. 'Guess what.'

'What?' I scowl at him.

'You didn't fail. So, stop thinking it, and just enjoy. Being out on a mellow afternoon with the most handsome and clever man on the planet.'

I slap him playfully on the arm. He can read minds, as well as all his other skills. 'My husband's not here, is he?' We smile at that and walk on.

At the end of the garden is a brick shed hidden behind a screen of ragged conifers. They need pruning. My granddad planted them as saplings to hide what would probably be called a man-cave now. *Daddy's in his den*, my grandma would say. She always called him Daddy.

We use the shed as a place to store garden tools and plastic tubs, and anything else that becomes homeless in your home. Piles of *National Geographics*, that kind of thing. Freddy is opening the back gate. He bends forward, peers around the old wood frame. His dreadlocks fall over one shoulder. Then he straightens up and steps through, into the back street. I follow; without thinking about it too much, I follow.

'Quick. Grab my arm,' he says, and crooks his elbow towards me.

I do as he says.

'Now. Walk with me to the front of the house. Why is there even a back street?' He runs his hand over the crumbling red brick of the wall. 'Is this as old as the house?'

My legs are trembling. There is pressure in my stomach. Through my tight mouth I push out an answer. 'All the land around here once belonged to Blackthorn.' It's all I can manage.

'Oh.' He thinks about this for a couple of seconds. 'Was it built for a rich entrepreneur then? There were plenty of those in the town, back in the day.'

I shake my head, zoom through my racing thoughts for some kind of answer. I know the history of the house, but adrenaline has hidden it from me. And my brain is shaking now, too. We are at the end of the back street, the furthest I have been for two years. I can't breathe, but Freddy is still pulling me on. Going back to the garden gate is as far as walking along the main road to Blackthorn's front door. Both are too far. I will die right here, 100 yards from my home. My mouth is glued shut, but Freddy talks on.

'Industrialists they might have been, but they bled our town dry. Built their huge houses, claimed the town's farmland, then turned their back on the locals when Irish labour proved cheaper.'

Across my fear, a lightning path is cut. Like a dragon breathing fire. He has it so wrong, and I must tell him.

'A colonel in command of the Barrow garrison built it, actually. He was well respected and loved.' I cough out the words, but Freddy doesn't notice.

'I stand corrected,' he laughs. 'And here we are, back at the front door.'

I let go of his hand and run up the drive and push open the big Victorian door. Then fall into the hall. Freddy stays behind me, lifting me from my knees so that I can walk into the lounge.

'Sit,' he commands, 'and let it all out.'

And I do. I sob and shake and twitch. Fold my arms, unfold them, take the kitchen paper that he offers me. Blow my nose. Fold my hands between my knees. Sip the tea he makes me. Realise I am still alive. And start to calm down.

The apple logs I put on the fire have burned down to glowing embers. Everything burns down, eventually, when the fuel runs out. Even the worst kind of flames.

'So, you didn't slap Tina Armstrong's face,' Freddy says, coming to sit beside me.

I shake my head. She got more than a slap, in the end.

He snorts lightly. 'She might have laid off you after a good slap.'

'Maybe. Or maybe that would have been fuel to the fire. Anyway, she didn't lay off me. Far from it,' I tell him, then I watch his face as he listens.

Chapter Twenty-One

'Denise's mum's died.' Alison Harman stopped her high-heeled stomp across the playground, coming to rest just in front of where Cassie was refereeing a breaktime kick-about. 'She's just telephoned. Poor lass, she was so upset.'

'Oh, no. What a shame.'

'She's going to be off for a while. We'll go to the funeral, shall we? Show her we're thinking of her.'

'Course.' Cassie shielded her eyes against the low-rise September sunshine, then blew her whistle. 'Let's take Becky, too.'

'Good idea. Anyway, I'll leave you to it.' She glanced at the football game, waving as a few of the children zoomed past. 'How's me'laddo been?' She pointed towards Iain McIntyre, who was charging about on the tarmac, shirt hanging out and red fringe plastered across his forehead.

'Getting there,' Cassie told her. 'And footy is helping. I'm using it as a bribe.' She held a finger to her lips. 'Just don't tell Mr McIntyre.'

'I won't.' Alison walked away, shoulders shaking.

Cassie turned back to the game. Sometimes competitive sport got through to children in a way that nothing else could. Georgia had been a case in point. Though she'd struggled with the traditional side of schooling, the child became herself when taking part in any kind of sport. Then, she found self-worth. Her face would be alight with confidence and laughter. And now, Iain McIntyre was punching the air and smiling, too. His kick had booted the ball between the two wooden posts at his team's end of the tarmac. Cassie gave a double whistle and held her hands out for the ball.

'That's it, for now. Breaktime's over,' she called. 'Come and line up.' She swung her arm across her body, beckoning them in, and laughed at the communal groaning. Then walked through the crowd of children rushing to get first place in their class lines.

A layer of mist had spread itself across the lawn of Blackthorn House. Smokey and soft, in contrast to the jarring in Cassie's stomach. She thought of Denise, burying her mother, today. How would that feel? Her own parents were only a telephone call away, but those conversations formed themselves from dissection of the weather or global news; there was no depth or empathy. She wanted to do better, but the thought of travelling a long way from Blackthorn House left her fearful.

There was a warmth to the autumn sunlight, and it soaked into her black clothing. She slipped off the jacket and smoothed it carefully across one bare arm, then turned her face upwards for a moment. Like it or not, she would have to spend the morning with Tina. The woman's behaviour, the words she used, that Cassie would be *right behind Judy* implied an elevated estimation of her power. Cassie took a deep breath and steadied herself. Perhaps there would be some waving of white flags, for the sake of Denise. Though she doubted it.

As she turned back to the house, Cassie let her gaze wander over the dark red brickwork and sash windows, unchanged for so many years. Today, all she wanted was to huddle down inside its walls and keep to herself.

'I'm just going to walk with the girls, Cass. Will you still be here when I get back?' Si. Standing at the kitchen door, dressed for a day of tree-pruning.

Cassie stepped towards him, careful in her heels. 'No. I'm heading off, now. We're meeting at school first.'

A frown spread across Si's forehead. 'Are you okay?' he asked.

'Fine. Why?' A lie.

'You've been quiet, this morning. That's all.'

'I'm always quiet.' Cassie leaned in for a kiss. 'And be careful on that.' She looked at the huge wooden double-ladder propped against one of Blackthorn's outbuildings. 'We don't have life insurance.'

'You say that every autumn, yet, here I am.'

Cassie slapped him lightly on the top of his arm. 'Don't tempt fate. I'll see you later.'

She called a goodbye to Helli and Janey, then clacked down the hallway. Her special handbag hung off the banister. It contained a packet of tissues from the last funeral she'd attended. Mick Ripley's. The school had closed for the day, and hundreds of people, dressed in blue and white at Becky's request, had lined the road leading up to the crematorium. Mick had been a life-long fan of the town's football team and his dedication rubbed off on many of Parkhouse's families. There had been lots of tears, as far as Cassie remembered. Today, though, would be all about showing support for

Denise. Tricky, when she hardly had a relationship with the woman.

As she pulled her car away from Blackthorn, Cassie tried to visualise a plan for the day, one that would provide dignity instead of friction. She would offer to drive them all, would smile and try to make some sort of eye contact. After all, Tina could hardly ignore her with Alison present. How would that look?

The traffic formed a slow line along the main road, nose-to-tail, in no hurry, as though the mellow light and golden warmth had changed a busy morning into a languid summer evening. But Cassie had somewhere to be. She wasn't buying into the Californian vibe one little bit.

Finally, she arrived at the entrance to Parkhouse. The car park was full. She rarely arrived this late. When Jax was in charge, she liked Cassie to keep out of the way. A glance at her watch told her there was enough time for a quick coffee and chat with Alison. And she would catch Tina's eye and offer a lift to the crematorium.

Cassie pushed open the front door and peered into the office through the glass partition. Tina was at her desk, all sharp-suited and ironed hair. Laura Pearson was standing alongside her, grim faced, glancing to see who'd come in. Neither woman acknowledged her. So much for planning.

The school was quiet. Most classroom doors were closed. Children were heads down and working or reading. To be a teacher, and be on the outside of that, felt strange. Unsettling.

Like when you were a child, on a sick day from school.

She sneaked a look through her own classroom door. Jax had everything under control, and she didn't want to disrupt that. The shuffle of heels on carpet made her turn around. Alison was coming towards her.

'Cass.' A rustle of grey silk. 'Tina said you were going straight to the crem. We were just about to head up there.'

Something snapped inside Cassie's brain. Her plan, cracked in two by brittle and harshly-meant words. 'Tina said. It's always *Tina said*. Like a weird game.'

Alison stretched her face so that her mouth fell open. 'My office, Mrs Clifton.' She glanced along the corridor. 'Now.'

'No. I'm not going to your office. I'm going to drive myself to this funeral.' Cassie turned sharply and walked away.

'Cassie.' There was a warning in Alison's tone. 'I need a word. Please.'

There were two choices. Cassie could storm away, face the funeral, then take the consequences of refusing her boss's request. Or she could offload her angst about Tina Armstrong, now, when they were all feeling edgy, anyway. She chose the latter and pushed her way into Alison's office.

'I never said any such thing to Tina.' Cassie folded her arms and raised her brows. 'And anyway, the woman never speaks to me. So, we could hardly have had a conversation about driving to the crem.'

Alison lifted a black blazer from the back of her chair. 'I'm not being funny, Cass, but is everything okay? I thought once Judy had gone, you'd stop being so—'

'So what?'

'Oh, I don't know. So wary. Tina's made a mistake, probably. That's all.'

How could this be happening again? Cassie feeling like she was the naughty schoolgirl, being soothed as a way of exerting control. A shudder crept across her shoulders when she remembered having to tell Alison what had happened with Judy Barker. The humiliation. The clutch of entrapment, like a tight band around the top of her ribs.

'I know you told me to rise above it, Alison. Rise above back-biting and school politics, you said. And I am trying. But what happens when you're the victim? Is your advice to just keep quiet and hope it'll go away?'

Alison's head snapped towards her. 'I'd never say that. I don't say it to the kids, and I'd never say it to my staff.' A pause. 'Are you saying you're being victimised?'

Cassie shrugged.

'If you are, we need to formalise things. Do it all properly.' *Again.* Alison hadn't said that word, but it was implied. It caused a blast of adrenaline that whizzed from Cassie's stomach to the top of her scalp.

I can't go through all that again.

'Can we just go to the funeral. We'll be late, otherwise. I need to think about things first.'

'Fair enough.' Alison slipped her arms into her jacket, watched as Cassie pulled open the door and stepped into the corridor. 'Tina can take us all.'

Becky Ripley was waiting in the car park, smart in a navy-blue trouser suit.

She waved a hand at Cassie.

'Hello, poppet.' She slid her gaze over Tina and Alison. 'Hello. Can I cadge a lift with you?'

'Course you can,' Alison said. 'Tina's driving.'

Tina led them to her car and pointed her key fob to open the doors. It was such an ordinary moment, a group of colleagues travelling together to attend a funeral, supporting each other in a quiet way, grateful for the chance. So why did Cassie feel like she'd been cracked open, exposing the raw version of herself to the vultures? She pressed her hand against her chest and gulped down some breaths, then let herself be ushered into the car. She sat behind Tina, and Becky climbed in next to her. Alison slid into the front passenger seat, tugging at her seat belt while they moved to the car park entrance.

A smooth flow of traffic was heading towards the town centre. A bus slowed down to let Tina out and she pulled at the steering wheel, guiding the car in the opposite direction.

'Poor Denise,' she said suddenly. 'It's awful when a parent dies.' She let out a small sigh. 'When anyone dies.'

Becky shifted position. 'Tell me about it,' she muttered. 'Losing Mick like that, it cut me in half. The finality of it. Never being able to have that life again, that you loved so much.'

Cassie couldn't believe what she was hearing. Joe's words crept into her mind. *Tina and Mick were kissing when I walked in.* There couldn't be any truth in that, could there? Becky would have known, surely.

Alison jumped in. 'How are the boys, Becky? Bet they miss him as much as you do.'

'He never got to see his latest grandchild. That hurts.'

'You'll have to make sure they all know what a great guy he was.' Alison looked over her shoulder at Becky. 'And so well loved by the Parkhouse community.'

'He was,' chimed Tina. 'You just never know, do you? When your time's up.'

'My Mick was a fit and healthy guy,' snapped Becky. 'His time wasn't up, as you put it.'

Cassie caught Tina's eye in the mirror. A blink. Nothing more.

'That came out wrong, sorry,' she said. 'I only meant that even if you look after yourself and do all the right things, you just never know. Denise's mum was only sixty, and in good health until a little while ago.'

Tina pulled up at a set of traffic lights. Becky didn't reply for a moment, then she said, 'You run, don't you, Tina? Is that to help you keep well?'

'I suppose so,' came the reply. 'I just pound the pavements around my estate.'

'Where is that?' Becky asked.

'Old Roose, actually.'

'I could never run,' laughed Alison. 'My thighs chafe too

much. It's bad enough walking.'

'Too much information,' said Cassie, and the tension eased slightly.

As Tina pulled the car between the gates of the crematorium, Cassie stared through the window. The wide green slopes gave a perfect view across the industrial landscape of the town centre, and out towards the gentle sweep of the sea. A similar view to the one from the woods on the far side of Blackthorn. And she wished she was there now.

Cars lumbered past, full of sombre-faced people, smartly dressed, at odds with the brightly floral landscape.

'I'll pull in here.' Tina nudged the car in between two others, then switched off the engine. 'There's a lot of people. Look at the queue.'

They climbed out and walked together, Alison in front with Tina, and Cassie next to Becky.

'Are you going to be okay with this?' Cassie asked, as Becky clutched her arm. 'It was my idea to ask you along, and now I feel bad.'

'I needed to be here. I haven't been visible enough lately. With Mick, and stuff. And I want *her* to see me.' She tilted her head towards Tina. 'Really see me.'

Cassie said nothing. This was Denise's day. She was about to bury her mother. Whispering behind hands was the last thing needed. The four of them joined the long line of people standing outside the chapel. There was a warmth in the sun. It seemed to mock the nature of the day.

'We can stand in the foyer, if needs be.' Alison clicked her heels together. 'These services are never that long.'

Tina moved slightly ahead of them, poking at the screen of her phone. Then the crowd fell silent.

Three dark blue Daimlers crawled past and stopped at the entrance to the chapel. Cassie let her gaze rest on the middle car. A man, sharply dressed in dark grey, stepped out, then held the door. Denise followed, blonde head down and shaking out her coat. Other people emerged from the third car, and followed the lifted coffin into the chapel.

Inside the hush of the main room, Cassie managed to find a seat alongside Alison. She was flicking through the order of service when Cassie sat down.

'All right?' A smile that seemed genuine.

Becky slid in beside them, and Tina took an empty space just in front.

Throughout the service, as tales were told of Denise's mother, Cassie watched Tina's back. She remembered the moment when the woman had issued her first threat. It had been a warning to others that they should be careful around Cassie. Why had she done that? Then there'd been the constant spitting and snarling, the pointed ignorance, and these fresh threats that Cassie would be thrown out of her job. This woman certainly hated her.

Cassie shuddered. Could she be in actual danger? Surely not. She thought about her own family. How would her girls cope if she suddenly wasn't there? And what about Si? She pictured him rattling around in Blackthorn without her. Then shook away the thought, and tried to focus as the pastor read the service.

In My Father's house are many mansions. If it were not so, I would have told you. I go to prepare a place for you.

Something about those words snatched at Cassie's breath. Her eyes darted to the doorway. Closed. Alison shifted in her seat. In front of her, Tina, head down, plucked at a wad of tissue. Cassie felt the muscles of her neck and jaw tighten. She dragged air in through her nostrils and pushed it away through puckered lips.

'Are you okay?' Becky glanced sideways.

But Cassie had to get out. She slid her hands across her thighs and rocked forward slightly. Then looked at the door again. Before her rational brain could react, she got to her feet and knocked against Becky's knees in an effort to get to the aisle. Without a backward glance, she made her way to the door and wrenched it open, desperate for escape. Then stumbled outside, ignoring the flashes of concern from two men in dark suits who seemed to be standing guard.

Becky was just behind her, running a hand across her shoulder and guiding her to a wooden bench at the side of the building. There were hushed offerings of help and orders to take deep breaths, but Cassie couldn't respond. She sat down and put her face in her hands, willing the world to not be there when she looked up again.

But there it was, with Alison's scowl and Tina's melting make-up and a whisper that they would go to Denise's house to show their faces. Cassie's stomach flipped over. Tina Armstrong could make her feel like an offcomer with just one glance. And now she was going to have to watch her fawning over Denise.

Denise's house was a large terrace, not far from the centre of town. The smell of coffee filtered out from the hall as the four of them made their way inside. Every door was open, showing high-ceilinged rooms and groups of people, balancing plates and, it seemed to Cassie, fraudulent smiles.

'You go and get yourself a cuppa, poppet. I need to find a lavvy,' Becky whispered to her. 'I'll be back in a mo.' She winked.

'Will do.' She watched Tina walk into a room on the left. Alison followed. Cassie needed to put some distance between herself and Tina Armstrong. She stepped towards what she thought might be the kitchen. It ran across the back of the house, and was stylishly modern, all chrome and black granite.

Denise was standing at the sink, a green floral pinny thrown over her black dress.

She turned as Cassie walked in.

'Oh. Hello. Thanks for coming.' There was a slight smudge of black under each of her eyes. 'I'm just trying to keep busy. Feeding everyone.'

'So sorry about your mum.' Cassie stepped towards her, not sure if there would be a hug.

'Thank you. I don't think it's hit me yet.' She slid her arms loosely around Cassie's shoulders, then let her go again. 'Dad hasn't said much, either. I'm worried about him.'

'Poor guy. Had they been together for a long time?'

'Almost forty years.' A pause. 'I've asked him to move in with us. He won't cope on his own.'

Cassie let her gaze travel around the huge kitchen. 'You've got loads of room here, haven't you? Will he want to move in, do you think?'

'I'm not sure he knows what he wants, at the moment. But I'll have to give up work, if he decides to come here. I can't move him in, then disappear off every day. That wouldn't be fair.'

'No, I guess not. Could you afford to stop working?'

'I could.' Denise sighed. 'Don's job would keep us going. And I wanted to get away from Parkhouse, anyway. I think I've told you that before.' She bit down on her bottom lip. 'Haven't I?'

'You did mention it. But we never talked much, did we?'
Might as well bring it up.

'No.' Denise grabbed at a tea towel and dried her hands. 'And that's one of the reasons I can't work there anymore.'

'What do you mean?'

'Her.' She flicked her gaze into the distance. 'Tina. Something's not right with her. She helped me a lot when I first started the job. I thought she was a lovely, kind woman. Then I realised she wasn't like that with everyone, though she always had her reasons. And I believed them. But I can't do the things she says anymore.'

'Like what?' Cassie's heart jumped against her ribs. What was this?

'Like telling me how I should lose a bit of weight. Like making me feel guilty if I've brought in a hefty lunch. Bringing me glasses of water and hot lemon. Saying it'd fill me up, and I could skip lunch and save calories.'

'I can't believe it. Your food intake is none of her business.'

'There were other things, too. She started to comment on the clothes I wore. You know. For the office. Saying there was a dress code. One time, when we were both wearing a burgundy-coloured blouse, she suggested we communicated about choice of clothing for the day. Texted each other or something, so we didn't clash.'

Cassie let out a loud snort. 'I hope you told her what you thought.'

'I didn't. Because, well, I saw what she could be like, when someone crossed her. She was livid when Laura didn't get the deputy's job. And I mean livid.' They were interrupted by the click of heels against wood.

'Denise. You poor thing.' Tina Armstrong.

The heels moved closer, then Cassie felt herself nudged out of the way, as Denise was sucked into a cloud of Black Opium. Alison was just behind, holding an empty glass.

'How are you?' Alison's outstretched arms.

Cassie's gaze slid momentarily over Tina and Denise, locked in an embrace. Then she stepped past Alison and out of the room.

In the lounge, a mismatch of wooden chairs and stools had been placed in every space between sofas and armchairs. Most were filled with people, Sunday-best covered in pastry crumbs, and holding conversations that would be deemed respectful.

Cassie didn't know any of them. She found an empty chair and smiled at anyone who met her eye. But her thoughts were firmly fixed on Denise's words. In them, hidden away between the ridiculous notions that women sometimes had, was the implication that what Tina Armstrong wanted, she got.

Chapter Twenty-Two

Sixty faces peered up at the sandstone clock tower.

'It's almost fifty metres high, and one hundred and twenty-four years old. Not bad, eh.' Cassie was glad of the mellow October sunlight, but she was having to squint at every landmark, which wasn't helping her headache at all.

Cassie understood the phenomenon of school-trip anxiety, but was convinced hers was self-inflicted, brought on by the adrenaline shots her body had taken to doling out every time she left Blackthorn. Si had told her to make an appointment with her doctor, that she was likely to be suffering from too much stress, but Cassie wasn't so sure. And she didn't want to take pills anyway. *Tranquillisers, or some such nonsense,* she thought. *I'd be laughed out of the surgery if a doctor looked at me.*

'The sandstone used to build it came from round here, too. Up by the hospital. Near my house. There's a quarry up there.' She caught the eye of a long-limbed boy with dark hair. 'You've been there, Michael, haven't you?'

He gave the tiniest lift of his head. They both knew he'd recently been brought home by the local police because he'd been climbing on the prohibited site. Jax glanced at her. Michael wasn't proving to be as problematic as Iain McIntyre. She held the red-haired boy's hand tightly, but his attention was fixed firmly on a man walking towards them, with a Staffordshire Bull Terrier on a leash and muzzled. Kevin Noble flashed a look at Cassie, a subtle tilt of his head towards their destination.

'We'd better keep going,' she told the children, 'or we won't even get there by lunchtime.'

'Yay! Lunch. C'mon, kiddos.' Joe Smythe, dressed for warmth in a bobble-hat and fleecy jacket, led them away again, with Cassie and another teaching assistant bringing up the rear. Having Joe back in their team was proving to be a huge asset. He had energy, and foresight. He'd prepped the risk assessment for this local trip and collected together everything they'd need to keep the children interested.

Cassie let her mind wander back to last winter, when she'd taken the previous year six children to Kendal for skiing, with Judy Barker who'd been more interested in getting into Nobbs's pants than she had been in keeping children safe.

Thank God that's over. Thank God for Joe.

They were heading to a local museum, built over one of the original graving docks, from a time when the town functioned as a port. Now, its biggest employer was an aeronautical firm, where the controversial nuclear-submarine-building programme was in full swing. Which meant money invested into a reclamation project for the old docklands, including the museum and quite a few miles of pathways and gardens running right along the edge of the town, and taking in coastal views of Walney Island, and its natural and local history.

'Smell that,' breathed Joe, as they arrived at the museum. 'Sea air. Fill your lungs, kids. Ten deep breaths before we walk any further.' Sixty pairs of eyes fixed on him as he led the deep-breathing exercise.

Cassie looked out across the water. The silver glitter of sunshine spread across its blue-grey surface, and a pair of herring gulls laughed down at them all. A man dressed in navy-blue, hair pulled tightly back in a ponytail, waved out a greeting and introduced himself as Gary. They were in for a treat, he said. Inside the warmth of the museum, the children fell into a hush without it needing to be mentioned, though sideways glares from silver-haired members of the public, helped.

'You can leave your bags and coats in here.' Gary pulled at a huge set of sliding doors. 'And you can eat lunch here, too.' He smiled at Cassie. 'Is that okay?'

'Great,' she told him. 'But can we have lunch now, then we can have our tours and a bit of fun outside. We'll have to be gone by half two.' She grinned sheepishly. 'Sorry.'

Gary laughed. 'I was a teacher, once,' he said. 'It's all go, isn't it?' He stepped away from the doors. 'I'll leave you to it. Shall we say twenty minutes?'

'Oh, you remember lunchtimes, then.' Cassie knew a few sandwiches and a drink would never last more than ten to fifteen minutes. But she could stretch it to twenty, with Joe's help. 'Thanks. See you soon.'

Kevin and Joe were settling the children on chairs and the floor, while Jax tussled with those who needed a more direct approach. Rucksacks were unzipped and the brown paper bags of free school pack-ups were doled out.

The children ate in sociable silence, sharing crisps and swapping bananas for apples. Cassie wandered amongst them, drinking bitter-tasting tea from the plastic cup of her thermos flask. She could never eat on school trips, preferring to keep topped up with cups of sugary tea and a few boiled sweets.

And today, her stomach was more knotted than usual. But everything seemed to be running smoothly, thanks to her staff, who were busily hoovering every scrap of leftover packed lunch into their mouths.

'Finished, miss. Can I go to the toilet?' Kaci Brown. First at everything. No depth, just speed.

'I'll take you,' groaned Cassie. 'Anyone else?'

The toilet run took the rest of Gary's twenty minutes, and the last sandwich-muncher was just finishing when he returned, sleeves pushed up and ready for action. His tattooed forearms attracted immediate attention, and Cassie winked at him when these became the first part of his story. She'd heard it many times before. It was all part of the town tour he was about to give.

By two o'clock most children were at the end of their reserve of listening politely. Some had more than others. Kevin and Joe were switching off, too, whereas she could have listened to local history and examined artefacts for the rest of the day.

'Time for some running along the walkway, then the park, Mr Noble?'

Kevin grinned. The grin of someone who had found an open gate after being locked in for so long. 'Yes, please.'

Gary picked up the vibe, too. He fast-tracked to his funny finishing story about Sir James Ramsden, one of the founding fathers of the town, being a model for The Fat Controller. The children howled with grateful laughter, and Cassie led the applause.

'And you can leave your coats and bags in the studio while you enjoy your run about,' he said. 'Okay with you, teachers?'

Cassie nodded her agreement. An unfettered run along the coastal pathway would pick up energy levels for the long walk home.

'You take your phone, Whites, and I'll grab the first-aid kits for me and Jax.' Kevin moved ahead of them, eagerness in every step. The children followed, all elbows and stepping on the backs of each other's trainers. The museum was a wonderful resource, informative and stunning in its design, but young minds needed a blast of action in between learning, and now was the time.

Outside, the tide was up, sending a slap of sharp spumy air onto hot faces. Energy was restored and Kevin led the charge of children as they jogged along the paved walkway leading to the play area. The museum faded into the distance, as the landscape changed. A mile of sea, sky and open views, straight up to the western fells of Cumbria. Free of coats and bags, the children flew, but Kevin and Joe were faster. Cassie and Jax brought up the rear, with Iain McIntyre, still handfasted, and some of the children who were unable to keep pace.

Suddenly, the pack stopped. The shout went up. More of a scream. Cassie left Jax and her mob and sprinted towards the middle of the line, noticing that Kevin was doing the same. The children were eerily quiet. Sixty of them, and not a sound but the screech of gulls and one voice, crying loud and clear.

Cassie got there first. A child, a small girl with a long blonde braid and a pink anorak, had fallen over and was lying, front down, her hand to her head.

'Lexi.' Cassie knelt beside her. 'Lexi, what's happened. Let me have a look.'

Blood seeped between the child's thin fingers. Then the crying stopped. Kevin arrived. 'Don't you look, Mrs Clifton. You know what you're like with blood.'

She stepped back, moving the children towards Joe, who was getting them into a line, quietly commanding.

Kevin knelt by the side of the now dazed Lexi and began talking to her. Cassie watched him lift her hand away from her forehead, watched him blanch as he looked at the injury.

'You telephone for an ambulance, Mrs C,' he said, low and

calm, their code for panic, 'then phone school and get them to tell Lexi's parents to meet us at A and E. Okay?'

Joe and Jax were moving the other children away, keeping their backs to where Lexi lay. Cassie fumbled for her phone and made the first call.

'Ambulance on its way, Mr Noble,' she told him, when she'd finished. He had unpacked a wadded bandage and was applying it to Lexi's head, holding it firm, and talking, his face close to hers. 'I'll phone school now.'

She punched in the number and waited. And waited. Disconnected herself and tried again. Nothing.

'They're not answering, Mr Noble. No answer.'

She looked across to where Joe and Jax stood, talking to the children, and using any distraction they could think of.

'Did either of you bring your phone?'

Jax shook her head and Joe patted his pockets for a moment, then did the same.

'You've just used yours. What's wrong?' He frowned. 'Give it here.'

As though Cassie was somehow not able to make a simple call. But she handed it over. Joe couldn't get an answer either. A siren wailed, close by. Cassie's heart was thundering in her chest. They needed to contact Lexi's parents. Not only protocol, but a necessity, should anything surgical be needed. *In loco parentis* was all very well, but she'd rather not be the one to invoke it. Nor would she want to put that onto Kevin.

'Shall I run back to the museum and phone from there?' suggested Joe. 'See if I can get through. Will you be all right?'

'Thanks, Mr Smythe.' Cassie wanted to kiss him. 'We'll be fine. Won't we, kids?' There was a subdued gasp of agreement. 'Let's all wave to Mr Smythe. See how long it takes for him to get there.' Cassie's stomach was threatening to come up through her mouth and create further problems. But it wasn't Lexi and her blood. It was the thought that Tina Armstrong had deliberately chosen to ignore her phone call. Surely not. But Cassie knew. And she was going to find out the truth at some point. For now, she could see two paramedics making their way along the path. Lexi was sitting up, laughing with Kevin, an outsized pad of cotton wool pressed against her small head.

The paramedics wanted to take the child to hospital. The wound needed stitching and possibly an X-ray.

'I'll go with her,' said Kevin, relief relaxing his face again. 'You get the others back. Hopefully Smiggy will have got through to school.' Then he lifted Lexi and walked away with the paramedics. Cassie and Jax rallied the children.

Joe appeared when they were almost back at the museum. 'I got through to school on my phone, no problem,' he called as he came out to meet them. 'Lexi's mum is going straight to the hospital. Mrs Armstrong got in touch with her; I take it that's where they've gone?'

Cassie nodded. 'She was very brave.' Then louder. 'But these others have been brave, too. Treats all round tomorrow, I think.' She put her arms around the nearest children. A small cheer went up. 'Time to go.'

The journey home flashed by in a collage of cranes, sandstone buildings and heavy delivery lorries. Cassie ran up and down the long line of children, chasing stragglers and applying brakes to the kids at the front. She put herself in the way of traffic as they crossed roads, and held her jaw in a rigid smile. But Joe saw. And he knew. His offerings of distracting anecdotes were kind, and Cassie clung to them as best she could, though all she wanted was to be home.

Later, when the accident forms had been filed, and the angst of the day had been reduced to the simplicity of aching muscles and a migraine, Cassie sat with Alison in her classroom.

'I don't know how you keep up with everything, Cass.' She sighed. 'I had to man the office while Tina had an early lunch. She was back by noon, but just being away from my desk for that hour has set me back by about a day, I think.' She ran a hand across her forehead. 'We'll have to look at replacing Denise with a temp. Just until she decides what she's doing.'

'Can you not just shut the office for an hour. When Tina's not there? She could put calls through to your phone. And if anyone came to reception, I'm sure they'd ring.'

But Alison was shaking her head. 'Oh, no, no, no. Tina wouldn't be having that. You know what she's like. She won't even go to the loo and leave her empire unattended. As I said, we need to find a temp.'

Cassie knew exactly what Tina was like. Though she doubted Alison did. There was a very fine line between being conscientious and being a control freak.

Alison stood up. 'I'll let you get off home.' She glanced at the clock. 'And, Cassie—'

'What?'

'Don't give me anymore heart attacks.'

'I'll try not to.'

Once Alison had gone, Cassie picked up her own phone, and walked along the corridor to the office and reception area. If Tina was still there, she would ask her about the call. Not that she'd get an answer. But it was late. The office was empty, though the aroma of Black Opium lingered.

She closed the door quietly and sat down in front of the main landline telephone. Then rang the number, just as she had earlier. The desk phone began to ring immediately. And *Cassie Clifton* flashed up in black letters on the olive-coloured digital screen.

October 2019

Freddy is silent. The evening has closed in on us now, and the lounge is dark. Only firelight allows me to see him. I watch his face and feel like there's been a shift in his understanding. He slaps his hands against his thighs. The sound startles me.

'You must have gone to your boss about that,' he whispers. 'Tell me you did.'

'Yep,' I reply. 'But Alison was more bothered about Lexi and her fall, than anything else. I told her I'd tried to telephone the school. I don't think it registered. Or she didn't want to know.'

'And Denise Kelly's comments. I guess you kept those to yourself, too?'

'Look, Freddy,' I say, exasperated, 'I was supposed to be on Alison's side of the desk. She took me on for just that reason. I was already feeling like a shit manager, as it was.'

He shakes his head and watches as I get to my feet. It's getting late. Time for him to go home. And I need a lie-down.

'I didn't appreciate being dragged out into the street earlier,' I grumble. 'That isn't why my husband asked you to help. I don't need immersion therapy. Like those babies that are thrown into the swimming pool, so they learn to swim.' But my lips twitch. Then turn upwards. I'm not angry, just wrung out.

'Hey.' He points his index fingers at me. 'There was no dragging involved.'

I let out a small exhale.

'There wasn't,' he protests, 'and anyway, you did it. Walked out, I mean. You had success.'

'Call that success?' I snap back. 'I had... I had a—'

'Panic attack. Say it, Cassie. That's all it was. Nothing bad.

Not a wrap of speed or a shag with a man you don't know.' His face has taken on a different quality, the expression lit up with something elusive. Intelligence? Knowledge? He's in charge, that's for sure. And I'm not used to it. I control me.

'All right,' I say. 'A panic attack. And I've had plenty. Had one on the way home after the head injury incident actually, because I was so annoyed with Tina *pigging* Armstrong.'

He makes no move to stand up from the sofa. 'No fucking wonder you've got a form of PTSD. You can't ruin your life out of sheer politeness.'

Did he just say PTSD? I have to think about this for a moment. I'm a nobody. I haven't fought battles or saved lives or chased armed criminals. What is he talking about?

'I admit I was in a pretty dark place by then, wasn't enjoying my work, always watching what other people were doing. Especially Tina Armstrong.' I hesitate. 'And before you tell me again that I should have talked about it; I did.'

Freddy's mouth forms the shape of an O. But he says nothing.

'I spoke to Joe. Well, he asked. About the phone call. And I told him the whole Judy Barker and Tina thing. Unprofessional, I know. But I did.'

In my mind's eye, I can see myself as I was, after that visit to the museum, taut as a guitar string, just before it snaps. Joe had offered to be with me when I went to Alison with a formal complaint, but in the end, I couldn't do it; either way, I knew the string was about to break.

Freddy does stand up now. He moves towards the fire and throws on two more logs. 'For Christ's sake, stop apologising for everything. Who cares what's professional or unprofessional? This was bullying, Cassie. Something had to give.'

'Bullying is what children do to each other. Nasty. But pretty simple.' I don't even like the word. *Bully.* It conjures up images of comic-strip boys in stripy jumpers, looming over their puny peers in some epic way. Whatever Tina Armstrong was doing was invisible and corrosive and extraordinarily complex.

'There's need for a better word, I'll give you that,' Freddy says, 'but in the absence of it, *bullying* works as a label for people to understand.'

I sigh. 'Having a label wouldn't have helped me. Or Becky or Joe or Denise. Now, can we just leave it? Want a last cup of tea before you get off?'

'Go on then.'

He follows me out to the kitchen.

We both stand, socks on the cold floor, listening for the kettle. The garden is in grey twilight. One star is twinkling its way across the early evening. There will be more later. I stand and look at this view often. Wish I could just go out there and experience it more fully, let the night-time soak in, make me real again.

Suddenly, Freddy clicks off the kettle. 'Let's walk around the block again. Come on. No thinking. No boots.'

He takes hold of my hand. His is cold. And I do think. I think of that star. The soak of evening. The sharp grey air. The wet grass, icy water and moss, creeping up into my socks. The shadowy trees. My fast breathing. The gate. Freddy's shoulders, the dreadlocks, ropes of darkness now. The hard surface of the street. The terrible thud of my heart, but thrilling too; the gothic streetlamps outside Blackthorn, the pools of silvery cold light on the pavement, the mock of the woods, and finally the welcome of my front door. I have done it again. There is less panic. It feels diffused, somehow.

'Now we'll have tea,' I laugh, pushing into the hallway. 'But take off your socks. Put them on the radiator.' I tilt my head towards the metallic monstrosity in the corner. 'It'll come on eventually.'

We are leaving wet footprints on the floor tiles. Similar sizes and similar shapes. Freddy really is a small man. I am having the usual rush of adrenaline. But it is lifting me up. I can still feel the night air on my cheeks.

'By Christmas of that year,' I say suddenly, 'Tina Armstrong had me in a head lock. Metaphorically, that is.' I find I want to tell him how bad things got. Now I'm finally realising they were bad.

'Hit me,' he says.

Chapter Twenty-Three

Laura Pearson was in the staffroom when Cassie went to put her lunch in the fridge. The weather had taken a wintry turn. Ice crystals covered the drive and garden walls of Blackthorn House, and the roads twinkled with a diamond frost. Staff had reverted to sweaters and boots, and even Laura had ditched her usual smart suit, replacing it with a thick cardigan and roll-necked layers.

She was leaning across the easy chairs and pinning something onto the noticeboard.

'Morning. It's a chilly one.' Cassie peered over Laura's shoulder. A poster. With holly leaves, and a snowman wearing a red-and-white Nordic jumper.

'Morning.' Laura let out a heavy breath as she pressed down on the corners of the poster, then, 'Excuse me.'

Cassie stepped sideways. However much she tried to square things with the woman, dislike radiated from her, icy and jagged. Laura pushed herself away and disappeared. Cassie leaned towards the poster, and the bottom dropped out of her world.

Bring Judy back for Christmas! read the headline.

Underneath were details of a party at a local hotel. With Judy Barker as the special guest. Everybody was invited; wearing a Christmas jumper was a necessity. And there was a special grid for people to sign up for the event, a column to tick when they'd paid their £30 fee. From what she could make out, Judy was coming back home for Christmas, the perfect chance to meet up.

A shockwave of emotion flooded Cassie's body. Her heart jumped. She clutched at her chest, wondering if she was going to faint. This felt like an attack, yet she was standing in a room by herself, with only a piece of paper for company.

Two names were already on the grid: Tina Armstrong and Laura Pearson. In Tina's tiny squared-off handwriting, with a jaunty tick that held so much mockery.

Cassie backed away, tried to steady herself and think. Here was a party she couldn't attend. It was as though the whole thing had been carefully orchestrated to exclude her, yet she was going to have to watch as people signed up for it and listen as it was discussed. She checked the poster again. The tenth of December. Three weeks of watching and listening. She wanted to tear it down, to rip it into hundreds of pieces and tip them over Tina Armstrong's head. But how could she?

A poster for the Christmas party went up every year. She wouldn't be allowed to object to this one, even though it was breaking her heart. Most of her colleagues would think nothing more of it than a party to herald the end of term.

To Cassie, it would feel like every person who signed their name on that list was somehow making a move against her. Perhaps she should add her own name. If the poster was on general view, it wasn't meant to exclude her, surely. But at this moment she felt as excluded as if Tina Armstrong had handed out an invite to every colleague except her.

The staffroom door opened. Two of the infant-department

teachers came in and saw the poster. A low rumble of voices and laughter.

'Hey, Cassie,' one of them called. 'Can husbands come to this?' She tilted her head at the noticeboard. 'Or partners, I should say.'

Cassie turned to face them. 'Not sure,' was all she could manage.

Don't sign up. Please, don't sign up.

But it was already done. Two more names on the list. And these colleagues can hardly have registered Judy Barker's existence. To Cassie, they felt like traitors.

Joe came in, all soft wool sweater and neatly pressed slacks. 'Hi,' he called. 'Cass?'

'Hello.' Cassie wanted to escape.

'What are we looking at?' He watched as the other staff members wandered away, then craned towards the noticeboard. 'Ha.' He turned to Cassie. 'Won't be going to that.' A sardonic grin. 'Not for you, either, I guess?'

'I just want to tear the bloody poster down. Or maybe go and punch Tina Armstrong's lights out.'

Joe shook his head. A sly grin spread across his lips. 'You and me both. But you know we wouldn't do it. However fucking annoying she's becoming.'

'I'm sorry, Joe,' Cassie said. 'I shouldn't be talking like that. She's not been at you again, has she?'

Joe tilted his head towards the kitchen area. 'I'm just going to get a coffee.'

Cassie followed.

'The weird thing is,' he whispered, under the sound of the kettle filling, 'she's being nice to me. It's creepy.'

'Nice? Are you kidding?'

'Honestly.' Joe leaned his elbow on the worktop. 'She even offered to do my register numbers the other day.' He pushed his tongue into his cheek. 'No one gets that, do they?'

'No,' muttered Cassie, 'they don't. Can I ask you something?' She glanced through to the staffroom. It was empty now. 'Do you really think she and Mick had something going on?'

'I don't *think*, I know. I liked Mick, and we used to talk, sometimes. About cycling and skating and stuff. He told me his marriage was struggling. Fragile, he called it.'

'Oh?'

'Yeah. I had a feeling he wanted rid of Becky.' He stirred his coffee. 'Why would anyone want rid of Becky. She's ace.'

'She is.'

The staffroom door opened again.

'There you are, Smiggy. And Whites. You hiding, or what?' Kevin Noble. In shirt sleeves, despite the weather. He stood with his hands in his pockets, and peered at the noticeboard, then let out a low whistle. 'Nice.'

'You'll be going to that, Kev, won't you?' Joe laughed softly. 'You love a Christmas jumper.'

'Will not. Neither will Whites.'

Cassie shook her head. Tears were scratching at the rims of her eyes. She didn't want an audience when they overflowed. 'You're right I won't. See you in a bit.'

She fled towards the nearest washroom. Once inside, she locked the door and leaned against it. What was happening to her? This was simply a poster about the staff Christmas party, yet it had grown teeth and was snarling from the noticeboard. She turned on the cold tap and water splashed into the sink, splattering the mirror while she patted it onto her cheeks and forehead. The cool shock was distraction enough to give her some breathing space.

While she dabbed herself dry with a paper towel, Cassie looked at her reflection. Here was a person she hardly knew. She had to get her control back. This was only her job, her workplace; it wasn't family. That had been her advice to Joe.

Why was it so hard to believe it herself? She breathed deeply for a few moments, then unlocked the door and made her way back to the classroom.

Through the window, she could see groups of children dragging along the pavement. Most wore coats and hats and leaned into their groups of friends. There were smiles and icy puffs of laughter. She thought about Helli and Janey, walking to school with Si, sliding across the glittering pavements and looking forward to the day. Where had her own feelings of optimism gone? Where was the lurch of freedom that came from a splash of blue sky, or the smell of frosty earth?

She had little choice but to keep going, to ignore the screaming and raging inside her head, to present a calm and measured face to her colleagues. But inside, she was dying, sinking, drowning. And here was Jax, smiling at her from the doorway, a piece of toast from Breakfast Club halfway between her hand and her mouth.

'Morning,' she said through a mumble of crumbs and butter. 'Cold weather makes me starving.' She narrowed her eyes at Cassie. 'Are you okay?'

'No, but I will be.'

'Hey. Tell Aunty Jax.' She sat on the edge of a table, brushing crumbs from her skirt. 'Actually, I think I might know.'

Cassie glared. 'Oh?'

'Just seen that poster, haven't I.' Jax patted the corners of her mouth. 'Bloody Judy Barker. What do we want her back for? Ireland can keep her, that's what I say. Plenty of dumb men there.'

'Mrs T, you're a terrible person.' But Cassie was chuckling, despite herself. 'That's a former colleague you're talking about.'

Jax harrumphed. 'Don't care. Let's have our own Christmas party. Select guests only.'

If that were possible, Cassie would gladly organise it. But she was a manager, someone who was supposed to be impartial and equitable. Her only option was to laugh in the face of everything weighing her down.

'Come on, Mrs Clifton,' Jax was saying, 'we'd better get on with things. The kids will be here in just over half an hour, and there's not a pot washed.'

They fell into their familiar routine. Setting up exercise books, photocopying, piling up resources on tables, making the classroom warm and bright and ready for the energy the children always brought. Cassie was glad of the distraction, but for the rest of the day, she didn't dare go back into the staffroom, dreading the sight of the party list, overflowing with the names of her colleagues and friends.

In the weeks that followed, an almost constant migraine hammered away from the base of Cassie's skull to the front, and she lost her ability to sleep. Nights would be spent walking through the rooms of Blackthorn, peering in at her daughters and trying not to wake Si. And daytime was worse. Her head heavy with worry, she would crawl through the endless hours, trying to pretend enthusiasm for the burgeoning Christmas festivities that grew and grew in every school at this time of year, fuelled by childish energy and a few snowy mornings.

Iain McIntyre, astute as any child used to having things exactly their way, was alert to the change in his teacher's focus. Both she and Jax had to nag him relentlessly, yet he'd still managed to throw a handful of Lego into another child's face and tip a carton of milk over the keyboard of Cassie's laptop. And there was still a week before the end of the term.

By the time the weekend of the party came around, Cassie was wandering around school in a daze of back pain and adrenaline. Most of her colleagues had signed up. Apart from Jax and Joe, and Kevin. For that she was thankful.

Christmas jumpers were discussed at length, though most staff, she suspected, hadn't even realised Judy Barker would be there. That had been engineered specifically, by Tina Armstrong and Laura Pearson, to bring Cassie to her knees. And it was working.

Things got worse as the week progressed. Both Jax and Joe found themselves the subject of Tina Armstrong's cajoling to sign up for the party; sometimes when Cassie was in the room with them. In the end, Jax had snarled at Tina, telling her exactly what she thought. That had been reported to Alison straight away, and the teaching assistant had been reprimanded for her unpleasant language.

It was the final straw for Cassie. She'd asked Alison for some time to discuss a few things. Her answer had come, in the form of a huff of air and a scratch of scalp, but she'd stood her ground. Insisting, against the millions of words in her head telling her she was becoming paltry, on a meeting.

'I want to talk about this Christmas party,' Cassie told her boss, when they finally managed some time together. 'The one Tina Armstrong is taking great delight in organising.'

An artificial tree, aggressively silver, stood on the coffee table between them. It was covered in cardboard decorations scribbled with holly and reindeer, and all manner of strange-looking angels.

Alison sighed. 'Like I haven't had enough of Christmas, Cass.' She put her head in her hands. Grey root growth showed through her brassy hair. Every bit of anger Cassie felt, every one of her sleepless nights, became tangled with sympathy, so that the story flipped in her head.

But she wasn't going to be deterred.

'I don't like the way Judy Barker is being promoted.

Especially with this party. It's being done to get at me, I know it is.' There. She'd said it, and how whiny it sounded.

Alison looked up. 'It's a bloody party, Cass. That's all. I can't tell my staff that they can or can't have parties.' She folded her arms. 'You're not going, anyway, are you?'

Cassie blinked. 'No, I'm not. But Tina is making damn sure everyone else is.'

'What are you saying?' Alison's nostrils flared.

'Judy Barker sent an awful text about me. I don't want her promoted in my workplace. That's what I'm saying.' Her last word escaped as a croak, making Alison frown.

'You're overtired.' She lowered her voice. 'You've had a lot on, this term. Let them have their party. Then it'll be over, and Judy will be back in Ireland.'

Her tone irritated. Cassie didn't want to be soothed.

'This party is being used as a tool to hurt me,' Cassie snapped. 'Jax and Joe don't want to go, but Tina has been chasing them, trying to make them change their mind. That's not a coincidence. Is it?'

Alison raised her brows. 'Don't talk to me like that, Cassie. We've all got things going on at the moment. Mine are a bit more pressing than a bloody Christmas party.'

'Fine.' Cassie jumped up. 'I'm alerting you to some social bullying in our workplace, and you're dismissing it, because it's me. The deputy head.' She stepped towards the door. 'Thanks for your support.' Then stomped out.

In the corridor, she passed Kevin Noble, heading home for the weekend. 'See ya,' he called.

She stormed past. Didn't want one word of kindness or concern because the floodgates would open.

'Whites? You okay?'

She kept walking. Marching. Charging. Her breath had gone, choked away by another adrenaline squeeze.

In her classroom, Jax was pulling on her coat. She turned as Cassie walked in.

'I'm getting off early, if that's all right, Cass. Picking Meggy up myself. I've hardly seen her lately.'

'Sure. I'm going now, too. I've had enough.'

'Are you all right? Did you see Alison?' Jax was a flurry of hands and care. 'Cassie?'

'I can't talk now.' Her voice crumbled. 'Sorry.'

She snatched up her coat and bag and fled. Pounded along the corridor. Crashed her shoulder into the coded door. Tried three times before she finally escaped, then jumped into her car and flew all the way to Blackthorn.

October 2019

When I got home that day, after asking for Alison's help, I was in a complete daze, gasping for breath and for words. Helli and Janey were already there, sprawled across the sofa, long navy-blue socks rolled down as far as their skirts were rolled up, mobile phones stealing priority from food and boys. The distraction of making them tea and getting them out of their uniforms and into Friday-night mode had calmed me down. I'd managed to eat and join them on the sofa for some TV and social media; their Facebook, and my reruns of *Morse*.

Later that week, when Janey had asked me why I wasn't at the party, I'd been confused. Until she showed me a photograph of three of my colleagues, happily posing in Christmas jumpers and paper hats. Though I was aware that teachers and teaching assistants had been advised to lock their Facebook profiles, obviously someone hadn't. I'd sent a message to Joe, who informed me that there were lots of photographs of the party. Stupidly, I'd begged him to give me his log in details. He could hardly refuse. And I'd spent the rest of that evening prowling about the Facebook profiles of my colleagues, looking at their party photographs and silly comments.

Some weren't so silly.

Tina and Laura had posted many photographs of themselves and Judy, embracing, fooling about, holding their thumbs up, with comments about the fun they were having, and their total joy at seeing Judy again. All for me, and as sharp as a knife, stabbing away at my fragile mental state. Those photos and the comments, the smiling faces of my colleagues, made me feel like I didn't exist. Made me wonder if I'd died, and this was someone's idea of hell, especially for me. I vowed, that night, never to go back to my school. Though, in the end, I did.

'Bloody mobile phones,' Freddy spits. 'I won't touch the things: they're toxic.'

'I agree... but try telling that to my daughters. Losing their phones is the only thing they seem to panic about.' I huff in a bitter way. 'They don't know what a real *panic attack* is like, do they.' The word flies out of my mouth and lands between my curled fingers.

He leans against the kitchen counter, one bare foot on top of the other.

'I didn't make up that name, Cassie,' he says. 'Why do you dislike it so much?'

I push back my hair. My scalp is tingling. 'Because I don't panic. I'm calm. Controlled. Well, that's what I thought I was.'

'Just the type of person to suffer from a panic disorder.' He glances at his watch. 'What time is your husband home?'

'Why?' I'm surprised at his question.

'I wanted to talk to you about hypnotherapy. Maybe try some.' He turns to face me. 'And don't look at me like that.'

I am smiling. 'Like what?'

'Like I am the quack you keep accusing me of being.' He walks towards the kitchen door. 'But, it'll keep. I'm coming back tomorrow, I presume?'

He walks into the hallway and lifts his socks from the radiator, sits down on the stairs and wriggles his feet into them.

'I have a man in my house, barefoot, and I know very little about him,' I say playfully. 'If you're coming back tomorrow, you have to tell me your story, as well.'

'If there's time, maybe. But you're the priority now.' He thinks for a moment. 'By the way, you do know that your boss was very wrong to dismiss your worries, don't you? She had a responsibility to you, to all her employees. Whatever stress she was under herself.'

'That's all very well,' I say, 'but it doesn't work in the real world of schools.' Of which he knows nothing.

'No, Cassie. Stop trying to explain things away,' he snaps at me. 'Sorry. But you've suffered acutely from what happened in your workplace. Are still suffering, actually.'

He lifts his coat from the line of pegs alongside the stairs, slips it over his shoulders, then bunches up the dreadlocks and pulls them from his collar. I wonder what his story is, wonder how he knows exactly the right things to do and the right words to use.

'Hey. You've got me around the block today. That's got to be progress, right?

'Right.' He gives me his hand. 'See you tomorrow, then.'

I hold on to him for just a moment longer than I need to. 'Bye.'

The evening air comes in as he opens Blackthorn's front door. Earthy and rich, and full of possibility. But not for me. I am wrung out. When the door closes again, I rest my head there for a moment. I haven't told him about my Facebook stalking; I'm too ashamed.

By the time I have tidied around the kitchen, Si arrives

home. He carries with him the scent of an autumn evening, ice and dying leaves. He takes off his cycle helmet and runs a hand through his flattened hair. 'Freddy gone?' he asks, looking over my shoulder, into the kitchen.

'Yes,' I tell him. He leans in to kiss my cheek. 'How's work been?'

'Work's work.' He begins to unzip his bright yellow cycling jacket. It crackles with energy. 'Has today been useful?'

That word. *Useful.* As though Freddy is a new ergonomic computer chair for my bad back. A wash of emotion hits me suddenly, making the tears flow and my shoulders shake.

'Hey,' Si says, putting his arms around me. 'If it's too much, I'll tell the guy not to bother. We don't want you going back to how you were.'

How I was? I want to scream. He has no idea how I was. From the outside, I looked like someone who was suffering from burnout. The fatigue, the tears, that was all real. But he couldn't see the burning, seething anger that was corroding my spirit. And the reason? I'd been told to rise above it. So, that's what I'd tried to do. I'd been told there was nothing to be done, so that's what I believed. And now, two years later, I want to wallow in it, I want people to know, I want something done.

'Sorry, Si, but I'm exactly the same as I was.' I can hear the pitch of my voice rising. For once, I just let it. 'What happened at Parkhouse, it shouldn't have happened. It wasn't me at fault, it was them.'

He tries to hug my tears away, but I tense my shoulders. Not this time. I don't want to be soothed. I'm bored of it, quite frankly.

'Cass,' he says, stepping away, 'I never thought it was your fault. You're the one who wanted to put it all behind you. I thought you did remarkably well, considering.'

'It's never been behind me. It's always been underneath

me, ready to ignite. I've been a Guy, on a bonfire. And Freddy's thrown in a lighted match.'

He shakes his head. 'That's it. I'm phoning him. Telling him not to bother, if he's upset you.' He picks up his backpack and starts rummaging around in one of the pockets.

'I've walked around the block today,' I say suddenly.

He stops rummaging. 'What?'

'I've gone out of the garden gate, walked along the back street, and onto the road. Then to the front door. Twice.'

He stretches his mouth. Frowns. Then smiles. 'Never?'

'Yep. And what's more, I'm going to do it again, with you. After tea.' I flutter my eyelashes, and he laughs. 'Might even go a bit further. Who knows?'

I somehow manage to get to the edge of the woods. I am clinging to Si's arm, but not fighting my panting breath. I am just letting it come. The sky is a deep violet-blue, wide open and full of stars. A twiggy silhouette creeps along the horizon. I won't go to the woods today, but I am close. My legs tremble, and a hand of sweat has formed across the back of my neck. But I allow those things and tell my husband all about them.

'I'm a bit shaky myself,' he says. 'Normal, after a hard day.'

Yes, it is. Normal. But the blackbird that darts across in front of us, drilling out his alarm call, that's not normal, that's wonderful. The scratch of cold air against my cheeks, that's far from my normal. But I love it. And my cloudy breath, hanging around me in rags, then floating away on the silvery light. That's just perfect.

I turn towards Blackthorn House; the place is calling me back. Tonight, I am able to resist its call, though my mouth has almost dried up with terror. The place has saved me, protected me, but also entrapped me. I have to free myself; I have to. So I keep Freddy and his advice in my mind's eye and only allow myself to *stroll* back home. The house tugs and twists at my guts, but I stroll.

And in the morning, when Freddy appears at my front door, I am ready for him.

'Something has happened to the weather,' I laugh, as I let him in. He is wearing an old-fashioned khaki mac. An oilskin, I think I've heard it called. Water pours from the hood and shoulders as he takes it off. I carry it through to the scullery. He follows me, boots in hand. I find a towel, and he rubs it across his face and the back of his neck. His dreadlocks have been pulled back into a bun today, with chunks escaping and sticking up like a set of feathers at the top of his head. We stare through the kitchen window, watching rivers of rain blur the view.

'You should have sent a message,' I tell him. 'Si could have picked you up.'

He rubs his hands together. 'It's fine. I'm not keen… erm, I mean, I like the rain. Could do with a cuppa, though.'

I haven't slept. After the three trips outside on the previous day, so much cortisol is sweeping around my system that I cannot relax. This is how I was, in the final days before I left Parkhouse, and for months afterwards. Insomnia became a frightening new presence in my life. It never leaves me, waiting in the wings to do its worst when anything unsettling happens.

'Kettle on, then. Coffee for me: I didn't sleep.'

'I thought you looked a bit ropey. No offence.' He forces a smile. 'I've had my share of insomnia, believe me. It's the enemy.'

I nod my agreement, fill up the kettle, leave a space to see if he says anything else.

He does. 'One of the reasons I studied hypnotherapy and guided meditation is because I was crippled in my late teens and early twenties, by not being able to sleep. It brought me to my knees, Cassie. I don't think people can appreciate how destructive it is if they haven't experienced it.'

'In your uni years, then?' I ask.

'In my uni years. And before them. I wasn't the happiest of young men. But I could step back from my misery and understand my own brain was causing a lot of it.' He pulls out a chair and sits himself down at the kitchen table. 'Enough about me, though.' He takes the tea I offer. 'I want to know what happened after that party. Was that when things came to a head?'

I sit down at the kitchen table. Exhale sharply. 'You could say that.'

Chapter Twenty-Four

DECEMBER 2016

The classroom felt as hollow as Cassie's stomach. Everything that usually resonated with her, the warmth and brightness despite the cold dark on the other side of the window, the cheerfully fake Christmas tree, Jax's collection of knitted nativity figures, it all caused pain. That she needed to see a doctor was blindingly obvious, and she'd argued with Si about it. Getting to the end of term was the only thing she could focus on. Inside the walls of Blackthorn, she could live with her low mood; at Parkhouse, it was killing her.

'There's a parent to see you, love.' Dot put her head around Cassie's classroom door. 'Tina asked me to come and get you.'

I bet she bloody did. 'Thanks, Dot. I'll come now.'

She followed the older woman out through the door and walked with her up the bright corridor.

'Have you heard my news?' Dot squared her shoulders. 'Eh?'

'No? What?' Cassie hardly had time to hear anyone's news in the last week. Not even her own.

'I'm retiring in February. About time, too.'

'Dot? You're never? How will we manage?' Cassie arranged her face into an expression that would show Dot her concern, but in truth, she couldn't feel anything, hadn't been able to, since the Judy Barker party and the Christmas joviality that followed. While Cassie had been struggling to put on a production, other staff had been gathered in little cliques enjoying the camaraderie that came with the festive season. Not one of them had asked how she was doing, and only Jax and Joe had offered any help.

'Look at that blessed tree,' Dot was saying. 'I don't know who you'll get to hoover the needles up, next year. But it won't be me.' She shoved her hands into the pockets of her blue tabard. 'I'd better clear them up. The kids will be here soon.'

'Thanks, Dot,' Cassie called after her, watching her trundle away. She was well past sixty-years-old. Why shouldn't she retire? But she would be a real loss. Like losing a parent.

In the reception area, a young woman waited, hair pulled into a high ponytail and frantically chewing gum. Her hands rested on a small pushchair.

'Hello,' said Cassie, opening the door. 'Did you want me?'

'Yeah.' More aggressive chewing. 'I'm Ethan's mam. Ethan Holland.'

Cassie hadn't met the woman, despite having the boy in her class for a term. Some parents never made contact, except to complain. Experience told her that complaining was exactly what this one was about to do. 'Oh. Hello. I should have guessed. You look just like him.'

'Yeah, well.' She hesitated. 'I want summat done about that new kid. Iain McIntyre. He's been making our Ethan's life a misery.'

Cassie held out her arm, aware of Tina Armstrong's halfway glance through the glass reception panel. And Laura Pearson's. They were huddled together, giggling about something on a phone in Laura's hand. Giggling, but listening.

'Do you want to come somewhere more private? The library, or my classroom?'

'No, I bloody don't.' The woman stared out through the open front doors. 'I've got to get this one to nursery.' She nodded towards the child in the pushchair. 'But our Ethan's getting bullied by this kid. And I want it stopped.'

'Don't worry,' Cassie said. Reassuring. 'I will look into it today, and ring you later. Is that okay?'

'It'll have to be,' she muttered, then she pushed her way out through the doors, calling her thanks in a way that left Cassie in no doubt they weren't intended. She would have to keep more of an eye on Iain McIntyre. He'd been pushed from class to class in the previous week, whilst dress rehearsals and communal singing had taken her attention.

As Cassie pulled the front doors closed and watched the parent bustle away in her beige parka and Ugg boots, she could hear the muffle of voices behind her. Two teaching assistants had joined the crowd in the reception area, perching on the edge of Tina's desk and snickering along.

Like a landfill site full of squawking gulls. And she was about to throw in an eagle. 'Off you go to your classes, ladies,' she called in through the office door, 'I'm going to ring the bell.'

Silence.

There had been no need to say it, but she couldn't resist. If they hated the management that much, best give them a tangible focus. Then she reached around to the electronic bell and pushed, kept her finger pressed down, let every bit of her anger flow into the jangle it caused. The corridors were soon filled with beaming, striding children. Coats and bags hung off their shoulders, and the excitement of Christmas flashed between them.

'Morning, miss.'

'Hiya, Mrs Clifton.'

'I liked the show, miss.'

And some of Cassie's anxiety dissolved in their collective joy.

In her classroom, Jax was laying out a morning task on each child's place. An idea that had been generated by the energy of seventeen boys bursting through the doors, and seventeen pairs of twitchy hands that needed to be occupied. Today, it was a very simple piece of origami, requiring small squares of red and green paper. But Ethan Holland was crying.

Cassie lifted his backpack gently away. 'Come and tell me what's wrong,' she whispered. 'Over here.' He let himself be led, just as Iain McIntyre burst through the door, laughing, and shoving another boy, who happily shoved back.

Ethan sobbed so violently that the other children looked like they might join him.

'I know what's wrong, miss.' George. Straight faced and even straighter natured. 'Iain's been slapping him around and saying horrible things.'

A few other children were listening in, tears forgotten now that there was the possibility of a scandal.

'Has he now?' snapped Cassie, looking across at the red-haired boy. A raise of her eyebrows, and she got a response.

'What?'

'Don't speak to me like that, Iain McIntyre. What's happened to Ethan?'

'Dunno.' The shoulder-shrug tipped Cassie over the edge.

'Well, you can wait outside until you do know. Out!'

Iain McIntyre gave a little huff and strutted back through the door. The children fell silent. Jax broke the tension with a loud rendition of 'Joy to the World', and they all laughed. But Cassie was surprised at how she'd gone from calm to full teacher anger in just a few seconds. It was the bullying. The bully.

'If you all get settled, Mrs T will sing the instructions for her Christmas puzzle while I sort out the registers.' This for the children as much as for her own sanity.

Jax tilted her head, pulled a wry smile. 'Just call me Mrs Claus.'

When she felt calm enough, Cassie put her head around the doorway and scanned the corridor for Iain. He was sitting on the floor, holding his head.

'Right,' she said, 'I want you in here, head down and working. And thinking about why Ethan was crying.'

The boy didn't move.

'Iain. I'm talking to you.' She stepped in front of him. 'Up.'

'Can't. I've got a migraine.' He lifted one eye towards her, kept the other hidden by his hand.

'You don't have a migraine. If I had a migraine, I wouldn't be able to have a go at anyone, or slap them, or call them names. I'd be lying down in a darkened room.'

'That's you. Not me.'

Cassie flipped again. 'Get up. Up.' She put her hands under his arms and lifted him. 'Into the classroom. Coat off and sit down. I'm not in the mood for this today.'

He wriggled out of her hands and stomped over to his table. She looked across at Ethan, raised her brows slightly. He smiled. Iain McIntyre did as he was told, but when he sat down, he swept a hand across his table and knocked all the paper, pens and scissors that had been laid out, onto the floor. Then his head went down, hidden by his linked arms.

Cassie picked up his resources and put them on another table. 'You can do your morning task at playtime,' she said coldly, then walked away.

The day didn't get any better. Twenty-two tired and over excited children in a hot room, then freed to mix with another 200, then locked down again: not ideal, but typical of the end of the Christmas term. Cassie and Jax did what they could to juggle the day and keep their class of children smiling. Iain

McIntyre recovered from his migraine enough to play football at breaktime, then play up for the lunchtime supervisors, leaving Cassie no choice but to send him out to work with Jax on his own. Which he didn't like, because she could be a hard taskmaster when she wanted to. But it meant that the rest of them had a lovely end of the afternoon, with even Ethan smiling.

'Ask your mum to pop in and see me after school, or in the morning,' she told him as he put on his coat, 'and we'll make sure she knows Iain McIntyre has had a telling off. And you need to tell me straight away if he starts anything else. Okay?'

'Yes, miss.'

'Bye, Ethan. See you in the morning.'

'Bye, miss.'

Jax brought Iain back in. Cassie sat on the edge of a table and waited, Eventually, he shuffled his way towards her.

'You, young man, need to think about what you're saying to other people. And how you're treating them. I won't have Ethan upset again. Do you understand?'

He looked at the floor, said nothing.

'Iain?'

Nothing.

She stared down at his small, gingery head, large ears standing proud. This one might be difficult to win. Change tack, that's what she usually did.

'Did you get any of the work done with Mrs T?' She glanced at Jax, who was sitting on a table nearby. 'Did he?'

'He's worked hard out there with me, Mrs Clifton. So, he *can* do it. And he made this.'

Jax held up a small origami box, half red and half green, neatly folded and precise. Iain lifted his face slightly.

'Wow,' exclaimed Cassie. 'It's one of the better ones. Some were a disaster.'

'Mine's the best,' mumbled Iain, craning to see the line of other boxes on the window ledge.

'Could be,' she told him. 'You can take it home if you want. Show your mum.'

He nodded lightly. 'Okay. Can I go now?'

'Go on.' Cassie grinned. Teaching was all about empathy, in her opinion. Some of her colleagues could do with learning a small slice of that, too.

'Bye, Iain,' called Jax, as the red-haired boy grabbed his coat and bag, and pushed his way out of the classroom.

'Now,' she breathed. 'Let's get cleared up. You wash the glue spreaders.'

'Cheeky. What am I? Your slave?'

'That's exactly what you are.'

Within an hour, Cassie and Jax had straightened up the classroom and laid out resources for the following day. They sat, side-by-side, talking about their own arrangements for Christmas, and their ideas for the spring term. Suddenly, Alison put her head around the door.

'Hiya, you two. Is all okay?'

Jax held her thumbs above her head, making Cassie laugh.

'Great. Not long to go now.' Alison smiled, but Cassie knew that look. An upturned mouth, a lying smile.

'Can I have a word, Cass. In my office.'

Cassie walked along beside her boss, trying to guess what new problem had arisen. There was a tiredness in Alison's expression, a mix of grey shadows and feverish flush, a taut jaw: every staff member looked the same at the end of Christmas term.

The classrooms were quiet. Some teachers sat at their desks, heads down over books, or peering at their mobile phones. Survival was key, in this last week. As were the small artificial trees with their overabundance of decorations that enlivened every shadowy corner. To come to work in darkness then arrive home again without having experienced more than a few minutes of daylight, gave Cassie a sense of disorientation not unlike jet lag. That, and the sinking sensation in her stomach every time she saw a huddle of colleagues she thought would be picking over her bones.

'I guess this is about Dot,' she said, as they walked into Alison's office. 'Hers will be hard shoes to fill, but we'll have to find someone, pronto.'

No response.

Alison pointed to the chair at the other side of her desk and flipped open a spiral-bound notebook. Cassie sat down and watched Alison's hands as she stroked the writing on the open page.

'This isn't about Dot. We've had a complaint.'

'What sort of complaint?' Cassie's heart performed a gigantic thud. Her stomach knotted, making her inhale sharply.

'Apparently, Iain McIntyre's parents came into reception after school. Ranting at Tina.'

Cassie couldn't speak. She stared as Alison scanned down the page.

'He told you he had a headache. You laughed? Said he couldn't have a headache if he was being naughty?' There was fury in her expression. 'Is this true?'

'That's not the context,' she replied, sifting through her thoughts for the actual event. 'I had a go at him for bullying Ethan Holland, and he didn't like it. He must have gone straight out of school tonight and told his parents what I'd said. But he is an arch manipulator, as we all know.'

Alison returned to her notes. 'Then, you sent him out. A kid who's just told you he wasn't well?'

'Why are you reading from that page,' Cassie cried. 'Haven't you spoken to the parents?' It was as though she was in a courtroom and her offences were being listed.

'Don't take that tone with me,' Alison snapped angrily. 'Tina was completely shaken by their shouting. Writing everything down was the only thing she could do to calm them.'

'I bet,' muttered Cassie. Tina? What had she got to do with this?

'Did you say this stuff to the kid or not?'

'I did. Yes. But Jax was also there, as were the other children. They could all vouch for the context. But I guess you're not interested in that. Because *Tina said*.'

Alison's tongue was pushed into the front of her bottom lip. She was tapping her gelled nails up and down on the desk. 'Tina has made a fuck-up of this too, for your information.' She shook her head slowly. 'She's told the McIntyre parents they can go to OFSTED if they want to complain further about you.'

Cassie's shoulders slumped. Tears welled up and spilled. There was nothing she could do or say. Alison filled the heavy silence.

'They were demanding you were sacked, and she couldn't think of how to get rid of them. OFSTED sounded important, so she said it. And I get that. Poor woman was panic-stricken, there on her own with the McIntyre dad shouting at her. Have you seen him?'

'She was behind a bloody glass panel and a coded door.' Cassie's breath was threatening to choke her. 'She's said that on purpose.' She jumped up from her chair and put her hands on the edge of Alison's desk. 'Get her in here. Then we'll find out who's in the wrong.'

Alison stood up, closed the notebook, and ran her hands across her face. 'I'm not going to continue this conversation with you, Cass. Not when you're in this state. I know you've been going under for a while. It's probably why you snapped at young Iain. I've got the parents coming in to see me tomorrow.

I'm going to have Becky there, too. Hopefully, between us we'll be able to save you from any threats they are making.'

Cassie didn't wait. She pushed back the chair and dragged open the door. Heard it clunk shut. This had gone on long enough. And if Alison wasn't going to do anything about it, then she was on her own.

Tina was in her office, zipping herself into a black padded parka. She slid a glance towards Cassie, then lifted her handbag.

'I want a word.'

Tina twisted her lips but didn't respond.

'I said, I want a word.' Cassie stood in the doorway. Tina was going nowhere.

'And what *word* would that be?'

'You can quit that. You and I are going to have a conversation. And I'll start, shall I? Whatever you think I've done, I don't care. This nasty little victimisation plan of yours, it stops. Now.'

Tina slammed down her handbag. 'You don't get to tell me what to do. You're not my boss. You're not anybody's boss actually. And you're a crap deputy head.' She flicked her hair. 'Look what you did to poor Judy.'

'And what was that?'

'She had to leave a job she loved, because of you. The text wasn't even bad, was it? You just used it.'

Cassie folded her arms, waited.

'As soon as Judy showed an interest in Kev, you jumped on her, didn't you?' Tina's chin jutted forward. 'Jealous bitch.'

'That old story. Judy was just a pawn, wasn't she? Your end-game was me.' Cassie stepped towards her. 'You can't stand me. Because I got the deputy's job instead of your precious Laura.'

Something flickered across Tina's face. She blinked it away before Cassie could put a name to it.

'I can't stand you. You're right,' she hissed. 'But then, not many can.'

'In Tina's world, maybe not. And that's a crazy place, from what I've heard.' A pause. 'I know about your affair with Mick, by the way.'

Tina glanced across the reception area, towards the front door, but kept her lips pressed together.

Finally. She's having a think.

'Whether you like it or not,' Cassie continued, softer, though her legs were trembling. 'I am deputy head. So, we need to move on from this… situation. I'm prepared to. Are you?'

No answer.

'Tina? Shall we just agree to be politely indifferent? I'll keep out of your way if you can't stand the sight of me. And you leave me alone?'

'Blackmail.' Tina spat out the word. 'That's hilarious. Well, I've got news for you, Mrs Clifton. Everyone knew about me and Mick, including his wife. So, your little plan's failed.' Then she slid her handbag over her shoulder and pushed her way out of the room.

Cassie watched her totter through the front door and across the car park. Becky knew Tina and Mick were having an affair? That didn't make any sense. Why had she never mentioned it? But would she have, given Cassie's status as slightly more than a colleague but a bit less than a friend? Now, though, there was a bigger problem. The McIntyre's complaint. Whoever instigated it, there would be consequences. Unless she could prove there was no case to answer.

Back in the classroom, Jax was just turning off the lights.

'Oh, God. What's happened?' she said as Cassie ploughed past her.

'Please go and see Alison, Jax. Tell her about what

happened with Iain McIntyre today or I'm going to be in a lot of trouble.'

Jax held out her arms. 'I will. I will. But let me look after you first.'

'No. I have to get home.' Cassie backed away, searched for her handbag then grabbed her coat.

Jax watched from the doorway. She passed her a handful of tissues. 'Drive carefully,' she called.

Blackthorn House stood, as it always did, with its arms wide open in welcome. The lounge curtains weren't closed, and warm orange light shone out through the big bay window. Cassie could see Si moving about. He would be wearing his slippers and making the place comfortable for them all. The girls would be in their rooms, sprawled on their beds, immersed in their digital life. And the house would settle around them, stoic and elderly, elegant and protective. Tina Armstrong could go to hell.

Cassie climbed out of the car and slammed the door, walked up the drive and let herself in. Si came from the kitchen, bringing with him the smell of something cooking.

'Hi, my darling. You're early.' He leaned in for a kiss. He looked at Cassie's face and let out a small sigh. 'What's happened now?'

'Oh, sorry to be a burden,' she snapped, then burst into tears.

Si put his arms around her, though she fought against him, trying to push herself away.

'Stop,' he murmured, 'just stop.' And held her still. 'Something needs to give, Cass. That school is making you ill.' He led her into the kitchen and closed the door. Cassie sat at the table, sobbing into a tea towel, while he made her tea and sat beside her, waiting.

'I've had enough, Si,' she said finally. 'Parkhouse is killing me.'

'Tell me what's happened today.' He lifted her hands, hesitated for a moment. 'But it's more than today, isn't it?'

Cassie inhaled deeply. The choked feeling was calming down, as it always did once she was back home. She blew her nose on the tea towel. They both laughed at that.

'I don't know what's happening to me, Si, and that's the truth.' She pressed two fingers to her temples. 'I told a kid off today, then found myself getting into trouble for it. And somehow Tina Armstrong's involved. Again.'

'She's a bloody secretary. But her name keeps coming up. Who did you get into trouble with? Can you tell me?'

'Oh, yes, I can tell you.' Anger was rising again. 'Alison called me into her office. Gave me a dressing down because the child's parents made a complaint. And somehow, sneaky Armstrong had managed to make things worse.'

Si shook his head. He got up from his seat and took the tea towel from the table, then peeled off some kitchen paper from the roll and ran it under the tap. He passed it to Cassie.

'Wash your face over. It looks sore,' he said, 'then we need to come up with a way to sort this situation out. It's bullying, Cass. And it turns my stomach.'

October 2019

We are standing at the kitchen door, watching water pooling on the concrete of the yard. Today, I see the fresh colours painted by the rain, as though for the first time. Between me and the world, there has been a disconnect; of that I'm aware. What I hadn't realised, until this morning, is how easy it would be to build a bridge over the gap. My mistake has been to assume the world would meet me halfway. So I've been waiting. For two years, I've been waiting. And it never has. But in just one day, with someone to show me how, I'm heading out there again.

'I hope Alison Harman realised she'd dealt with you very badly,' Freddy is saying. He has a biscuit in one hand and a mug of tea in the other; he is the hungriest adult I have ever met. Most are worried about their waistlines or their health. Freddy hoovers up anything.

I shake my head. 'Far from it,' I tell him. 'Iain McIntyre's parents wanted me sacked. Alison, with help from Becky Ripley I guess, appeased them by promising to remove the child from my class and put him into Kevin Noble's.'

He blinks then stretches his eyes.

'I know,' I say. 'But Alison insisted it was the only way to stop them from taking things further. When all I'd done was reprimand a kid. Great boss she turned out to be. And as for Tina Armstrong...' I leave him in the doorway and step back into the kitchen. 'She was far from done with me.'

'Can I ask you something about her?' Freddy looks thoughtful. 'I shouldn't really. But I need to know.'

He's captured my interest. 'Oh? Ask away.'

'Is she... I mean was she... erm... Is she married?'

I have to think about this. Did I ever encounter a Mr Armstrong? Or hear about him? And why would Freddy be interested?

'I'm not sure,' I tell him. 'But poor guy, if she was.'

He doesn't laugh.

'Why do you want to know?' I ask.

'I was just thinking about her affair with Mick Ripley, that's all.'

I had wondered about this myself. I couldn't believe Tina would be a different person in her family life. If there was a family life. I think I remember mention of a son, too. How little I knew about her, in the end.

'Talking about husbands,' I say. 'Tina took a swipe at Si, too, you know. Suddenly, I wasn't enough of a target.'

'Or too much of one,' he snaps. 'What happened?'

I tell him about the business Si used to own. About his use of Facebook as an advertising tool. About how a malicious report had closed down the page, and caused some customers to wonder.

'There's no smoke without fire, isn't that what they say?'

Freddy scratches at his chin. He has reached the point, as I did, where disbelief trumps normal human reaction. How many times can sympathy be shown before the brain starts to say *now hang on a minute.*

'Are you saying Tina Armstrong got his Facebook page shut down?' he whispers. 'Was it definitely her?'

'Who else would it have been? But *Clifton Welding* lived to fight another day. Si had a website and lots of other ways of promoting his firm. But–'

'What?'

I sigh. 'It knocked him sick. The thought that someone hated him enough to do that.'

'I don't think it was about hatred, Cassie. It was about power. And control.'

I look up at the kitchen skylight. The rain is smashing against the glass and bouncing off again. But the house was built for rainy days. However cheerless they are, Blackthorn is a water-tight presence, an ark. Floating on a sea of my regret. The best place to be in the rain is in the cellars. They run underneath the main rooms, seven feet high and as long as the house itself and are accessed by a flight of steps leading down from one wall of the scullery. Now, they contain plastic storage boxes full of books and magazines, Christmas decorations and well-used toys.

I tell Freddy about the rooms, hoping for a distraction. Talk of power and control, it scares me.

'We started to convert them a few years ago, but the money ran out. And so did our patience. The more the builders unearthed, the more they found needed to be done. We called a halt to it, in the end.'

'I'd love to see them.' He's on high alert, suddenly. Then, 'Sorry. You must think I'm so pushy. It's small-man syndrome.' He laughs, but I hear no fun in it.

'What do you mean?' I ask.

'You've never heard of small-man syndrome?'

I had. But only in the sarcastic context of explaining why men of five-foot-six or less appeared to have a chip on their shoulder. Freddy doesn't strike me as someone who would subscribe to this sort of populist psychology.

I shake my head.

'To be honest, Cassie, neither have I. But I know I was tormented mercilessly right through school because I was this little guy. Even at sixteen, I only had size four feet and wore a ten-to-twelve-year-old blazer. My mates called me *Midge*. So, I felt the need to fight everyone, and shout my mouth off.'

In other words, he was the victim of school bullies, too. It's just a pity mine were also supposed to be responsible adults.

'Not nice, is it,' I say.

He shakes his head. 'No.'

'Cellar?' I ask.

'Yes, please.'

I take him through the scullery door and down an open staircase. It leads into a small, dark hallway. I fumble for the light switch, white plastic and hanging loose from the bare brick wall. One bulb lights up, harsh and bright. On either side of this small space are pitch-pine doors with white porcelain handles and scratch plates. The greasy fingerprints around each, tell their own tale.

'Jeez,' exclaims Freddy. 'It's like a whole other house.' His eyes roam around, blinking and darting, but he hasn't seen anything, yet.

'Go through that door,' I say, thumbing to the left.

He pushes it open, and light floods the hallway.

'This was the servant's kitchen,' I say. 'That window is at ground level with Blackthorn.'

Each of the bays at the front of the house has another window underneath, the same width but half as high. Freddy walks into the room, and stands, open-mouthed. I point out the dusty blacked range under a brick supporting arch, the row of bells with room numbers underneath, and the huge pot sink. He runs his hands over the built-in dresser and cupboards, and kneels to touch the quarry tiles, bone-dry, despite the rain.

'We've gone back in time,' he gasps. 'This is amazing.' I find I'm liking him more and more. He feels the house, like I do.

'This room could certainly tell some stories. Though I think the colonel who kept the place only had a small staff: butler, cook, parlourmaid and a poor old scullery maid. She'd have hardly left the kitchen.' I laugh. 'That would have suited you. Plenty to eat.'

'Have you never thought of restoring this room? Or converting it?' He splutters a little. 'Sorry. I know it all costs money. But... wow! I'm just stunned.'

'We started a conversion. I'll show you, but the money did run out, sadly.'

I walk back through the open door and across the hallway. He follows me, running his hands over every surface, saying nothing. I push open the matching door, and once again, light floods across us.

'This room was the servant's parlour and dining hall. They lived here, basically. We stripped it out and had a membrane system put in, but that's it. We're using it for storage at the moment.' I pull at the thick plastic liner that protrudes from the wall. 'I don't think we needed to have this done, to be honest. The rooms aren't even damp.'

There is little left of the original stone fireplace or green flock wallpaper. The stairs to the outside privy have also gone, but we brought down the soil pipes and water supply, in case we ever found the money to add a bathroom for the girls' den. Unlikely, now. Freddy is very quiet.

'What do you think?'

'Where does that door go?' he asks, nodding towards what was the entrance to the toilet and coal hole. His face has taken on an intensity I haven't seen before. Like a kid, when they've been told to wait, even though the object of their desire is right there.

'Have a look,' I say.

He pulls at the thick wooden door. It opens easily, onto nothing.

'Oh,' he says. 'What was there?'

'Step into the gap,' I tell him, 'and you'll probably be able to work it out.'

I watch as he walks into the dark void and looks upwards. 'There's half a staircase here.' He laughs gleefully. 'I'm guessing that would have led to the netty.'

'Where?' I shriek.

'You know. The lavvy. The outside loo.'

'You're right. But what's the netty?'

'It's what my nan called this brick outhouse where there was a toilet. In her back yard. She tore sheets of newspaper up and hung them on a hook outside. Only *The Times*, mind. She was very particular.' He switches to a high-pitched long-syllabled way of speaking, and it makes me howl. Freddy, a comedian? Who'd have thought it?

'We were going to put in a new one, down here, with a shower, possibly.' I perform a dramatic shrug.

'No money,' he laughs. 'A place like this could bleed you dry, if you're not careful.'

We walk back out into the hallway. He closes the doors very carefully, then follows me back up the stairs.

'Almost lunchtime,' I say, in the kitchen. 'Do I need to ask?'

'No.' He sits at the table. 'But can I ask you a few things, while you're making it. Oh, God. That sounds so cheeky. Sorry.'

I pull open the fridge.

'Don't worry about it,' I say. 'Turkey sandwiches okay? And a bit of salad?'

He nods across at me. Rests his elbows on the table and rubs his hands together. I wait for his questions. I've kept quiet for so long about what happened. Thought if I told people the raw details, I'd lose something of myself, though in the end, there was nothing left of me, anyway. But a new me emerged. One I quite liked. Up until I met Freddy. Now I realise I haven't felt safe in my own body for more than two years, and I have somehow caused that.

I move between the fridge and the pantry, opening cupboards and knocking knives and cutlery against themselves. I have my back to him, but I can hear the cogs of his brain, whirring towards me.

'Have you realised that both Judy Barker and Tina Armstrong were responding strongly to how you were, Cassie?' he says suddenly. 'Perhaps projecting their own problems back onto you?'

I lay down the knife in my hand. It has a creamy coloured ivory handle, the dregs of a set left by my grandparents. The girls hate those knives. Say elephants have died for them. They are correct, of course, but I have never been able to throw them away. That would seem like a waste of the elephant's death.

'That sounds like you're saying what happened was my

fault.' I face him and pull back my head in shock. 'You've said this once before. Is that what you think?'

'There's my point. You've gone from calm to cross in one second. But I bet the old you never reacted to anything they did, in front of them.'

'Course I didn't. I had a persona to keep up, as I've told you. It didn't stop me feeling angry, though.'

I turn back to the sandwiches, sprinkle salad across the turkey and lay another slice of bread down on the top. Then I use the hated knife to divide them into neat triangles. Freddy smiles as I push the plate towards him.

'What?' I mutter.

'None of what happened was your fault. But your resistance to it is what made you ill, not the thing itself. I'd have gone ape-shit every time one of those two women did what they did. Whether it got me in trouble or not, because the long-term effects caused by refusing to acknowledge your emotions was far worse, in the end.'

'Blah, blah, blah,' I say, but I am laughing.

Freddy laughs too. Then picks up a sandwich. 'Got any salt?' he asks.

I bang the salt pot down in front of him. He picks it up. 'Nice, he says. 'Cornish Ware. Original, by the cracked lacquer, too.'

'You are so predictable,' I groan. 'Perhaps you should come and live in Blackthorn. Everything here suits you so much.'

He peels back the top layer of his sandwich and sprinkles the salt. Some of it misses and drops onto the table. 'Oops,' he says, then scrapes it off again with the side of his hand. 'Think about this then, Cassie. My interest in this house. You're talking about this house. It's part of your therapy.'

He has my full attention now. I put down my sandwich. 'So, your interest in Blackthorn has been fake?'

He shakes his head. Finishes chewing. 'Far from it. This

might sound showy, but I'm going to say it, anyway. I'm a really intuitive therapist. I picked up on what your area for safe discussion would be. Houses. And I tapped into that to show us both how you relaxed within that subject.'

'Bloody hell, Freddy,' I interrupt. 'I feel like I've been played.'

'You haven't. I tapped into your safe place, because it's mine, too.' He chews thoughtfully and waits.

I wonder if I should ask. But I do. 'Are you having problems? Why would a psychotherapist need a safe place, as you call it?'

'Two reasons,' he says. 'One, the amount of angst we absorb from listening to patients means that we have to have regular psychotherapy ourselves.'

I think about this… it makes sense.

'And two, I, personally, have suffered at the hands of other people – idiots – and had to find a way through it. Still am, in a way. Anxiety never leaves you. I still have my phobias.'

'Great.' I huff out the word. 'No hope for me, then.'

'Oh, there is,' he smiles. 'Hope, I mean. Whether you were depressed or not, after you left Parkhouse, you're not, now. I can tell. You're primed and ready to live the questions about your recovery, your reprogramming of response. I know you can do it.'

I beam. I can't help myself. He is saying just what I have had buried in my brain and can't find words for.

'But, Cassie,' he says as he finishes his last bit of sandwich, then runs his fingers over his plate for crumbs, 'you haven't told me about those last days, yet.'

Chapter Twenty-Five

DECEMBER 2016

Becky Ripley was standing on the doorstep of Blackthorn, darkness behind her, all frosted breath and shiny faced. Cassie pinched at the collar of her dressing gown as she opened the front door. Visitors were the last thing she wanted. Not after a *holding* day. Jax had coined that term: the last day before a holiday held no educational value whatsoever. Children were simply being held, penned, whilst they fought for freedom.

'Come in,' she said. 'You'll have to excuse the nightwear. It's more comfortable when I get home from work.'

Becky stepped inside and began to unfasten her coat. 'Just checking you're all right, poppet. I won't stay long.'

'It's fine. Really. At least have a drink.'

She followed Cassie into the lounge. Helli and Janey lay on the sofa, feet resting on each other and staring at the television.

'This is Becky. From Parkhouse.' Cassie patted their bare legs. 'These are my daughters. Helen, and Jane.'

The girls grinned then clambered away with a swish of ponytails and school blouses.

Becky ignored them in favour of the room. 'This is some

house,' she breathed, as she ran her hands over the fireplace. 'You don't see black marble very often.'

'Have a look around while I make us a drink,' offered Cassie. 'Give me your coat. I'll be in the kitchen. It's at the back.' She made a dive for the open door, but Becky followed her along the hallway.

'I don't like to poke around other people's houses,' she said, handing Cassie her coat. 'And anyway, I came to see you. Are you happy with the outcome of the meeting with those parents? The McIntyres, wasn't it?'

'Happy's not the right word. Whose idea was it to remove the child from my class?'

Becky's expression changed. She opened her mouth to speak, but Cassie cut in. 'Sorry. I know you can't tell me that. Just ignore me. I'm so touchy at the moment.'

She turned away to fill the kettle and heard Becky dragging out a kitchen chair.

'I'm not being very sociable, am I. Should have said sit down.'

Becky peered across the kitchen. 'You don't need to keep apologising, poppet. And it was my idea to suggest the McIntyre child be moved to Kevin Noble's class. It stopped the parents in their tracks, that's for sure. They were threatening to go to the newspapers. Or their MP. Or even the police. It was ridiculous, Cassie. They're awful people.'

'Tell me about it.'

'Alison Harman was a bit out of her depth, if you ask me. Putting the school's reputation before her own staff. Mick would never have done that.' Becky chewed at her nails. 'And she was reading from a set of notes made by that bloody Tina Armstrong. Well, I wasn't having any of that.'

Cassie filled two mugs with the boiled water, sloshed in some milk then pushed one across the table towards Becky.

'Do you take sugar?' she asked.

'No thanks.' Becky took a sip of her drink. 'Anyhow. The McIntyres went away quite calmly. So that was something, seeing as they were baying for blood when they first arrived.'

'My blood, I guess.' Cassie could feel her anger rising, twisting up from the pit of her stomach and threatening to choke her. 'Honestly, Becky. I can't think how the situation got so out of hand.'

'Can't you?'

'No.'

'Look no further than that bloody bitch of an admin assistant. She's the one who told those awful parents they could go to OFSTED. It would never have crossed their minds, otherwise. The whole thing should have been shut down at the door, if you ask me.'

Cassie rested her elbows on the table and put her head in her hands. Tina Armstrong. Each time something bad happened, that woman's name came up. So much for getting back to normal once Judy Barker left. More than anything, Cassie just wanted to do her job. And not to feel terrified every time she walked through the doors of Parkhouse.

The tears came then. They spilled into her hands while she waited for Becky to notice.

'Oh, my love,' the other woman said. 'You can't go on like this.'

'You're right,' gulped Cassie, taking the kitchen paper Becky was pushing towards her. 'But I've tried to tell Alison. She's not interested. I've even asked Tina to lay off me. Pathetic, aren't I?'

'That woman's going to get what's coming to her.'

The burst of words made Cassie look up. *Becky knew about Tina and Mick. Of course she did.*

'And she will,' Becky continued. 'I'm a great believer in karma, even if it's a bit slow to show itself.'

Cassie realised she needed to shut down the conversation.

Something about Becky's tone was wrong. There was a professional distance to maintain here, however tempting it was to offload. 'Ignore me, Becky. I'm being a sap.'

'Just you give as good as you get, that's all.' Becky sounded more like herself again. 'Now, are you going to show me around this house of yours? We'll leave the outside for another day.' Her eyes flashed across Cassie's nightwear. 'When you're dressed for the occasion.'

Chapter Twenty-Six

JANUARY 2017

By the time the Christmas holidays were over, Cassie had passed all of Iain McIntyre's books and records to Kevin Noble. He said very little. There could be no refusal to take the child in support of his colleague: not without damage to his own reputation. And that was far from perfect. The action had been purely to placate the child's parents, Alison told her. But it felt like a bomb had been dropped on the twenty years of Cassie's teaching life, and she would have to spend the next twenty picking over bits of charred paper and burnt ideals.

Joe pointed out that she should be glad to offload Iain McIntyre, that he and his parents would now be someone else's to deal with, but the humiliation burned deep.

After a few days of the new term, the child was causing problems again. Perhaps it would make his parents realise their little darling was the issue, rather than the teaching staff. Either way, the worry of it all brought Cassie to her lowest point, and one Friday night she went to bed with a sore throat, and did not rise again for a week. Then, she managed to lie on the sofa in Blackthorn's lounge with a blanket over her for a further four days, before Si realised he might have to talk to the doctor.

She listened to Cassie's chest and pronounced a pneumonia in one lung – a common symptom with this year's new strain of influenza – and ordered her back to bed. And Si was to call accident and emergency if her breathing got any worse.

After another week's rest and a strong dose of antibiotic, Cassie was well enough to allow Jax a visit. They laughed at tales of the disastrous string of supply teachers, brought in to cover her class, and how Alison Harman was now teaching alongside them, to keep order.

'She's found out just how tiring it is to teach, day-in, day-out,' Jax told her, 'and she keeps getting Tina coming in to make her sign things or answer phone calls.'

'That'll be the first time Tina has seen the inside of my classroom for years.' Cassie turned the situation into a joke, but she hadn't missed the toxic actions of Tina Armstrong. And staying within the comfort and protection of Blackthorn had given her time to think.

When she was fit to return to her workplace, she was going to challenge every marginalising or spiteful action that came her way, regardless of consequences. If that meant she clashed with colleagues, then she would have to live with it.

Becky had been right. *Give as good as you get* was going to be her new motto.

On the morning Cassie returned to work, the first miniature daffodils of the season had opened in Blackthorn's front garden, and the air tasted crisp enough to bite. A month away from Parkhouse had healed over the surface of the deep wounds inflicted by Tina Armstrong. If the scabs held, anything was possible. Cassie smiled as she climbed into her car. If she could just find her feet again this week, it would be half-term.

Jax was already in the classroom, sitting at a table, gluing worksheets into exercise books. She beamed as Cassie walked in. 'Thank God,' she said. 'I had this terrible fear that you wouldn't be back in today. It's been hell-on-Earth without you.'

'Well, here I am,' Cassie twirled around. 'You'll be sick of me by the end of the day.'

'Never.' Jax stood up and walked over for a hug. 'But you've lost weight. Are you sure you should be here?'

'Make your mind up,' Cassie sighed. 'You either want me here, or you don't.'

'I do. I really do.'

Cassie pushed her way into her stockroom and hung up her coat. The tiniest flicker of optimism, as light and fresh as a sea breeze on a summer's day, made its presence felt behind her eyes.

At half past eight, Kevin Noble put his head around the door, all smiles, and a cleanly shaved face. 'Whites. Nice to have you back. Shout if you need anything. Oh, and Tina just asked me to bring this down.' He pushed a yellow piece of paper across the table towards her. 'Just needs signing.'

'Thanks,' Cassie replied, too brightly, she thought. 'We'll have a catch-up later.'

Alison put her head in to say hello. Followed by Joe. Then one or two other staff. Just before the children were due to come in, Cassie smoothed down her skirt, straightened her blouse and called across to where Jax was sharpening a tub of coloured pencils.

'Wish me luck.' She snatched up the yellow absence form and marched out of the door. Kept on marching all the way to the office.

Tina Armstrong was sitting at her desk, sipping a tall glass of steaming water with a slice of lemon floating on the top. She turned her head away very deliberately when Cassie walked in. There was no greeting, no asking after her health. Nothing.

'Morning, Tina,' she said, fraudulent in a way the other woman must have heard and understood. 'If you want me to sign this,' the yellow form was slammed down, 'you will have to ask me yourself.'

Then she stepped lightly away, though adrenaline was rushing through her body making her legs as heavy as slabs of granite. She pressed the electronic bell as she passed, and it started the avalanche of distraction typical of a working day.

The yellow form didn't materialise again until Cassie was putting her coat on to go home, much later.

Alison walked into the room. 'How's it been?' She hid a yawn behind her hand.

'Fine. And Jax has been brilliant. She should have been a teacher.'

'Good.' She held out the yellow form. 'Sign this, will you, Cass?'

Cassie tutted, then took the form from her hand. 'I guess Tina's been to see you, then.' She rummaged around in the pot on her desk for a biro.

'She has.' Alison matched her eye-roll. 'I know she can be bloody difficult, but you're the one with the power, as I've told you before.'

Cassie leaned over the desk and scribbled her signature on the form. 'She's the one with the problem, not me. She didn't even ask me how I was.'

'Build bridges with her, Cass. That'd make everyone's life easier.' Alison picked up the form. 'I've seen you in action. I know you can do it.'

There was nothing Cassie could say to that. She didn't trust herself, anyway. A light cough was all she could manage.

'Okay.' Alison looked out of the window. 'Have a good evening. And try to rest a bit. You still look tired. Are you going to be able to come to Dot's retirement party on Friday?'

'I am. Joe put me on the list while I was off. Si and I will both be there.'

'Great.'

'Have you managed to get anyone to replace her?' Cassie was usually involved in staff recruitment, but the last few weeks had been something of a blur.

'I'm going to use an agency team to manage the site until we can find the time to get together properly.' She spread her arms wide. 'I need you, Cass. Supporting me. I'll cover you for a day, after half-term, and we can get on with everything. I'll see you later.'

Then she stepped towards the doorway, and was gone.

As Cassie moved to follow, her mobile phone began to ring. With a sigh, she rummaged in her handbag. The screen showed the call was coming from Helli and Janey's school.

She pressed the green *accept* button. 'Hello. Cassie Clifton speaking.'

'Hello. This is Marion Green. Headteacher of Friar's School. Am I speaking to Helen and Jane Clifton's mum?'

'You are. Is everything okay?' Cassie's heart gave a lurch. She sat down at her desk.

'Nothing to worry about, Mrs Clifton. I've got Helen and Jane here with me. They're absolutely fine. But I wondered if you could pop up to school for a little chat. Now?'

Cassie clutched at the phone. 'Why? What's happened?'

'Come up to school, please. And don't worry. I'm sure everything will be fine. I'll talk to you when you get here.'

Then a distant click, and Marion Green was gone. Cassie grabbed her handbag and rushed from the room, propelled along by her mental picture: one of the girls bleeding, dying, needing her.

By the time she reached Friar's School, Cassie had managed to calm herself. Mainly by breathing through her nose and counting. And repeating Marion Green's words over and over: *Helen and Jane are absolutely fine.*

The school was quiet. One or two children in sports kits and blazers shuffled their way down the drive, bags slung over their shoulders and attention firmly on their phone screens. Cassie rang the intercom bell and waited. Eventually, Marion Green appeared. In person. A headteacher who could never be contacted, and whom half the children had never even seen.

'Mrs Clifton?' Cropped, grey hair and a tilt of her head towards Cassie. 'Hello. Don't look so worried. I'm sure everything will be fine.'

'Would you mind telling me what this is about?' Cassie followed the woman, staring at her burgundy-clad shoulders as she strode forwards through the wide white corridors. The clinical feel was punctuated only by arty photographic panels showing smiling pupils engaged in fabulous activities: goggled up and holding test tubes or peering at Apple Mac screens, or even rustling up a stir-fry in the school's food-tech labs. Cassie preferred to see children's work on the walls, however much it left Blu-Tack stains or pushpin marks.

Helli and Janey were sitting together on a row of plastic chairs outside the headteacher's office. 'Girls.' Cassie knelt in front of them. 'What's happened?'

Helli screwed up her face. 'I don't know.'

'We were just told to come and wait outside Miss Green's office. And that you would be collecting us.' Janey seemed anxious. 'Are you all right, Mum?'

'Course I am.' Cassie looked towards the office door. Marion Green held it open, a benign smile playing on her lips.

'If I could have a moment, Mrs Clifton?'

'Don't move, you two.' Cassie stood up. 'I'll be back in a sec.'

Inside Marion Green's office, another woman was already

seated at the side of the huge oak desk that dominated the space. She smiled a hello at Cassie, and shifted position, gesturing at another seat directly opposite Marion's.

'I'm Susan Coward. Jane's head of year.' She held out her hand. 'I think we've met, actually. Helen's head of year couldn't join us, I'm afraid, but he's been briefed.'

'Briefed about what?.' Cassie sat down. 'Please tell me what this is about. Has Jane done something?'

Marion Green leaned her elbow on the desk and glanced at the notepad in front of her. 'There's no easy way of telling you this, Mrs Clifton. We've had a call from the hub. The social services hub. About both your daughters. Well, about your family, actually.'

'What?' Cassie shook her head. Something exploded in her stomach. 'Saying what?'

'Calm down, Mrs Clifton. We don't think there's any cause for concern. But we have to follow up these reports.'

'What reports? What's been said?'

'Whoever made the call said they thought the girls were in danger because of the comings-and-goings at the house where they live.'

Comings-and-goings? Cassie flung back her chair. 'I don't know what's happening here, but I'm furious.' The words came out with such force that Susan Coward reached for her arm and patted it. As though she was calming a childish tantrum.

'We know the report was malicious, Mrs Clifton. We've checked on Helen and Jane, and there are no concerns.' Marion Green held Cassie's eye. 'But there are protocols we must follow with reports like this. Just in case the children involved are in any danger. I'm sure you appreciate that. You've probably had to dance to that tune in your own job.'

Checked on Helli and Janey? What was she talking about? They didn't need checking on. And if they did, it was Cassie's job. Nothing to do with the school. 'Would you mind telling me who made this report. And what exactly I'm being accused of.'

'You'll appreciate, Mrs Clifton, we can't give you that information.' Marion Green clasped the heavy silver pendant that hung around her neck. 'But you will get a visit. Also routine, as you know.'

'A visit? To our home, you mean?'

Susan Coward reached over, again.

'No. don't touch me,' Cassie hissed. 'This is becoming so ridiculous, I'm starting to think it's a joke.'

'No joke, Mrs Clifton. I can assure you. And if you want my opinion—'

'I don't, thanks.'

A light cough from Susan. Then, 'Well, here it is, anyway. To get through to the hub, you've got to know what buttons to press, as it were. So, whoever made this report has done some kind of research or has been involved with social services themselves. And they definitely wanted to cause trouble for you.'

Trouble? That was an understatement.

'Probably a disgruntled parent,' Marion Green continued. 'This happens more often than you would think.' She flicked over the top page of her notebook. 'I knew it was malicious as soon as the hub telephoned me, though you have been assigned a temporary social worker. Just to make the home visit and sign off the paperwork.' She peered at the new page. 'It's Viv Hale. She knows what's what.'

'I'm sure she does,' fumed Cassie, 'but she's not getting into my home to check on me. No way.'

'It's the only way to get rid of her, Mrs Clifton. And she's very nice. She'll know there isn't a problem. Probably won't even want to talk to the girls.'

'Damn right, she won't.' Cassie stood up, inhaled deeply, and tried to swallow down her choking rage. She glared at

Marion Green, hard enough to send the woman sinking into the back of her seat. 'Now. I'm taking my children and I'm going home. You will be hearing from me again. Because I intend to find out the truth behind what is, quite frankly, a load of shit.'

Chapter Twenty-Seven

By Friday, Cassie was exhausted. After her encounter at Friar's, she'd marched the girls out, vowing to change their school and sue every one of the teachers.

When she'd explained everything to Si, he'd persuaded her Marion Green was doing exactly what Alison would have done in the same situation. The system of reporting existed for a reason. To put the safety of children before any sort of embarrassment behind which abusers could hide. But he'd been as angry as she was. And he'd put voice to the thoughts swirling through Cassie's seething mind. That Tina Armstrong had somehow been responsible for the whole situation. Who else would be able to make a call to social services, without any mistakes? Only someone who knew the system. There had been the closing down of Si's Facebook page, and now this threat to Helli and Jane. Neither of which was traceable. Both of which had caused untold damage.

Through the rest of the week, Cassie kept to herself, the simmer of her anger lying just beneath her teacher persona. And she'd watched Tina Armstrong like a hawk watches its prey. From high-up and out of view, ready to drop at any moment. But the effect of so much tension was taking its toll.

Now, she lay on the sofa in Blackthorn's lounge, watching the fire roar up the chimney. The room smelled of pine from burning the last small boughs of their Christmas tree. Helli and Janey sat together in the big armchair, flicking through music channels on Sky TV.

'I want to go tonight, Si, but I'm so tired,' she yawned. 'And it means we'll have to see *her*.'

He lifted Cassie's feet onto his lap and sat down. 'I'm not fussed, either way.' He stared at the TV. 'You decide. But don't let the Armstrong woman stop you from going. You know what we agreed.'

In the face of Cassie's spiralling mental health, they'd decided to write down everything that had happened; the whole Judy Barker and Tina Armstrong debacle. Then they would take the information to the next level, whatever that was.

'We'll go. Just for an hour. Say our goodbyes to Dot.' She swung her legs over the end of the sofa and sat up. 'You girls make sure all your schoolwork is done. Don't want to be charging round trying to sort it out next Sunday.'

No response.

'Girls.' Si grabbed the TV remote from Janey's hand. 'Your mother's speaking to you.'

'We'll do it,' sighed Janey. 'You don't have to go on.'

'When you've gone,' added Helli, 'can Jack come over, and help?'

Si treated them to one of his best frowns. And a growl. 'Who's Jack when he's at home?'

'God, Dad.' Janey again. Indignant. 'He only lives along the road. You've seen him loads of times.'

'Jed's lad? Oh, all right then. But we won't be late. And I don't want him here when we get back.'

'All right.' Agreement from both girls: a bonus. Si threw the remote back at them.

'Now, wife,' he said, holding out his hand, 'let's go and get spruced up, and get this over with.'

Within an hour they were driving out past the edge of town and along the main route into the Lake District. The metallic blue of an early evening sky opened out in front of them, and the gentle grey slopes of the low fells felt close enough for Cassie to reach out and touch.

A familiar knot of nerves had formed in her stomach as soon as they'd driven away from Blackthorn. But she was getting over her anxieties, wasn't she? Tonight though, she would have to be in the same room as Tina Armstrong, watch her groom and scalp-hunt, and be missed out from any greetings, and from her circle of chairs. She would just have to handle it. There were many other colleagues who would talk to her, and Becky would be there, she was sure.

Fifteen miles from Blackthorn House was the Lakeview Hotel. On the shores of Lake Windermere, and a rather expensive place for a site manager's retirement party. But it had been Dot's choice. And her money. As Cassie opened the car door, she could smell the cold edge of water. She'd had a meal at the hotel, once before, and remembered the proximity of the lake. From the conservatory, it was possible to step up onto a choice of two wooden piers and get even closer.

'I wish I'd stayed at home,' she said with a shiver, then peered up at the slate façade of the building. Inside would be Tina and Laura and their whole exclusion game. Si came up behind her and slid his arms around her shoulders, then rested his chin on the top of her head.

'What's done can't be undone,' he cackled.

Cassie could smell his shaving cream, citrusy and sharp. She put her hands on his arms and leaned in for a moment. 'Macbeth? What are you trying to say?'

'Just drawing your attention to *the witches*.' He thumbed towards the hotel. 'In there.'

'Not helpful.' She would square things with Dot, then try to get away again. Keep Tina and her cronies at a distance.

Inside the hotel were people and noise, balloons and bunting, and Cassie relaxed a little. Dot would hardly notice if they didn't stay for long. And here she was, carrying a small child in a pink sateen frock; a perfect match for Dot's own.

'Cassie, love.' The child reached out a hand. 'And this here's Ella. My youngest grandchild.'

'Hi, Dot. Everything's in full swing, I see.' Cassie kissed her. 'Si's here, too.'

He smiled. 'Couldn't let you go without one last snog, Dot.'

'Cheeky,' she beamed. 'And that was you, anyway.'

There was a longstanding joke between them, after a Christmas party years ago, when a drunken Dot had draped herself across a much younger Si and demanded a kiss.

In the days when I could just socialise with my colleagues, without agendas. That had changed when Cassie had become management.

'I'll drive home, if you want to have a drink,' she said to Si as he moved towards the bar.

'Soft drinks for both of us, I think. We don't want to get too settled.'

She scanned around the room for a moment. And there was Tina Armstrong, in a sleeveless red dress, standing with Laura Pearson, Kevin and Joe. A laughing huddle. Laura met her gaze, then looked away quickly, leaning forward to say something to Tina. Someone came to stand next to her. Jax.

'Hi. I thought you'd be collapsed on a sofa somewhere.' Grey curls and red lipstick.

'Nice blouse,' laughed Cassie. 'Haven't seen you wear that for work.'

'Can you imagine.' Jax smoothed down the cream chiffon.

273

'You look nice.'

They chatted. Something fizzed in Cassie's stomach. It made her legs feel weak. Dot's grandchildren ran about, weaving between the groups of adults. Si came over with their drinks, joked with Jax about working with control freaks.

Time passed. Kevin finally came to say hello. Cassie found a seat at a table near Alison, and they talked about work for a while. Becky arrived and Jax drifted away. Cassie's shoulders drooped. She would see the site manager presented with her gifts, then she'd have to go home. Every adrenaline surge was leaving her feeling scattered and numb.

A sideways glance showed her a group had formed at the bar. Tina, and some of the lower school staff, with Laura Pearson, and her swish new hairstyle. Their grins reminded Cassie of *Maleficent* in the Disney cartoon, smiling malice with a hint of vomit. Their voices had taken on a sharpness. Tina hauled herself up onto a bar stool, leaned forward to say something in the ear of the young barman. Her elbow slipped and she fell against him, making the others shriek with laughter.

'Look at the state of her.' Becky Ripley slid into the seat next to Cassie. 'I'd heard she was a hard drinker. Doesn't tally up with the little-miss-prim act she puts on in that office, does it?'

'Oh, hi. I wondered if you'd be here.' Cassie patted her hand. 'And no, it doesn't. But she's consistent with me. Consistently absent.' They looked at Tina again, and laughed as she slipped off the stool while rummaging in her glittery handbag.

Becky let out a long sigh. 'Never mind, poppet. You've got a week off now. Use it to recharge. You've had a right old time of it.'

Which was exactly the wrong thing to say. Kindness was only adding to Cassie's fragile state of mind. Confusing, but that's how it was. The more people tried to hold her up, the more down she felt. As though the props of support caused damage, ripped holes in what they were trying to protect. Her throat tightened.

'Thanks.' It was all she could manage.

Becky jumped up. 'Let's go and raid the buffet. That always cheers me up, anyway.' She tugged on Cassie's hand. But Tina and Laura got there before them. Cassie went to back away, then felt Becky's hand on her arm.

'Don't let her get to you, Cassie. Remember what I said.' She lifted two plates and pushed one into her hand. 'This looks lovely.' Too loud.

Laura began piling her plate with a pink-tinged pasta salad. She did the same for Tina. Cassie and Becky sidled along behind them. There was no conversation, no banter. Just Becky's eyes on Tina's tiny waist and the back of Laura's head bobbing up and down with her whispering. Then a burst of laughter that jangled Cassie's nerves and turned down the corners of Becky's mouth.

'Did you say something, my dear?' Becky peered over Laura's shoulder, aiming her words directly at Tina.

She spluttered then spun away from them, shoving her plate into Laura's hand. 'Won't be a minute,' Tina hissed. 'Bit crowded in here. I need some air.'

Cassie watched her totter towards the conservatory door. Then she opened it and was gone.

Around the room, small conversations were taking place. People were huddled together over plates of food and sparkling glasses. Si was laughing with Kevin Noble, and nobody was looking at Cassie.

'I'm going after her,' she muttered.

Becky smiled, just slightly. 'About time,' was the last thing Cassie heard as she hurried away.

Outside, a sweet-water smell hit the back of her nose. She

picked her way across the slate-shingle beach, to the edge of the lake. The whole expanse looked like a huge black puddle, fragmented only by moonlight and the occasional ripple from late-moving watercraft. Tina had stepped onto one of the wooden piers and was scrolling through her phone. Cassie stepped up onto the slippery wood and watched. She continued tapping on the screen, then walked further out, holding the phone to her ear. A conversation started up.

Cassie waited.

'No. I told you ten and I meant it.' Tina had reached the end of the pier. As she turned, she caught sight of Cassie, then slid the phone away.

'Problems?' Cassie smiled into the darkness.

Tina flicked her head. 'No. Not that it's any of your business.' She stepped forwards.

'And my business isn't anything to do with you, either.'

'What do you mean?'

'I mean, not so long ago, I told you to leave me alone. So now you've started on my family.'

Tina twisted up her top lip. 'You're fucking crazy. Do you know that?'

But Cassie wasn't about to let it go. 'I know you phoned social services, Tina.'

She waited, watched for a reaction that didn't come.

'I have no idea what you're on about,' Tina sneered, 'and I don't give a toss anyway. Now, let me get past.'

Her head went down, and she stumbled slightly.

'Got nothing to say, all of a sudden?' Cassie stepped wide and blocked her.

Silence. Just for a moment.

'Oh, I've got plenty to say, believe me.' She narrowed her eyes.

'Go right ahead, then. You've had it in for me since the day I got the deputy's job. That's a long time to be festering, Tina.

Go on. I'm the bad guy. So, you might as well tell me what I've done.'

Tina's head shot forward, bringing her face close to Cassie's. 'Okay. You want to know. Well, here it is. I dislike everything about you. The way you walk. The way you talk. The things you say. Your clothes. Your face. That creepy husband of yours. Everything.'

Cassie snapped out a laugh. 'Don't hold back, will you.' She watched as Tina trembled a little. 'It is personal, then. I told Alison it was. She thought it just had something to do with me being management.'

'Alison. What a joke. *I told Alison*,' she mimicked. 'Like she was going to do anything.'

'What is wrong with you, Tina? You don't get to run the world. I can be how I want and do what I want. I don't give a shit if you find me offensive.'

'Oh, but you do. Look at you. You're shaking.' She tried again to push past. 'I'll give it a few more weeks. Then you'll be gone.'

'Like Mick, you mean? I doubt it.' Those words escaped before Cassie could do anything to stop them. And now they hung in the chill of the evening. Until Tina bit down on them and swallowed hard.

'No. Like Judy. The woman *you* chased away.'

Cassie sang out a sigh. 'Here we go again. Judy left because she'd been played. My only mistake was that I thought Kevin was the player. But it was you, wasn't it? You used her for one of your little games. Where I was the target.' The swirling anger in Cassie stomach was gathering itself, forming a ball of energy that needed somewhere to go. It found its way along her arms, and she pushed hard against Tina's chest. 'Well. I'm not going to be your target.'

Expecting Tina to retaliate, Cassie moved away quickly, leaning sideways into the middle of the pier. But no retaliation came. Tina staggered backwards and her last footfall was against thin air. She tumbled into the water with a loud scream and a messy splash. Without thinking about it, Cassie jumped in after her.

Cold-water shock shot the breath from her lungs. Tina was gasping beside her, slapping her arms on the water's oily surface, and screaming at the top of her voice.

'Cass. What's going on?' Kevin Noble, running across the shingle beach. 'I came out for a fag. Saw you two on the pier.' The pitch of his voice made Cassie hesitate. Just for a moment, then she reached for Tina's bobbing shoulders and pressed down.

October 2019

The kitchen is silent, save for the rain beating against the skylight. I chew at my thumbnail, trying to control my rising panic. Then remember not to try and control it. Freddy looks directly at me. He reaches across the table and gives me his hand, then holds my gaze and leads me through some deep breathing. I keep my attention focused on his face; it's a soft face. He has blond eyebrows and lashes, but the eyes are steely.

I've never explored what I did to Tina. There is only the relief that nothing was followed up. I've had my story ready, my justification, but if Kevin hadn't turned up, I would have fought to keep the woman underwater. Whether that would have amounted to murder, I don't know. That she'd brought me to this low point in my life is something I'm certain of, thanks to Freddy. Up until now, I'd always blamed myself.

'I really lost it that night,' I tell him when I find my voice again. 'I hardly recognised myself.'

His expression says it all. He thinks I wanted to kill Tina.

'Bloody hell, Cassie.'

'Oh, don't worry,' I say. 'Tina lived to tell the tale. Not that I gave it much thought at the time. You probably think I'm a terrible person now, don't you?'

'You'd had a taste of what drives people to commit acts like that,' he murmurs. 'I don't think you're terrible.'

I shake my head and dip my face to hide how much I loathe myself. My hand is released, and I hear Freddy get up, then feel him settle beside me. An arm slides around my shoulder.

'Oh, God,' he whispers. 'I'm so sorry. Did someone call the police? You weren't arrested, were you?'

'No. I wasn't arrested,' I tell him. 'And Kevin *superhero* Noble fished Tina out of my grasp before anything bad happened.'

'I bet she was gunning for you, after that.'

'Strangely not,' I say, and shake away his arm. 'It was all a bit of a blur. Becky was there, I think. And Alison. I was crying and apologising, but no one seemed to be taking any notice. Most people were too busy looking after Tina, who told them she'd slipped, that I'd gone in to help her. And if Kev saw what I did, he never said.'

Freddy's lips are pressed together, eyebrows rigid.

'I didn't go back to Parkhouse, though,' I continue. 'She got her way, in the end. It was a kind of trade-off, I guess. So, here I am.' I use my hands to illustrate this, and he laughs softly.

Then he jumps up. Throws our plates and mugs into the sink. Turns the tap full on, and screams at the top of his voice. I stare at his back. Could I do the thing I so want to do? Cut my anxiety loose? See where it goes? I watch the push and pull of Freddy's ribs. Then I let go and allow myself to match his shrieking. I add some thumps on the table with my fist, for good measure. Water splashes up the front of Freddy's green sweatshirt. He turns the taps off again and gives a few punches into the air. We both stop and stare at each other across the silence. And burst into laughter. I can't control it. Tears stream down my face, and Freddy puts his arms across the table and rests his head there, shoulders shaking.

When we can finally look at each other, I find I can speak without panting and gasping.

'That felt good.'

He agrees.

'It's a bit like birds. How they shake away excess energy from their wings when they land. You don't see birds suffering from anxiety attacks, do you?'

'That's just plain silly,' I tell him. 'But I see what you mean; kind of negates my swan analogy, though.'

He frowns. I explain how I always chose to glide over the surface of murk, making sure I looked pristine and cool. Though I was frantically paddling where no one could see.

'Swans don't do that,' he says. 'They *are* cool. And they bite at anything trying to ruffle them. I'll say it again. You should have bitten back.'

Telling me this won't alter outcomes now, as Freddy knows; he's the psychotherapist. I'm only the amateur, trying to get by. Once I'd left Parkhouse, people remembered they should have helped me more.

Guilt makes saints of us all.

'You wouldn't believe the text messages I got on the drive home.'

Freddy cocks his head. 'What? Who was texting you?'

'From people wondering where I was. Asking if I was okay. Telling me about Tina's little accident.'

'Who?'

'Joe. Jax. And Becky. When all I was expecting were police sirens and a road block.' I shudder as this memory creeps back to me.

'Had none of them seen what happened on the pier, then?'

I shake my head in a dramatic way. 'Apparently not. Though I'm sure Becky was there. On the beach, I mean.'

On the drive home, I'd had the worst panic attack of my life. Si was going to pull the car over and call an ambulance. But all I could think of was those police cars.

Once we'd got back to Blackthorn and I'd realised neither Kevin nor Tina was going to tell anyone what happened, I made a vow to myself. I would leave my job, leave teaching altogether. Make another life for myself.

My way out was engineered by Alison. I gave her no option, told her that my mental health had deteriorated to such an extent that I wouldn't be a safe bet as a teacher. This frightened her, I am sure. She let everyone know the flu had taken hold again, and I was struggling. I guess they had to accept it.

'You should have taken legal advice at that point,' says Freddy.

I agree. It's what most people think. But they are not me. On that night, I had decided to terminate my connections with everyone associated with Parkhouse School. Even the colleagues I'd regarded as friends. Such was the bleakness of my thinking, at the time. I could trust none of them, I reasoned. Not Becky, not even Jax. Though she sent me a phone message from time to time, I couldn't bear to reply.

'Maybe I should have. But then I'd never have been free of those people. So, I walked away quietly, in the end.' I stretch my arms above my head, let out a sigh of relief. 'The truth is, Freddy, I was extremely unwell at the time. I just wanted it to stop. The panic, I mean. As you call it.' I grin wryly. He returns it.

'That's when you should have called me.'

I laugh softly. 'What were you doing two years ago?'

He thinks for a moment and stares down at his hands. He's counting.

'I was working in Salford. In a therapy centre for traumatised children and young adults. And trying to get clean.'

'Oh, God. I'm sorry. I didn't mean to be nosy.'

'Like I am, you mean.' He smiles sadly. 'It's not the sort of clean you're thinking though, Cassie.'

Now I am confused. Really confused. Drug or alcohol dependency had flashed into my mind, and now he is telling me my thoughts are wrong. But what else could it be? Freddy watches my face.

'I had an anger problem,' he says. 'Stemming from my treatment as *Midge*, at school. He was a very different guy to Freddy, believe me.'

'Still intelligent, I suspect.' It's all I can think of to say.

'Oh, yes. Too intelligent for my own good. Every single jibe about my height and lack of stature felt like a poisoned arrow. After I'd analysed each one, I wanted to kill the archer.'

An image of this man, with his dreadlocks and love of houses, holding his fists up to a group of baying, testosterone-fuelled contemporaries, shocks me. I find it hard to believe.

'And did you manage to find a cure. For your anger, I mean?'

'For my anger, I did,' he says. 'And I want to share it with you. That's why I suggested hypnotherapy the other day.'

This is where he loses me. Hypnosis? To cure anger or panic? It sounds like some strange kind of New-Age thinking. And though I'd assumed something like that about Freddy, when we'd first met, I have come to realise that he is a purist in his field, and very knowledgeable with it. Not the quack I'd called him.

'I'm not sure about that. Being hypnotised, I mean.'

A small burst of air escapes from his nostrils. 'It's not *being hypnotised*. It sends your brain into a deeply relaxed state. Teaches it how to get there itself. Especially after a trauma.'

'I haven't had a trauma.' I shoot out those words, but he holds out his hands.

'You have.' He reaches for me. 'Cassie, you have. Trust me.'

I lay my cold hands over his, find I do trust him. And I'm interested. In this moment, not in the past, and in how this could work for me. He stands up and leads me into the study. The light is poor in here, especially on a rainy afternoon.

'No,' he whispers, as I reach to flick on the blue and jade Tiffany lamp that was my grandma's pride and joy. 'You can sit or lie, and put that over yourself.'

He lifts the thick woollen blanket I keep on the back of the sofa.

'I'll lie down.' A nervous giggle escapes. I am tired. If I somehow fall asleep, it will be a bonus. I wriggle down and let Freddy fluff the blanket over me.

'Close your eyes,' he says, sitting on the floor and leaning his back against the sofa. 'And just be open to what I say.'

I laugh to myself. There is a level of control here I am expected to relinquish, that I've never allowed before. But so much of what Freddy says makes sense. Can I let him access my brain in this way? I can try. I owe him that much, at least.

'Think of the muscles in your scalp becoming warm and relaxed,' he says. 'And they will do exactly that.' His voice becomes low. But as clear as the trickle of icy water over rock. I try my best.

'And as these muscles relax,' he continues, 'you will become aware of your forehead tensing a little. Let it relax.' It does, and I do.

'Now, let the relaxation spread all around your face; across your cheekbones and lips. Focus on my voice, let that be everything to you.'

I allow myself to stop thinking. Only respond to his voice and his instructions. My breathing becomes very shallow and quiet. As I follow his words, I sink into the soft velvet of the sofa. It becomes one with the muscles of my back and shoulders. Freddy uses guided relaxation to make me aware of my whole body and the tensions that hide there. I am very close to sleep when he guides me away from my body and into some other places: a forest, a glade, a pathway to the future. Some of these, I can't imagine, but it doesn't seem to matter. There is a calm in my body I haven't experienced for many years. But I am conscious, still.

And then I'm waking up. The delicious awakening that comes after a long and refreshingly warm night's sleep.

'Hello,' Freddy says, as I sit up. 'I realised you'd gone spark out, so I stopped talking. That was about half an hour ago.'

I run my hands through my hair, smooth down the strangely matted lump I can feel at the back of my head. The room is dark, but the central heating has kicked in. I am in the centre of a safe cocoon, yet my world seems to have shifted. Freddy is sitting on my office chair, near the window. I can't hear the rain, but there is no sign of any light. He is in complete silhouette. The lamp is within reaching distance, and I flick it on. Bright jewels of blue and turquoise and white fill the room.

'I must have fallen asleep. Sorry,' I say, and he laughs.

'That's the point, Cassie.'

'What do you mean?'

'I calmed your brain down enough for you to fall asleep. Imagine if you could do that for yourself.'

I think about this, think about the episodes of heightened panic I have experienced. In those moments, tracking Freddy's voice, I found the complete antidote. How could that be?

I stretch my arms above my head, then stand up. 'Imagine,' I reply coyly.

'I'm being serious. I used recordings when I first started trying to treat myself. CDs on a CD player. You can get podcasts and downloads now. I have my favourites. Usually soothing American voices. You just have to do some research.' He looks at me, tongue-in-cheek. 'Some phobias can be stubborn to treat; it depends on the personality. You've surprised me. I thought you'd be more resistant.'

I had thought this myself. 'There you go then... a surprise-a-minute, that's me.' I pad across the room and stand next to him then lean forwards to look at the sky.

'It's clearing a bit,' I say, 'but it looks like evening, not late afternoon.'

'We could try a walk to the edge of the woods. Make the most of your calm state.'

Nothing jolts. Nothing inside me jumps in fear. 'Could do.'

'Just long enough for the kettle to boil,' he laughs, then makes his way into the hall. Blackthorn House is dark and quiet. Settled, somehow, the weight of its presence not quite as stifling. I click on the hall light and lift my coat from the peg. Freddy has slipped his boots on.

'Can I borrow one of your husband's jackets?' he asks. 'Mine's probably still dripping in your scullery.'

I find him one of Si's padded anoraks, grey with a red trim. It swamps him, but he draws the elastic tightly around his thighs.

'Perfect,' he says.

I push my feet into my trainers. I am worried that I'm not worried. I say as much to Freddy.

'Stop thinking, then. You've already used up your lifetime's ration of thinking. Eke out the last bit. Save it for when it's needed.'

'Kettle,' I say, pointing my thumb backwards. 'I'll wait on the step.' He watches as I run through to the kitchen, turn on the tap, fill it and switch it to boil. Perhaps he thinks I am stalling, but I'm not.

We are soon standing at the edge of the wood. The rain has turned everything to a shiny version of itself, washed and ready for me. Clean and metallic. A swish of car tyres passes behind us.

I am gripped by a sudden urge to stand under the first clump of trees: birches with silver paper bark. Just that far. No further. I keep stepping forward, across the crunch of the footpath, the splash of standing water. I fix on those trees. Just to lay my hand on their trunks, that would really be something. And I do. Freddy is just behind me. Further along the path, the spikes of Blackthorn and the beech coppices stand together, silent and watchful, jealous.

I will come and see you another time, I think. For now, the papery birch trunks print a message on my hand.

We've been waiting, they say.

I turn to Freddy.

'Okay?' he asks, cocking his head slightly.

'Okay,' I say. 'Now, tea.' I can't help myself. I slide my arm through his. We are shoulder to shoulder as we walk. Talking about how the house looks, square and solid and regal against the pure black sky. A smear of light filters through from the kitchen, giving the downstairs bay windows a warm glow, sleepy somehow.

'I'll have a cuppa. Then I'll have to get home. That's three days of intensive work, Cassie. I'm not going to see you for a while. What you do in that time is up to you.'

'You're giving me the brush-off? Just when we were getting on so well?' But I am smiling, and he knows it, sees it in the cold flush of my cheeks, the splash of light where there has been pallor.

He shakes off his boots, and steps in through the open front door, then hangs up Si's coat. 'You need to build up what you do. Every day, a new slice of challenge. And write everything down. Not that there's anything wrong with your memory. You're a sharp one, you are.'

I'll run with that.

When I left Parkhouse, there was a void in my life. And I fell into it, couldn't sidestep it or find another way to ignore its presence. It got me. Swallowed me up, made me a shadow. Learning how to escape from that gave me insights, and a new version of myself. But not real freedom.

'There's something else,' Freddy says suddenly. Worry snakes across his forehead.

'Oh?' I give my coat a shake and hang it up.

'What if it wasn't Tina who reported you to social services? Have you ever thought about that?'

'She must have.'

'Why bother to deny it then? When she'd already admitted just about everything else?'

What he's doing now is unearthing an event that I wanted to keep buried. I don't like it. There has been a certain satisfaction in blaming Tina Armstrong for everything that went wrong for me at Parkhouse. I can't lose that.

'She hated me, Freddy. It was made very clear. The fact that I didn't deserve it is what flipped me over the edge, in the end.'

He drags out a chair, sits down and lifts one foot so it rests on the opposite knee.

'It's funny,' he says without a smile, 'but I keep returning to one thing you said earlier.'

'What's that?'

'Correct me if I'm wrong. But didn't you mention that Becky said Tina would *get what was coming to her*?'

'Well remembered,' I tell him. 'Poor Becky. I've never heard from her again, you know. But Alison did tell me what happened.'

Chapter Twenty-Eight

APRIL 2017

C assie watched as the package was pushed through the letter box and clattered onto the floor of the hall: a cardboard shell, with a logo in the bottom corner. Blue mountains and lines of sea, on a white background. She knelt to pick it up.

'Anything for me?' Si came up behind her, dodging sideways and peering at her hand. 'Oh. That looks official.'

'It'll be my end-of-contract papers. P45 and the like.' Cassie turned away from him and shuffled back to the kitchen.

'You'll have to open it,' he called after her. 'Then file the papers away somewhere and forget about them.'

Easy for him to say. But just the sight or sound of something from her old life was enough to send Cassie into a crying, seething meltdown. This letter represented much more than the termination of employment. It was a flag of triumph for Tina Armstrong and her crew, a banner of her success in ridding Parkhouse of its most hated member of staff. Or, at least that was how Cassie viewed it. The truth was, Alison Harman had tried very hard to provide support and persuade her to stay, had offered sabbaticals and counselling and reduced hours. None of which were a route out of the anxiety Cassie felt whenever she thought of her workplace. And so, she'd given in her notice, and presented a sick note from her doctor, in the interim.

'I'll open it later,' she told him. 'Today's going to be difficult enough.'

After weeks of pestering, she'd finally agreed to a visit from Alison, and the presentation of gifts and flowers. A final shove from Tina Armstrong was how it felt.

'I hope you're going to get dressed.' Si sat down beside her at the kitchen table and topped up his mug of coffee. 'No one but me should have to bear witness to that scabby old dressing gown.'

'What else are husbands for?' But Cassie's stomach clenched at the thought of choosing clothing and making small talk. For the past two months, her life had consisted of wandering around Blackthorn, cleaning, cooking and pretending there was no world beyond its thick brick walls. She hadn't even been able to manage a walk in the garden. One step outside led to an out-of-body experience. As though she was watching a greasy-haired, grey-faced woman, from some place high above. The top of the beech trees, perhaps.

'And talking of what husbands are for,' he said. 'I can be here today, if you want.'

Si had passed some of his welding jobs over to another business so that Cassie wouldn't have to cope with her breakdown on her own. Not that she thought she was breaking down. But a visit to her doctor told her different. A scribbled prescription for antidepressants and sleeping tablets had been pressed into her hand whilst she'd sobbed and worried about how to get back to Blackthorn.

'Up to you,' she said with a shrug.

Upstairs, she pulled open her wardrobe and looked along the rows of shirts and trousers, sweaters and skirts. All reminders of a Cassie Clifton that didn't now exist. But she would put on a front for Alison, let her think she was healing and that there were no hard feelings. Neither of which were true. Every over-bright message she received from Jax, each letter from her own children's school, most news items about education; all caused a visceral pain, a twist in the gut of her recovery.

She chose a pair of jeans and a navy-blue sweatshirt. Might as well look like a student. Then she locked herself in the bathroom and turned the shower on to full blast and heat.

When Alison Harman arrived in the early afternoon, Cassie watched her through the lounge window. She slammed her car door, then stared up at Blackthorn before pulling her phone from her pocket and scrolling for a few moments.

The April weather was soft and mild, with pastel-blue skies and air that tasted of hope. The tubs and terracotta pots on Blackthorn's doorstep were blooming with narcissi and early white tulips.

'They're gorgeous.' Alison pointed her thumbs as Cassie pulled open the door. Then held out her arms. 'How are you?'

Cassie saw genuine warmth in her smile. She allowed herself to be hugged, though she struggled to return it. Here was the woman who expected her to rise above something she herself wore a flack-jacket against.

'I'm okay.' Cassie stepped back and beckoned Alison in. 'Getting there, as they say.' Then, 'We'll go into the kitchen, if you like. I'm sure you could do with a brew.'

Alison followed Cassie as she slapped her feet along the hall floor.

'I love your house,' she said. 'It's huge.' Her eyes stretched as they followed Blackthorn's staircase upwards, then roamed across the white plaster cornices and architraves.

'Thanks.' Cassie took Alison's jacket, orange and padded, and watched as she laid two large carrier bags on the table. The lilac-and-yellow faces of a chrysanthemum bunch peeked from the top of one. She turned away. Was she really going to be given gifts? After everything that happened. 'I'll put the kettle on. Coffee for you?'

'Yeah. Sure. I've got some things for you.'

The moment stretched. Cassie watched the flow of water from the tap, wanted it to last for ever. But she would have to turn around eventually.

On the table were the cellophane-wrapped flowers, and a large gift box. And a stack of paper envelopes. Alison picked them up. 'People wanted to send you individual cards,' she tilted her head towards the stack, 'but we clubbed together to get you this.' The box was pushed across the table, aggressively floral, with a loose lid. 'Open it. Go on.'

Alison let out a small cackle. It tapped its way down Cassie's spine, making her shudder in a way she hoped couldn't be seen. Would Tina Armstrong have contributed to this gift?

Hypocrisy abounds in a den of thieves, as her granddad had liked to point out. *He must have known some of the people I worked with.* And here she was, about to play the same game.

'That's so kind. I don't deserve it.' She lifted the lid of the box and was greeted by a layer of pink tissue paper, which she peeled back, to reveal a buttery leather handbag, and a long blue envelope marked with the silvery logo of a local restaurant.

'We got you an Abbeyvale token, too.' Alison lifted the envelope. 'For a twelve-course taster-menu experience. Everyone loves the place.' Her grin was soft and red. It had a finality. As though the whole gift-giving scenario should be closed down quickly. Cassie wanted to rip the token into tiny shreds and throw it into the range. To fling away a handbag which she would never use. Instead, she turned those emotions back on themselves. Then they'd be hidden. Tears could mean she was simply happy with the gifts.

'I don't know what to say. That is lovely. Thank you so much.' Cassie reached in for a hug. 'Please pass on my thanks to everyone else. I'll read the cards later.'

'No worries.' Alison held on to her for just a little bit longer than she should. 'Anyhow, I'm glad you're feeling a bit better, now everything is settled. I miss our little chats, you know.'

Behind her, Cassie could hear the bubbling of the kettle, rattling lid, and splatters of steam. She stepped away and began gathering cups and milk and spoons, each sound a welcome addition to the paper-thin atmosphere in the kitchen.

Those little chats. The ones where Cassie had taken her instructions for the day, then been dismissed. The ones where she'd offered up every shred of her knowledge, hoping the favour would be returned, should it be needed. When she turned back again, Alison was sitting at the table, scrolling through her phone.

'Thanks, Cass.' She reached out to take her coffee. 'They can't leave me alone for five minutes.'

'Is everything okay?' Cassie's stomach twisted. Did this woman have no idea what she was suffering? Her job, her life. Passed over as easily as a moan and a screen-flick.

'It'll have to be.' She thrust the phone away. 'But I'm not going to appoint another deputy. Not yet, anyway.'

'It's a lonely job,' Cassie snapped. 'I wouldn't wish it on anybody.'

'Meaning?' The headteacher was back.

'No colleagues on your level. No real support. But always having to give it.'

'I supported you, Cass.'

Cassie had no idea how to reply to this. Not without

compromising the last shreds of her own integrity. Then suddenly, it didn't matter anymore.

'You did, yes,' she said, 'and I'm grateful for it. Just not cut out for management, that's all.'

The lies people told; places told. It was a disease; by the time symptoms were visible, the damage was done.

Alison cut in, frowning slightly. 'You were the best damn manager I ever had. I learnt a lot from you.'

If she was supposed to say thank you for the compliment, Cassie couldn't bring herself to do it. Was this woman ignorant of the facts? But she seemed so confident. Once again, the doubt crept in. Had her extreme reactions, her anxiety, her panic, been separate from the actions of other people? How much did Alison know of those actions? And how much did she want to know?

'Well, you've got the chance to branch out on your own, now. I feel like I was just complicating things.' Cassie was struggling. There was so much she wanted to say, but those things would turn her into a wheedling subordinate.

'How?' Alison picked up her coffee. Took two mouthfuls.

Cassie crossed her arms and rested them on the table. 'Too many people didn't like my management style. You must have seen how Tina was with me.' There. She'd said it.

'Oh, her.' Alison's nostrils flared. 'She's like that with everyone. Her husband's found someone else, apparently; she's even fallen out with Laura now. But at least I've managed to persuade Denise to come back. Temporarily.' She laughed. A brittle laugh. 'And if you're feeling better, getting away from the place was probably the best thing.'

It wasn't the place's fault. 'Anyway,' Cassie said, grappling for safer territory. 'How have you been? I'm sorry I left you in the lurch.'

'Don't worry about it, Cass. You had to get yourself right.

And Kev's been really supportive. So's Laura. She's practically running the lower school at the moment.'

'She always had it in her.' Cassie's lie slipped off her tongue and joined the others zipping around her kitchen. 'I'm glad she's put a bit of distance between herself and other influences.' She felt the roots of truth sprout from her mouth, and spread across the room. Twining around Alison's wrists and ankles, making her jolt upwards, startled. And whatever Kevin Noble had seen, he was keeping his mouth firmly shut.

'Changing the subject, have you seen anything of Becky? I know you and her were friendly.'

Friendly? The woman hasn't been near since she left Parkhouse. 'No? Hasn't she been around school?'

Alison laid her phone, screen-side down, on the table. 'She resigned from the governing body. I thought you'd have known.'

'I didn't.'

'I don't think she's well, to be honest, Cass.'

'What's wrong with her?' Cassie shook her head. 'Sorry, that sounded rude. You don't have to tell me.'

'I'm not even sure,' said Alison. 'When she came to hand in her resignation, there was something odd about her. Scruffy, not very clean. She bit Tina's head off in the reception area, by all accounts.'

I'm sure Tina deserved it. Cassie said nothing.

'I'd better get going, actually,' Alison huffed. 'It's been good to see you. You'll keep in touch?'

'I will.' Cassie lifted Alison's coat from the corner of the scullery door. As simple as that, then. Three sips of coffee and some insincere gifts, and she was cut loose.

October 2019

Freddy shakes his head. 'That ex-boss of yours. She was a right one, wasn't she? You were better off away from that place, by the sound of it.'

'She was new at the time,' I tell him. 'A bit naïve. And I quite liked her, actually. There were some good people at Parkhouse. Not that I hear from them much, now.'

He stands up. I know he has to go home, but I don't want him to. He has a life. It's not my life. I can't expect him to listen to my bleating for ever.

'My opinion is this.' He stretches his arms above his head and yawns slightly. 'Your psyche was trying to get you away from that place. And it did whatever it needed to. Time to work on what you want to do next. Leave the past where it belongs. In a box marked lessons and resources.'

I groan.

'Do you like what I did there?' he says.

'Ever the artful psychotherapist.' I can say this to him now. Because we both know that's not what I think.

His face becomes serious, the mischief gone. 'There's something else, Cassie.'

'There always is,' I spit.

'Have you thought that your friend. Becky, that is. Have you thought she might also have suffered because of Tina Armstrong and her behaviour?'

If I were to be totally honest, I'd tell him I hadn't thought of anyone else much, these past two years. Yes, I've taken care of my family and they've returned the favour, but my own self-indulgence has crowded out everything else. That Becky was in her home, trying to come to terms with her grief and her rage hadn't occurred to me.

'Let's sit down again for a minute,' I say. 'You should be used to my overreacting by now.' I shoot him a grin. He sends it back. Then we shuffle into the study. I think back to our first meeting. I had been determined to dislike him, to chase him away with my indifference to his finely honed skills. I'd seen them as medicine, in a way. To be rubbed on the wound so that it healed. I never thought they'd be able to burrow down and heal from the inside out. The body does that, but it has to be coaxed.

We stand together in front of the window and look into the grainy darkness of the garden. The rain has stopped, but an arc of diamond droplets still hangs from the top of the panes. Freddy shivers.

'I feel guilty now. More than usual,' I tell him. 'But you can see my problem with visiting people. It's just not possible. I've never even used that restaurant token.'

'I don't suppose you have.' He is thoughtful for a moment. 'Did you ever telephone Becky?'

His comment makes me laugh. 'I just wanted away from everything to do with Parkhouse. So, no. I never telephoned Becky. Or anyone else.'

'Here's a thing,' he says. 'I think you should make it one of your targets. Going to visit someone. Becky, preferably.'

'Here's another thing,' I tell him. 'You should go home.'

When Freddy arrives the next day, unexpected and grinning, I haven't the heart for turning him away. For half the night I have paced my bedroom, ranting at Si and lying to myself. Though I have used many excuses as to why I couldn't possibly pay a visit to Becky Ripley, none of them are valid. I'm scared. That's all there is to it. And I don't like being reminded of just how scared I am.

'I'm here again,' Freddy says from the safety of the doorstep. 'You look rough.' He is wearing a multicoloured hat and has his hands pushed into the pockets of the checked jacket I have seen once before. The day is bright and blustery, and for me, completely terrifying. Walking around the block from Blackthorn is one thing. Climbing into a car and driving, even a couple of miles, would feel like a first trip into space.

'Thanks,' I say. 'And if you've come to force me out for a visit, I'm not going. Not with you or Si or anyone. I'll see Becky another time.'

He rubs his hands together, and blows into the palms, then stares at me for a moment.

'Let's catch a bus,' he says, as though this will placate me. 'It'll be good for you.'

'No.'

'Come on,' he says. 'Using public transport is a well-accepted step to recovery for agoraphobics. Let's do it.'

'I said no.' Though the bus stop is only a short walk away from Blackthorn House, I can't imagine sitting with the public, having a full-blown panic attack and trying to swallow it down, but Freddy is persistent.

'Stop thinking about the worst thing that could happen and get your trainers on. You've got this.'

'I haven't.' I peer at him. 'Unless—'

'Come on. Tell me.' Freddy takes my hand. 'What?'

I glance at my car keys on the hall table. 'I'll drive us. If you trust me.' My heart is hammering against my ribs at the mere thought of this, but I just might be able to do it.

Freddy is shaking his head. There's an expression on his face I haven't seen before: the sunshine has disappeared.

In that moment, I stop thinking and turn on my personal autopilot. I slip my feet into my trainers, pick up the keys but leave everything else, and storm down the drive, shoving him out of the way. I'm shocked when the car springs into life, at my bidding. Freddy hovers around the door for a moment, and I wonder if he's going to get in. When he does, I rev the engine loudly.

'Easy,' he mutters. His hand on my arm explains what he means.

'I drive how I drive,' I tell him. 'Live with it.'

He fastens his seat belt and turns to look out of the window.

We are soon heading towards the last place I knew Becky lived. She may not even be there anymore. My breath is catching in the back of my throat and not making it to my lungs, but I am surprised to find a clarity of thought I wasn't expecting. When I'd taken that final journey, from Lakeview back to Blackthorn, there had been fear; mind-numbing fear. It's still there. And it's still making me feel pathetic and useless. But Freddy knows about it, understands it and has me convinced I still count. So, I keep on driving.

'Prepare yourself for Becky not being in,' Freddy says suddenly. 'It's what a person would normally do. They wouldn't catastrophise that they were about to die.' He looks pale, and I wonder how safe I actually am behind the wheel.

'You don't know what I'm thinking,' I snap, then laugh. Of course he does.

He cocks an eyebrow at me. There is the faintest trace of sweat on his upper lip.

'If she's not in,' I say, 'we'll wait. How about that?'

'Or we could leave a note. No need to drag things out.'

I'm trying to concentrate on driving, but there is something in Freddy's tone that seems a little off. It's like he's lost interest in my plight, like he's in a different place altogether.

The roads don't feel busy. Which is a surprise, considering it's a Saturday lunchtime. When we pull up in front of Becky's house, the street is deserted. But there is a car on the drive and I'm pretty sure it's hers.

I clutch the steering wheel and wait for a major blast of panic to hit, now the driving muscle isn't being used and the distance from Blackthorn has opened up. I feel like I will only be able to breathe when I'm back there. But I can't get back there.

'We'll have to go and knock,' says Freddy, unbuckling his seat belt. 'Don't think about it, just do it.'

'Will you stop with the bloody mantras,' I mutter. 'I need to get home.'

'No.' He pushes open the door and takes some deep breaths. My driving must have been worse than I thought. It looks like Freddy suffers from motion sickness. 'No one is going home.'

My knuckles are white with the effort of holding on. Freddy is on the pavement now, and massages his temples. I'm about to ask him if he's all right, when the front door of Becky's house opens, and she is walking towards us.

'Can I help you?' she calls. 'Excuse me, but you're blocking my drive.'

I force myself out of the car, then wait until she catches my eye. She has half a head of silver hair now, and the rest is a straggly brown. Her face is thinner, and I can see the bones of her shoulders through a saggy T-shirt.

'Oh, Cassie.' A flash of something crosses her face. Surprise perhaps? Or annoyance? 'I'm not really... I'm...' She doesn't finish, just puts her hands over her face and turns away.

'We came to see how you are,' I say, though my mouth is so dry my tongue feels like it's stuck.

The driveway is now completely choked with weeds. Most are brown and dead and falling over. Every window has curtains pulled tightly closed.

'You'd better come in then,' Becky is saying. 'Is this a new boyfriend or something?' She peers at Freddy.

'It's Freddy,' I tell her. 'He's kept me company on the drive. I'm not so good at doing things by myself. As you've probably heard.'

We follow her into the house. Everywhere is in darkness, and no dog comes running to greet us.

'Where's your lab,' I ask. 'Mini, wasn't it?'

'Gone,' she says. 'She was Mick's dog, anyway.'

I can feel Freddy's presence, just behind me. I know he would be telling me to act and not think, and I'm trying. But I can hardly breathe and I'm sure Becky must be able to see my pulse throbbing in my neck and under my right eye.

'Did you want something in particular?' she asks.

'Cup of tea?' I suggest, then wonder what I'm doing. Although I know, deep down. 'Tea and sympathy?'

But there's nothing. No smile, no banter, no interest. Becky is a cold, hard shell. I know this because it's how I've been. Past tense. I see that now.

'Have you cut all ties with Parkhouse, Becky?' I ask. 'Like I have?'

She mutters something about being ignored and abandoned, then leads us into the living room. There is a smell of trapped air and rotting vegetation. A plant is dying somewhere. Nothing is different from the last time I was here. Except there is now a layer of greasy dust over every surface.

Freddy has taken off his hat and is wiping his face with it. I briefly wonder why he hasn't said anything. But what would he say? He knows nothing about Becky that I haven't told him. There is no common ground.

'How are your boys?' I ask. 'There was another grandchild on the way, wasn't there?'

'Can we stop,' Becky spits. 'Stop this ridiculous talk. I've been festering in this house for the last two years. Waiting. Waiting. Waiting—' This last word is delivered with a grimace that sends a fresh burst of adrenaline through me, and I want to run.

But I don't.

'Becky,' I say, low and smooth. 'Something's not right, is it? Let's talk.'

This is all it takes.

She smashes her hand into the line of photographs on the mantelpiece and sweeps them onto the floor. Freddy jumps away.

'I'll tell you what's not right, shall I?' She turns to face me. 'You didn't drown the fucking bitch Armstrong when you had the chance, that's what's not right. You were meant to help me. Why didn't you help me?'

What is she saying? Me? Drown someone? Is that what I was going to do? Is that what people think? My stomach hits the floor. Like when the cliff edge is there, and you look over.

'I was in a bad place,' I tell her. 'I'd never have drowned her. Or anyone else. Why are you saying that?'

'Christ.' She yanks at her own hair. 'Because I wanted rid of her. That's why.'

Freddy is standing by the door. He catches my eye and lifts his eyebrows towards freedom. But Becky is right in front of me. She smells of old sweat.

'I got rid of Mick. So that just leaves her.' This last word comes out with such force I think she might vomit. What is she talking about? *Got rid of Mick?* I reach out a hand to her. It is slapped away. Then she walks towards a small cabinet in the corner of the room. When she opens it, I see an array of medicine bottles and a plastic asthma spacer, similar to the one we kept at Parkhouse, for emergencies.

'See this,' she is screeching as she rifles through and pulls out a blue inhaler. 'His Ventolin. He needed it, that day. But I'd hidden everything. His lips were purple, but I just laughed. Told him to call his precious Tina. See if she could help him.'

Freddy has grabbed my hand, and he's pulling me out of the room.

'I'm going to get her,' Becky screams at us. 'I've got nothing

301

to lose now, have I? When you report me, tell them the lot: tell them I set you up as well, but you were too weak to follow it through. Tell them anything, I don't care. I'm going to get her.'

But we're out of the front door and running towards my car. Becky doesn't follow us. Instead, she stands in the doorway, her face distorted, her mouth still calling out.

'Jeez,' whispers Freddy as we reach the car. 'We can't just leave this, Cassie. We can't. The woman needs help. Let me stay with her.'

'And do what?' I am absolutely certain I won't be able to drive back to Blackthorn if Freddy isn't in the car with me. But he is right. We shouldn't leave Becky.

'I need to think,' I say. 'Did she just tell us she'd killed Mick? Did I imagine it?'

'She did.' He eyes the car. 'We can't ignore that.' He pats the pocket of his jacket and pulls out a tiny leather wallet. 'I have a number for the community mental health team.' He rummages and finds a card. 'Could you telephone them?'

'I didn't pick up my phone.'

He groans. We look at each other for a moment. I shake the car keys.

'Let's get back to Blackthorn,' I say. 'You can phone from there. I doubt Becky would let you back inside now.'

A door slams. Then Becky is climbing into her car and reversing it off the drive. Freddy's expression slides.

'Get in the car,' I hiss. 'Quick.'

Freddy hesitates. I wonder if he's going to walk away and leave me.

'Freddy?'

He holds up his hands. 'Right. Okay. I'm getting in the car.'

Even as he slides one leg across the passenger seat, I'm not convinced he won't get out again. Becky is speeding away. We need to follow her. I start the engine and listen for the slam of Freddy's door.

'I'm in,' he says eventually.

I want to ask him what is going on, but he has opened the window and is leaning out as far as he can. I decide now is not the time for talking, and I set off in pursuit of Becky.

We catch up with her when she gets snared between two vans in a long line of traffic.

'Keep your eye on her,' I tell Freddy. 'It's all we can do, for now.'

Becky leads us across town, away from Blackthorn. Her words stay with me, flowing like the traffic queue we have joined: in front and behind and at every junction, forcing us into a position where we can't escape.

You didn't drown the fucking bitch Armstrong when you had the chance... tell them I set you up as well, but you were too weak to follow it through.

I watch my hands, clutching at the steering wheel, skin stretched taut over bone. Becky was behind those last few things I blamed on Tina: the Facebook hack, the phone call to social services. Those things were meant to tip me over the edge. And they did. The pain I was feeling by then was almost unbearable. But I would never have killed anyone. That, at least, was a terrible judgement on Becky's part.

The procession of cars is leading us through the town's industrial heartland, then it thins out towards one of the more modern housing estates. Where Tina Armstrong lives. When I say this to Freddy, his shoulders sag.

'Let's just go to the police station,' he says. 'Tell them what we know. Becky can't hide. We've got her address and the licence plate of her car. They can follow things up.'

'We're not in some kind of television drama,' I hiss. 'Becky's in a bad place. You, of all people, should know that.

303

When she stops, we'll talk to her. Get the truth and see what help she might need.'

I haven't forgotten how terrified I was, the night I snapped. Fear of police or medical intervention had me looking for a way out. I'd even fantasised about walking to the edge of Blackthorn Quarry and flinging myself towards freedom. Thank goodness I'd had Si, fighting my corner and knowing the truth. If Becky's in trouble, I'm going to do the same for her.

Freddy slides down in his seat and looks away. I feel like I'm on my own with this. And the strange thing is, my fear is receding. The huge wave that hit me earlier has done its worst and is now only a gentle lapping on the shore of my thoughts.

We drive slowly, taking in the street names – they're mostly tree based, Chestnut Walk, Aspen Drive – keeping Becky's car close enough and hoping she can't see us. Then she pulls up.

The road is wide, with grass borders and tidy pavements. Most houses have a wall or a hedge. I stop my car a little way behind Becky and wait for her to climb out. She doesn't.

'What's happening?' whispers Freddy, drawing out that last word. He's struggling, I can tell. Him. When it should be me.

'Don't know. Can we just wait for a minute? See what she does?'

'Okay.' He pulls the sunshield down and settles back into his seat.

I peer through the windscreen and wonder if any of the houses belong to Tina Armstrong. The one with the fading cherry tree in the middle of the garden perhaps, or the whitewashed one with the double extension. I couldn't begin to guess. There was never any normal conversation between us; none of those boundary-setting chats. We just traded insults. When I think about this now, I still don't understand it. Had it only been about competing for power? Not something I was ever interested in, yet I became a threat. But Becky's loathing of Tina comes from a place of betrayal. And it has been putrefying for years.

'She's not moving.' Freddy's voice cuts across my thoughts.

I'm about to climb out of the car when I catch sight of something in my wing-mirror.

A figure.

Running.

Decked out in a tracksuit and plugged in to headphones. In the moment it dawns on me that this is Tina, I hear Becky's car start up. Freddy slides forwards in his seat.

'She's on the move again,' he sighs. But I don't respond.

Tina passes my car. Then reaches Becky's. There is a roar of engine noise, but she keeps on running.

I can only think to press down on my horn. Freddy looks at me in horror. 'What the—'

Tina turns just in time to see Becky's car speeding towards her, just in time to look for a way out. From where I am, it doesn't look like she's found one. The car hits a wall and Tina disappears from view.

Time slows.

Freddy and I sit there for an eternity before we react. Yet we are out of the car within seconds.

Tina is lying on the far side of the wall. The one that has been almost destroyed by Becky's car. And she is screaming at the top of her voice. To me, that is a good sign. But Becky is right behind us, hurling insults and scrambling over brick rubble. Freddy grabs at her arm and she tries to throw him off. I kneel by Tina, and she goes quiet for a moment, blinking at me, then at Becky.

Suddenly, she starts up again. 'What's happening. What's happening.' The same words, over and over. And I see she has a large cut on the back of her head. It is gaping and leaking a lot of blood. A man has come out from the house opposite.

'Ring an ambulance,' I shout at him. 'Get help. Just get someone.'

Becky has fallen to her knees and Freddy has his arms around her. She is shaking.

And then there are sirens and people and the bright bluster of white clouds and sunshine.

Epilogue

I look through the window of the car at the brick-built 1950s block, with add-ons of more modern glass, and a flat roof. I am terrified to be here. And thrilled. Three miles from Blackthorn's pull, the furthest I've been on my own for more than two years. The gravity of that thought zings through my veins more than any amount of adrenaline. Yes, I have the pound of my heart and the pant of my breath to contend with. I can't speak. Brain-fog is threatening to overwhelm me, but I am here. Picking up my daughters from their trip to Edinburgh. It sounds so normal. I am normal; Freddy was right.

Freddy. Who knew the poor guy was suffering from a phobia of his own. After the accident – that is how we refer to it now – he'd sat with me at the side of the road while we waited for the police to tidy up, and he'd explained everything. He hadn't been in a car since he was fifteen. On the farm where he'd lived, driving tractors and other utility vehicles on their private land had been an expectation and a much-anticipated adventure. Except he had crashed. The jeep he was driving, unlicensed and *on his own,* hit a wall, killing one of the farm dogs and trapping him for more than an hour. Being inside a small moving vehicle has terrified him ever since. He never took a driving test. When I laughed and told him the trip he took with me might have been a cure, he didn't understand my humour. Instead, he explained how difficult he'd found therapy, so he'd given up in the end. He quite enjoys buses and trains, apparently. I do, too, and we have made a pact to take a train journey together one day.

For now, I've been reshaping my life to include walks and shopping trips. All unaccompanied, all outside. On one glorious morning in the middle of November, when a layer of icy diamonds covered the roads, and my garden had turned from green to feathery white, I even managed to walk through Blackthorn Wood, across the frost-hardened ruts of mud, winter sunshine giving everything a heroic glow. It lifted my heart so that I floated back home again.

Today, I am determined to meet my girls as they climb out of their carriage. Even if it means there is no breath left to speak to them. I swing my legs out from the driver's seat, pull down my woollen hat and step into the cool evening air. The zip of my parka catches, and my legs wobble as I try to tug it free. In a small corner of my consciousness, something is screaming at me, telling me I can't do what I'm about to do, that I need to get home. But thanks to Freddy and his hypnotherapy, I have learnt how to confine the screaming voice. Allow it but confine it.

I focus on the smell of the waiting room, disinfectant, and copper coins, and adjust to the brash white lights above me. Then I stroll onto the platform as if it's the most normal thing in the world. My heart is hammering against my ribs, but I don't run. Instead, I stamp my feet, as though I'm colder than I am.

Whatever happens in a panic attack, Freddy told me, *try to make it worse. Double the feeling.*

What has surprised me about panic attacks is that they can galvanise you into action. When Becky had driven her car towards Tina, those same feelings made me blast my horn then dive from the car to try and salvage something. Freddy had seemed calm. He told me later he felt numb from trying to take his own advice. Panic had freed me from myself, that day. And now, it's going to do the same thing again.

I am startled by the low rumble of the train. Then, the two notes of the horn. It chugs into the station, headlights flaring, the drag of diesel and goodbyes coming from under its wheels. But this is a hello for me. I peer, chin forward, like a schoolkid waiting for Santa. Then I see the girls. They're part of a crowd, small faces, and long fair hair curling from the bottom of their hats. They wave. Get up. And they are suddenly out on the platform with me. Hugging. Grinning. A normal family greeting.

Freddy comes to visit us a couple of days later. He brings a splash of damp air and wax-cotton jacket in with him.

'I love your tree,' he says. 'This is a house that's perfect for Christmas.'

Si takes his coat, and he kicks his boots into the scullery.

'I remember the house rules.' Freddy's wry laugh. I have missed it, though we've spoken on the telephone often. 'I've been so busy. It seems everyone is worried about their mental health, all of a sudden.' Then he stops. Shrugs sheepishly. 'That came out wrong. Sorry. And a lot of my work has been with kids. Teens. Young men. Referred by worried family members. And schools. I'm even getting private work from schools. That's a worry, in itself.'

'Sit down,' I say, pointing to the kitchen table. 'I'll make you a drink. You sound as though you need a break.' I point towards an old Quality Street tin next to the fruit bowl. 'And there's mince pies. You'll be starving. You always are.'

He doesn't allow a second of politeness to pass. Just reaches for the tin and helps himself. 'How are things?' Words and a spit of crumbs. 'Heard any more about Becky Ripley? Or the dreaded Tina?'

'Things are good,' I say. 'I've been getting out. I even went to the train station on Monday. By myself.'

Freddy clutches at his chest. 'Wow. You're a fast learner.'

'The police have been in contact,' I tell him. 'They've opened an investigation into Mick's death. Becky's been sectioned. She's in Guild Lodge. That's Preston, isn't it?'

He shudders and scratches at his chin. 'Poor woman. Tina Armstrong. What an utter, utter destroyer of lives.'

'She's tried to contact me, you know.'

'What?'

'Hard to believe, isn't it? She's still in hospital, leg in traction, but she's been messaging.'

Freddy slaps his hands across his face.

'Jeez,' he whistles. 'Finally. You're going to be allowed in her gang.'

We both laugh at that.

I pass him a mug of coffee and a plate. He slurps noisily and burns his mouth.

'Nobody's waited on me since... since I was here last, I don't think. It's all take, take, take. I could do with you at my house, keeping me going.' He smiles up at me. The dreadlocks have been trimmed slightly. They lie neatly across both shoulders. No ragged ends. And he is clean-shaven.

'How are things with you,' I ask tentatively. 'With the... I mean the...'

'I know what you mean.' He leans back and folds his arms. 'The therapist getting a taste of his own medicine.' But he is smiling.

'I'm interested, that's all.'

He catches at my gaze. 'I've buried it for years, Cass. I have a colleague who is prepared to help me, but I'm not sure it's worth it.' He makes a peace sign with his fingers. 'Down with the combustion engine, man.'

'Don't be ridiculous,' I say. 'What do you think powers a bus?'

'Yeah, okay. Point taken.' He sips his coffee. 'I've been so busy; my own therapy will have to wait.' And when my mouth drops open, he continues. 'Don't look at me like that. Next time I see my own counsellor, I will cut my problem loose. Promise. But working with you has caused a bit of a clog-up to my list.' He smiles. 'I enjoyed it, though.'

'And you enjoyed the money.' I wink.

'Cheeky.' He gives me a mock-slap. 'But, yes. So now, I've had to turn my back room into a waiting area to deal with the overflow. It's not great. Especially as it means leaving the dog in the kitchen, where he wails and tries to dig his way through the door.'

'Good that your practice is thriving though, mate?' Si comes to sit with us at the table. 'You'll be raking it in.'

I shoot him a frown. This is people's mental health we're talking about.

'What?' he laughs. 'Why don't you look for premises, Freddy. There's plenty around.'

'I have been thinking about it, actually. But haven't had the time to look. I might sell my house and buy somewhere bigger, with office space. Or some extra rooms, at least. Now,' he reaches for another mince pie, 'tell me the best... and worst thing that's happened since I last saw you, Cass.'

That makes me smile. Cass. Our relationship has moved onto a footing of mutual trust and likability. Freddy is the first person I have built a relationship with since I left my job. He likes this version of me. He never met the old one. And he never will. She has gone, needed to go. This man has helped me to grow into the person I was meant to be. As has Tina Armstrong. I must thank her, one day.

'Best thing: I met my girls from the station. Worst thing: Joe Smythe. From Parkhouse. He's going to pay me a visit. It's freaking me out.'

Freddy finds that amusing.

'How's the sleeping and the zingy nerves?' he asks.

He knows me so well. 'The hypnotherapy podcasts are brilliant. I do one every day. Honestly, it's made such a difference.'

'So, I was worth the money?' He tilts his head. 'Cass?'

'You were.'

Si interrupts. He is holding his chin in his hand, resting his elbow on the table. Staring straight at Freddy.

'You could use the cellars,' he says. 'Our cellars, I mean. Get the whole place properly finished, then rent them from us. There's tonnes of room down there.'

None of us speak. We look at each other and we wonder: could Blackthorn find a fresh purpose? The thought sends a shiver down my spine.

Finally, Freddy smiles. 'You think?'

'It's possible,' says Si. 'You've been down there, haven't you? It's a whole other house.'

'You could come and work with me, Cass.' He is laughing. Then he stops. 'No. You could. Really. God, I could do with someone like you. Organised. Clever. Bloody fucking hell. This is a real possibility.' He looks at Si. 'You weren't joking, were you?'

'I wasn't joking,' says Si.

Later, when we've poked around the cellars and talked grand plans, Freddy and I are sitting in the study, making lists. Neither of us wants to believe there will be an end result to this huge plan. But we're going to try.

'Get your coat, Cass,' he says suddenly. 'Let's smash some more boundaries.'

I'm not sure. I'm feeling a little disorientated, and besides, it's drizzling. But Freddy is insistent. He walks to the front door and lifts his jacket from the peg. And mine.

'Get our boots, will you?' It sounds so normal, but already, I can feel the catch of my breath somewhere in the back of my throat. There must be a way to put him off. I'm not in the mood for boundary smashing. Not with him. Not yet.

'Boots.' It's Si. 'Get me a paper, if you're passing the shop. I'm just going to get the Blackthorn deeds out of the loft. There's all sorts of information in the pack. Might be something of interest. I'll see you in a bit.' He hands Freddy his lace-ups and me my Uggs. Then he takes the stairs two-by-two, calling to Helli in her bedroom to help him with the loft ladder.

'Paper shop it is then.' Freddy stands up and pulls open the front door. 'Ready?'

I'm not. But I step outside, anyway.

Freddy chatters on about how we could turn the cellar plans into a reality, how we could convert aspects of the place to suit his needs, how much everything would cost. I try to focus on what he is saying, but I'm becoming more and more aware of how far we are from Blackthorn. I try to stop thinking about this, but the pull is there. A string from my heart. The further it is stretched, the faster the beating. Freddy holds out his elbow. I am glad of it. I slip my arm through his and it bolsters me, somehow. A car flashes by. And a bus. This is my body, trying to protect me. That's all it is. And it's not subject to mind control.

'All right?' Freddy asks, patting my hand.

I sigh. 'Do you know what? I think I am.'

THE END

Also by Paula Hillman

Seaview House

The Cottage

Acknowledgements

Blackthorn Wood was a difficult story to write. As a teacher, I spent many hours working with problematic behaviour, and trying to sort out many types of bullying. The hardest of these to deal with was the kind of victimisation that happens within the friendship groups of girls. Often, the perpetrator had an unshakeable belief that the victim was deserving of their treatment, as she had done something that didn't uphold the subtle power dynamics of the group. Others in the group may have felt uncomfortable, but were very careful to watch their own backs. I've seen this happen in the world of grown-up girls too: hence the Blackthorn Wood story was born.

I live near the beautiful fifteen-acre How Tun Wood. It is managed by the Woodland Trust, and is a match for the Blackthorn Wood in my story. My family and I walk there often, as do many people in our town. I sometimes wonder what it would be like not to have access to nature. What if you could see it but were not able to get there? The spine of Cassie's story came from these thoughts: Freddy is almost my alter-ego, cheering her on to get better.

As always, I must thank Betsy Reavley and Fred Freeman for their continued support with my writing. The Bloodhound team are exceptional, particularly my editor Clare Law, and proof-readers, Abbie Rutherford, and Tara Lyons. Clare's insights on girl-bullying have been vital to the final manuscript. My family are my writing cheer-leaders, but I now also have a fan base, who are eagerly awaiting the publication of Blackthorn Wood: I hope it lives up to their expectations.

A note from the publisher

Thank you for reading this book. If you enjoyed it please do consider leaving a review on Amazon to help others find it too.

We hate typos. All of our books have been rigorously edited and proofread, but sometimes mistakes do slip through. If you have spotted a typo, please do let us know and we can get it amended within hours.

info@bloodhoundbooks.com

Milton Keynes UK
Ingram Content Group UK Ltd.
UKHW040629181123
432822UK00004B/68

9 781916 978058